The Broken Wolf

Natalie Baulch
Edited by: Rianna Cuddy

Copyright © 2022 Natalie Baulch

All rights reserved

The characters and events portrayed in this book are fictitious. Any similarity to real persons, living or dead, is coincidental and not intended by the author.

No part of this book may be reproduced, or stored in a retrieval system, or transmitted in any form or by any means, electronic, mechanical, photocopying, recording, or otherwise, without express written permission of the publisher.

ISBN-13: 9798475690178
ISBN-10: 1477123456

Cover design by: Art Painter
Library of Congress Control Number: 2018675309
Printed in the United States of America

To all the people who read my book on Wattpad, you have given me the confidence to believe in my book.

To my family for putting up with my constant stories since I was little.

I couldn't have done this without any of you.

Finally, to Rianna, my amazing editor! Thank you for offering and following through and being the most amazing friend! Thank you for caring about The Broken Wolf as much as me.
You have made this Final Edition with me and I will forever be grateful!

Lilla

1 year earlier

All I have to do is jump. Not even jump, but just step over the edge. Keep walking until I'm falling. That seems simple enough.

I want to die. I can't live life like this. The pain, the loneliness, the guilt, I can't live with any of it. All I have to do is take a deep breath, lift up my foot and step over the edge.

Should I say something? Should I whisper my goodbyes into the silence surrounding me? With no one around to hear them, is there even a point? Maybe I should just think them?

To be honest, I don't want to think at all. I just want to feel nothing, to be numb. To be gone.

So I take a deep breath, lift my foot, and step over the cliff's edge.

*

Wrinkling my nose, I open my eyes, curious to see what tickles my face. I slam them shut as quickly as I open them, finding the sunlight too harsh.

Letting out a breath, readying myself, I open my eyes slowly. Green streaks are everywhere, and as my eyes adjust, I realise it's grass.

With my muscles stiff and aching, I turn over, groaning as I land on my back. The bright blue sky greets me, and I can't help the smile that grows on my face. A blue sky in the morning will do that to you, even with my view being obscured by tree branches.

I let out a sigh, my smile disappearing as I realise I'm in the woods, on the muddy grass, where the insects hang out. That thought alone makes my heart race. I know I'm a Wolf, a Rogue even, but insects scare the crap out of me. I become a frightened little girl with a high pitched scream when I see them. The worst one? Spiders.

I sniff the air expecting to smell the different trees and flowers, the different animals I'm meant to hunt.

Instead, the smell of nature is hidden under the scent of the boys changing room. Sweaty and gross laced with the distinctive smell of Werewolf.

They move into view, blocking the blue sky, creating a shade over me. Topless men in shorts, every woman's dream, right? I sigh heavily, waiting for one of them to talk.

I realise I've left myself at a disadvantage as they tower over me.

"You are in Freedom Howlers Territory, Rogue." He sounds stern and as annoyed as I feel, I'm disrupting his day.

"I'm sorry, I'll leave." I say and resist the urge to slap myself, although being as weak as I am right now, I doubt I'd even be able to do that. Realising I have to get up, I sigh and roll back onto my stomach. They take a few steps back, giving me room, and slowly I begin to move.

Impatience and annoyance roll off of them as if they think I'm being slow on purpose, and at that moment, I wish I could revel in it. I manage to get up on one arm, but before I can bring my other arm to take some of my weight, I collapse. I try again and fail.

"Shit," I roll over onto my back and stare at the now frowning faces of the men. I let out a chuckle.

"Could you maybe carry me off of your Territory?" I joke; they don't laugh. Note to self: sweaty, topless men have no sense of humour.

"Why are you so weak?" The same voice speaks again, and I turn to look at him. Handsome, like all Werewolves. I've tried looking for ugly ones, but they don't seem to exist. He has jet black hair and brown eyes, staring at me with... amusement? His annoyance is gone and I seem to be entertaining him.

My eyes trail down his body, taking in his toned muscles. I blow out a breath, he isn't doing anything but standing there, yet I find him just as entertaining as he finds me. He emits power but not enough for an Alpha.

"You're the Beta. Is your Alpha too busy to deal with me? Should I feel insulted?" I ask, cheekily. I always push my limits, not too bothered about what happens to me. To my surprise, the Beta laughs.

"Our Alpha is on his way. He loves to deal with Rogues." I can hear the slight threat in his words, but all I do is chuckle back.

"If I was going to be killed by an Alpha, I probably wouldn't be standing here today." I state, honestly. I notice they all tense at my words, and I can see them having a conversation in their minds, trying to decide if I am a threat. I wait patiently, trailing my eyes across the abs of all the men around me, appreciating the sight I've woken up to.

"Our Alpha is one of the most vicious Alpha's in the country when it comes to your type. Instead of rolling around in the grass, laughing and having fun, you should be worried. Or need I remind you that you are a Rogue." The Beta says through gritted teeth, annoyance with me set in. I held my breath for a moment but then remembered that I didn't recognise the Pack smell, and he said a different Pack name. Freedom... something or other.

Relieved, I chuckle, "Firstly, do I look like I'm rolling around?" I leave out the having fun part, up until this moment, it has indeed been fun messing with them. "Slightly dramatic on your part. Secondly, I can handle your Alpha." I say with confidence, more to myself than anything. That doesn't go down too well with the Pack members in front of me as I dismiss their tremendous and powerful Alpha.

"You're too weak to take on an Alpha," he remarks. He has a point; I am having a bad day. "Why are you in our Territory?" He asks, getting back to the main point as his annoyance with me continues to grow. I guess I'm not as entertaining as I was a few minutes ago.

"Well, the original plan was to kill your Alpha and take over the Pack, but as you can see, that plan isn't going too well." The sounds of their collective growl erupts at the threat to their Alpha.

Additional note to self: they don't get sarcasm either.

On a sigh, I continue, "I honestly don't know how I got here. I was running last night, and the next thing I know, I'm waking up here with you lovely people. Shouldn't your Alpha be here by now?" I ask the Beta, growing slightly bored of this. The sooner the Alpha gets here, the sooner this can be over.

"I've been here since you asked for me the first time, Little Rogue." I shiver with pleasure at the sound of his voice and then wince. His scent hits me, the salty freshness of the sea, one of my favourite smells in the world. I find myself struggling to breathe. My emotions don't know what to do. Feel pleasure or pain.

"Do you know how rude it is to keep a Rogue waiting?" I try to joke; he laughs. The sound causing me to cry out as a sharp pain radiates through my body.

He's by my side in seconds, and I close my eyes before I find myself looking into his.

"Look at me, Little Rogue," he urges, softly stroking my cheek. My skin begins to tingle beneath his touch before the pain takes over, like fire coursing through my veins. I squeeze my eyes shut tighter, so I don't do what he says, even though every fibre of my being wants to listen to him, to please him.

"Open your eyes." His voice stern, but still I refuse. I know what will happen if I look into his eyes; the pain will be excruciating. I can feel his anger rolling off of him in waves, and I squeeze my eyelids tighter together.

"Open your eyes and look at me!" His tone is an Alpha command.

"No." I whisper just before the pain of hearing him, smelling him, touching him, leads me into darkness.

Dayton

I'm shocked as I stare at her unconscious body. She denied my Alpha command. Something almost impossible under normal circumstances, let alone her being so weak. She doesn't emit the power of an Alpha or Beta; she is just an ordinary Wolf. In terms of power, she was ordinary, but looking at her was like looking at a perfectly cut diamond.

Her long black hair was darker than night and flowed effortlessly over her shoulder. Her full, natural lips were a deep red, and all I wanted to do was kiss them. A sculptor couldn't have fashioned her face any more perfect. Her elegant, button nose was covered in black smudges, as was the rest of her, but her eyes stood out. Before she passed out, I saw her striking purple eyes, so unusual. Now that I'd seen them, I couldn't imagine her having any other coloured eyes, they wouldn't suit her.

Her clothes were filthy and torn, unsurprising for a Rogue. Her skin was tanned and covered in dirt; it looked like she hadn't showered in days. This was surprising for a Rogue; it usually would be weeks or months between showers. She was thin but looked like she ate well, which pleased my Wolf. I'd hate to think she had been starving for weeks.

She wasn't particularly muscular, she had curves, but she couldn't have weighed more than 7 stone. So small for a Wolf.

"Alpha?" My Beta comes up behind me. Austin is my best friend; I sometimes think he knows me better than I know myself.

I pick her up and begin my journey to the Pack doctor. The men disperse, but Austin follows me; I know he's confused. Rogues killed my parents; I didn't have sympathy for them. Usually, their passing out made it easier for me to kill, unlike those who tried to run.

As the wind hits me, so does the smell of violets which I know belongs to her. My Little Rogue. The pet name popped into my head the moment I arrived.

Hearing her talk was like listening to angels sing; her voice was so soft and sweet I knew I could hear her speak for the rest of my life. My Wolf agreed.

"She ran circles around you," I remark as Austin meets my stride. "She was so light and breezy, making jokes, despite how riled up you were getting. I can see how she survived as a Rogue."

"So that means we keep her?" Austin asks on a laugh thinly veiled curiosity.

"She's my Mate." I tell him, glancing down at her.

"Well, she'll be running circles around you too then." Austin chuckles, finding this amusing. Of course, my Mate had to be a Rogue.

"I wonder what's wrong with her." I say, worry strong in my voice, deciding the doctor's office is so far away all of a sudden.

"Maybe hunger? Exhaustion? She said she'd been running all night." Austin tries to reassure me.

"No, it's something else, she winced at my presence, Austin. I physically caused her pain. That's not hunger or exhaustion." I say as we finally reach the doctor's office. I had felt her pain, as Mate's do; it had made me grit my teeth to stop myself from crying out. That sort of pain should only happen when violence occurs, but nothing violent had happened. The only logical explanation was that it was me. She was fine before I came along.

"What happened, Alpha?" The Pack Doctor asks, beckoning for me to put her on the hospital bed. I did so delicately, not wanting to cause her any more pain.

I catch the flash of confusion across his face as he catches the smell of

Rogues. Packs have certain smells, as do Rogues, so that we can tell which Pack wolves belong to, and it helps us tell the Rogues apart. When the Ancestors created us, they were smart about it.

He tries to hide his confusion as he gets to work checking her over. I explain the meeting in the woods, the worry in my voice evident, but he doesn't question it.

My Wolf won't settle down as we watch the Doctor examine her, not liking another Wolf touching her. As much as I agree, I'm also shocked, we hadn't locked eyes yet, so I shouldn't feel protective or her pain. None of this makes sense, and it's not how I pictured meeting the love of my life.

"She couldn't even stand; she tried but kept collapsing." Austin informs the doctor before we fall silent, watching him work.

All of a sudden, he sucks in his breath sharply.

"What?" I ask, panic-stricken.

"She has a Venom Mark, she–" Doc is interrupted as Little Rogue begins to stir. He places her hair back in place.

I grab her hand and stroke her forehead with my other hand, "Little Rogue?" She winces and pulls her hand away, clenching her eyes closed.

"Please stop. Please don't talk to me or touch me. I can't handle the pain. Your smell is suffocating me; I can barely breathe." She whispers hoarsely.

She wraps her hands around her body as if trying to hug herself. I hold back a growl as my Wolf, and I hate being spoken to and disrespected, even by our Mate.

"Why are your eyes closed?" Austin asks, taking over as I take a step away from her.

"I can't look into his eyes, and if I open them, I will feel the pull even more, and I can't handle that much pain."

"Can we take her with us?" Austin asks Doc on my behalf rather than responding to her.

"Yes, you can; she just needs rest."

Take her to my house, set her up in the opposite bedroom. I mind-link to Austin before leaving her, even though every part of my being is dying for me to go back to her.

Lilla

I wake in a strange bed. In a strange room, sweating from the summer heat. Kicking off the covers, I'm relieved to see I'm still in my clothes. Filthy as they are.

I do a quick check, racking my brains on how I got here. I don't feel unsafe, which is odd. Feeling completely safe is an unusual feeling for me.

Then it clicks.

My Mate.

I feel myself start to panic. How did I find him? That should be impossible. I must have been mistaken. No longer weak, I decided to get out of bed and investigate. Maybe because I was weak, I was wrong about the situation. That must be it.

When I open the door, his scent hits me. Salty sea smell. Feeling slightly dizzy, I shake my head and follow the smell.

I can't help but smile as his scent reminds me of the good memories I have of my family.

I find myself just outside the kitchen, the sound of multiple voices sounds through the door and I hesitate. Part of me wants to leave them to it, but the need to know if he is my Mate forces me to open the door. Silence fills the room as they all stop to stare at me. The atmosphere now thick and heavy with my presence. Six sets of eyes watch me, waiting. No one seems to be sure of what to do or say.

"Well, this is awkward." I say for lack of anything else. One of the guys around the table smiles; I instantly liked him.

"Are you okay? Do you need something?" The Beta asks; he is the only person I've spoken to in this Territory. He is my new favourite person.

"Names," I find myself saying, and he frowns slightly. I can feel the Alpha staring at me, his eyes causing my skin to burn.

"I don't know your names." I whisper, hating myself. I never sound so unsure of myself; I'm a Rogue, I always act confident, but suddenly under their scrutinising eyes, I'm acting like a frightened little girl. It sickens me.

I receive a friendly smile from the Beta.

"I'm Austin; this is my Mate Aria. Blade and his Mate Blaze, and that's Russell." They all wave at me, and I smile back.

"Blade and Blaze, huh? You guys were made for each other just based on your names alone!" I say with a smile, and they chuckle.

"People can never really believe that's our names. They always assume they're nicknames or something." Blaze tells me with a welcoming grin.

They all seem extremely friendly, so I relax slightly. I notice that they haven't given me their Alpha's name, but I don't ask, unsure if I even want to know. I'm still trying to decide if he's my Mate, although there is strong evidence to support this theory. From the way he smells and from the burning feeling on my skin as his eyes trace my body. The pull to face him and look him in the eyes is intense, but I hold off.

It's impossible for me to find my Mate.

I let out a sigh.

"What's your name?" Austin asks.

"Lilla."

"That's just as unusual as ours." Blaze says.

"It's not a common name. It's Swedish for little. I was the runt of my former pack... so..." I trail off, shrugging. They can see from looking at me that I'm the runt. I'm tiny; I never bulked up like all the other Wolves. You wouldn't

tell I have muscles by looking at me; I've always been skinny. I'm not exactly tall either. It is helpful, though; people look at me and underestimate me.
Silence falls across the room.
I let out another sigh.
Who am I kidding? It may be impossible, but clearly, there is something between this Alpha and me.
"What's your name?" I ask, turning to him but avoiding his gaze, my eyes falling on his chest. He doesn't speak; I glance at his face, wondering if he even heard me, and our eyes meet instantly.
I wait for the agony, the sharp pains to fill my body, but nothing happens. He looks just as confused as I feel. I wasn't the only one expecting some sort of pain to happen to me.
"Dayton, my name is Dayton." he says softly. His voice still causes me pain, but it's no longer a sharp and agonising feeling. It's a dull pain, like someone pinching me. I can handle that.
I step towards him and then freeze, nervous. He stands and begins making his way over to me, closing the gap between us.
His hand softly strokes my cheek, "Are you okay?" He asks, worried.
Mate! My Wolf cries out, and I gasp in shock, almost keeling over. I haven't heard her voice in over a year, and I've missed her. I try to hold on to her, but she is gone just as quick as she arrived.
Pulling away from his hands, I turn and run out of the room as the silent tears spill over.

*

A knock on my door startles me but before I can say anything the door opens and Dayton walks in.
He stands at the end of my bed awkwardly. I sit up, leaning against the headboard.

"It's funny that we've barely said two words to each other but you already mean more to me than my own life." Dayton breaks the tense silence, looking down at the floor.

"That's Mates for you." I whisper, my heart aching. I would give anything to hear her again, my Wolf.

He smiles slightly but his eyes don't leave the floor.

"I'm sorry. I know this isn't how you imagined meeting your Mate would go." I admit and he finally looks up at me.

Our eyes drawn to each other and we just stare as if the rest of the world has fallen away.

This is what it's meant to be like. Pure love at first sight. Nothing else matters. Just us.

Except...

I look away first.

"I don't know how to do this. You are my Mate and every part of me aches for you, but it's not as easy as that for me." I say, now it's my turn to look at the floor.

Dayton sighs and sits down on the bed opposite me. He frowns slightly and shakes his head as if ridding himself of a thought.

"We go at your pace. I'm not stupid, you are a Rogue for a reason. I would like to know why. God, Little Rogue I would love to know everything about you. Every inch of your soul. I just want you to know that there is nothing you can do or say that will push me away. You are right. I didn't imagine meeting my Mate would be so dramatic and difficult but this is better. This is real. This feeling we have is real. Us. No matter what."

My heart feels full for the first time in years and all I want is him. I push away the niggling thought in my mind.

I lunge at him, wrapping my arms around his neck, hugging him. He immediately wraps his arms around me and we sit there holding each other, no more words need to be said.

*

After Dayton left my room, I spent the rest of the day under the duvet and wrapped in my thoughts. I wake the next morning with dry eyes. Stretching out my muscles, I decide to have a much-needed shower. Slowly making my way to the en-suite, I peel off the dirty clothes stuck to my skin. It takes me a second to figure out how the shower works and I have to hold back a moan as the heavenly water cascades down my body when I do.

When I'm clean, I get out of the shower and wrap a towel around myself. I sigh, annoyed; I hadn't thought this through; I have no clothes. I sniff the air searching for his scent as I walk out of my room.

I think back to seeing him yesterday. His t-shirt was tight and showed his defined muscles. His face was remarkable; with his high cheekbones, piercing blue eyes and pink lips. He had shaggy blonde hair that I just wanted to run my hands through. He was a thing of beauty, a true and pure Alpha.

Making my way down the hallway, I hear him talking with a few other people, the same ones from yesterday. This time, however, they are in the living room at the bottom of the stairs. I go to round the corner and start descending but stop when I hear my name, curiosity getting the better of me.

"You all have the freedom to speak; I won't hold anything against you. I'm just curious about what you think of Lilla." Dayton says; I shiver with pleasure as he says my name and then wait to hear the answers.

After a breath, Austin speaks, "She seems funny."

"She didn't seem bothered that she was a Rogue trespassing; she acted like it was no big deal that was pretty cool." Someone else speaks, but I don't recognise the voice, which means it must be Russell, the only man not to talk to me yesterday.

"She is one of the most beautiful people I've ever met," Blaze speaks, and everyone agrees with her. Feeling slightly uncomfortable, I decide I should interrupt them when Austin speaks again.

"I like the way she treats you." I hold the banister in a loose grasp as he says speaks and make my way down the stairs, surprised no one has noticed me.

"What do you mean?" Dayton asks, confused.

"I think he means the way I talk to you. I don't treat you like the big, bad Alpha that you are." All eyes turn to me, and before I can blink, Dayton is standing on the step below mine, trying to shield me from view.

"You're in a towel." he says, and I can hear the lust in his voice.

I look down and feign shock, "I am? I thought this was a dress, but now that you mention it..." I look down at myself again. "It does look like a towel!" I say sarcastically, and he growls at me. I roll my eyes, though I'm pleased I don't feel any sharp pain, only the dull throb I can handle.

"I don't have any clothes, and I figured you would probably appreciate me walking around in a towel rather than naked." I didn't mention that I would never walk around without any clothes in a million years. He turns me around and pushes me back up the stairs, down the hall and into my room.

"I had Russell shop for you yesterday. He hung it all up while you slept. He is normally good at that sort of thing, so..." he trails off as I walk into the massive wardrobe. My mouth falls open; this is amazing. There are hundreds of clothes and shoes in a deep L shaped wardrobe.

"How does he know my size?" I ask with a frown, as Russell walks in.

"I'm good at guessing people's size from just looking at them; it's a talent." I nod, and he winks; I smile, running into his arms and hug him as thanks. He reminds me of my brother, who I miss terribly.

Dayton leaves us to it, and I start scanning the clothes, turning back to Russell.

"What should I wear?" I ask, barely containing my excitement.

Dayton

She wasn't in pain anymore. Well, not enough for me to feel. I was happy; she had looked into my eyes. I couldn't keep the smile from my face, even when she ran from the room with tears in her eyes.

I didn't follow her yesterday simply because I could tell her tears weren't because of me. I didn't want to push her; so much had happened to her in the last day, so I left her to herself for a little while before checking on her.

Now she was in her room with Russell going through the clothes he had brought her. Her eyes had lit up when she saw the entire wardrobe, so I promised myself to try and make her that happy again, no matter what it takes.

I can't feel her Wolf. My Wolf interrupts my thoughts.

What do you mean?

I mean that I can't feel her Wolf. The connection is there, but I can't reach or feel her. I frowned, he was ruining my good mood, so I shut him out and push the thought to the back of my mind.

I wish my parents were alive to meet Lilla; they would love her to pieces. Especially the way she speaks to me, something I wasn't too thrilled about.

Lilla walks into the room laughing at something Russell said. She is wearing shorts and a vest, she looks stunning with her toned, tanned legs on show, but my Wolf and I do not like that she is walking around like this when other un-Mated Werewolves could see her.

She turns to look at me, "Do you like it?" She asks, sounding slightly uneasy. Part of me wants to tell her she looks fantastic, which gives her confidence. But a stronger, more possessive side wants me to drag her away from anyone who can see her.

"I'd prefer if you didn't walk around showing your legs or really any part of you to anyone but me." I try to sound nice, but it comes out as a growl and her eyes narrow, the smile from her face dissipates.

"Oh, okay. Should I go change into something that shows no skin? Will that please you, Alpha?" She asks sarcastically as she walks further into the room.

"You're my Mate." I state through gritted teeth, as though she had forgotten.

Lilla clicks her fingers, "I knew there was a reason to stick around!"

I let out another growl, she is testing my patience, and I don't know how much longer I can keep my Wolf under control. Something about her gets under my skin easier than anyone else.

"Go and change." I use my Alpha command.

"No, I like what I'm wearing." she argues.

I pushed away from the table and stood up; I knew I was overreacting, but my Wolf had been dying to get out since Lilla arrived in my Territory. I had managed to keep him at bay until now. At the act of defiance to my Alpha Command, my Wolf breaks out before I can control him.

Lilla

He was breath-taking. The Wolf standing in front of me was mesmerising, and in a different situation, I would have gone up to him and touched him. His fur wasn't the colour of a typical Alpha. They tend to be as black as my hair, but the Alpha in front of me was chocolate brown, like a Labrador, although he is definitely bigger than a dog.
I make a mental note not to tell him I referred to him as a dog, men and their ego's and everything.
Even standing from a distance, I could tell he came up to my shoulder; he was chunky too but it was pure muscle; he fits perfectly with his human counterpart.
My simple act of defiance had angered his Wolf, not necessarily short-tempered, but I had felt his Wolf's need for a run since I got here; I just simply did what I do best and pushed him too far. His Wolf needed out, and I granted him that; I did him a favour if you ask me.
I knew I could go up and change, but it's not in my nature to do what I'm told. If I listen to him now, he will always think he's in charge, and there is no way I would let him or anyone be in charge of me again. Besides, I'm a Rogue. I don't like being told what to do; he should get that. If he had asked me nicely, I would have considered changing, but no, Mr Alpha had to try and command.
I let out a sigh.

"Maybe you should go for a run and calm down. I will not be told what to do, and you shouldn't be trying to scare me into it. I'm your Mate, not a Prisoner."

Dayton growls, clearly unhappy with my response. Anger leaks through my emotional wall. Something I had taught myself to do to avoid the pain emotions cause me.

"Do not growl at me. I will wear what I want; I will not be a 'yes man' because you are an Alpha; that's not how we will work. You are starting to me piss me off, so go for a run and let your Wolf's energy out and come back to me calm." I say through gritted teeth, pain bouncing around my body as anger fills me.

I breathe in and out, calming myself and resetting my wall. The anger seeps away, and the pain lifts; he stares at me, and I decide to go towards him; I stroke his head, and he leans into me.

"Your Wolf needs a run; go, calm down and come back to me, okay?" I say softly, adding a tinge to my voice which I know he will listen to. He nods slowly before running towards the front door.

*

I'm lying on the sofa, my feet over Russell's lap, as we spend the afternoon watching TV, although we are chatting the whole way through, putting holes in the movie we are watching.

I get along really well with Russell, I feel so comfortable around him, and the fact he didn't ask me any questions about my life before, made it even easier to relax around him. Dayton is still out running; he clearly has a lot of pent-up energy.

"If they had a kid in real life, it would be stunning." I say, Russell agrees.

"Her dress reminds me of–" he stops mid-sentence and sits up straight.

"What's wrong?" I ask, frowning, sitting up and bringing my feet to the floor.

"Austin and Dayton found another Rogue. He is less ... manageable than you; they are fighting. I have to go help, stay here. Dayton would kill me if you were put in harm's way." Russell tells me, and I nod; as much as I hate the instruction and the Rogue in me wants to disobey, I don't want to go. I can't help fight the Rogue, so what's the point in going?

Russell is gone in seconds, and I watch through the window as he shifts.

I go to sit back on the sofa when an familiar voice breaks through in a panic. I run, following Russell's scent, the smell of freshly cut grass. I come through the clearing to see Wolves fighting. Two against two. I frown; Russell said it was one Rogue.

Dayton catches my smell and turns my way, distracted. The Wolf he is fighting uses this to his advantage and overpowers him.

More Wolves appear, but I know the Wolf he fights, white as snow with grey paws looking like he is wearing socks, will have killed him before any of them get to him.

"No!" I scream, and the white Wolf hesitates and looks right at me. Everyone freezes, the fighting stops and all the Wolves look in my direction. It's strange to think my simple cry caused this.

The Wolf now standing with the white Rogue looks at me gratefully, and I look into his eyes, surprised.

"Russell?" He bows his head in response.

The Rogue gets off Dayton and starts towards me, but Dayton shoots up and stands between us, growling.

Calmly I speak, knowing the situation needs to be diffused before anyone gets hurt. "I need everyone to shift back; I can't speak or have a conversation with you all as Wolves." No one moves.

I look to Dayton, "Shift!" I demand, and with a growl, all the Wolves disappear into the tree line and come back putting on shorts. I frown and make a mental note to ask where the shorts come from, now is not the time.

The Rogue appears and slowly walks towards me, weary of the Alpha even though Dayton hasn't reappeared yet.

The tears spill down my face, and I throw myself into the Rogues arms, sobbing; he holds me tight and soothes me. I hear a thunderous growl, but I don't let go, frightened that if I do, the Rogue will disappear before my eyes. He doesn't budge either as he strokes my hair, whispering soothingly that everything is okay.

"I'm here now, Lil; it'll all be okay." He promises, oh how wrong he is, but nice to believe, even just for a second.

Dayton growls again, and I let go and turn to my Mate. I reach out a hand, knowing that he needs to touch me for reassurance.

"What are you doing here?" I ask the Rogue.

"I was looking for you, Lil! I've been to so many Territories, but your scent is so faint, it's hard to keep up. Strong here though, you staying here?" Alec responds.

"Yeah, he is my Mate, so I'll probably stick around." I smile, nudging my head in Dayton's direction as he squeezes my hand gently.

No one else has spoken, the Wolves around us are used to Dayton being in charge, but he is unsure of how to proceed now it's clear I know the Rogue.

"Mate? I didn't think... Congrats!" He quickly changes his wording at my slight shake of the head.

"You're a Rogue!" I point out the obvious.

"I am?" He feigns shock before smiling. "I went back to our old Pack; she told me everything. I left quick to come to find you." His voice breaks at the thought; he shakes his head to clear it. "You haven't joined your Mate's Pack yet?" Alec asks.

"We are having issues." I wrinkle my nose, which causes Alec to laugh.

"What issues?"

"He keeps trying to tell me what to do." The exaggerated disgust is evident in my voice, and Alec chuckles.

"Oh dear, no one tells Lilla what to do!" He directs at Dayton, who snarls, clearly not happy with this situation or being told about his Mate.

I decide to bring the conversation back to the situation at hand; our catch up can wait.

"Why the fighting?" I ask Alec

"I thought you might be in danger, hence the..." he trails off and points at his temple, the sound of his panicked voice as he called my name still fresh in my mind.

"So why were you fighting with him?" I ask, turning to Russell.

"Erm, well, I didn't intend to, but I got here and ...erm... he's my Mate." Russell bursts out, excitement in his voice but a hint of sadness as he takes Alec's hand. My eyes widen, and I squeal happily, letting go of Dayton's hand and hugging them.

"You can join the Pack too!" I say excitedly to Alec, happy to know he won't be leaving anytime soon; I glance at Russell to see sadness take over completely.

"No." Dayton says from behind me.

"Why not?" I ask, confused, turning to Dayton.

"He used to belong to the Midnight Moon Pack, Lilla; they are a huge no-go for this Pack, a kill-on-sight sort of situation." Russell says sadly, clutching Alec's arm. My stomach lurches.

"For Russell's sake, we agreed not to kill him, but he must leave now." Dayton says, his tone not to be argued with. So, naturally I argue.

"For Russell's sake? You are better of killing him than having him separated from his Mate," I spit out.

"Russell is more than welcome to go with him."

"So I have to go to then?"

Dayton looks at me, confused. "What do you mean? Why would you?"

"Dayton, before I was a Rogue, I was in the Midnight Moon Pack. I escaped. Alec is my brother."

Lilla

No one moves. Silence settled around us. I knew this moment would come; he was going to reject me. Tears slide down my face, I didn't even think it would be possible for me to have a Mate, but now I do; I don't want to lose him. I've seen what that does to a Wolf. I shudder at the thought.

Finally, Dayton speaks, "How long ago?"

"Did I escape?" I ask; my voice is raspy as my mouth and throat are dry, "a year."

"What about you?" He turns to Alec.

"Three years ago. I went back briefly a month ago looking for Lil."

Dayton nods, contemplating his response. "Then it's not an issue. Alec, you were gone before they turned, and you, Little Rogue..." he trails off as he pulls me towards him. "You are my Mate, so I don't care where you came from."

"So you won't reject me?" I murmur, looking up at him, my chin on his chest seeking comfort.

"The only thing in the entire world that would make me reject you is if you killed an Alpha." He chuckles, looking down at me with warmth in his eyes. I smile softly as he slowly places his lips on mine. I take in his scent and try and pull him closer, feeling safe in his arms. His hands tighten around my waist, his tongue traces my lips, wanting access but a throat being cleared stops us.

Alec looks at me amused. Embarrassed, I want to bury my head in Dayton's chest, but I fight the urge and pull away.

"So are we just meant to watch you guys make out or...?" Alec asks, relaxed now he knows Dayton has no objections to his presence. Russell is beaming now that his Mate has been accepted.

"Oh my God, there's two of them!" Austin groans, and Dayton chuckles, the sound causes me to shiver with pleasure.

"What do you mean?" Alec asks

"Well, Alec, I think he is talking about our people skills, good looks and witty banter." I joke, moving towards him.

"Oh, of course! What else would he be talking about?" He puts his arm around my shoulders.

I hear Austin groan again.

"Come on, Lil, show your big brother around our new home."

*

"Okay, so maybe it wasn't the best idea." Alec looks at me with a "duh" expression before walking on. I was trying to show Alec around, but I didn't know the Pack, so we decided to just wander and see what there was. The place was bigger than we thought. The Pack takes up a whole town; they have their own schools, shops, and hospitals; it's a highly populated Werewolf area, with the odd Human who knows about us. The town is surrounded by woods, making it easier for our species to run. Training grounds include a running track, an obstacle course, and an empty ring where fighting and sparring occurs. The training grounds are made specially to test people in Human and Wolf forms. The houses are close together, and there are lots of them. There are at least over three hundred in the Pack, at a guess.

We had decided to make our way to Dayton's house, which was the biggest pack house I had ever seen, even bigger than our old Alpha's. The issue is that we didn't know which way it was. I had suggested a shortcut through the woods, and now that we were lost, Alec wasn't impressed.

"Can you just call someone or something?" Alec asks, turning to face me.

"How? I don't have a phone, and I wouldn't get a signal in the middle of the woods even if I did!" Alec walks on, muttering to himself about never listening to me again.

"Remind me to kill you when we find our way back to your Mate's house!" Alec calls, and I roll my eyes.

"Did you guys get lost?" We see Austin and Dayton staring at us, desperately trying not to laugh.

"No, we were just casually strolling." I say nonchalantly, but Alec runs over and throws his arms around them dramatically.

"Thank God you found us! I thought I was going to die out here!" He says as he pulls away.

"So, you did get lost?" Dayton asks, coming towards me.

I fold my arms, "I knew where I was going." He wraps his arms around my waist and chuckles.

"Of course, you did, Little Rogue. Come on, it's getting late. I wanted to stop off at Doc's office to check you over, see if you can start training." With one arm still around my waist, we walk back toward civilisation.

"Training for what?"

"So you and your brother can complete the tests to join our Pack."

"What tests?" I frown; I was never any good at tests.

"Just to see what you and your Wolf are capable of." He shrugs his shoulders like it's no big deal.

"Do I have to go to Docs?" Alec asks, shooting me a worried look; he knows the issue I have with the tests already.

"No, you can go find Russell and meet us at his office; you guys are coming over to mine for dinner. Little Rogue has to go because of how we found her." I had told Alec how I got here and what happened, so he just nods, and Austin takes him in search of Russell.

Doc is expecting me, and Dayton agrees to wait outside after some persuading.

"How are you feeling today, Lilla?" He asks, gesturing to the seat opposite his, a small desk between us.

"I'm fine; Dayton just wants to clear me for training."

"What do you suppose I do?" He asks; his voice is cold and detached.

I shrug, "Clear me, I guess."

"Clear you? Say I do that; what happens when you wake tomorrow barely able to move? Or you collapse during training because you are too weak?" His eyes are dead, his eyebrows pinched together.

"I don't know, I didn't think–"

"No, you didn't think. You didn't think when you came onto our Territory, you didn't think at all." His voice is full of disgust. This is not how I thought the conversation would go. I thought he would look me over, run a few tests and then tell me I was fit and ready.

"I'm sorry, but did I do something to offend you?" I question, racking my brains trying to think of what I could have done to have him have such a strong reaction to me.

"You turned up in our Territory. Only the most vindictive and awful people who commit heinous crimes get the Mark you have, and I'm not surprised since you belonged to the Midnight Moon Pack. You don't deserve to be part of this Pack or Mated to our Alpha. You should just tell him the truth and quick so he can reject you and move on." Doc finishes, he stands and moves away, turning his back and dismissing me.

A tear slides down my cheek; I knew Dayton would reject me when - if - I told him the truth. A part of me had hoped that he would accept me, but the Pack Doctor thinks Dayton will reject me. With this once conversation, all my hope has diminished, and all that's left is fear.

I push open the door and breathe in the evening air, trying to calm myself down, but tears continue to slide down my face.

"Little Rogue, are you okay?" Dayton asks, moving from his position of leaning against the outside wall of Doc's office. He places a hand on each side of my face and wipes the stray tears. Just having him near makes me feel better.

"I'm fine." I say, leaning into him, taking in his scent.

"What did he say that has you so upset." Dayton asks softly, but I can feel the anger beneath the surface.

"Nothing, Dayton, please just leave it." He shivers as I say his name, and his anger is replaced by lust. "Can we go now?" I ask, hopefully.

"Lil?" Alec shouts and starts to run toward us, dragging Russell behind him. "Have you seen Russell's house? It's amazing!" He stops in front of me as I turn away from Dayton to face Alec, and he frowns when he sees my tear-stained face. "What's wrong, Lil?" He asks worriedly.

"Nothing." I repeat for Alec's benefit, but he just raises an eyebrow. Before I have time to say anything else, he grabs my hand and pulls me a safe distance away from prying ears.

"Tell me what happened!" Alec demands, and I burst into tears before "nothing" passes my lips for the third time. He wraps his arms around me, and when I've calmed down, I tell him what Doc said.

*

"Alec! Just leave it!" I beg as I run after him. He growls and slams the door behind him, shaking the whole office. Dayton and Russell stare at me with wide, questioning eyes; I follow Alec.

I gasp when I open the door to see he has Doc by the neck, yelling at him.

"Let him go, Alec!"

He growls in my direction and turns his attention back to Doc, who looks petrified. I push my own fear aside and try to get through to him.

"Alec!" I shout, and he growls louder, causing Dayton and Russell to come in. Dayton tries to pull me out of harm's way as Russell makes his way over to his Mate, wanting to calm him down.

I get out of Dayton's grasp and block Russell's path; he will only get hurt, and Alec will never forgive himself.

"Enough is enough! Alec, I said let him go!" I let the anger seep into my voice and use the commanding tone that runs in our family. I collapse in pain, and just before everything goes black, I see Alec release his grip from Docs' neck.

Dayton

"She is showing her brother around, I have pups keeping an eye on them so they don't get lost, they'll keep me updated." Austin informs me, dropping down next to me on the sofa in my office.

I nod and take a sip of my Whiskey.

"Drinking before midday, what's going on?" He asks, taking the glass from me and helping himself.

"Do you remember when we were kids? How simple life was? We didn't have anything to worry about. So carefree." I muse and Austin smiles.

"We used to run wild, didn't we?" He says, laughing at the many memories we shared.

"I wish I could be a kid again, no worries, no drama, just running around playing, nothing to do." I sigh, as Austin hands me back my glass.

I look around my office. It used to be my dad's and I didn't change any of it. I couldn't bring myself to. Bookshelves full of books behind the desk, I've never even touched them, but the memories of my dad pouring over them made me keep them.

"Look Dayton, I know you better than anyone, if a best friend Mate existed, mine would be you," he said with a smirk. "You were always doing something, some job you had to help out with. You weren't as carefree as you think. You just love the idea of doing a job without the consequences of being in charge. You didn't have to worry about making the wrong decision, messing everything up. Now, you do."

Austin is right and we both know it.

I sigh.

"They were part of the worst Pack in the world. Can I really make the decision to bring them in? What about the safety of my Pack? They are unpredictable." I rub a hand over my face, feeling the weight of the world on my shoulders.

"Actually, are they unpredictable? She is your Mate, from the moment you met her, you knew her better than anyone else. Yes, you've technically known her 5 minutes but your Wolf's instinct with his Mate means you know her. That makes her predictable. The same with Russell. Which makes Alec predictable." Austin finishes of the shared glass of whiskey and goes quiet, listening to the voices in his mind.

"They are lost, we should go help them." Austin stands up.

"Can I really ask the Pack to take these to Rogues in?"

"You are the Alpha, you technically don't have to ask. But also, this Pack would do anything for you. We trust you. We would never ask you to turn your Mate away. You never would anyway."

I stand up and stare at my best friend.

"This could lead to a war." I state and Austin laughs.

"Over those too? Your girl said it herself, she was the runt of the Pack and Alec isn't special either. Yes, the Midnight Moon Pack is psycho, but they won't go to war with us over a couple of nobodies."

I smile and feel the weight lift.

"You're right I suppose! Come on then, let's go help them, but let's watch them for a distance for a bit, this could be entertaining."

*

She is keeping something from me. I knew it, my Wolf knew it, but what?

I couldn't understand why she winced at my voice or touch when we met, but that pain she felt made me buckle. Why was she feeling pain at all?

She had looked as white as a ghost when she told me she used to belong to that Pack. I shudder as I think about it. How did my Little Rogue belong to them once? What would she have been forced to do?

Her brother was a male version of her, the humour, the sarcasm, the witty banter. Even their looks were the same, the black hair and the unusual purple eyes. They could pass for twins easily.

"How is she doing?" Alec comes in and sits down on the bed next to her. When we had run into Doc's office and seen Alec holding him by the throat, my Wolf was torn. Do I protect Lilla? Or do I protect my Pack from the Rogue attacking?

Lilla won.

It turned out, however, that she didn't need my protection. She used a commanding tone. I could feel the power, but I didn't recognise it. And with it, more questions about my Mate filled my head.

Alec must have recognised it because he snapped out of his anger immediately. The pain was unbearable as Lilla collapsed, even I fell to my knees. When it subdued, I picked her up and carried her home. Alec blamed himself; it was all over his face as he sat watching her.

"The same, hasn't woken yet," it had been a whole day and she was still out. "Alec, what happened?" I asked. Alec sighed, running a hand through his hair.

"It's not my place to tell you, but you must know I wouldn't have attacked a Pack member if I wasn't protecting her." I nodded; he was sincere in his words.

"I have so many questions about her." I say as I stare down at my sleeping Mate. Alec looks at me, sadness in his eyes. He opens his mouth to speak, but he is interrupted by a knock at the door. We both turn as the door opens, and Austin comes in.

"Everyone's ready." He informs me; for a second, I'm confused before I remember I had called a meeting after Alec had turned up. I look over at Lilla.

"I'll stay with her; go be an Alpha." Alec reassures me with a smile before I turn and follow Austin out the door.

*

Silence fills the room as I walk in and sit at the head of the table. I look around at them all. Austin was on my right, next to him was Blade, on my left Rowan, the Pack Trainer, next to him Jace, my best tracker and Russell sat at the end of the table opposite me. My most trusted Pack members helped me keep this Pack in check. They all had their uses.

"Two Rogues slipped through our borders. I realise she is my Mate and her brother, but it still shouldn't have happened." I say, addressing the main issue. I look at Jace, "Double the patrols and send a few Wolves out to the edge of the borders to make sure our scent is still strong, have them mark it if not." Jace was in charge of border control; he nodded in understanding.

"The training with the Rogues needs to start soon." Rowan explains, he hadn't been introduced to Lilla and Alec yet, neither had Jace.

"Start with Alec immediately. Once Lilla wakes, we will see if she's strong enough; we may have to wait until she recovers." Rowan nods.

"Is Doc okay?"

"He's fine, a bit shaken, but Alec did no harm," Austin informs us. "He won't tell us what it's about though." I slam my fist on the table, anger rising. Why were people keeping secrets from me?

I'm the Alpha.

"Anything else?" I snarl, the room is quiet, but I look up to see them shake their heads. I stand up and walk out, making my way out of the house. I wanted to go back to Lilla, but I knew I needed to go for a run first.

*

By the time I made it home, night had fallen and I decide to go to sleep and see Lilla in the morning. As I opened the door, the sound of laughter travels through the house. I found myself climbing the stairs and letting myself into her room. Lilla and Alec sat laughing hysterically in bed, and immediately my heart warmed.

My Little Rogue is awake and happy.

Her striking purple eyes glance in my direction and light up when she sees me.

"What are you two up to?" I ask, moving towards her.

"Nothing." Alec says innocently, then kisses her cheek and leaves.

I raise an eyebrow at her, and she chuckles.

"How are you feeling?" I ask her, sitting in the chair next to her bed.

"A little weak but fine."

"How weak?"

"Well, weaker than the other day when you found me," she says softly while picking at lint on her covers. She was fragile then; was it possible for her to be even weaker?

"What happened with Doc? What did he say to upset you?" I asked. I had to know; it was like an itch that needed to be scratched.

"I'm broken," she whispers, barely audible. I wait in silence for her to continue. "Doc knows that I'm bad for the Pack and told me my worst fear would come true." She isn't looking at me; instead, she plays with the duvet, tracing the design.

"What's your worst fear?" I ask

She sighs, "That you will reject me." I sit shocked for a second before getting up and walking around to the other side of the bed. I climb on the bed, wrapping my arms around her as she rests her head on my chest.

"I told you the only thing that would make me reject you is if you killed an Alpha, so please stop worrying. I'm not going to reject you." I say strongly.

"We'll see. Can I take a nap?" She asks, quickly changing the subject. I try to get up, but she grabs my arm, stopping me.

"Can you stay?" Her voice was once again barely audible. I relax into the bed and with her head on my chest, my arms wrapped around her, we both fall asleep.

Lilla

I was first to wake up; I looked up at his face, so peaceful when he's sleeping. Without even thinking, I bring my index finger to his hairline and then begin to run my finger down his profile. As I reach his lips, I see they have a slight smile on them. I look up into his eyes to see him watching me. I turn over fully so that I'm on my stomach and stare at my Mate.

"Hi." He silently watches me as my fingers continue to trace the outline of his lips. "Sorry if I woke you." I add and pull my fingers away, suddenly embarrassed.

"I don't mind; you can wake me up anytime." He says with a grin, and I smile at him. "How are you feeling?"

"Better, I'm still weak but I feel like I'm strong enough to move around." Before the sentence has barely left my lips, he flips us around so that my back is firmly on the bed, and he is hovering over me, holding his weight with his arms on either side of my head. My breathing increases, and I'm sure he can hear my heartbeat as he stares into my eyes. His eyes trail down my face and land on my lips; suddenly nervous, I lick them, and his eyes darken with lust. He moves forward until his face is inches away. I wait expectantly for him to kiss me, wanting – no – needing him to do so.

Growing impatient, I lean forward the rest of the way and peck his lips softly. That was all the encouragement he needed as his lips crash against mine, my head falling back onto the bed. His tongue traces my lips, and without any hesitation, I open my mouth, and our tongues intertwine.

I wrap my arms around his neck and run my fingers through his hair, forcing him closer to me. His lips leave mine, and he begins to trail down my neck with his tongue. I bite my lip, fighting a moan when he freezes.

The only sound is our heavy breathing, and I wonder why he has stopped. Is there someone at the door? He is pulling away from me, and I feel cold. A small part on my neck still tingling from where his lips had been seconds ago.

That's when it hits me. My hand flies to the last spot he kissed, searching for the strap that has been hiding my secret. The strap is no longer there; instead, I feel it hanging off my shoulder, and immediately I pull it back and sit up.

Dayton is watching me; his eyes darken in anger rather than the lust they were a second before. I open my mouth to speak, but with a growl, he turns and leaves. I run after him, calling his name, begging him to listen.

He makes his way down the corridor and quickly down the stairs before he stops in the front room, where I see Alec, Russell, Blade, Blaze, Austin, Aria and two other men I don't recognise standing there watching us, unsure if they should leave.

"Dayton, please! I can explain!" I beg, leaning against the bannister at the foot of the stairs; I was still weak, and running after him had made me tired.

"There is nothing to explain. You are already Marked! You belong to someone!" His voice cracks as he says it, and tears spring to my eyes.

"No, I –"

"Just tell me something, do you love him? Does he make you happy?" His voice is full of hurt and sadness; tears are running down my cheeks, his pain and my pain holding on to each other.

"Dayton–"

"Who is he? The man you love enough to let him Mark you." He continues to ask me questions, not letting me answer.

"He's my–"

"Don't tell me! I don't want to know." He growls, his hurt turning to anger, and I flinch at the sudden change.

I can feel his anger boiling over, he turns to open the front door before he shifts, leaving shredded clothes in his wake.

*

Still too weak to stand for long, Alec grabs me a chair. I can feel everyone watching me. I sit facing the front door, waiting for him to come back.

He has to come back.

"Lil?" Alec has been trying to get me to talk; I had been uncooperative so far.

"He didn't give me a chance to explain," my voice falters, and the tears start again.

"How did he find it?" Alec asks, kneeling in front of me.

I look down at him and raise an eyebrow. "How do you think?" I say, annoyance creeping into my voice.

Alec grimaces. I place my hand over the strap. The Mark was just on the collar bone; it was painful. It had to be; it was punishment. It wasn't big, just two teeth marks, like a vampire would leave behind. I could easily cover it, which is why he hadn't seen it, why no one had seen it.

I groan, and I place my head in my hands. "How could I be so stupid?"

"You got caught up in the moment, Lil." Alec tries to comfort me, but I can hear the discomfort in his voice.

"I should never have let my guard down. I should never have...." I trail off as I break down in tears. "He didn't give me a chance to explain," I sob.

Alec puts his arms around me, and I fall into them, they are comforting, but they aren't the arms I want.

"He was mad; he couldn't let you explain. He nearly shifted while shouting at you; he could have hurt you. He knew that. He needs to be calmer to hear the truth." Alec reassures me, rubbing his knuckles soothingly over my back.

I relax slightly, but the tears continue to run. "Then he will reject me." I feel sick at the thought.

"Of course, he will reject you!" I look up to see one of the men I don't know staring at me with nothing but disgust.

"Rowan, leave it." Austin says, but Rowan ignores him.

"You are Marked by another Wolf, and you still try to seduce our Alpha? That is sick. How could you be so heartless and cruel?!" He spits out.

I stand up; as much as I want to watch the door until he comes back, I needed to leave; I don't need people saying horrible things to me right now. I make it to the stairs before Rowan starts talking again.

"I just don't get how you could let someone Mark you when they aren't your Mate."

I turn and face him, "I didn't *let* anyone do anything." I say through gritted teeth.

"What does that mean?" We all turned to the source of the voice, but I knew who it was. Dayton stood in the doorway staring at me.

"You're back," I say apprehensively. He wasn't gone long; he can't have calmed down yet.

"I need to know the truth; I need to know why and who Marked you. Otherwise, no matter how much I run, I won't get the anger out of my system. You said you didn't let anyone do this?"

"I was forced," I look down at my hands, my throat killing from my sobbing.

"By who?" He asks, his eyes narrowing, his anger radiating, but I feel slightly at ease as I don't think it's directed at me.

"My Uncle."

*

This is not how it was meant to go. I planned on telling him when I was ready. When I could face the truth. It was meant to be a conversation between him and me. No Audience. Instead, I had told him a partial truth. He'd have questions. He'd expect answers. The answer I wasn't ready to give.

The air around me was thick; no one knew what to say. Aria had gasped at my words, and Blaze had her hand over her mouth; the men just stared at me; even Alec looked at me with wide eyes. He didn't think I was going to do it like this either.

My knees buckle because I've been standing too long, my whole body feeling drained. Dayton picks me up in his arms before I have a chance to hit the ground; I lean into him instantly, my head on his shoulder as he carries me to my bed.

Without a word, he tucks me in and goes to leave.

"Dayton?" I begin to panic, and he turns to face me, worry written all over his face. "Where are you going?" I couldn't have him leave me again; what if he didn't return?

"I was going to leave you to sleep," Dayton says, standing by the door.

"Please, stay?" I beg, and without any hesitation, he climbs into the bed next to me and wraps his muscular arms around me.

"I'm sorry," I manage before sleep beckons me.

*

I wake the following day feeling empty. I turn over and begin to panic. Dayton is gone. He left me. Jumping out of bed, I notice that I have my strength back. Today is going to be a good day. I search for his scent and follow it, it leads me to the front door, and without thinking, I open the door and continue my search.

As soon as I see him, I begin running. He is watching something, so are other members of the Pack. It's a big crowd, but I don't pay any attention, my eyes firmly set on my Mate. I push through the crowd getting odd looks from them, but I don't stop. There is a space between my Mate and me, and I run for him. His head snaps up, catching my scent, and he turns my way as I fling myself into his arms.

Immediately his arms wrap around me, and I place my head on his shoulders, leaning towards the crook in his neck, inhaling his scent.

"What's wrong, Little Rogue?" He asks as my legs wrap around his waist, his hands land on my butt, holding my slight weight.

"I thought you had left me. I thought..." my throat catches, and I snuggle closer as his arms tighten.

"It's okay, Little Rogue. I'm not going anywhere." I begin to relax, and then I start to hate myself. How have I become someone who relies so much on one person? I have made sure to only ever count on myself, yet I had run out into a town I barely knew, in my very skimpy pyjamas, all in search of Dayton.

Dayton snaps me out of my thoughts as he lets out a growl. I snap my head up and look at him. "You are in your pyjamas, in front of my Pack." I roll my eyes. I'm surprised it took him so long to notice.

"So? They can all see me in your arms, and I'm pretty sure most of them saw me running for you like a maniac." I see most of the Pack had stopped watching whatever they were watching before I arrived, and now they were watching us.

The Alpha and the Rogue.

"Alpha?' Rowan calls, and Dayton turns in his direction, with me still wrapped around him. I turn my head to see two Wolves standing side by side, one of which I recognised, watching us.

"We stopped the fight; you said you wanted to see it."

"Fight?" I asked, turning back to face Dayton.

"Alec's training." Dayton says, and I jump down.

"Oh... Can I have a go?" I ask excitedly, remembering after the words had slipped out my mouth, it was the worst idea.

"Are you strong enough?" Dayton asks, unsure, and I try to think of a way out of this.

"I have good and bad days. I will never be 100% strong, but I understand if you don't–" I'm interrupted by a snarl coming from Alec, and before I can ask what's wrong, I pick up the scent. Panic sets in, but knowing I have to protect this Pack - My Pack - I push it down and take control.

"Stay here," I snarl at Alec, and as I start running toward the scent, a man jumps through the trees, heading straight for me.

*

"Keep him away!" I tell Alec, talking about Dayton; he doesn't argue; he shifts into Human form and, grabbing a pair of shorts, places a firm hand on Dayton's shoulder. I see him say something, but I face the man in front of me.

"Well, well, well. Look at Little, all grown up. I have to say you look ravishing in that little outfit." The man speaks, giving me the once over. I hear Dayton growl behind me, and I hope Alec has a tight enough grip on him.

"What are you doing here, Luke?" I ask, stepping slowly forward.

"Alpha Drake has had me searching for you since you left. Or should I say 'escaped?' You didn't make it easy; I'll give you that. Always moving, but you've been here a bit too long. So, let's go. Alpha Drake isn't done with you." He says casually as he beckons me to follow, like he expects me to just leave with him.

"Well, I'm done with him." I retort. Luke laughs.

"You are so cute when you try to be strong. Come with me, Little, or I'll make you." He threatens.

"So make me," I tease, and he shifts into a Wolf as he runs for me.

No one moves; Alec commands everyone to leave us alone. Luke's black Wolf lands on top of me and goes for my throat. I can feel his hot breath on my skin, making me shudder in repulsion. I bring my hands to his snout and pull back, my fingers starting to pour out blood as his teeth sink into them. Despite the pain, I continue to pull, not giving him the chance to snap down on my fingers. When I see his neck, I grab it and squeeze, causing him to whimper in pain. I push him off and stand up. He circles me, snarling and growling. He comes at me again, but I jump and land on his back, bringing him down.

He struggles beneath me, but I have my Human teeth at his neck before he can do anything, and he freezes. He may have under-estimated me, but he knew what I could do to him in just one bite.

"Shift back, or I bite." I warn, and beneath me, I feel him shift. "He didn't tell you what you were up against, did he?" I get off him, and Alec throws me shorts without me asking. I throw them at Luke as he gets up and faces me. "No, all he said was that it was you. I remembered you; I knew you would be easy to bring back."

"Poor naive little boy. Go, now." I order, and he frowns, putting on his shorts.

"You're letting me go?" He asks, disbelief painted over his face. Mercy and kindness were not something they were used to.

"Yep, and you will give him a message for me. Tell Alpha Drake that the next person he sends to bring me back, I won't hesitate. I will take a bite and make them walk back just to die in front of him." I watch Luke begin to leave, "Oh and Luke? Tell him I found my Mate."

"Why would he care about that?" Luke asks, frowning.

"Trust me, he'll care." With that, Luke runs off in the same direction he came from. I turn round to see that I have an audience. I catch Rowan staring at me with an impressed look on his face. I think I've earned a little respect.

Dayton growls, and I turn to him. "What the hell were you thinking? Fighting a Wolf in Human form? He could have killed you!" He comes forward, free from Alec's command.

I snort, "No, he couldn't."

"He is a fully grown Wolf, Lilla! If he wanted to kill you, he would have. You're only small; he was going easy on you." Dayton snaps, and I snarl, keeping my anger at bay.

"You have no idea what you are talking about, pup, so drop it." I snap, and I hear an audible gasp around me. I had just referred to their Alpha as a pup. Very disrespectful.

"Lil!" Alec shouts, shock written all over his face. Even he thinks I've pushed too far. Dayton is in front of me in seconds, hand wrapped around my throat. I look into his eyes to see his Wolf has pushed through.

Fear and instinct take over, and before he can react, I sweep my leg, causing us both to fall. We land with a thud, and his hand has left my throat as he tries to protect me from getting hurt. Protectiveness beats the urge to show dominance, which I'm counting on. My legs are on either side of him as he lies on his back. The anger is still there, but he gains some control over his Wolf. The area is silent; no one moves, no one speaks; they all just watch to see our next moves.

"You ever touch me in anger again, and I will rip your throat out without hesitating. Mate or not, I will not go through another abusive Alpha." I stand up and walk away, leaving a stunned Dayton on the floor and his Pack members staring after me, mouths wide open.

*

Alec follows me back to the house, calling my name. When I reach the stairs in the front room, I stop and turn. "What, Alec?"

"You have to apologise to him," he says simply. My eyes widen. I hear the door open, but neither of us pays any attention to the figures in the doorway.

"Why?"

"You disrespected their Alpha! You called him a pup and floored him!"

I breathe in and out, refusing to get angry.

"You heard what he said, right?"

"Yes, he underestimated you, as everyone else does," Alec shrugs, not getting it.

"Exactly my point, Alec! Everyone underestimates me, and in some cases, like with Luke, it is beneficial but to have your Mate not think you are capable..." I trail off. "It hurts."

Alec sighs and rubs his temple, trying to ward off a headache. "Okay, I get where you are coming from, but he is their Alpha, who you disrespected and then showed dominance. You can't do that; his Pack will see him as weak; they will try what you tried." Alec says, trying to make me see sense.

I don't say anything, so Alec continues, "You have to do what the Alpha says, and he knows what's best for us." His words hit me, and I suck in my breath sharply.

"I need to leave; I can't be here with you right now." I start to panic and turn to the door. I see Dayton, Austin, Rowan, Blade and a man I don't recognise staring at me. I push past them and sigh as the night air hits. Alec follows, clearly not done with the conversation.

"Lil-"

"You sound just like her," I accuse, and Alec frowns.

"Like who?"

"Mum! Telling me the Alpha knows best. I have to do what the Alpha says. You sound like just like her!" I can't keep the disgust from my voice.

Alec points his finger at me, warning, "She didn't do anything wrong!"

"How the hell would you know, Alec? You've been gone for three years." I turn away and run into the woods, not waiting for his response.

Dayton

Her scent is nowhere. Like she never existed. She ran off after an argument with Alec, and we left her to cool down, she needed to be alone, but hours later, no one could find her and I had the whole Pack looking for her. No scent made it impossible. I head to my room; my Wolf and I are too anxious to think clearly. What if she has been kidnapped? Killed? What if she left and is never coming back?

I needed to think as an Alpha, not as a Mate. I needed to be alone.

Opening my door, her scent hits me, and I immediately calm down. She is sitting on my bed in my hoodie, her bare legs crossed, leaning against my pillows.

"Little Rogue? Are you okay?"

I mind-link the Pack to let them know I've found her.

"I'm fine; I came in through your window. I figured your Pack would be searching everywhere, and I didn't want to be found," she says softly. I decided not to ask how she climbed two storeys to get to my room.

"How long have you been here?"

"About as long as you've been looking for me. I found your hoodie," she looks down at the writing: Göteburg. "So, you've been to Sweden?"

"Only once; it was a very short visit. My Dad was creating a treaty with an Alpha there; he wanted to show me how it was done. He brought me that hoodie as a reminder." I sit down on the bed at her feet, her legs now out in front of her, slightly bent. "What about you? Ever been?"

She shakes her head, "Our Alpha was Swedish; he is the one who gave me my name," she looks at her feet.

"Your Alpha named you?" I ask, frowning, she nods, and we fall into silence.

"I'm not going to apologise to you. For what I did or said." She says suddenly, snapping her head up at me.

"I didn't think you would," I admit. "I shouldn't have done that to you, though. I shouldn't have let my Wolf take control like that. I was scared for you; fighting a Wolf in human form is dangerous." I explained, even though there was no excuse for how I treated her. I'll never forgive myself.

The fear in her eyes as my hands wrapped around her neck, her words *'I will not go through another abusive Alpha,'* made me shudder. To think what my Little Rogue has been through.

"You aren't my Alpha; you can't treat me like a disobedient Pup. You can't decide for me what I'm capable of. Like you, this Pack can't see me as weak. If I'm to be the Luna here, you must treat me as an equal." Silence stretches out between us.

"Why couldn't I move?" I frown, and before I can ask any more questions, Lilla kisses me. I know this is a tactic to distract me, but I kiss her back, and her kiss becomes more urgent.

She bites my bottom lip, and I open my mouth as our tongues entwine. She grabs my shirt and pulls it towards her as she leans back into my bed. I follow, trailing kisses down her jawline and neck, causing her to moan. I come across her Mark as I move the strap and stop. Breathing heavily, I lean my head on her shoulder. The Mark is unusual, but it's still a Mark that isn't mine.

"Dayton," her voice is full of lust, and I shiver as she says my name. I pull away, and she sighs.

"I can't; you belong to someone else."

"My uncle, and it's not even-"

"It doesn't matter. You should go to your room and sleep. I've moved the tests to tomorrow." I climb off of her, and she sits up.

"Why?" She asks; I notice the panic in her voice, probably because she hasn't done any training.

"We have an Alpha coming to visit; he is looking for someone. I won't have them thinking of you as just a Rogue. I want you to be in the Pack and seen as the Luna, whether we are Mated or not."

"Which Alpha?" She asks as she gets to the door. She is standing in my hoodie, her legs on show; she never did change out of her pyjamas. I look away quickly before I change my mind.

"I don't know. Austin ran into him; he doesn't recognise his scent but says he barely escaped with his life. We need to be ready."

Lilla

I close my door in my room and put my forehead on the wood, groaning. I was meant to have more time to get out of it, to think of an excuse.

I snap my eyes open when someone clears their throat.

"Sore throat?" I ask sarcastically, and the figure on my bed chuckles.

I fall onto the bed, lying on my stomach, my arms under the pillow.

I close my eyes and sigh, "the tests are tomorrow." I say, but he doesn't respond.

"What did she do?" He asks softly, I know who he is talking about, but this isn't a conversation I want to have. Now or ever.

"What?" I ask, eyes still closed, pretending that I'm drifting off to sleep.

"What did Mum do?" He asks again.

"Nothing, she did nothing." I admit.

"Nothing? But you said-" I sit up abruptly and look into my brother's eyes.

"Alec, she did nothing. She stood by and let him do whatever he wanted. She told me he was doing what was best for the Pack." The venom and hatred in my voice shocked him.

"Oh, God!" Alec rubs his face violently. "What the hell happened in the three years I was gone? It wasn't that bad when I left, was it?" He removes his hands and faces me.

"Alec, I'm exhausted. Could we leave this until tomorrow?" I get out of bed and make my way to the bathroom.

"Lil, please!" Alec calls, standing up. "Tell me, what happened?'
"You left! You walked away from your Pack, your family. You walked away from me. You left, broke his heart and then more drama happened, and you weren't there to help us. You ran, and now we are here, with tests tomorrow that we both know I will fail. I get why you did it, but you had me. He would have accepted you, gay or straight, he didn't care, and honestly, if you had been around, maybe I wouldn't have this Mark." Drained, I walk into the bathroom, close the door and sit on the floor, waiting for him to leave.
I had been too harsh; he would take it the wrong way. I should go out and apologise, but instead, I lie down on the tiled floor and fall asleep.

*

I wake up stiff. Sleeping on a tiled floor will do that to you. I get up slowly. At least I wasn't weak. I shower and dress, ready to face the day.
The tests, I groan as I remember.
What the hell was I going to do?
I walk downstairs to find everyone waiting. I see Alec, and my chest hurts at the harsh words I had said to him yesterday.
"Alec!" I call, and he turns to me, coldness in his stare.
"I'm sorry," I say with a pained expression.
"I'm the one who is sorry," he says, and I frown, confused. "I'm sorry that my being gay was the cause of all your pain."
He turns and leaves with Russell. I sigh, I knew he'd take it the wrong way, but I have to deal with these tests first. I can deal with Alec later, one thing at a time.
"Should we go?" I ask, and Dayton nods. I feel my legs shake as I walk, and I begin to sweat. My stomach is in knots, and the feeling of nausea hasn't left me since I woke this morning.
"Don't worry, you'll be fine." Dayton says, wrapping his arm around my

waist. Usually, his touch calms me, but today it doesn't; I give him a nervous smile before I pull away, not looking at the hurt expression that I knew would be on his face.

*

"Okay, first we want to see you run in Human form around this track, as fast as possible." Rowan says to us; I glance around nervously at the formed audience. The excitement rolls of them, causing bile to rise in my throat. Little children are on their parent's shoulders to get a better view. I find Dayton, who gives me a reassuring smile and then when Rowan blows the whistle, Alec and I run.

*

So far, we have completed the tests in Human form. The agility, where I had beaten the fastest Wolf in the Pack and Alec. The obstacle course was my favourite as I had picked different ways to overcome each obstacle. The fighting - which was challenging, to begin with - with their best fighter was tough, and I didn't want to hurt anyone, that was until someone mentioned his name. After that, I saw red. Alec had to save the man before I killed him, and then he had to calm me down. Now we had to do it again in Wolf form; of course, it wouldn't be the same, and part of it included the woods.

"Shift." Rowan commands, and Alec does so next to me. I just stand there looking at him. I had been good all day. Doing everything that was told of me, even though I wanted to rebel, but this was something I couldn't do.

"Shift!" Rowan shouts at me, and I stand in front of him frozen; I needed to think of an excuse, but my mind was blank as I went into panic mode.

The audience is silent, and Rowan turns to Dayton, confused. Dayton comes forward and stands in front of me.

"What's wrong, Little Rogue?" He asks, voice filled with worry; I stare up at him.

"I can't do it." I whisper as I begin to shake.

"Hey, yes, you can. You already did the tests in Human form. The Wolf part is kind of the same, only a little different. You'll be okay, Little Rogue." His voice is full of pride and reassurance.

"No, Dayton, you don't understand; I can't do it!" I say with more force, and he frowns.

"All you have to do is shift; don't worry about your clothes." It's my turn to frown now. Does he think I'm worried about ripping my clothes?

"No, I-"

"Just shift." Dayton interrupts with more force. He has to stop interrupting me. It was becoming a habit, one I intended for him to break.

"Dayton." I say, and he shakes his head.

"You are beginning to embarrass me in front of my Pack. Again. Shift, Lilla!" His hands that are on my arms tighten slightly. I step away from him, pulling my arms with force out of his grasp.

"I wouldn't want to be an embarrassment now, would I?" I say as my eyes water. He knows he's hurt me, and he takes a step forward. I can see and feel everyone watching us. It's so quiet you could hear a pin drop, so I know everyone listened to every little word we have said.

I walk around Dayton and start to walk away from the training grounds; I turn to face him as I near the crowd. "I'll be packed and gone before you come back," my throat tightens painfully as I push through the crowd, heading for the house.

*

Ten minutes later, I'm standing in the doorway, arms crossed with two Werewolves next to me. Dayton stops when he sees me, Austin, Rowan and another man, who I still didn't know the name of, but have seen with them multiple times now.

"I tried to leave, but they wouldn't let me." I point at the Wolves.

"I don't want you to leave Lilla," he says.

"I didn't finish the test, and I'm an embarrassment to you and your Pack." I shrug my shoulders as if it isn't a big deal, but we can all hear the hurt in my voice.

"I didn't mean what I said. I just..." he trails off.

"Your Wolf retaking control?" I ask bitterly.

"No, I just... You wouldn't shift, and it was embarrassing for me as an Alpha, not as your Mate."

"You should have let me explain!" From the corner of my eyes, I see Alec and Russell appear, hand in hand.

"I know, and I'm sorry." He is, I can hear the raw emotion in his voice, but I'm still angry.

"You constantly interrupt me before I have a chance." I continue, and he looks down. We wait silently for him to say something.

"So, tell me - us. Why didn't you shift?" Dayton says, looking back up to face me.

"I can't."

"What? Like stage fright? Everyone gets that the first time shifting in front of a Pack. You just got to push through the nerves and shift." Austin says, and I rub my temples warding off a headache. Why aren't they getting what I'm saying?

"It wasn't nerves. I can't Shift!" They fall silent as I say the words, confusion written over their faces.

The question is all on the tips of their tongues: What kind of Werewolf can't shift?

The answer: A Broken One.

Dayton

This morning the air was thick with tension when Lilla came downstairs. Alec and Lilla had fought last night, we could all hear them shouting, but we gave them their privacy and didn't listen. Of course, the temptation was there; I would have loved to have learnt more about my Mate by listening.

His last comment to her this morning was about being gay and her pain. I didn't ask, although, again, the temptation was there, even for my Wolf.

He shut up quickly when Lilla's nerves hit us. I automatically tried to reassure her, but she dropped my hand and walked ahead. My Wolf was hurt; he just wanted to reassure his Mate.

Feeling how nervous she was, I wanted to cancel the tests, but it was a Rite of Passage for every Wolf joining My Pack. Even the Luna. Especially the Luna.

It turned out she had nothing to be nervous about. She is magnificent. She is the fastest Wolf, faster than Alec and faster than the fastest in my Pack. The obstacle course was unexpected; with all the different ways to beat each obstacle, Lilla did the ones I never thought of. My Mate, the Luna of this Pack, was pure talent.

The fighting is where it all went pear-shaped. Alec went first, it wasn't easy, but he won. Then it was Lilla's turn.

Rowan and Austin held me back as she was thrown about like a rag doll. I was stunned each time she got back up, considering how weak she could be. I could see and smell the cuts on her, but she was so focused like she hadn't noticed. Maybe the adrenaline had something to do with that. I did see, however, that she wasn't healing, and I wasn't the only one.

She was just thrown against the side of the ring when someone from my Pack shouted, 'Come on, Derek.'

Alec tensed next to me as Lilla stood up, almost robotic. Her expression and her body language changing. She had become someone I didn't recognise, someone, fit to be in the Midnight Moon Pack. She wasn't the Lilla I loved, but this cold, stone-faced, heartless creature.

The fight changed; no longer was she thrown around like a rag doll but instead the one doing the throwing.

Alec swore and ran towards them. He got there before any real, life-threatening damage could be done.

Alec held her and whispered in her ear repeatedly until my Little Rogue came back.

*

I had regretted the words as soon as they left my mouth. I wasn't embarrassed by her but by the situation; that's all I meant.

"I can't shift!" She explains, frustrated. We all stare at her in confusion, not knowing what to say or do.

I knew something was wrong.

I told you I couldn't feel her Wolf.

My Wolf says in a righteous tone. I ignore him and stare at Lilla, trying to form words.

"What do you mean you can't shift?" Austin asks from next to me.

"What kind of stupid question is that?" Alec snorts. "She can't shift; there is no hidden meaning behind those words!"

"Why can't you shift?" I find my voice, and Alec and Austin go silent, though I can feel Austin glare at Alec.

She frowns and stares at me. "It hurts," she says, her voice breaking, causing my heart to break a little. "More than anything I've ever experienced. It hurts to even try." She wipes away loose tears roughly with her fingers.

"Is it your first time?" Rowan asks softly. I try to hide my surprise. Rowan is never soft with anyone, first time-shifting or not.

She shakes her head, "No, my Wolf is...." she pauses looking for the right word, "blocked. Anything I do that involves my Wolf causes me pain. Like meeting my Mate, the one thing that is meant to be the most amazing experience for us causes me intense pain because my Wolf is trying to get through." She stares down at herself, taking in the injuries and the blood. "Healing doesn't work either." She stares at us as we once again fall into silence.

"How?" Jace asks, and we all turn to him. "How is your Wolf blocked?"

We turn to Lilla, waiting for her to answer. She opens her mouth to say something but then closes it. Her broken expression changes to the one I saw when she was fighting.

"It just is." She replies coldly before turning around and heading to her room.

Lilla

"It just is?" Alec follows me into my bedroom. The bed suddenly looks uninviting, so I just stand in the middle of the room. Alec moves around me and sits on the bed facing me, one leg hanging off the end of the bed while the other is curved under him.

"What else was I supposed to say?" I ask, throwing my hands up.

"The truth never crossed your mind, huh?" He raises an eyebrow; our argument is temporarily forgotten in the drama.

"I can't tell them the truth." I tell him like I'm stating a fact.

"Yes, you can." Alec rolls his eyes as if I'm being unreasonable.

I shake my head and he frowns, "Why not?"

"Did you know that there is a difference between being lonely and being alone?" I ask, finally sitting on the bed as the need to sit down wins over. I copy Alec's sitting position, facing him.

"What's that got to do with anything?" Alec questions while his brain tries to piece the two things together.

"Being lonely feels like something is missing, but you are surrounded by people who want to help. When you left the Pack, I was lonely even though I had a Pack who tried to help and tried to understand, but I knew the only person who would get it would be you, so without you, I was lonely.

"When I became a Rogue, I was alone and not by choice. Which is its own form of torture. I had no one. No one to support me or help me. No one understands my situation. No one to call for help. Alec, I had no one to love me.

"Now, I'm still lonely, but again I have a Pack around me, willing to support me and try to understand. You saw them trying to support me without even knowing the truth. If I tell them, they will throw me out, and I'll be alone again. So, I can't tell them the truth because I'm scared. I'd rather feel lonely for the rest of my life than be alone ever again." I finish explaining and watching as Alec tries to follow my train of thoughts.

He finally sighs, "Lilla, what happened? What made Dad change? Was it me leaving?" I stare at my brother, his eyes pleading for the truth, the look of guilt all over his face. I caused the guilt, and I knew I owed him the truth. Our truth.

"My dear, dear brother, no, it wasn't your fault, but please know that what I'm about to tell you doesn't change us, okay?"

"Why would it?" Alec asks, the guilt leaving his face as bewilderment takes over; he looks at his foot as it moves around the carpet. It's my turn to sigh.

"Dad changed because his Mate died," I rush out the words before changing my mind. Alec's head snaps up to stare at me.

"I saw mum when I went back," Alec states, clearly thinking I'm lying. I push away the voice in my head demanding to know about him going back to the Pack and seeing mum. I had to deal with this before I dealt with that.

"Mum is his wife, not his Mate."

Alec scoffs, "Who told you that?"

"Mum did. When Dad first started changing, she decided I needed to know, so I could understand why he was suddenly becoming this way and why he wouldn't be my dad anymore." I wipe away the tear that falls down my face roughly, refusing to cry.

"Okay, so tell me everything." Alec finally decides, and with a nod, I begin.

*

"When Dad was 21, he was made Alpha, and he decided that he wanted to be seen with the most beautiful woman in the Pack. Mum said he was young and foolish. His eyes landed on Mum, and he knew she was the one he wanted. Her Mate had died before he could Mark her, so there was never going to be another Mate that got in the way, and she wouldn't go mad. He was too impatient to wait for his Mate, but I think he thought that he could just ditch Mum when he did.

"But he fell in love with Mum, no one believed they weren't Mates, they were best friends, you've seen them together, up to this moment you would never have guessed they weren't. Mum fell pregnant with you, so Dad decided to marry her; they both ignored the elephant in the room, which was what they would do if Dad met his Mate. Dad was over the moon when you were born; Mum said she had never seen him that happy.

"Then he found his Mate. I saw pictures of her, Alec; she looked like a Goddess. Long blonde hair, blue eyes, she was stunning. Mum gave Dad an out because she didn't want to stand in the way of two Mates, but Dad refused to leave his wife and his son. So, they all agreed to an affair, which sounds ridiculous but considering the circumstances, it was probably the most honourable way. So, Dad and his Mate had an affair, and Dad still had his wife and son, and Mum told me that they were honestly happy, that for whatever reason, it worked.

"Until his Mate fell pregnant, obviously they couldn't get rid of it, it was two Mates child and Mum wouldn't have that. I was born nine months later." I take a breath and watch his reaction.

"But we look so alike." Alec stares at me, trying to see any differences.

"Alec, we both look mostly like Dad, the only feature I got from her was the blonde hair, which I don't even have anymore." Alec picks up some of my hair and lets it fall slowly out of his hands.

"Then what happened?"

"She didn't want me, she couldn't have a family with her Mate, not properly, and she was worried she would resent me because I look so like Dad, so she gave me to Mum. I guess she was trying to be a good mother. She asked her to raise me as her own, and Mum did. I never would have thought she wasn't my mother; she didn't treat us any differently.

"After I was handed over to Mum, Dad and his Mate continued their affair, like nothing had happened, and so for years, that's what it was like.

"Then you left, three years ago, Dad was upset, and he didn't understand, but he survived; he knew you'd come back one day. He was so sure of that. It all changed when the Rogues came.

"They came at night, and Dad and his Wolf were torn, but he protected his wife and daughter. He chose to protect us over his Mate, who the Rogues killed without a second thought. He started to change after that. You know how it goes, a Wolf who loses his Mate when they are Mated drives the Wolf mad." I finish.

Alec pulls me into a hug, and we stay there for several minutes.

"What's going to happen about the tests?" I ask, remembering this morning, which feels like days ago.

"Dayton postponed it to this evening, but now he knows you can't shift; I have no idea what he's going to do."

*

I let out a high-pitched squeal and jumped onto the bed. Dayton and Austin burst through the door, looking for danger. Seeing none, they turn to me. It was the afternoon, and after Alec and I had a long talk, I wanted to nap. He had left me to it, and I went into the bathroom to pee.

"Little Rogue? What's wrong?" Dayton moves towards me, worry written over his face.

"Spider! In the shower! It was moving!" They both wince at my high-pitched tone.

"A spider?" Dayton asks, frowning.

"A huge motherf-"

"We thought you were being attacked!" Austin interrupts.

"I was! By a spider! Don't judge! You haven't seen it!" I yell, and Austin goes into the bathroom to check it out. I still haven't moved from my stance on the bed, and Dayton is standing at the edge, watching me with curiosity. I move towards him, looking down at his face. I couldn't help the smile that formed on my lips. We hadn't spoken since this morning but seeing him there, I wasn't mad at him, and from the look on his face, neither was he. I drape my arms around his neck as his hands find my waist.

"I like being taller than you." He lets out a growl, obviously not agreeing with me.

"Don't get used to it."

I laugh but stop abruptly when Austin appears with the spider in his hands. He makes his way towards me.

"Lilla, he wants to say hello!" He teases, and I scream and hold on tighter to Dayton.

"Dayton, please make him stop!" I beg, and I hear him chuckle. I push him away and glare at him.

"It's just a spider, Little Rogue." I can see the amusement in his eyes as Austin continues forward.

"Dayton," I can't help but whine. I've said it before, and I'll say it again. Frightened little girl when I am around spiders.

I see him shiver as I say his name. I change tactics.

"Dayton, make him stop." I say, using his lust to my advantage by putting on a hopefully, alluring voice.

"Austin, kill it and get out." Dayton orders, and within seconds the spider and Austin are gone. I relax, and Dayton moves forward; I climb off the bed and close the distance between us.

"What's going to happen with the tests?" I ask before our lips meet. He sighs and looks at me. "Alec will still do them. You won't."

"Won't people ask why? I don't want anyone to know." My voice goes small, and he pulls me closer. The lust and need for my kiss are gone as he tries to reassure me.

"They can ask why all they want, but I'm the Alpha; they can't argue with my decision. Besides, this Alpha is coming tomorrow. No one recognises the Pack smell, so we are all on edge." I wrap my arms around his waist and breathe in his scent.

"I'm sorry." I whisper.

"What for?" He asks, tightening his hold on me.

"Being a hassle, I'm probably not what you expected for a Mate."

"You are not a hassle, and you are more than I expected." He kisses the top of my head. "Now go take a shower; you and Alec are joining the Pack tonight."

Dayton

I sit on Lilla's bed as she jumps in the shower, the feeling of exhaustion taking over. I lean forward with my elbows on my knees. This has been the longest week of my life. So much has happened since meeting my Little Rogue a week ago. A lot to process.

They run through my mind. I let out a sigh

We are stuck with her.

My Wolf pipes in, reminding me as if I would get rid of her or something.

I wouldn't change her for anything. I just need her to trust me. To stop hiding things from me.

I hear the shower stop, and I realise I have been sitting here a while, lost in my thoughts. She may keep things from me, but I know enough about her to know she wouldn't be happy if she saw me waiting for her to come out of the shower in her towel.

As I make my way out, my eyes are drawn to the slightly open bathroom door, and before I can turn away, my attention is captivated by the movement of my Mate.

I know it's wrong, and I should leave, but the instinct to stay, because she's my Mate, won over.

She steps out of the shower delicately, and my eyes trail up her perfect legs; she turns to grab a towel and my eyes land on her perfectly pert bottom.

Before she can get the towel around her body, my eyes are on her back.

The scars are red and raw, and the bruises are blue and purple; as she turns around, I can see the scars on her stomach and her ribs. The lust for my Mate is replaced with pure anger.

I barge into the bathroom, causing her to jump and scream; she protectively wraps the towel around herself.

"What the hell are you doing?" She shouts at me. I ignore her and pull her towel away, wanting to see the damage up close. I turn her around repeatedly in my arms, taking in her scars and bruises.

"Who did this to you?" I growl, causing her to flinch. The anger leaves my body as I feel her shaking beneath my hands. I let go realising I'd scared her. She slowly wraps the towel around her.

"I'm sorry, Little Rogue, I just..." my voice breaks, and she just looks at me, almost assessing the situation.

Unexpectedly she wraps her arms around my waist, hugging me. For a second, I didn't react; I expected her to be angry at me. I wrap my arms around her as she presses against me, tight. We stay like this for a while. Until Lilla is dry. Both needing the comfort of our Mate.

*

When Lilla is dressed, she comes and sits next to me on the bed.

"Dayton, I've not had the easiest life, okay? You know what Pack I'm from. Just because I haven't told you any of it yet, doesn't mean I don't trust you or don't want to get close to you. I'm just not ready to talk about it. It's hard enough living through it, but to say it out loud, I just... I'm not strong enough to put myself through it again. Not yet, okay? Please give me time. Please be patient. I know I've been a handful since I got here. Not exactly Luna material, and I'm sorry for that. I'm sorry that you are stuck with me."

I let out a slight growl and pulled her close, taking in her scent. Eventually, I let her go, holding her face, making her look me in the eye.

"My Wolf said that to me earlier, '*We are stuck with her*', but there was no regret in his voice. It was pride and happiness and reminded me of what I have. You have gone through a lot, and I know that, and we are proud of how strong you are and happy that we are stuck with you. I wouldn't change you for the world, Little Rogue. Take as long as you need. I will still be here when you are ready to talk about your past."

Lilla

We are joining the Pack in an hour; my heart is racing as I stare at the clothes in front of me.

"Nothing to wear?" Russell asks, causing me to jump. I hadn't even heard him walk in. I shake my head.

He disappears as he walks further into the wardrobe. I still wasn't over its size; I doubt I'd be able to wear all the clothes here in my lifetime. While Russell is busy searching for an outfit, I wander around looking at all the clothes. I stop at a floor-length dress and pull it out.

The top crochet half of the dress is stunning, forming a choker-like halter neck, while the bottom half is plain, so it's not over the top. It's a navy blue colour with a bodycon fit that makes the whole dress fit together perfectly. I just hope I have the chance to wear it.

"A bit formal for tonight," Russell appears, holding a red skater dress in one hand and wedge sandals to match.

I put the dress back and take Russell's offering; he disappears again, muttering something about jewellery while I change. Once I'm ready, Russell gives me a nod of approval.

"What about your hair?"

I sigh as I look in the mirror, it was currently sitting in a messy bun, where it had been since my shower.

I loved almost everything about my hair. Its length reached my bum as I didn't get it cut often. It was fine but there was loads of it, which meant it didn't hold a curl; as much as I tried the minute after styling, it would be dead straight again.

I didn't mind; it never got a kink in it when it had been up all day, so it took minimal effort to manage and was full of volume.

As I said, I loved my hair, except for one thing.

The colour.

My hair used to be this natural dirty blonde; it was just gorgeous, like my birth mother's.

Now, however, it was as black as ink. Unnatural against the paleness of my skin. Yet another thing that's taken away from me.

I take it out of the bun, and we watch as it falls down my back. I pull it all over my shoulder to cover my Mark.

"I think I'll wear it down."

*

"We are standing here today to welcome two Werewolves into our Pack. Alec and Lilla, both Rogues, please voice any reason why they cannot join." Dayton's voice travels around the room, where all three hundred of the Pack is standing. I would never have thought everyone could fit in here, but apparently, they could. Dayton, Alec and I were standing on a makeshift stage at the front.

"They belonged to the Midnight Moon Pack!" Someone shouts, and immediately people begin to murmur their agreement. The thing with joining a Pack is that everyone has to decide, not just the Alpha. It doesn't even matter that I'm the Alpha's Mate; we still need to be accepted by everyone. It also means they can voice their concerns without fear of being punished by the Alpha.

I roll my eyes; of course, this was an issue. "How do you respond?" Dayton asks us, and before Alec can say anything, I answer.

"Alec left three years ago, before the Midnight Moon Pack changed, so he is nothing like them. I left the Pack a year ago, deciding I would be better off a Rogue than in that Pack." I answer they seem to accept this as another point is raised.

"She didn't complete the tests!"

'No, I didn't, but you all saw me handle that Wolf from the Midnight Moon Pack; I can handle myself quite well. I also managed to protect this Pack, even though I am technically not a part of it."

"Any other concerns, or do we accept them?" Dayton asks after a moment of silence. We wait patiently for another counter argument but receive none.

"We accept." Three hundred voices say at once, and I fight the urge to cover my ears at its loudness.

"With the acceptance of the Freedom Howlers Pack and the acceptance of the Alpha, I Alpha Dayton, make you one of us." Dayton produces a knife, and I flinch automatically, something he notices but doesn't say a word, a frown cutting across his face. He holds his hand over a goblet and slashes his palm with the blade, causing me to wince at the pain he feels. He sends me an apologetic look as he squeezes his hand, causing the blood to trickle into the goblet.

He then holds the cup up and hands it to Alec, who drinks and passes it to me. I drain the rest of the blood, and as it trickles down my throat, I feel a buzzing in my veins as I'm accepted into a new Pack. I catch Alec smiling; he felt it too.

The smile I place on my lips disappears as the pain starts. I should have known. I should have been more prepared. This is something for my Wolf to be part of as well. I double over as the pain intensifies, and Dayton runs over. I grip his shirt and lean against him, his arms wrapping around me. The pain dulls but not enough to handle as I fall to my knees, pushing Dayton away. I hear people asking if I'm okay, but I don't answer. Instead, I close my eyes and curl into a ball, waiting and hoping the pain will fade.

Dayton

The pain was excruciating. I had blocked it out so I could help Lilla but standing watching her on the floor, the pain she felt was pushing through the mental block I had put up. Unlike the other times, she didn't blackout. She is shaking, though, and I don't know how to help her.

The Pack watched her; Doc tried to come forward, but I had growled a threatening growl, and he is now frozen to the spot.

Suddenly, the pain is gone. Lilla uncurls herself, breathing heavily. She rolls onto her back and stays there for a moment, unmoving.

I watch as she stands up slowly, and then she turns to face the Pack, the most dazzling smile on her face, showing her pearly whites. Everyone begins to relax, but I notice the smile doesn't quite reach her eyes.

"Shall we get this party started or what?"

Soon, everyone is having fun. Music is playing softly in the background; those over 18 are getting drunk, some are playing darts and pool while others are sitting and chatting. I see Alec run around, followed by a dozen children; he runs past Lilla, who, when seeing him, bursts out laughing.

"Help, please!" He begs his sister as he collapses on the floor. The children surround him and start jumping around, trying to get him to get up.

The women that were talking with Lilla are now laughing along with her. Lilla stands from her seat and claps her hands loudly, causing people to turn to her, but she doesn't notice, her attention on the pups.

"Who wants to hear a story?" She asks as they stare at her.

"What story?" One of the children asks curiously.

"How about..." she trails off for a second, "the one about the Ancestors," she smiles at them.

"Never heard it," another tells her, questioningly.

"Well, if you sit down and are quiet, I'll tell you." She sings, and immediately they leave her brother alone and sit around her.

She hasn't realised that the music is off, and everyone is silent, wanting to hear the story too.

Not many people knew about the Ancestors, and every little detail was important; the most we knew was that they were the rule makers, higher than Alphas. Like Royalty, but no one knew their story, most of what we did know were just rumours.

*

"Hundreds and hundreds of years ago, five children were born simultaneously on a night of a full moon. They were the five who were to fulfil the prophecy." Lilla took a breath, but an impatient child asked a question before she could continue.

"What prophecy?"

"A prophecy made by..." she hesitates, frowning slightly, "well, no one knows who made it, but we do know they were powerful. The prophecy stated:

> "On the night of a full moon, five children are to be born,
> One girl, four boys, unrelated, an alliance shall be sworn.
> Abandoned by their own, they will create a Pack,
> For on their sixteenth birthday, their bones will start to crack.
> They will be the making of a new species,
> Creating more of their own, forming treaties.

Rules and laws shall be set,

And those who have been created will forever be in their debt."

Everyone was staring at her, mouths open. How did she know the prophecy? Off by heart. I saw Alec watching her, though he was the only one unfazed. Did he know it too?

"True to the prophecy, their parents abandoned them in the woods. They found each other, almost like a pull leading them to one another. They became a family of their own, a Pack. Though they were all equal, no Alpha's or Betas.

"As the Prophecy had stated, they were to be unrelated, but two boys were brothers. Twins, to be exact, which also went against the prophecy because it meant they weren't all born at the same time. Nothing was different; it didn't matter that the two were blood-related they were a family anyway.

"When the first full moon that fell on their birthday arrived, it was their 16th and together as a family, as a Pack, they changed, bone by bone, slowly and painfully, their Human bodies shifted into Wolves. After this, they began to fulfil their destiny; they changed Humans that were worthy into Werewolves. They created many Packs, always leaving someone in charge, the Alpha, who chose his right-hand man, the Beta. Soon, they had created Packs worldwide, so they created laws for the Packs to abide by. They called themselves the Ancestors, and with that, a new species had been created."

Lilla stops talking and looks at the faces of the children. I looked around the room to see everyone had moved closer and were sitting down, either on a chair or the floor, hanging off her every word.

"Is that it?" A little girl asks.

Lilla shakes her head. "As you know, ordinary Wolves Mate for life. They find their other half, have pups and grow old together. Humans seek this, love at first sight and destiny. They find someone to love, marry, and have children, though it isn't always for life.

"The Wolves in us crave for a Mate, and the Humans crave to be loved, so when the Ancestors created Werewolves, the need for love and a Mate twisted and wound its way together, helping make the bond between them two Werewolves. So soon, the Packs began to change, people left, and people joined.

"The Ancestors have some unique gifts that make them superior to the other Werewolves. So, they made a few changes. They created a ritual that had to be followed to join a Pack, the one Alec and I did a couple of hours ago. They gave each Pack the gift to communicate between themselves through their minds, and they created the Mates Mark. So that everyone knew whose Mate was whose to stop blood being shed. They made it so that the initial of your Mate would appear inside a full moon where they had bitten.

"The Ancestors, however, were not to have Mates. They weren't to have children either; all they could do was change Humans to Wolves. Though there is a rumour that one Ancestor met his Mate and had two children, it was never confirmed, so I can't say for sure, but the Ancestors know everything. They have informants and hear the rumours; they don't appear much for anyone anymore but essential issues.

"The people that meet them say they have more special abilities than we can ever imagine. They are the Ancestors and the first Werewolves."

*

I jolt awake when I hear a scream, my Wolf whimpering. I know it's her. I get out of bed, and as I open my bedroom door, I meet Austin and Aria, as they are the only other two who live here. I need to have my Beta close, we had learnt from our mistake of living apart when Rogues attacked, so they had moved in.

"Another spider?" Austin jokes, and I laugh, but a blood-curdling scream bounces around the house before I can answer. Immediately all three of us run to Lilla's room, bursting open the door; we find her thrashing about in her sleep.

"Nightmare?" Austin asks, watching her.

"Probably. Should we get Alec?" Aria asks. I was going to tell her not to bother him, but then we heard it. A bone break. I nodded at her, and she left quickly.

"What do we do?" Austin asks as we hear another bone break, and she screams. I place my hand on her arm, hoping to have a calming effect, but I snatch it back just as quickly.

"She is burning. We have to do something!" I say, and Austin looks at me with worry. Alec bursts in and stares at his sister, Aria and Russell, appearing behind him.

We hear more bones snap and crack, and I grit my teeth, feeling it too. "The pain reminds me of my first shift." I say, and Alec's eyes widen.

"Shit. Okay, we need to cool her down. Fill the bath with ice." Alec says, and without arguing, we all begin to get to work, listening as her bones break.

"She can't have any more bones left to snap!" Austin says as I pick up my Mate and bring her into the bathroom.

"What is happening to her?" I ask as I place her in the bath, surprised to see she is still asleep. She continues to thrash around, soaking us all with ice water.

"She is trying to shift." Alec says, pushing her head down under the surface of the water.

Lilla

2 years earlier

I stare down at the innocent new-born in my arms. His eyes are closed, his little heartbeat beating steadily, no idea of the danger he is in.
"Kill him." My Alpha shouts into the deathly quiet room. The whole Pack is here. They are to watch as I kill the bundle in my arms just to show the punishment for trying to leave.
"Kill him, Lilla!" His voice takes on a commanding tone. I have no choice now; you can't go against a command; it could kill you. The pain is unbearable.
I look at the Pack as they stare at me, wide-eyed. The new-borns parents stood in front of me crying quietly; they had been commanded not to make a sound.
With the pure silver knife in my free hand, I hold it over the day old baby boy's heart as he wakes from his sleep; his crystal blue eyes stare at me. I take a breath, readying myself to kill the innocent new born.

*

Cold. Painfully cold. Stinging-my-flesh cold. I open my eyes to see nothing; everything is blurry. I take a breath, only for my lungs to fill with water.
I begin to panic, which only rises when I feel the hand on my head holding me down. He has found me; this is my punishment. Of all the ways for him to kill me, I didn't think it would be by drowning. I don't fight; it's pointless fighting. I won't win.

Dayton. What about him? Is he okay? Did he kill my Mate as more punishment? What about Alec? Did he slaughter this Pack because of me?

The hand holding me down disappears, and I pull myself up, instinct fighting the death I know is coming. I cough up the water I've swallowed and gulp down the air around me as it burns my lungs.

I stare at the five people surrounding me; they are staring at me expectantly. Was I supposed to say or do something? I open my mouth to speak, but my throat aches, closing it again. I begin to shiver as the feeling of cold hits me again.

"Shit! Take her out!" Dayton commands without a second thought, immediately ten hands pull me out and wrap fluffy towels around me.

I nearly collapse at having to hold my weight, and Dayton wraps his arm around my waist, holding me up. I barely notice as my wet pyjamas disappear and I'm standing naked. New, dry towels are wrapped around me before I'm carried to the bed, and the duvet is wrapped around me tightly as I continue to shiver. Ten pairs of eyes watch me as my shaking subsides.

"You tried to shift in your sleep. You were burning up; we had to cool you down." Alec says after a while. They were trying to help me. Not kill me. I relax, knowing I'm safe, and my eyelids droop. I feel exhausted, my muscles and bones are aching, and I drift off to sleep without fighting it.

*

"Lilla?" Alec's voice breaks my sleep, and I open my eyes. He is staring at me with worry.

"Leave me alone." I push his face away from me and close my eyes.

"Not weak then," he says, relieved, and I turn over, grunting.

"Lilla, you have to get up." He says, and I groan. The back of my head comes into contact with something soft yet solid, and I start laughing.

"Did you just hit me with a pillow?" I turn to face Alec, who is looking at me innocently.

"I have no idea what you are talking about. You have to get up! That mysterious Alpha is on his way to the house. Dayton went to meet him, and he asked me to check on you. He said if you are okay, I had to get you up and ready to meet the Alpha and his Beta." He pulls the duvet away from me. "How do you sleep all night, tossing and turning but manage to stay wrapped up in a towel?" He asks, and frowning, I look down to see that I was indeed in a towel.

"Where are my pyjamas?" I ask, confused.

"Do you not remember last night? The ice bath we gave you?" Alec reminds me.

"Shit! That actually happened? I thought it was a dream." I sit up out of bed. "Is it just an Alpha and his Beta? Why isn't he bringing backup?"

"I don't think he wants to be seen as a threat. Dayton doesn't recognise the Pack scent, though, so he is very wary. Now go have a hot shower, get dressed, and I'll meet you downstairs." Alec orders and I do as I'm told with a salute.

*

"How long until they get here?" I ask impatiently; we hear a car pull up before Alec can answer. My heart rate increases, as does my nerves. I was acting as a Luna today, and I was petrified.

"Take a deep breath, in and out. I'll do it too." Alec says, and together we breathe in through our nose. The familiar scent of musk fills my nostril; I stare wide-eyed at Alec to see he recognises it too. We run to the front door and open it to see Dayton standing laughing with an Alpha. I'm unsure how to feel, scared because he's found me? Angry because he is here, and I need to protect my Pack? Or betrayal because Dayton is laughing with the enemy?

Alec growls behind me, and they both turn to us. Dayton's eyes light up when he sees me, but I'm not focused on him. My protective instinct takes over, knowing he could kill Dayton at any second.

"This must be your Mate, the future Luna; it's a pleasure to meet you." His voice sends chills down my spine, and he steps forward. I begin to panic; the idea of being strong gone as fear sets in.

Alec growls again, causing Dayton to frown, "Lilla, Alec, this is Drake," Dayton introduces but fails to mention the Pack he owns; it hits me, he doesn't know! Why wouldn't he ask? Why bring an Alpha here when he doesn't know which Pack he belongs to?

The Alpha steps forward, arm extended towards me, ignoring Alec.

"Hi, I'm Alpha Drake of the Midnight Moon Pack."

Lilla

Dayton's smile disappears, and I feel the Pack surround us, although hidden from view.

Dayton growls, his stance changes from friendly to ready to attack, and all Drake does is smile.

In surrender, he holds his hands up, "I'm just here to meet the Mate of a former Pack member. I was intrigued. Now that I've met you and seen Lilla and Alec, I'll be on my way."

He turns to walk away but stops as if remembering something.

"There is one other thing, though." He turns to face Dayton with a smirk. I tense, recognising the glint in his eyes, and I know what he is about to do. I run for Dayton, Alec shifting as he runs by my side. I push Dayton behind me and let out a thunderous growl, the pain is immense, but I bite my tongue, determined not to let him see me in pain anymore.

"If you want to do something, do it to me, but you leave Dayton and this Pack out of this." I find the strength I've been searching for as the need to protect my Pack and my Mate pushes down my fear.

"Where is the fun in that?" Drake laughs, the sound making my skin crawl.

"You want to see me suffer; you don't want to kill me yet." I realise, and his eyes narrow. "You have spent the last year searching for me so you can punish me again and again, which means you don't want to kill me. You want me alive for this sadistic game you're playing. You came with only your Beta knowing there wouldn't be a fight. Knowing that if I want to kill you, I can't just rip your throat out in front of so many witnesses, it's the worst crime a Werewolf can do, killing an Alpha. So why are you here? You aren't here to see us all grown up and happy, so tell me, Drake, why are you here?" He growls at my disrespect, it's the first time I have ever called him by his name instead of Alpha, and he doesn't like it.

Eventually, Drake sighs as if I have caught him out. "Okay, you are right. I'm here to give you some news, and I wanted to see your faces when I did." He smiles like a small child getting a big bar of chocolate.

"What news?" Dayton asks from behind me.

"How long ago did you meet?" He asks, ignoring Dayton.

"A week ago," I answer without hesitation.

"The Mark on your collarbone," Drake says, causing me to frown. Why does he keep changing the subject?

'The one her Uncle gave her,' Dayton says, and for a second, Drake looks surprised, but he quickly recovers.

"Yes, the one her Uncle gave her. It turns out he had a backup plan."

"What do you mean?" I ask as my heart rate increases again.

"I mean, he knew it wouldn't work fully on you because you're too powerful. He also knew it was more than likely you would find your Mate. So, he added a clause to the Mark." Drake can barely contain his excitement, my heart pounds as I exchange a look with Alec.

"A clause?"

"You have three more weeks of happiness with your Mate, and if you haven't rejected him by then. He dies."

Lilla

No one moves. As if we are playing musical statues and the music has stopped. Drake disappears before I can even catch my breath. No one chases after him. No one moves. After all, the music has stopped.

Drakes smiling face is imprinted in my mind as if this was part of his plan. I glance around to see people starting to move, Pack members leaving, some I recognise going into Dayton's house. My house. I can't move. I can't breathe. I'm drowning.

I watch the world move as I stand there; when did the music start playing again? I can't hear it, so I stay still. Am I breathing? It doesn't feel like I'm breathing. Have I forgotten how to breathe?

"Lilla!" Dayton shakes me slightly; I stare at my Mate. There are no words, he puts his hand on my face, and I lean into it.

Neither of us has the words.

What is there to say?

His hand leaves my face and trails down my neck and arm, and he grabs my hand.

He started to pull, wanting me to walk. I look down at my feet as they move; they don't look like they belong to me.

We walk into the house to see his most trusted members waiting. They are all watching us.

"She's in shock," Alec states, walking over to me. He pulls me into a hug; I feel numb and pull away, looking around.

Who's in shock?

"What do we do?" Russell asks the room

"We find a way out of this clause thing," Dayton says as if it's obvious.

"You can't," I say; my throat feels dry as I speak.

"So, how do we do that?" Jace asks as if I hadn't spoken.

Had I spoken? Did I say the words out loud?

"You can't," I try again, but they all continue speaking as if they can't hear me.

Am I speaking out loud? Am I going crazy?

Pain shots through my body; I grip the chair closest to me until the pain subsides. I don't have long.

"We could try..."

"This could work..."

"What about..."

I can hear them all discussing it, but I don't focus on their ideas; what's the point? None of it will work.

I feel invisible and numb. Part of me wonders if I'm still outside and I'm having an out of body experience. Then they say something; they have an idea. One word that grounds me, snaps me back to reality.

"...Ancestors?" I no longer feel numb as I look at Jace and reply before anyone else can.

"No." With that one word, they all look up at me. They finally see me; they hear me. For a split second, they fear me.

"But if we can contact them, they could help?" Austin says

"So, what? You want to pick up the phone and call them?" I ask. "Or drop them an email? How do you propose we get in touch with them?" I ask the room.

"They are just trying to help,' Alec tries to calm me.

"The Ancestors are not the solution. They are never the solution. They are the problem. Dangerous and too powerful for their own good. This Mark isn't something they or we can fix." A tear slides down my cheek. "This breaks my heart to admit, but..." I take a deep breath. "There isn't a solution to this. It can't be fixed. The only way for this to work is for me to reject Dayton."

"No, you'll go crazy!"

"I won't." I lie. "My Uncle's sole purpose is for me to suffer; if I go crazy, I'll forget you. I'll end up killing myself. He doesn't want me to die. This Mark will prevent that, another clause, no doubt. He knows I won't let you die. He wants me to be here but not be able to be with you. He wants me to be in love with you and watch you move on and hate me."

Silence fills the room. Pain shoots through me again. I double over. My skin begins the burn. I'm out of time.

I stand up and face everyone. "I'm going to go to my room; I'm going to lock the door..." I keel over as a bone snaps. I take a breath and calmly continue. "What you will hear won't be pretty, but I'll be okay. So, please. Leave me alone." I turn and leave slowly and calmly. I lock myself in my room and wait for her to begin.

*

I wake oddly refreshed. She hadn't managed to break free as she snapped and cracked every bone in my body. I couldn't decide if I was thrilled or disappointed when she gave up and retreated.

I frown as I walk into the kitchen, I was forgetting about something. I shrugged the feeling off and grabbed some coffee.

"Morning, Lilla, how are you feeling?" Russell asks, walking in and heading towards my direction.

"Much better, thank you." I sit down as Russell grabs his coffee.

"Have you seen your brother? He wasn't there when I woke up; I assumed he came to check on you." He sits down opposite me

I shake my head, "I just got up; you are the first person I've seen."

"Lucky me!" Russell smiles, but it doesn't reach his eyes; he's worried. "I can't mind-link him, he's blocked me out, and I have to go into a Pack meeting in a minute."

"I'm sure he's fine, probably out for a run, wanting alone time or something." I tried to comfort him; I wasn't worried; it's not like he'd been missing long.

Russell pulls out his phone as we sit in silence drinking coffee; he laughs at something and turns his phone to show me a meme. He accidentally locks the phone before I can see it; I go to tell him but stop when I see the date. My blood runs cold.

Alec? Where are you? I push through the block.

Russell glances at the clock, "I've got to go; if you see Alec let me know," he kisses my cheek and is gone.

*

I find him sitting on the edge of the cliffs, I quietly join him and we watch the water crash against the rocks below.

"You're stealing my spot; I like to come to cliffs in moments of crisis. It's my thing," I say, trying to lighten the mood.

"I'm going to kill him," Alec ignores me; I frown but don't speak

"Whoever killed Dad, I'm going to find him and kill him."

Bile rises to my throat, and I try to swallow it back down to speak

"Alec, when you saw mum, what did she tell you about Dad's death?"

"Not much, there wasn't much time. They were hunting me down for sneaking in, so she told me what she could before I had to go. She didn't get time to tell me who killed him." I feel nauseous; I can't be near him; I need to leave.

"Dayton needs me; I better go." I lie, "You should talk to Russell; he's worried about you." I get up and walk slowly away on shaky legs. I need to talk to Dayton; I need my Mate.

*

I take in my appearance, pale and drawn; I had thrown up when I got back and looking at my complexion, I look ill. What am I going to do? I can't tell Alec.

I head towards Dayton's office; not bothering to knock, I open the door to see the meeting still going on.

"Little Rogue, are you okay?" Dayton stands up, worry etched on his face; I don't blame him, considering what I look like.

"Russell, Alec is at the cliffs; he's fine but could do with talking to his Mate." I say, and Russell looks at me, relieved. "The rest of you need to leave; I need to talk to my Mate."

I hold the door open and wait. They look at Dayton, who nods, "Jace, get on that," is all he says as they leave.

"What's wrong, Little Rogue?"

"I need to tell you something because I need someone to talk to. I need advice, but you need to promise you won't ask questions; I'm only telling you as much as you need to know."

"Okay, no questions, I just want you to talk to me."

"It's our dad's birthday today; Alec is upset and wants to kill the person responsible." My voice is wobbly as I get more and more nervous; I can't believe I will say this out loud after so long.

"That sounds fair," Dayton says, unsure of the issue.

"Dayton, I killed our dad."

Dayton

"What?" I stare at this girl in front of me. I misheard her. I must have. This Little Rogue of mine couldn't have killed someone.

She was a Rogue. She must have killed someone at some point; my Wolf is quick to remind me of something I'm always quick to forget.

She was so confident as she said it. Cold. I shudder. No one should be able to say that and be okay with it.

"I killed my dad," she repeats, less confident. More unsure of herself. There she was, my Little Rogue was back.

"You mean you blame yourself? You think it's your fault?" That must be what she meant. That sounds right.

My Wolf laughs.

"No, I mean, I grabbed the knife and stabbed him myself." She informs me like she is telling me it's raining outside. No emotion on her face or in her voice. How can she say it like that?

"Why?" I ask the obvious question.

"I said no questions; you promised you wouldn't ask," she states, folding her arms across her chest protectively.

"Ha! That goes out the window when you tell me you killed someone and not just anyone but your father. You expect me not to ask you a single question, don't be so stupid."

"I expect you to trust me," she says it so quietly; I pause for a moment, thinking I imagined it.

I need air; I need out of this room. I need away from her.

"I can't look at you right now." I walk out, leaving her in my office.

"Dayton! Wait! You don't understand!" She runs after me, shouting, clearly not caring who could be listening.

"What don't I understand?" I turn around so quickly she almost runs into me. She takes a step back when she sees the disgust on my face. "You killed someone, and you don't care. You're right; I don't understand that."

"We aren't humans. We have Wolf in us. We kill." Her voice had lost the desperation when she was chasing after me. She's gone cold. Who is this girl?

"We aren't just wolves; we aren't wild animals killing left, right, and centre. We have humans in us to stop that. To feel. To know right from wrong. We have our laws. All of this would be anarchy without them. You can't kill people and expect to not even explain yourself."

"I have an explanation; I have a really good reason." Back to emotions, a tear slides down her face.

"You probably do, and I want to believe you do. God, I want to believe that my Little Rogue has the best explanation with all my heart. I want to trust you and just accept it, but at the end of the day, you won't let me ask questions because you don't trust me. How am I meant to accept all you tell me without question when you won't accept me as your Mate?"

She opens her mouth to say something, but Rowan interrupts awkwardly. "Sir? Sorry, erm, you said to inform you when it was done." I turn and nod at him, and he runs out the door, happy to leave us arguing in the hallway.

"What's done?" She asks, and I frown at her. Was that it? The discussion over, we just moved on? Is that what she thinks?

I sigh; the energy to keep arguing with her is gone. "The Ancestors, I had Rowan spread a rumour about killing an Alpha unprovoked to get them here. To help."

She pales. "You what? How could you not talk to me about this?"

"That's a bit rich coming from you, don't you think?" I say venomously.

She flinches. "You don't know them. They are cold and Ruthless; they kill for no reason. They are vicious and cruel. They won't help."

"Really? To me, it sounds like you'll get along swimmingly." I turn and walk away from her.

I'm the Alpha; I make the decisions. I don't need her opinion as long as she refuses to explain. If she doesn't see us as Mates, why should I?

*

She looks breath-taking. Stunning. Gorgeous. Beautiful. I am running out of words to describe how my Mate looks as she walks into the room. We were hosting a formal party to introduce Lilla to the Alphas in the territories around us. One or two couldn't be here, but most had turned up, including my best friend, Daniel.

Unfortunately, this was all organised before our argument, so we had to go ahead, but thankfully the event had kept me busy. Too busy to see her and too busy to think. But through Russel, we had agreed to put on a pretence that everything was fine; I don't need Wolves outside my Territory knowing my business. Especially not Alphas.

The event was being held in my living room; if it was big enough for my Pack meetings, it was big enough for an event. I had had most of the Pack running around doing errands to get the room to look as formal as possible. A long table was pressed against one wall full of foods, and I had some of the lower tier Pack members dress up to play waiters, holding trays of champagne. Daniel had arrived with his parents, his Beta and the Beta's Mate Julie, leaving the third in command in charge of his Pack and Territory. Daniel had arrived earlier than other Alphas as we all needed to catch up. Now he and the other Alphas were watching Lilla walk down the stairs like she was royalty.

We may be at odds, but my heart stopped when I saw her.

The room had gone silent as she entered; I don't think she was expecting it as she quickly looked down, her long black hair falling in front of her face. She was wearing a blue strapless, floor-length dress with diamonds scattered around it. No wonder my credit card bill was high after Russell had gone shopping.

I couldn't help but notice how even though she hasn't done anything new or special with her hair, it sits on her shoulder, covering the Mark her Uncle gave her. She scans the room looking for me, but they land on the Alpha to my right.

Her face lights up, and she runs into his arms, "Danny!" She screams excited, and he laughs, hugging her back. How did she know Daniel?

Lilla

1 year ago

I felt an arm wrap around my waist and pull me back from the cliff I was about to step over. I begin to panic. Has he found me? The arm spins me around, grabbing me by the shoulder, he shakes me.

"What the hell do you think you are doing?" I don't recognise the voice, but he could have sent anyone; would he sound so angry if it was him? Maybe. I think he'd like to kill me himself; taking my own life would ruin it for him. The angry man is still shaking me, and I close my eyes and feel myself go dizzy.

"You will hurt her," another voice pipes up; he stops shaking me, but his grip tightens against my shoulders like he's worried I'll disappear if he loosens it. I keep my eyes closed while the dizziness subsides because I'm too scared to open my eyes. Not that that would change my situation; if he were here to bring me back, he'd bring me back if my eyes were closed or not.

"Why were you trying to kill yourself?" He's annoyed; I open my eyes and tilt my head at this man. Why is he so annoyed? He doesn't know me. It's not like he'd miss me if I died.

Realising I'm in no danger - yes, I'm fully aware I'm with strange strong men, but if they were going to harm me, they would have just let me go over the cliff - I begin to relax. I stare at the man who saved my life. His short spiked sandy-blonde hair made his bright blue eyes stand out. He was taller than me with huge muscles (no surprise there), I could feel the power of an Alpha.

"Well, you see, my life is picture-perfect, and I just couldn't handle how

unbelievable happy I am," I answer his question sarcastically; his eyes widen in surprise at my attitude. "Why do you think?" I add when they just stare at me. His grip loosens slightly, "You could have gotten yourself killed!"

"Isn't that the whole point of trying to kill yourself, or have I got it wrong?" I stare longingly at the cliff.

"You know what I mean," he pulls me further away from the cliff; I had missed my chance. I was so close to all of this being over.

"Actually, I haven't got a clue what you mean; why did you save me anyways? I'm a Rogue, isn't having me dead the point?" Annoyance creeps into my voice as we begin to walk.

"I know you are a Rogue; we've been watching you since you walked onto our property. Rogues tend to be liars, so I like to watch them, see what they try and get up to. Though I wasn't expecting that." He gestures towards the cliff and frowns.

"That doesn't answer the question of why you saved me," I grumble. He pulls my arm slightly, so I'm facing him, and I watch him stare intently at me, searching for something. A glimmer of disappointment flashed across his face, but it was gone just as quick. I felt guilty when I realised he was looking to see if I was his Mate. If I were, he'd never find out anyway.

He starts walking again, members of his Pack slowly walking, all eyes on me in case I do something. Shaking off the feeling, I start walking again, catching up to this stranger.

"There is something about you, every fibre of my being told me I had to save you." That's why he thought I could be his Mate; the guilt washes over me again. We all walk for a little while in silence; I suppose there isn't much to say to a stranger you felt you had to save.

"Where are we going?" My voice is loud against the silence.

"My house." I freeze; I guess I was wrong when I thought they wouldn't harm me.

"Why? If you are going to kill me, just do it. You don't need the whole Pack as an audience. My dead body will be enough."

"I'm not going to kill you; I'm just taking you to my dad, he's still in charge, and by law, he has to meet all Rogues." He grabs my hand to get me walking again. I groan slightly but follow; I have completely misread the situation. I thought he was Alpha. I don't have the best track record with parents. Why did I have to hesitate before I walked off that bloody cliff? If I had just stepped over without thinking about goodbyes and all that crap, I wouldn't be in this mess right now.

As we get to the house, he watches my reaction expecting me to be in awe of it, but it's no big deal; I've seen Alpha homes before.

What is a big deal are all the Pack members we come across as we get nearer, they are all walking in for a meeting that I'll be the centre of attention. Getting quite a few looks of hatred and disgust, I find myself holding on to the man who had saved my life.

"Bring her forward," a voice beckons as we enter the house. I don't move. I grip his arm tighter as he tries to extradite himself. Panic fills me at the idea of dealing with his father, and I put my arms around him, burying my head into his neck. Taken by surprise, his arms stay out, not touching me, then suddenly they are wrapping around me and holding me tight.

"Please, just let me go. I won't do anything, I promise. I'll leave your Territory. Please!" I whisper in his ear, begging. My past with Alphas, causing panic to grip my entire body as I start to shake.

"Hey, it's okay. Nothing is going to happen to you," his hand strokes my hair, trying to assure me, but my grip tightens.

He isn't my Mate; hell, he isn't even my friend. He's a stranger, but I feel safe for the first time in a long time. It makes no sense because I know he will be Alpha one day, yet he saved my life. I don't think I'll ever understand why but he did.

"Please!" I continue to beg for the life I was just trying to take.

"What happened to you?" A woman's soft voice comes from behind me, and I turn to look at her, not once letting go of the Alpha's son. I find that she's not looking at me but instead, her eyes are focused on my back. While I was stretching myself to stay attached to this stranger, my thin vest had ridden up, *and she could see parts of the scars and bruises. Her hand reaches out, but she stops as I shake violently.*

"Please," I beg, but at this point, I don't know what I'm begging for anymore.

*

"Little one!" He chuckles as he steadies himself, unprepared for me to fling myself at him. I feel Dayton and his friends join us. "Why am I not surprised! Which poor sod are you manipulating here then?" He asks as we pull apart; I feel the awkward tension settle on the group.

"Actually, I met my Mate," I leave out the part where he hates me right now; it's already awkward enough.

Danny starts laughing, (a bit too hard if you ask me.) "Good one! No, seriously, who's the guy?" Still laughing, he looks around at everyone to find he's the only one. He looks at Dayton, whose expression is thunderous; I wasn't sure if that was because of Danny's earlier question or because we are Mates and I had literally thrown myself at another man. Possibly a bit of both.

Danny looks at me and frowns, "but...?" the unfinished question floats between us. "We have a lot to catch up on." His voice was stern before turning back to my angry Mate.

The fantastic thing about Danny is he can smooth over any situation. The intense emotion you felt is gone before you have time to realise it, whether it's Dayton's anger at this situation or saving me from walking over the edge of a cliff.

"Sorry, mate; I didn't realise she would be your girl! Small world!" Dayton's anger simmers down, but it's still evident. He smiles and hugs the man in hello, and all is forgiven for Danny. He still won't look at me.

The awkwardness settles in the group as everyone says hello; I could feel their minds working in overdrive at Danny's first question. No doubt, all wondering just how much I had manipulated their Alpha.

I feel a hand on my arm and turn to see Danny's parents, Connor and Sylvie, Connor lifts me into his arms, and I can't help the laugh that escapes.

"You've been missed," Sylvie says once I'm back on solid ground, and I pull her into a hug. I breathe in the scent of the Pack, of my old family.

"So, how did this happen?" I hear Danny ask Dayton, looking at me. I feel Sylvie's eyes on me, watching my reaction.

"How about you boys go and chat, and Dayton can tell you and us girls will have a natter!" Sylvie recommends, although the tone in her voice suggests no one has an option. Before anyone can say anything, Dayton walks off. I feel my eyes sting and quickly turn away from his distancing figure.

Sylvie and I begin to walk away when Danny appears at my side and puts an arm around me, pulling me close. "I'm a girl for the evening," He explains at his mother's questioning look, and I smile.

We grab drinks from a tray and stand in the corner catching up about pointless things before Danny turns serious.

"What the hell? Mate!?" He exclaims, and his mum sighs; I'm guessing she planned on being a bit more tactful than that.

"I don't know how it's possible, but it's true! I woke up weak on their Territory, and you know the Law, Alpha has to meet the Rogue!" I smile slightly, which he returns.

"I had heard that somewhere."

"Dayton mentioned something about needing help for some issue?" I nod. "I'm assuming to do with you." It was a statement, not a question.

"Drake turned up; he warned us about the Mark. It's bad, guys, and Dayton has made it even worse." I feel sick every time I think about it.

"How could he make it any worse than that?"

"He asked the Ancestors for help."

They pale as they stare at me; the room feels like it shifts but everyone is still having a good time, completely unaware of the panic flowing through my veins. Alec is by my side instantly and begins pulling me out of the room.

"What are you-" I gasp as three figures appear before me. I feel Dayton reach me and brush against my arm, ready to protect me.

"Going somewhere?" I look at the figure who asked the question, but no words come out. Their power is overwhelming, and my head begins to feel heavy.

"Who are you, and why are you in my Territory?" Dayton demands, surely, he must feel their power? He was not in any position to demand anything from them.

"We are in your Territory because you wanted us here, but I am sorry for not introducing ourselves first. I am Cain; this is Emily and Blake. We are the Ancestors."

Lilla

The atmosphere in the room changes, the laughing and all the enjoyment of the evening is sucked out. Everyone had heard the extraordinary introduction. Ancestors in this Territory. This would be the biggest thing to happen to this Pack.

My head felt heavy, and I tried to shake it as I stared at them. Dayton's most trusted moving forward. I feel Danny stand behind me with his family. Alec is gripping my arm hard, his nails digging into my skin, but I feel numb. This is my worst nightmare come true.

"We heard an Alpha was killed?" Cain asks, looking around at his audience. The image of my dad flashes before my eyes, and Blake gasps. The heaviness leaves my head.

"You got here quick." Alec speaks; everyone else is unsure how to address them. They should be shown the ultimate respect. I look at Dayton; he should be talking; this was his fault. He is staring at the floor, and as I look around, all his Pack are doing the same, showing respect. Alec and I have always said that respect should be earned, not automatically given by rank, so we never showed respect to those 'above us.'

Emily looks at him intently and then slides her eyes over me; the heaviness returns twice as intense, I wince at the pain, and Alec growls.

"Move your hair." Blake commands, and I start to panic. They can't know this. They can't find out.

"We already know," Emily says as the heaviness disappears. I feel exhausted as I realise what they have done.

"You shouldn't do that without permission." I find myself saying. They scare me, but now that they know, I don't see the point in hiding it.

"Such a serious accusation means we can, now please, move your hair." Cain speaks.

Shaking, I lift my hand and push my hair off my shoulder away from my neck. They all stare at it, I watch them, it's clear they are talking amongst themselves via mind link, so I wait. Calmness washes over my exhausted mind and body as I realise this must be the end.

"We will come back tomorrow; we have many things to discuss with you," They disappeared before any of us had time to register what they had said.

"Why not just discuss it now?" Jace speaks to the room, confused.

"This isn't the setting; they'd want it to be more private," Alec says.

"Then maybe they shouldn't have come tonight."

I feel myself sway, too exhausted to stand. I grab on to Dayton before he has a chance to move; instead of holding me or helping me, he pulls his arm out of my grasp. I nearly buckle, but Danny grabs me.

"I'm going to say good night. I'm tired after tonight's events," I kiss Danny on his cheek.

"Do you need help to bed?" Danny asks, concerned after seeing my expression. Not one he'd forget, I assume.

"I'm fine, Goodnight," I say and leave before anyone can argue.

Once in my room, I step out of the dress and put on shorts and a vest. I sit on the edge of my bed and think everything through. I know what I need to do. Pulling together any energy I have left, I jump out the window and land - a little wobbly - on my feet.

I know I can't be here when the Ancestors come back. I can't be in their hands. So I run, and I keep running until I find what I'm looking for.

I let out a satisfied sigh when I reach the edge of the cliff, the sound of the waves crashing against the rocks below, the wind whipping against my skin; I feel at peace and smile. Everyone's misery will be over when I'm gone; Dayton will be better off. I faltered slightly at the thought of my Mate. "I knew you'd come here." I turn to face the voice and find that he isn't alone. Dayton, Austin and Alec stand with him.

"Lil, what are you doing?" Alec asks, and a tear falls down my face.

"Would you do this to your Mate?" Danny asks

"He's better off without me."

Dayton releases a deep growl. "How dare you decide that for me! I wouldn't be. I'm your Mate. I can't lose you!"

"You've barely even spoken to me since we argued, and you won't look at me even now."

"Enough! Lilla step away from the edge." Alec is furious, but I can hear the command in his voice. I gasp as I feel it run through my body and I step back off the cliff.

Dayton

Everything falls into slow motion as she walks off the cliff. I watch as everyone shouts or screams. My heart stops.

Do something! My Wolf growls at me. Everything returns to normal, and I run to the cliff's edge, ready to jump when I'm pulled back.

"You won't survive it," Ancestor Cain shouts as I fight against him. I see Ancestor Blake jump in after her. I stop fighting and watch over the edge like I'd be able to see.

"Then what's the point of Blake going? She won't survive it either. She'll be dead."

Ancestor Emily stands before me, forcing me to look into her eyes.

"Do you feel empty or lost? Is there a pain in your chest?" I shake my head in answer. "Then she can't be dead." She says bluntly, but I see the relief flash across her face before she can stop herself.

"This can kill her, can't it?" I have to ask, I have to know the truth, so I can prepare myself.

"She is more Human than Wolf," Alec states, and Russell wraps an arm around his Mate.

"Jumping over the edge of a cliff with rough seas and sharp rocks would kill any Wolf." Daniel snarls, clenching his fists at his sides.

I feel a pain in my chest, and I take a deep breath; my Wolf begins to whimper. No, please, no. I silently beg as the pain intensifies.

"Dayton?" Ancestor Emily calls my name, but she sounds so far away as grief engulfs me. I clutch my hand to my chest.

"Help!" We turn to see Ancestor Blake, dripping wet, holding a lifeless Lilla in his arms. "I was too late, she...." He trails off, unable to say the words; I fall to the floor, my legs too weak to hold my body up. My Little Rogue is dead. Gone. I was so angry at her. What an idiot. My Wolf growls at me in agreement.

Alec runs and grabs Lilla off him. Instinct wants me to rip her from him and hold and protect my Mate, but I can't find the strength to move.

I watch as he cradles her, placing her on the ground, her head resting in his lap as he kisses her forehead, tears running down his face. I feel them pour out of my eyes as I listen desperately for a heartbeat.

Alec glances at the Ancestors and almost stops whatever he plans on doing, but he shakes his head and focuses on Lilla. His canines extend, causing us all to frown. What is he doing?

Before we can react, he bites down on her neck; my Wolf doesn't even do anything; we all just watch.

Dayton

"What the hell was that?" When Alec pulls away from Lilla, Russell is the first to speak, her heartbeat returning to normal.

"We should get her inside," Alec says, sounding and looking exhausted. The Ancestors are the first to react, quickly picking her up and going back to the house.

Russell and I run to help Alec, who passes out as we reach him. I lift him as I'm the strongest amongst us and follow the Ancestors, all in silence, trying to understand what just happened.

I mind-link Austin, Rowan and Jace to meet us in Lilla's room, unsure if they had been at the cliff. My mind felt all over the place. Too much had just happened for me to comprehend.

I watch as Ancestor Emily orders everyone around in Lilla's room, unsure what to do with the body I'm carrying. I seem to have lost the ability to think for myself.

Ancestor Cain and Blake take Alec off me and put him in the bed next to my Little Rogue. Everyone is running around doing something, but I can't move or follow what's going on.

I snap to it when I hear a gasp leave Ancestor Emily's mouth. She has seen the scars and bruises covering her body while changing Lilla out of wet clothes. She continues to dress her and beckons for the other Ancestors to come over, lifting her vest slightly to show them. They growl at the sight, but the growl grows louder when Lilla's hair falls away. Ancestor Emily moves the rest of the hair out of the way, showing them all the Mark.

The three of them push past everyone and leave the room, I watch the Ancestors shake violently, as they lose control and their Wolves start to take over. I quickly glance at Lilla and hear her heartbeat, relieved it is still beating even if I don't know how it happened.

The house is empty of guests, and I silently thank my guys for dealing with the party and getting rid of everyone; I don't think I could have coped with that tonight.

"I am going to kill him!" I hear Ancestor Blake growl just as they burst through the front door. I race to the window in time to see all three of them shift at once.

My eyes widen at the Wolves standing in my territory. They were the biggest Wolves I had ever seen, but that isn't what's so captivating about them. The base colour of their fur is white, which covers their stomachs and legs with grey fur mixing in from their legs to their back, which turns to black as it reaches their face. Their tails stripped all three colours.

Werewolves are usually one colour; a rare few are two; I have never seen three colours on one before, all three of them the same. Even twins have a few differences in their fur, no matter how subtle.

They turn to look up at us, and I hear Russell gasp behind me; Wolves eyes were usually like the colour they are in human form, but theirs were blood red.

We all watch these magnificent creatures run off towards the woods, disappearing in the darkness with the sound of their heart-breaking howls bleeding through the night.

Lilla

This is what I wanted a year ago. Being free, like running as a Wolf used to feel. I always wondered if I would regret it, but I feel truly happy for once.

My body slams into the cold water, and I let myself sink to the bottom. I knew the jump wouldn't kill me as there is very little that can kill a Werewolf.

Our skin is hard to penetrate, so standard weapons wouldn't work; our claws can kill Werewolves; they are strong enough to penetrate the skin. Pure Silver can't kill us, but it can burn through our skin and weaken our Wolf.

Drowning is another thing that can kill us; your lungs can't fight against the water. There are a few others, but drowning is the most effective if you haven't got a Werewolf willing to slice your throat.

I feel tired as I run out of air, so I force myself to breathe normally and feel a burning in my throat as my lungs fill with seawater. I close my eyes and wait for death with a smile on my lips.

*

My eyelids feel heavy, but I open them anyway. I turn over to see a glass of water, and I grab it and drain the glass, cherishing the feeling of the cold water sliding down my dry and sore throat. Disappointment washes over me as I realise I'm alive, but I force myself to hide it.

"You jumped just because I commanded you. That's not a normal reaction."

Alec says, lying next to me. I have to remind myself he hasn't been there for years, so he doesn't understand the impulse I feel to go against a command. "What happened?" My brain feels foggy, but I know enough to ignore his statement

"Blake went in after you; he got to you but not in enough time, you were..." His throat catches, and I realise what he's saying.

"But then how?" I ask frowning

"Dayton thinks I brought you back from the dead." He chuckles at the idea. "He was lost in his grief; his senses weren't as clear. Your heartbeat was faint; you were probably seconds from death. I brought you back." Alec explains, and my hand flies to my neck. His bite had healed for the most part, but I could still feel it. There are only a few Werewolves capable of what Alec has done. The power in his Werewolf venom is strong enough to heal any damage done to another Wolf, to make a heartbeat again, and lungs recover from the damage of drowning. To heal the brain cells that are dying from lack of oxygen.

"I'm going to have a shower," I feel the sadness engulf me, and I know I need to be alone. I get out of bed, my legs weak, my body aching and tired. As I get to the door, Alec's voice pipes up with a hint of disgust.

"The normal reaction is to thank the person who saved your life."

I turn and look at him; the tears I was trying to hold back fall down my face. "Yes, it is. When you want to be saved." I close the bathroom door behind me and turn the shower on. I strip my body of my clothes and get in, letting the warm water wash away the memory of seawater. The familiar feeling of emptiness washes over me, and I let the tears fall.

*

I head downstairs to see everyone gathered in the front room – what is it about this lot that they need to be involved with every little thing? Is this how Packs are now? – all evidence of a party gone.

Dayton sits with his elbows on his knees, his face buried in his hands. He doesn't look up, although I'm sure he knows I'm here.

The Ancestors are staring at me, anger radiating off them; they make their way towards me and immediately I step back, hitting my back on the banister. They stop moving and watch me; my heart starts pounding.

"Why would you do that to me?" A low voice asks in the silence; my heart tugs at the pain I've caused him.

"I'm sorry," I whisper, knowing they can all hear. I may not be sorry I jumped, but I'm sorry I hurt him.

He scoffs, lifting his head and looks at me. "Sorry? That's it?"

I frown; what else does he want from me?

"We need to talk." Blake states before I can say anything. Fear grips me as he moves forward, but Blake holds his hands up, "We just want to talk," he repeats more softly.

"Aren't you going to kill me?" I ask, and Blake's face crumbles.

"No, Lilla, we aren't going to kill you." Emily steps forward, standing next to Blake, her voice soft and reassuring.

"Why should I believe you?" I ask warily. Cain growls, and I feel myself start to panic. Funny how I was ready to kill myself so quickly, but the thought of an Ancestor doing the job scares me.

"Cain! We are trying not to scare her!" Blake shouts at him.

"I'm sorry, I just... I hate that she doesn't trust us because of those Bastards! It's sick what they did to her!" Cain's voice rises, talking as if I'm not there.

"How do you know...?" I trail off and scan the room, looking for an answer. Do they all know?

"The pain in your head at the party last night was us looking through your memories," Emily reminds me apologetically.

"Why would you do that?"

"It was me; I did it first. I was intrigued by you. The fear rolling off of you at just having us stand in front of you made me curious, and the unusual eye colour added to that curiosity; I couldn't help myself. It shouldn't have hurt as much as it did, but you are weaker than I thought." Blake says, and I frown, pride pushing away the fear.

"I am not weak," I say through gritted teeth. I am still a Rogue at heart, and with the blood from my family running through my veins, I could never be seen as weak by an enemy, even if the enemy was trying to make peace.

He looks surprised by my sudden change, but something flashes in his eyes and speaks again. "You don't have your Wolf; you are weak."

The low growl that slips from my lips surprises us as I hold back a wince.

"Only the weak would try to commit suicide," he continues to taunt me. I narrow my eyes and clench my fists. "You are nothing more than a Human with a few extra abilities." Before I can think long enough to stop myself, I lunge at him.

He lands on his back, my legs supporting me on either side of him, my hand on his chest; I notice that he doesn't fight back, but amusement is written on his face. "Listen here, Ancestor, I've already taken out one of you, and I will do it again in a heartbeat!" I threaten, and he chuckles.

"I have no doubt you would; you truly are something else, Lilla." He looks at me with adoration, and I frown. "Something remarkable, something we both know shouldn't exist."

I stare into the eyes of Blake, unsure of what to say. How am I meant to respond to such a comment? Do I see it as an insult? Or do I see it as a compliment? I decide to ignore it, so I rack my brains for a change of topic.

"Do you think I deserved what happened?" I find myself whispering so low only the two of us can hear. He sits up slowly, and I end up in his lap, my legs stretching out behind him as we face each other. He brushes my hair away, and with his finger, he traces over the Mark.

"No one deserves this," he whispers just as low. From another point of view, this could be seen as intimate, the way he is tracing a spot on my collarbone as we speak softly, staring into each other's eyes, but for me, it's not an intimate position to be in. Instead, it's a frightened, damaged little girl trying to understand what she did wrong to deserve such punishment.

He wipes away the tears falling down my cheeks with his thumbs. He sighs, "I get it," he says louder.

"Get what?"

"Why everyone who meets you has the sudden urge to care for you." He smiles at me when I pull a face.

"If that were true, then none of this would have happened," I answer, and he raises an eyebrow.

"Are you sure about that?" We are talking normally now; no one else says a word; they all just watch us.

"What do you mean?"

"Through your memories, I saw what your Alpha did to the Midnight Moon Pack, it was inhumane, but he left you out of it. He cared for you, made sure nothing bad happened to you. No matter how much of a monster he became towards the Pack, he was always caring and loving towards you."

I raise an eyebrow as I answer him, "then you missed something," my tone is cold, and I see him flinch slightly.

"No, I meant before that," he says in a gentle tone. "What he did to the Pack was inhumane, but what he did - what they both did - to you, there are no words to describe how callous they were."

"Can you help us?" I ask him, looking down at my hands.

"I'm sure as hell going to try."

"So, I can trust you?" I still refuse to look at him as I ask my questions. He pulls my chin up until our eyes meet.

"When your father told you and your brother the Ancestors' story every night, did he ever mention the colour of our Wolves?" I knit my eyebrows together as he changes the subject. I shake my head, curious to see where this is headed.

"Black Wolves are meant to be seen as fierce and violent and great leaders, which is why most are Alphas." He stops, waiting for me to say what we both know I'm going to say.

"Dayton is a Brown Wolf," I inform him; he smiles and glances behind me.

"Yes, he is. Brown Wolves are meant to be seen as protectors, a security for a family, which is why Alpha's that aren't Black Wolves are Brown. Then you have the Grey Wolves; they are meant to be seen as balanced and patient; they normally make good Beta's."

"What about White?" I ask, slightly impatient.

"White Wolves are meant to be seen as pure and innocent. Ancestors are three colours. Black, White and Grey. We are to be seen as fierce and violent, balanced and patient, and pure and innocent."

"Why haven't you got any Brown?"

"Brown is for protection and security for the family, for a Pack. We don't have Packs to protect or a family; we are meant to be seen as the Law, in charge, it's not our job to protect."

"What's this got to do with whether I can trust you?" I ask; going back to my question, Blake chuckles.

"I'm saying that you can trust me - trust us - because even though it's not exactly in our job description, our Wolves are screaming and shouting for us to protect you."

Dayton

"No disrespect, Ancestor, but can you please let go of my Mate? My Wolf wants to rip your head off." I say as politely as possible, my whole body shaking. Despite everything she has done, she's still my Mate.

When Lilla had first lunged at Ancestor Blake, I was proud of her; she was standing up for herself against an Ancestor, which also had me worried; they were Ancestors; after all, where is her respect.

My Wolf became angry when she was sitting in his lap staring into his eyes, the position was far too intimate, and Ancestor or not, my Wolf wanted to kill him.

"Sorry," Ancestor Blake says, smiling sheepishly, and Lilla holds out her hands for help to get up. Alec moves forward, but I beat him to it, finding surprise written across her face. I may be angry at her, but since she nearly died all I've needed to do was hold her. I pull her close and take in her scent, letting the smell of violets calm my Wolf down. She folds into me, allowing me to hold her; we both needed this. Nothing was fixed between us, but we needed this.

"So, what's the plan?" She asks, letting go reluctantly and facing everyone.

Ancestor Cain glances at the other Ancestors. "We are going to bring down the Midnight Moon Pack." He says it so calmly that I wonder if I've misheard but looking at everyone's shocked faces, I know I haven't.

"What?" Lilla steps towards them slightly, clearly no longer scared of them.

"From all the information we have of them, it is safer if we dispose of the Pack." Ancestor Cain replies in his calm voice.

"Are you serious?" Lilla looks at them as if they have grown another head, and Ancestor Cain frowns.

"Yes, they kill innocent people, Humans and Werewolves. They need to be put down." He responds.

"They only did that because Drake commanded them. You can't kill a whole Pack because of what their Alpha commanded them to do!" Lilla's voice rises.

"Lilla, after three years of killing innocent people, most of the Pack has lost their humanity. We can't save them."

"You can try!" Lilla argues, and Ancestor Cain throws her a sympathetic look.

"Lilla-"

"No! If you fight the Midnight Moon Pack, I will fight alongside them." Lilla's voice comes in strong and confident, and I feel proud but outwardly scowl at her words.

"But you are in this Pack with your Mate..." Ancestor Emily points out.

"I'll leave; I'll become a Rogue again if it means protecting them from you." I let out a growl at her words, but she ignores me. I will not have my Mate leave my Pack.

"How can you stand up for them after everything they did to you?" Ancestor Emily asks.

"Because I know what it's like to be commanded to do something you don't want to do and what it's like to say no to the command. It's not their fault; it's Drake's." Silence falls, and it's clear the Ancestors are having a private conversation. Instead of waiting for them to decide, Lilla speaks again. "I was serious when I said I'd leave this Pack; I won't become a Rogue. I will join the Midnight Moon Pack, and then you will have to put me down as well."

"You can't just throw a tantrum when you don't get your way." Ancestor Cain speaks, and Lilla glares at him before turning and making her way to the kitchen.

"Where are you going?" Ancestor Blake asks, and without turning, Lilla replies.

"Leaving the room before I cause myself more pain or kill Cain," she slams the door, and we look around awkwardly.

"What do you think, Alec?" Ancestor Blake asks

"I agree with Lilla."

"You do?"

"Look, Lilla doesn't think as we do. When we leave a Pack, we move on and create a new family and friends; Lilla doesn't do that. She will always see them as her Pack; she won't move on; she will always try and protect them." Alec says, shaking his head slightly. "Our Dad taught us that the Pack you grow up in is important and should never be forgotten. With me that went in one ear and out the other, I was never meant to leave the Pack; the males rarely do. But Lilla, she took what he said to heart; she knew one day she would meet her Mate and would have to leave, so Lilla made sure she knew everyone in the Pack by name, she made sure she was friends with everyone so that one day when she left, she could phone her old Pack or visit and she could ask about everyone and talk to them. She knows everyone you are planning on killing; they are her family, so I agree with Lilla." Alec makes his way into the kitchen to join his sister while we fall into another awkward silence.

"So, what do we do now?" Austin asks his focus mainly on the Ancestors.

"For once, the Ancestor's don't know how to solve this problem." Ancestor Blake replies in the third person before placing his head in his hands, defeated.

Lilla

1 year earlier

"What's your name?" the Alpha's son asks me as he directs me into his room. When I wouldn't let go of him, he had taken me upstairs away from everyone. He points at a seat, and I take it.

"Lilla," I answer in a barely audible voice.

"I'm Daniel. Can I get you anything?" He asks, treading carefully like I'm about to break; I shake my head.

"Can I ask what happened to you?" He's referring to my scars. I shift uncomfortably, trying to avoid his gaze; what could I even say?

"I have to go. Stay here, lock the door behind me." Daniel says, running to the door.

"Wait, why?" I ask, standing, confused.

"There is trouble with some Rogues, don't worry. Just stay here and hide. You'll be okay." He smiles, trying to be reassuring, and then he's gone.

I make myself breathe slowly as flashbacks hit me without warning; this wasn't the first time I've been told to hide from Rogues.

Screams come from outside; I hear growls as they shift. I need to be able to defend myself. I look around the room for a weapon. Nothing. I begin to panic; I breathe in and out. I can't panic; I need to survive.

Kitchen.

If I can get to the kitchen, I can get a knife. Taking one more deep breath, I open the door and run for it.

Finding the kitchen, I start rifling through drawers when I see a set of kitchen knives on the counter. I find the sharpest, biggest knife and tuck it in the waistband of my jeans, the knife instantly cutting into my back, more scars; what difference will it make?

What now?

Do I go back upstairs and hide?

Do I help?

I hear another scream and the need to protect others brings out the fighter in me. I run towards the front door to see Daniel's mum, the Luna, watching two Wolves fight. One of them must be her husband or her son.

I watch as the Black Wolf with green eyes overpowers the other Black Wolf, who is already severely injured; she gasps.

Green Eyes must be the Rogue.

"Baby, please don't die." She breathes; it's her husband. The Alpha struggles against Green Eyes; he uses what's left of his strength and pushes him off. He is very weak. The Luna can feel his pain and is gritting her teeth against it. I put an arm around her, and she jumps away, relaxing when she realises it's me.

The Alpha must have felt her fear when she jumped because he turned his attention away from Green Eyes to check on her. That was all Green Eyes needed. He smacks the Alpha with his paw, with such force, the Alpha lands near us; the smell of blood coming from him is so thick, I gag.

He tries to stand up, but he's too badly injured. He won't survive this fight.

It's my fault, if I had just stayed in my room or hadn't put an arm around her. He wouldn't have lost his concentration.

Green Eyes heads for the Alpha, growling, teeth bared, he lunges at him, ready to land a killing blow.

Instinct takes over. After seeing first-hand what losing a Mate does, I couldn't let it happen again.

I run and lunge at Green Eyes using as much force as possible; he lands away from the Alpha.

He growls and turns to face me, anger filling his eyes. I can tell already that he is under-estimating me as I crouch slightly, readying myself for a fight. He lunges for me, and I duck, causing him to jump over me. I stand straight and pull out the knife that is already covered in my blood from scraping across my back.

I turn to face him as he lunges for me again, and I fall onto my back, dropping the knife. He immediately goes for my throat, and I use all the strength I have to keep him at a distance, my hands pushing against him as he uses more force to get his teeth closer.

I quickly glance around for the knife to see it about a foot away. As I let my arms drop down, surprising Green Eyes as he stumbles forward slightly, a plan forms in my head. I use this opportunity to move closer to the knife, my eyes on Green Eyes as he shakes his head before lunging at my throat again.

I use my arm to block him from my throat and scream as his teeth sink in, but it was all I needed to reach the knife, and with his teeth clenching my arm, I plunge the knife into his neck.

The blood begins to pour out of his body; he lets go of my arm, the effects of a pure silver knife weakening him, he stumbles away. Another Black Wolf appears, and using his claws, he kills Green Eyes. I sit up slowly, wincing in pain; I see Rogues being killed around me.

I hear a sob and look over to see the Luna pulling her Mate into her lap

'He is dying,' she says to no one as tears fall down her cheeks.

Daniel runs over and wraps his arms around his mother as she sobs. The Pack members surround us, bowing their heads in respect for their dying Alpha. His breathing and heartbeat begin to fade. I walk over and pull him from her lap, she tries to pull him back, but I shake my head; she lets me hold him as Daniel holds her to his chest.

I have to save him.

I'm probably too weak now I'm injured, but I need to try.

I sink my teeth into his neck.

My thoughts are filled with the need to save their Alpha, for his injuries to heal.

I block out everyone as I focus on what I'm doing, praying and hoping it will work. I may not have my Wolf, but I don't need it; this is all about my bloodline. Someone grabs me, trying to pull me off; they let go when they hear it.

His breathing starts to pick up, and his heartbeat strengthens; I feel the pain across my chest as his injuries become my own. When I know he has healed, I retract my teeth and look at him as he opens his eyes.

He frowns slightly as he stares at me. 'Thank you... Ancestor,' I nod my head as my eyelids begin to droop. I feel arms wrap around me, and I wince as the pain from my injuries intensifies.

'Will she be okay?' I hear someone ask, the voice sounds so worried, which makes me smile; when was the last time someone was concerned for me?

With that thought, I drift off into the darkness.

*

"What colours are your Wolves?" Blake comes into the kitchen with the others. My hand freezes before it reaches my mouth, I look at Alec, and he shrugs and reaches for more of the cereal in the box. I slowly bring the cereal to my mouth before tossing it in and returning my hand to the box for more.

Alec and I weren't in the mood to cook, but we were hungry.

"Why?" I ask before putting more cereal goodness into my mouth. Dayton comes over and grabs a handful for himself.

"I am curious to know the colour of your Wolves; we all are." He gestures to the other two Ancestors behind him.

"Mine's white with grey on the fur of my paws," Alec answers before stuffing more cereal into his mouth.

They nod, "Two colours, that sounds about right." I frown at Blake's comment.

"How can it sound about right? We aren't meant to exist; we are the only two who do, so how can you say that like it's what you expect."

"Well, we figure that Ancestors have the three colours, and as offspring of an Ancestor, you two would have two of the colours." Emily tells me, and I shake my head.

"I'm not two colours," I tell them, and it's their turn to frown at me.

I catch Russell, Dayton and Austin staring at Alec and me with wide eyes; they didn't know we were related to Ancestors.

"How many are you? One? Three?" Cain guesses, and I shake my head.

"I'm four."

"Four? How? Which is your base colour? Describe yourself!" Cain says, sitting down opposite me, his elbows on the table and his face in his hands.

"Erm... well..." I trail off as I think of my Wolf. "My snout is white until just about my eyes, a streak of black framing my Wolf's face. Then from my ears to just before my tail, my fur is grey. My stomach and legs are a chocolate brown, with bits of black fur scattered around. My tail is striped in all four colours. It's prettier than it sounds." I say quickly when I see their astonished faces.

"How is that possible?" Emily finally speaks.

I shrug my shoulders, "When I first shifted, my dad said it was because I was his Mate's daughter. Their connection was stronger than the one he had with his wife, making me more powerful. I don't think that's true, though. From what you told me about the colour of Wolves, it just sounds like my Wolf couldn't pick a personality." I look at the cereal box and pretend to find the cereal interesting as I feel everyone's gaze on me.

"I think that your Wolf became exactly what it needed to be for you to be here today." Blaze breaks the silence, and I look up and smile at him. He was becoming my favourite Ancestor.

"So, Alec and Lilla are children of Ancestors... how is that possible?" Dayton asks.

"We don't know. We were shocked when we found them. As I said, they shouldn't exist at all. Ancestors can't have children."

"You aren't supposed to have Mates either, but Dad did." I point out.

"Yes, he did. We have no idea how that is possible." Blake runs his hands over his face. "There was nothing in the Prophecy about you two, that's for sure."

"So, your dad is an Ancestor?" Austin asks slowly, just making sure he is following.

Lilla! Did you kill an Ancestor? Dayton's voice runs through my head. I can't help but flinch at the disgust and anger in his voice.

Lilla

"Dayton, wait!" I follow after him after he storms out of the room. He was angry with me before when he thought I killed just an Alpha, I couldn't imagine what he would think now.

"Were you ever going to tell me?" Dayton turns to face me abruptly. I nearly smack into him; he stops so quick.

"I thought telling you it was an Alpha would be bad enough, and let's face it, you've barely acknowledged my existence since you found out."

He scoffs, "You should have told me."

"When? It's not something you exactly look forward to telling your Mate. Hi, my name is Lilla, my favourite colour is purple, like my eyes, oh and by the way, I killed an Ancestor." I say sarcastically, and he growls at me.

"The one thing that could make me reject my Mate is if she killed an Alpha, I never thought I'd have to add Ancestor onto that!" He shouts, and I can see his struggle with his Wolf.

"Then do it. Reject me, Dayton, but don't you dare try and make me feel bad for killing a man who deserves to be dead!" I practically spit the words out, finding it hard to keep my anger down.

"Tell me! Tell me why he deserved to die!" Dayton demands. My anger vanishes as the feeling of emptiness takes over. My expression goes blank, and when I speak, my voice is cold; the need to make him understand is gone as I block the memories from taking over.

"No."

"No? You said your worst fear was being rejected. I am giving you the chance to tell me everything, and you say no." His voice comes out angry, but I can hear the pleading tone, which causes my heart to ache. He's begging me to not make him do this, but Rogues have to look out for themselves first.

"Then reject me." I say, keeping my voice cold and emotionless despite the pain in my heart. "Reject me, and all of this is over," I feel tears slide down my cheek, contradicting my emotionless mask.

We stare at each other for what feels like forever before he turns and storms out of the house, shifting.

I let out a sigh and wipe the tears away.

"Why don't you tell him?" Blake's voice says from behind me, and I turn to face the Ancestors.

"I can't do it. I'm not ready or strong enough to relive that part of my life." I shake my head to stop the images from coming forward, and the feeling of nausea hits.

"Cut the crap, Lilla, you are strong enough. You are stronger than anyone I have ever met. If you wanted to, you could face your past." Emily says, annoyed.

"I don't want to face it! It is unbearable, it makes me sick, and I don't want to have to face it!" I shout at them; Blake and Cain back away, a sign of submission, but Emily steps forward, challenging me.

"By keeping all these secrets, you will lose everyone you love, but if you just let go of the pain and fear, you wouldn't have to lose anyone." Emily says, and I shake my head.

"What's the point? I only have three weeks with him; we might as well reject each other now when he looks at me with such disgust, and his Wolf is so angry with me. If I tell him and he forgives me, we only have three weeks before he dies; he has to reject me for us both to survive. So, tell me, what is the point?" I ask, my anger rising, and the pain causing me to wince.

"So, you are giving up?" Blake asks, disappointed in me.

"I think after the shitty life I've had; I deserve to have the option of giving up. I have managed a whole year as a Rogue by myself, not depending on anyone else. I could keep my secrets without anyone getting pissed off with me. I could fight and kill whoever I wanted without worrying about repercussions or someone being angry because I put myself in danger. My life was easier as a Rogue for a year than it has been living with a Pack and a Mate for a week. So, I'm giving up. I'm giving up on my Mate, on both Packs, on Alec, and you guys." I point a finger at them, and their expressions of pity stare back at me.

"You are letting Drake win." Blake tells me, and I laugh a humourless laugh. "He was always going to win; he just wanted to see how long I was willing to fight. All of this was just entertainment for him, and I don't want to be his entertainment anymore." Tears are streaming down my face as I turn and leave the Ancestors. I walk out of Dayton's house, and I keep walking until I leave Freedom Howlers Territory.

Blake

We watch her leave; we know she is leaving the Territory, but none of us have the heart to stop her. She has a point, her life is just entertainment for Drake, and after all she has been through, I'm not surprised she wants to give up. I would have, a long time ago.

"What do we do?" Emily asks, and I shrug.

"Let's focus on something we can figure out." I say, feeling completely defeated. We have been Ancestors for thousands of years, and we have never had a problem we couldn't fix.

Until we met Lilla.

Walking into that party was all business; we were professional, we needed the Alpha to sort out the allegations, but I felt like I was being watched. Don't get me wrong, everyone had their eyes on us; we stood out, but I could feel one set of eyes piercing my skin. I sought them out and laid eyes on this breathtaking little thing. I focused on her and her group, but I couldn't help but notice that all the men, Mated and Unmated, were looking at her, not in a 'must have her' kind of way but with fondness like she lit up their lives and they wanted to protect this little Wolf from anything negative that could come her way.

I felt my power come through, as did the others, as our guard slipped for a brief second when we caught her eye. She gasped and went pale. Could she be the one we were here for? The one who killed an Alpha? Seemed a bit unlikely, but we made our way over, partly because we had this strange pull towards her but also, she was standing with three Alpha's, and we needed one.

As we got closer, we could see one of the Alpha's was her Mate; the love in his eyes as he stared at her, the protective stance he was holding and the connection we could see between them gave it away. It's an Ancestor thing being able to see a Mate's link.

While Cain spoke to them about the rumour we had heard, I was intrigued and completely distracted by the purple-eyed beauty. That should have made me realise who she was, but it didn't click; it only piqued my interest; the only purple-eyed Werewolves I know of are us. I could feel the fear roll off her, and I couldn't help but wonder why she was so scared of us. Curiosity got the better of me as I eased my way into her mind and went through her memories.

I could feel my Wolf growl with anger; how could we have let this happen? How did we not know this? I mind-linked with Emily and Cain to look through her mind as I had finished. I watched her as she struggled with the pain of having the three of us in her mind.

After looking at her Mark, we couldn't contain our anger anymore, so with a swift goodbye, we headed for the woods.

That's what we were doing when we saw everyone running towards a cliff. We shifted back, calmer now than before and getting dressed, we followed everyone, keeping hidden. My heart broke seeing Lilla standing at the edge, but I couldn't help but see that she looked utterly at peace for the first time since I laid eyes on her. That thought was gone from my mind the second she jumped. I followed after her, the need to protect and save her growing each second.

Before I could save her, Alec took charge; we were stunned; they were both more powerful than we thought.

We brought her back to her Mate's house, and I got changed and waited for Emily. She showed us the bruises and scars and the Mark when she called us back in. We had been through her memories, but nothing was to prepare us for actually seeing the damage.

That Mark shouldn't be on her at all. That Mark is cruel, unnecessary punishment that she didn't deserve, and frankly, it pissed us off. We didn't even make it to the front door before we shifted, our Wolves grieving for Lilla just as much as us.

"Something we can figure out..." Emily says, and I focus on the present.

"How about how she has so much power and has a four coloured Wolf." Cain says, and I give him a sour look.

"We don't know the answers to that either." I point out.

"Maybe her dad is right. Maybe it has got something to do with his Mate." Emily says, and I frown.

"What do we know about her?" I ask, referring to the Mate.

"Nothing," Cain says, annoyed with himself for not having any answers.

"Well, let's find out about her. Talk to whoever you need to. Let's just get somewhere with this." I say, and they nod.

"What about Lilla? She's leaving the Territory." Emily reminds me.

"She will be back; as much as she wants to leave all this behind, she still has the Mates bond; she won't be able to stay gone long." I say, and again they nod before all three of us get to work finding out as much as we can about Lilla's mother.

*

A few hours later and we have taken over Dayton's office. Neither he nor Lilla had returned yet, but we were too engrossed in our research to look for them.

"Okay, I have a name." Cain says, hanging up the phone.

"Let's hear it." I say eagerly. We had spoken to our informants who had got us in touch with someone who then got us in touch with someone else, this cycle continued for the past three hours; so far, my people had come up empty.

"Christina," Cain says, smiling triumphantly.

We both stare at him, waiting for something more, but it doesn't come.

"How do you know that's her?" I ask.

"One of my guys has a friend who knows everything about everyone." Cain says with a shrug.

"So, you have a random name of someone with nothing to back up the claim that Christina is her name." I say, and Cain growls.

"This is so hard!" Cain slams his hands on the desk, and Alec opens the door seconds later.

"What are you guys doing in here?" He asks, looking around at the mess we have made. To my surprise, my Wolf has no objections to his disrespect; I think it has something to do with the fact that he has Ancestral blood because it's the same with Lilla. Actually, with Lilla, my Wolf wants to submit to her, which confuses me even more. How does she exist?

"We are trying to find out who Lilla's real mother is. It might help us figure out how she is so powerful." I explain, and Alec frowns.

"You know Lilla has a picture of her real mother in her room, right?" He asks, and we stare at him open-mouthed.

"How the hell did we miss that?" I ask, referring to the fact that none of us remembers it from her memories.

"We were too focused on her other memories to care about the little ones," Emily points out, and I roll my eyes.

"Can you get it for us?" I ask Alec, and he leaves, returning a few minutes later with a photo.

The woman is beautiful, but she has nothing on Lilla. She had long blonde hair and blue eyes that sparkled with the smile on her face; she was truly happy.

"Shit," Emily breathed, and we turned to her.

"What?" Her eyes are focused on the picture as she takes it from me and stares at it intently.

"Emily, what is it?" I ask, and she looks at us.

"This is Layla, the first human I changed into a Werewolf."

"So, her name isn't Christina?"

Lilla

I'm no longer in Freedom Howlers Territory. I had kept walking, and now I was in another Pack Territory; I keep wandering, knowing I'm being watched. I need to play a part, back to my Rogue days when I needed to survive in other Packs. You assess the Alpha and see what he would fall for, the innocent lost girl or the feisty Rogue are two of my favourites, but I had lots of ways. I feel a powerful, heavy presence and quickly realise I'm now being watched by the Alpha.

"Are you lost?" I turn towards the voice and see the Alpha watching me, I assess him, but his face shows nothing but kindness... innocent lost girl it is.

I widen my eyes to look frightened. "Oh God, I've wandered into your Territory, haven't I?" I run my fingers through my hair, "I'm a Rogue! God, I'm so stupid!" I pretend to beat myself up and let a tear fall down my face.

"Hey, it's okay, you aren't in any trouble; tell me your Pack, and I'll take you back, and you can be accepted by your Alpha again; it won't be an issue." He gives me the most dazzling smile, and I return it with a hesitant smile.

"I'm so sorry, I'm new to the Pack, and I was out learning the boundaries and must've wandered off. I'm so sorry!" I sound exasperated, and he moves towards me slowly, like I'm a frightened creature that will bolt at any sudden movements.

"Come on, I'll walk you back." He offers. Well, no. That's not what I want! I hesitate for a second which he notices; he stops and waits.

"I fought with my Mate, a bad one, he threatened to reject me, I just..." I trail off and let more tears fall; rule number one of lying is keeping it as close to the truth as possible to avoid slip-ups later.

The Alpha thinks for a second, "So let's make him sweat, come up to my house, have a cup of tea, and make him wish he hadn't opened his mouth, teach him a lesson."

Now that's what I wanted. I smile and nod, wiping the tears from my face as together, we walk up to his house, his Pack disappearing as the Alpha has decided I'm no threat.

See. Playing Alphas is as easy as 1, 2, 3.

*

"What's your Pack called?" I asked absentmindedly, looking around as his house came into view.

"The Crescent Pack," he says, and I nod.

"What's your name?"

"Alfie, what's yours?"

"Lilla," I reply, and we smile at each other.

He opens his front door and gestures for me to go in before him. What a Gentleman. I mumble a thanks and step into his house to be greeted by seven Werewolves. Alfie steps around me and goes straight to a woman holding a baby in her arms.

"Lilla, this is my Mate Abbie and our baby girl Ava." He introduces, and I smile, giving a small wave. Trusting her Alpha and Mate even though he just brought a Rogue into the house, she smiles warmly at me.

"Hi, I'd wave, but... my hands are full," she gestures to the baby with her head, and I smile.

"These are my parents, Charlie and Lilly, my Beta and his Mate, Dylan and

Olivia and my third in command and his Mate, Finley and Evie." They all wave and say hi, and I do the same.

"Everyone, this is Lilla; she accidentally wandered into our Territory after a fight with her Mate," he tells them, and I receive suspicious looks from everyone. I immediately continue my persona of being sweet, innocent and slightly ditzy.

"We had this huge fight, and I just went for a walk. I didn't even know I was in the new Territory until Alfie pointed it out." I say, running a hand through my hair and staring at them with my best innocent expression.

It works on everyone but the parents who continue to watch my every move. No one mentions if they notice I used his name rather than calling him Alpha.

"Why don't you sit down?" Olivia asks, and I smile gratefully, taking a seat on the sofa opposite them.

"What did you and your Mate fight about?" She asks, pretending to act concerned when she is just being nosy.

"Oh, well, it's stupid, but he said I was keeping secrets and I'm not, and I told him so, but he didn't believe me and threatened to reject me if I didn't tell him. I walked away then because I didn't want him to see how much he hurt me." Even though I'm bending the truth, the tears that slide down my cheeks are genuine, and I quickly wipe them away.

"Oh, you poor thing," Olivia moves to place an arm around me. Before anyone can question me anymore, I'm saved by a Pack member who comes into the house.

"I'm sorry to disturb you, Alpha, but the third in command of the Midnight Moon Pack is requesting to see you." I stiffen in Olivia's arms, and she looks at me questioningly.

"Send him in." Alfie says with a simple smile, and my eyes widen.

I feel sick; this can't be happening.

I knew I should have killed him when I had the chance; instead, I let him go with a warning. A warning! I've gone soft since I met Dayton.

"Alpha Alfie, nice to meet you, I'm Luke." I watch Luke walk into the house and shake Alfie's hand, not paying any attention to anyone but the Alpha.

"Nice to meet you, Luke; how's Drake?" Alfie asks as I try and shield my face by leaning forward to rest my elbows on my knees and burying my head in my hands, acting like I'm distraught.

"He is good, thanks. He just wanted me to come here in person and express his gratitude for letting him stay here while he was conducting business with another Pack."

"No need for thanks. Why don't you stay for dinner?" Alfie offers. He is too nice for his own good.

"I don't want to put you out," Luke declines.

"Nonsense, we already have one guest; you can join us." Alfie says.

"Thank you. That is very kind of you." Luke smiles and takes the empty seat next to me. "I assume this is the other guest you were speaking of? Hi, I'm Luke; you are?" I still hadn't faced him, and he hadn't caught my scent by the way he was acting, which means he wasn't on guard. I lift my head and turn towards him with a smile.

"Hi Luke, I'm Lilla."

Lilla

He stares at me, unsure how to proceed, but I keep the smile on my face, and I stare at him; my heart is pounding, trying to figure out how to get out of this mess.

"Nice to meet you; I definitely can't say no to dinner when you have such a beautiful guest!" Luke finally says, playing along. This makes me more anxious, he is clearly up to something.

"You are out of luck; she has a Mate!" Alfie says, laughing, and Luke pretends to be disappointed.

"So, Luke, you are in the Midnight Moon Pack, right?" I ask; I don't plan to wait to see what he has planned, so I have to play my own game.

"Yes, I am. What Pack are you in?"

"So are the rumours true about your Pack?" I ask, avoiding his question. I didn't know how Alfie or his Pack felt about mine, so I want to avoid mentioning it.

"What rumours?"

"Well, I heard that the Midnight Moon Pack has changed in the last three years. I have nightmares about what I've heard you guys do and what the Alpha is like." I keep my answer vague and my voice light, remembering I'm still playing the innocent girl, but his eyes narrow slightly.

"We aren't as lenient as we once were," his answer is as vague as mine, and I give him a dazzling smile.

"You don't want a lenient Pack, right? People think they can walk all over you that way!" I say innocently

"You are right, Lilla," Alfie adds into the conversation, and I turn my attention to everyone else.

"So, tell us about yourself, Lilla," Alfie's Dad says, his attitude still suspicious towards me.

"Erm... well, what do you want to know?" I ask, slightly nervous, but I hide it with a light chuckle and a confident voice.

He frowns slightly; he doesn't trust me. Yet they are willing to trust the likes of the Midnight Moon Pack; maybe this Pack isn't where I want to be.

"What Pack are you from?" He asks, and I stare at him.

Shit, I should've seen this coming.

"Well, technically, I'm a Rogue now, but not on purpose," I laugh, trying again to avoid the question. I see Alfie stand and leave the room to talk to a Pack member, but his father doesn't let up.

"What Pack did you *accidentally* leave?" He emphasises the word accidentally; he would have made quotation marks with his hands if it wouldn't have made it too obvious.

"Why are you so interested?" I ask sweetly, and Charlie arches one of his eyebrows.

"I'm just curious, a Rogue comes into my Territory with a story about a fight with her Mate, though she hasn't been Marked; it just seems odd, is all." He replied honestly.

"Except it's not your Territory anymore, it's your sons," I say, batting my eyelids, acting as innocent as I can, though I'm getting bored of the whole thing. I was too tired to continue this charade.

"Maybe so, but he is more trusting in other's than I am," he returns calmly, but I can sense the warning in his words.

"So, what do you think I'm here to do exactly?" I asked, icy steel in my tone, goodbye innocent lost girl.

Everyone straightens, noticing the change in my demeanor.

"I haven't figured that out yet," he says, watching me.

Alfie walks back into the room.

"Your Mate is on his way up here to get you; you are welcome to stay for dinner."

I feel more confident, so I turn to Alfie's father

"The Freedom Howler's Pack, my Mate, is the Alpha," might as well be honest as Alfie obviously knew, and they'd find out anyway.

"Thank you for your hospitality, Alfie," I smile at him, "but I think we will head home once he's here." Alfie smiles and nods in understanding, sensing the tension in the room.

"That's very disrespectful," Luke says from next to me, and I turn to him with a questioning look. "You shouldn't be calling an Alpha by his first name; you should be calling him Alpha." Luke says, and from the spark in his eyes, I could see he was trying to wind me up.

"Luke has a point; as a Rogue and lower down than everyone in this room, you shouldn't be calling him by his name; you don't get to do that until your Alpha accepts you as his Mate." Charlie agrees with Luke, and his wife Lilly nods in agreement. Technically I was higher up than everyone in this room, but they don't know that.

"I think I'll stick to calling him Alfie," I say, shrugging my shoulders and letting out a little laugh.

"It is disrespectful!" Charlie growls.

"Respect needs to be earned!" I say through gritted teeth. I hear Luke snort behind me. This was his intention. He wants me to anger these people, anger a Pack and make a new enemy. I turn away from Charlie and face Luke.

"So what business was Drake conducting?'" His amused expression is taken over by a confused one. "You are here to thank Alfie for Drake's hospitality when conducting business with another Pack. What business?" I ask, and his eyes narrow suspiciously. I know he doesn't know the truth, and as he is away from Drake, I have an opportunity to tell him the truth.

"The Freedom Howlers, Alpha Drake wanted to give the Alpha and his Mate -you - some news." Luke says, watching me.

"What news is that?" I ask, and he frowns.

"I don't know. It is between Alphas. It has nothing to do with me."

"I can tell you if you want," more confident now that I can sense Dayton is close, not entirely sure how Luke will take my news.

"You don't have to; it's none of my business." Luke shrugs his shoulders and looks at his hands, he has been commanded by Drake like the rest of the Pack, but I can see his curiosity seeping through.

"He wanted to tell us that my Mate will die in three weeks." I keep my voice steady, and he snaps his head up to look at me.

"What?" He asks, his voice rising.

"My Mate will die in three weeks as punishment for killing my dad." I tell him, and his face twists into horror.

Luke shakes his head, the command running through him and his actual feelings pulling him in different directions.

"But you were saving us," Luke says quietly.

"I killed his brother, Luke. Drake doesn't believe a single word of what I told him my dad did." My voice is strained as I say it, and Luke stares at me. The pain of reliving that moment pulls his feelings to win over the command.

"I'm sorry, Little," Luke says, and I give him a small smile. My Luke was still in there.

"You guys know each other?" Alfie asks.

"Little Rogue?" Dayton says as the door flies open, his eyes landing on Luke and me next to him. He lets out a growl and races forward. I stand up and push Luke behind me.

"Dayton. Leave him." I say, and he stops frowning at my sudden defensive stance over him. "Please, it's not his fault." I say, and Dayton simply nods. He doesn't understand, but he's trying to trust me.

I turn to Luke, he's battling hard to fight the command, but it's winning over; I bend down and hold his chin, so he looks at me.

"I know it's hard, but keep fighting, okay? I'm going to help you all out from under him, just keep hold of any small feelings, try and be my Luke." I smile softly, and he smiles back.

"You'll help us soon?" He sounds like a little boy, and my heartaches; a tear rolls down my cheek. This was all my fault.

Dayton

The sudden shift in the Pack tells me that someone has left our Territory. I know who it is, but I ask anyway.

Who left?

Lilla, Alpha. The voice of a young Pack member waves into my mind, he sounds scared, and I don't blame him; telling your Alpha that his Mate left the Territory is not something anyone wants to do.

Which way?

Going into Crescent Pack, Alpha. I relax slightly at the words. Alfie is one of the nicest Alpha's I know; she should be safe. I run back to the Packhouse to see Alec and Russell watching TV.

Somehow, he had missed the argument between Lilla and me, so he was still oblivious to the fact she had killed his dad, and for that, I was grateful.

"Where are the Ancestors?" I ask, making my way to my office. I need to make a phone call.

"Your office," Alec replies, eyes never leaving the TV.

I open my office door to see the place is a complete mess. Pieces of paper are everywhere, on my desk, chairs, floor and the table big enough to sit everyone when we have a meeting. The Ancestors look up when I walk in, surrounding the big table.

"Hi, hope you don't mind, but we needed your office." Ancestor Blake says with a smile on his face.

"For what? A Paper Party?" I can't help but ask sarcastically, forgetting that they are above me and I should respect them. I walk carefully around my office until I reach my desk, and I place the papers on my chair on the floor and sit down.

"We are conducting some business," Ancestor Blake explains sheepishly as he takes in the room. "We'll tidy up when we are done." He promises, and I nod, although I'm surprised at his reaction. Have they forgotten they are above me?

I sit and think about the best course of action for a few minutes. Should I leave her with Alfie for a bit? Forever maybe? Seems simple enough.

My Wolf disagrees; despite our argument, her secrets, and everything, she's still my Mate.

I let out a sigh.

"She will come back," Ancestor Cain says, and I look at the three of them.

"I won't blame her if she doesn't. I told her I would reject her," I groan as I remember her face; that blank expression gives me chills, and I hate that I'm the reason behind it.

"You were angry; she knows you don't mean it." Ancestor Emily says, and all three of us men turn to face her like she's crazy.

"Ignore Emily because she doesn't know what she is talking about." Ancestor Cain says, and Ancestor Emily glares at him.

"Lilla left because she has given up on you guys, thinking you have done the same. She will come back because she can't stay away from you when neither of you has rejected each other yet." Ancestor Blake informs me, and I agree with him; my Wolf has been whimpering and howling since I walked away from her.

"How are you guys okay with what she did?" I ask them, and Ancestor Emily sighs.

"Dayton, Lilla does what she needs to do to protect those she loves; she puts everyone else before herself. What Lilla did, she did because she didn't have a choice. It was for completely selfish reasons. Even if she wants to believe she did it for everyone, she did it to save herself. It is the first time Lilla was selfish, and we don't hold it against her because of all the times for her to be selfish; she chose the perfect time to do so." She tells me, which only confuses me more. I let out another sigh.

"Go get her, I know it seems an impossible thing to forgive, but I promise you if she hadn't done it, if she hadn't killed her dad, you wouldn't have a Mate at all."

*

"I, Alpha Dayton of the Freedom Howler's Pack, accept Lilla, simple Rogue back into my Pack." I say the words as we walk towards the house, and I feel the shift in the Pack telling me she is back in. Lilla doubles over, and I block out the pain to help her by gritting my teeth.

I rub my palm into her back, and soon she stands straight.

"I'm fine now. Thanks." She smiles at me reassuringly, and I smile back; she may not have told me why and I may not have forgiven her, but what the Ancestors said have stuck with me. The thought of never having had the chance to meet my Little Rogue makes me feel sick.

"I am sorry, Lilla, for what I said. I could never reject you, no matter what you did. Besides, it was an Ancestor; my rule applies to killing Alpha's." I joke and turn to her as she stops walking.

"Dayton, my dad wasn't just an Ancestor. He was an Alpha too." She tells me, and I frown. I really should have figured that out on my own. Of course, an Ancestor in a Pack will be the Alpha; where was my common sense?

"Okay, I should have known that." I laugh awkwardly at my own stupidity. My smile drops when I see the worry written over her face, and I pull her into a hug. "I will not reject you, Lilla, no matter what."

"Promise?" She asks, her voice muffled as she is squashed against my chest.

"I promise," I kiss her forehead. "I'll tell you what we need to do." I offer, she moves slightly in my arms to look up at me, her chin resting on my chest.

"What?"

"We need to go on a date. Just you and me. No talking about the heavy stuff, just getting to know each other. Doing something a normal couple does." I say, my breath catching at the dazzling smile she offers me.

"I'd love to."

Lilla

A date. I was going on a date. Why did I agree to this? What could have been going through my mind that made me say yes?

Actually, I didn't say yes; I said I'd love to. Why would I say that?

I groan and flop down onto the sofa in the wardrobe. I should have just kept away from him when I left the Territory, but no.

"What about this?" Russell says, and I lift my head to look at the outfit.

"How do I know? You know where I'm going, I don't." I point out, and he sighs before disappearing again. I lean back down. "Can't you give me a clue?"

"Commanded not to," Russell says, and I groan loudly. "Okay, this is what you are wearing." I sit up, putting my arms behind me to support my weight. "Here we have a simple cream top with sequins making it seem more extravagant and formal, a pair of dark blue jeans and brown wedges."

"I can wear jeans?" I ask, trying not to get my hopes up.

"Yes, you can. It's probably best." Russell says with a shrug, and my mood brightens. I get to wear jeans, but I get to wear heels too. I frown slightly at the shoes.

"Have I got anything higher?"

*

"Should I be worried that you are taking me into the middle of the woods?"

I ask, laughing nervously as I look around me. It isn't so much the walking through the woods in heels during the night that makes me nervous but more to do with the fact that I'm going on a date. My first date.

It sounds stupid since I've literally made out with Dayton, and I've been living with him for the past two weeks, but when the word "date" is involved, my nerves spike, and I feel like a teenage girl.

"Trust me," Dayton says without turning around as he leads me further and further into the woods. "Maybe you should have worn more appropriate footwear." Dayton says as we reach a fallen tree that is blocking our path.

I roll my eyes, "If there is one thing you should know about me, Dayton, it's this. I can wear heels for anything, any occasion, any chance I get I will wear heels; I've been wearing them since I was five and they are my favourite type of shoe. I can walk, jump and run in heels, so please don't even try to tell me about appropriate footwear." I say it with a straight face because I need him to know I mean every word, but he laughs at me. I used to love wearing heels. I only stopped when I became a Rogue; you don't get many choices in footwear.

"Yeah, if you're so good in heels, get over this tree without my help." Dayton dares me, and I raise an eyebrow.

"Really, are we doing dares now?" I tease, and he shrugs, his face showing his amusement.

"I was just giving you the chance to prove how amazing you are in heels." Dayton says innocently. I narrow my eyes at him.

"Fine, I've already shown how good I am walking in heels, now for the running and jumping. I'm also throwing in the perfact landing for you." I tease as I walk back the way we came. I turn as I reach the corner and stare ahead at the tree. I don't need this much of a run-up, but I wanted to prove to him I could do this.

So, in my 7inch wedges, I run as fast as I can, jump over the log and land perfectly on both feet, throwing my arms up for dramatic effect; I turn to

Dayton to see him staring at me with wide eyes.

"I will never second guess your footwear again." He says as he jumps over the tree and joins me.

"Good," I say, desperate to have the last word as the nerves evaporate, and he simply shakes his head and chuckles.

*

"Here we go," Dayton says as we come into a clearing. I gasp as I look around. The trees surrounding the small open space are covered in tiny lights, creating the perfect romantic atmosphere. Candles are placed in parallel line forming a path before making a circle around a white table and chairs. I walk towards the table to see two red plates, wine glasses and cutlery opposite each other, with white and red candles in the middle.

"Do you like it?" Dayton's voice brings me out of my reverie, and I turn to face him. He hasn't moved from where I left him, and unable to speak, I simply nod. "The candles are electric, I wanted the real thing, but it was a health and safety issue," he informs me, and he continues to talk before I can say anything. "Do you recognise the place?" I shake my head, but I realise it does look familiar. "It's where we first met; you were lying on the floor at the time, in the exact spot where the table is. I can't help but think of this as our place, you know? Even though I only said a few words to you before you blacked out, but–"

While he was speaking, I had made my way over to him, and I decided to interrupt him as he rambled on by kissing him. We are the same height in my heels, which is an excellent advantage for me. I pull away from him before we get carried away and smile at him.

"This is perfect," I tell him, and he smiles at me before leading the way to the table. He pulls out my chair, and I sit down with a grateful smile.

As he sits down opposite me, two Pack members I don't recognise appear, one with a bottle of wine and the other with two wine glasses.

The glasses are placed in front of us, and I see they are filled with lettuce, prawns and lemons. "Prawn Cocktails for starters," the man who had carried them over announces while the other man pours wine into the glasses already there.

"Thank you," I breathe as they both leave. "This is amazing," I say as I pick up my fork and begin to eat.

"I'm glad you like it," he says and begins to eat. After our starters are finished, they bring out our main course, roast chicken, potatoes and salad. It tastes incredible, and we soon finish it, making small talk all the way through.

When they take away the plates, and we wait for them to bring out dessert, I take control of the conversation. "Okay, we are meant to be using this time to get to know each other, so what's your favourite song?" I ask, and he takes a sip of his wine.

"Stay Another Day by East17, my mum used to play it when I was young, and it became my favourite." He tells me, and I notice he saddens slightly as he thinks about his mum. "What about you? What's your favourite song?"

"I Would Do Anything for Love by Meatloaf, my Mum and Dad used to sing it to entertain us when we were young; they were awful singers, but it made us laugh and then Alec and I would join in." I smile fondly at the memory and then shake my head. "Favourite Colour?" I ask before taking a mouthful of my wine.

"Red," he says simply, "yours?"

"Purple," I answer, and he smiles.

"Like your eyes? Or lighter?"

"Dark Purple, like my eyes," I say with a nod. "Okay, tell me something I don't know about you. Remember, no heavy stuff."

"Erm... okay, this is something no one knows, but when I was 10, I decided I didn't want to be an Alpha when I grew up, so I decided to run away. My Dad found me about an hour later, and I told him being an Alpha seemed too hard and too much responsibility, and I didn't know how to do it. When my dad started to show me what Alpha's do, taking me with him to meet other Alpha's and to meetings, he showed me that it wasn't as hard as I thought, and I was overreacting. To this day, I don't regret running away because it brought my father and me closer and showed me how to be an Alpha." Dayton says, and I reach my hand and rest it over his.

"Thank you for sharing that,'" I say earnestly, and he smiles at me.

"Your go, tell me something I don't know about you."

"Okay... I don't know how you will react to this, but this isn't my original hair colour." I tell him, and he bursts out laughing.

"I tell you something heartfelt and honest, and you in return tell me you dye your hair," he says through his laughter, and I pull my hand away from him and cross my arms over my chest.

"I don't dye my hair," I say softly, and he slowly stops laughing and looks at me.

"But you said that's not your original hair colour," he frowns.

"No, it isn't. My original hair colour is blonde; when my Wolf was blocked, my hair changed to black." I tell him, and he stares at me intently.

"Either way, you are beautiful," he says after a few minutes, and I blush at the compliment.

"What's for dessert?" I ask, changing the subject. Both men return as I finish the question with martini glasses. They are placed in front of me with a small spoon, and I stare wide-eyed at them.

"Layered Chocolate Mousse," the man informs us, and they leave us to eat. White chocolate at the bottom, followed by milk chocolate and dark chocolate on top, I dig my spoon in, determined to have all three layers at once. As the first mouthful fills my mouth, I can't help the moan that comes out.

"Oh my God, this is the best thing I have ever tasted!" I exclaim, and Dayton chuckles; we eat the rest of the dessert in comfortable silence.

"Thank you for this," I say, gesturing around me. "It was perfect."

"Anything for my Mate," he answers.

"Well, isn't this cosy!" I snap my head around to see Drake leaning against a tree, surrounded by darkness. I stand up quickly, knocking the chair back and standing between him and Dayton. Dayton growls and moves forward, but I put a hand on his chest, stopping him.

"Don't, Dayton." I say, he stays behind me, but I can tell he isn't happy about it, his Wolf and instinct telling him to stand between his Mate and the threat.

"What do you want, Drake?" I asked, donning my emotionless mask.

"I just came here to remind you that you have two weeks before your Mate dies, unless of course, you reject him." He says, holding up two fingers.

"That's why you came all the way here?"

"I was staying at Crescent Pack; I was out while you were there, readying myself to leave until Luke mentioned you were still a happy couple. So obviously, you didn't get my previous message, and I'm fully aware the Ancestors are on the way," he smiles at us.

"So, what? You want to speak to them?" I ask, my voice cold, but I am beyond confused.

"No, this is a distraction."

"Distraction?" Dayton asks just as we hear a distant howl behind us, a heart-wrenching howl.

"I just want to hurt you more," Drake says, eyes never leaving me. 'Consider this just more punishment for killing my brother."

Dayton, Lilla, you better come back here. Austin's urgent voice fills my mind, and three Wolves come rushing into the clearing.

Both of you leave; we will take care of him. Cain's voice in my head makes me tear my eyes away from Drake to face them.

"But..." I trail off, not sure why I'm protesting, and when I turn back to where Drake was standing, the spot is empty. The three Wolves let out a growl and run in the direction I'm assuming Drake went.

"Come on," Dayton says, pulling me, and we both take off towards his house.

I see Russell sitting on the floor naked when we get there, and I freeze.

"Russell? What's wrong?" I manage to spit out, but the feeling of dread fills me.

"He's gone." Russell sobs, and I feel the bile rise in my throat.

"Who's gone, Rus?" I ask, mentally begging and pleading that I'm wrong.

"Alec, they took him, five men came out of nowhere, and three held me, two of them drugged Alec and took off; after a while, the three men let me go and disappeared. I didn't stand a chance; I tried to follow, but–" he's voice catches, and he breaks down crying again.

They took Alec, Drake took Alec. The anger boils inside, and I can't keep it down as it continues to rise. Dayton pulls away from me as I shake, and the sound of Russell's cries fade when we all hear the unmistakable sound of my bones snapping.

Dayton

It's like time stood still. We had seen it happen before, we had heard her screams and her bones break, but this time it was different. I could feel her anger radiate off her small frame and judging by Jace's and the rest of my closest Pack members faces, they could feel it too.

As the bones in her legs shatter, she falls to her knees, she cries out as they fracture, and falls onto her stomach. Everything is eerily silent as we stare at her. The only thing telling us she is alive is the sound of her heart beating.

"What happened?" Ancestor Blake runs towards us, the other Ancestors following closely behind. They stop when they see Lilla unconscious on the floor. Her bones still breaking; does she have any whole bones left in her body?

"I think she is trying to shift," I say, coming to my senses and blocking out my Wolf's cries.

"What do you mean trying to shift? She has already tried that once this month," Ancestor Cain says, and I shake my head.

"I don't know, okay? She heard about Alec, and she got angry, and then this happened." I point at her body that has fallen silent. No bones left to be broken.

The Ancestor's tear their eyes away from her, and we all do the same as we have unknowingly created a circle around her.

"What about Alec?" Ancestor Emily asks, and Russell lets out a cry. Aria appears from the direction of the Pack houses, Rowan with her. She runs over and wraps her arms and a blanket around Russell, comforting him.

"Drake took him; he came here to distract us while his men took Alec." I explain, and the Ancestor's exchange a look.

"What?"

"A brother for a brother," Ancestor Blake says quietly, and we all fall silent. A scream erupts from Lilla's mouth, causing us to cringe and cover our ears. We all stare down at her and watch as her bones begin to heal, reforming themselves.

"Is she...?" My eyes refuse to leave my Mate as she moves jaggedly on the floor.

"Drake pushed her too far; there is only so much she can take." Ancestor Cain says.

"What do you mean?"

"Drake not only took her brother, her family, but he took her Pack member. There is only so much a Brown Wolf can take; Drake has made a mistake taking Alec. He is underestimating just how powerful Lilla is."

"So, because she is angry, because Drake took Alec, she is..." I point at Lilla and glance up to see Ancestor Blake nod.

"Her Wolf is breaking free."

Lilla

1 year earlier

"Wakey, wakey," Drake's voice fills the room and groaning, I open my eyes. "Have a nice sleep?" He asks and then laughs. I simply nod, too terrified to speak. "Good, now come with me, Little." He grabs a fistful of my greasy, golden blonde hair and drags me until we reach a door. I frown slightly; usually, my torturing took place in my cell for everyone else to see how weak I was. Today, I was led upstairs into a living room, up more stairs, and into a bedroom.

"This is my room; what do you think?" Drake asks, and I begin to panic.

What are we doing in here? If he tries something, I'll rip his throat out! My Wolf growls protectively.

"It's perfect for an Alpha," I say softly, and he beams at me, clearly pleased with my answer.

"I agree. Now your punishment for today will be different from your usual. I want to spice things up a bit. I'm going to give you a Venom Mark," Drake states, sitting on his bed and patting the space opposite him. I walk over and sit down; no point in fighting.

"Do you know what that is?"

I shift nervously and offer a slight shake of my head.

"As an Ancestor, I have many abilities that other Werewolves don't have, and this is one of them. This Venom Mark is a Mark placed just below your collarbone; it will leave behind two fang marks and is permanent. I will bite down and release venom into your body, and it will trap your Wolf. This means *you won't be able to shift, you won't be able to connect at all with your Wolf, you will be Human but smell like a Werewolf and feel empty because half of you is missing."* He speaks so calmly I begin to wonder if he is saying the same as what I'm hearing. As if he's a doctor explaining a simple procedure, a teacher instructing their pupils, a demon describing my personal hell.

He lunges before I have time to react; he sinks his canines into me. I scream and begin to struggle, but as the venom moves around my body, causing me tremendous pain, I grow weaker and weaker until I can't keep my eyes open any longer.

*

ALEC!

That's my first thought as I open my eyes. I'm lying on my side, and I feel stiff and weird. I try to open my mouth to talk, but nothing comes out.

What's happened? Why can't I speak? I begin to panic when I hear Dayton call my name.

"Lilla, breathe, you've shifted, okay, just calm down." Shifted? Did he say shifted?

That's when it hits me. I feel weird because I'm no longer Human. I don't remember this feeling; I don't remember what it feels like to have paws or fur covering me. It's been so long.

How did I do this?

Wait. My Wolf! I close my eyes and search, calling out for her, but nothing happens.

"Lilla, you aren't free; she won't be there." Blake says, aware of what I'm trying to do.

I must be free; I'm a Wolf. I retort, having to mind-link, seeing as I can't speak out loud in Wolf form.

"We need to show her," Emily chimes in.

Alec! We need to find Alec.

I begin to panic; everything else can wait. I can't let Drake do to him what he did to me.

"We will make a plan, but maybe we should go to your room so you can shift back; we don't have any of your clothes out here," Dayton says; he doesn't want anyone to see his Mate naked.

"We can show her in the mirror too." Russell adds; I lift my head and look at him; his face is tear-stained, he sniffles, but he keeps staring at me. Still lying on my side, I turn my head to look at everyone; they are all staring at me, eyes wide. My description of a four coloured Wolf doesn't prepare everyone to see it.

Dayton is right; I can't help Alec like this; I need to be human and make plans. I can't even enjoy the fact I managed to shift because I need to save Alec.

I stand up slowly, stumbling slightly; I feel a bit like Bambi; there is no way I could even fight like this when I'm like a brand-new pup getting used to being on four legs.

Getting to my room, we all walk into my wardrobe... do they expect me to shift back with them here? I thought the whole point was that they wouldn't see me naked.

I turn to face them, about to ask them to leave, when I catch myself in the mirror.

Staring back at me is the same Wolf, I remember. The same Wolf I told everyone I looked like. White fur until my eyes, a streak of black framing my face, ears to tail is grey fur, my stomach and legs are chocolate brown, with tufts of black scattered, and my tail is striped all four colours.

There is just one difference, and that is the silver.

Silver fur wraps around my Wolf, from snout to tail, making it look like I'm wearing chains. She may have finally broken free, but she is still a caged animal.

I shake my head and turn away from the mirror. I need to shift back. I can't do this right now. I can't have questions; I can't panic. I can't be horrified. I need to get Alec back.

Please leave.

I say to them all, and they leave me alone; I close my purple eyes and concentrate on being Human. Once I shift back, I glance at myself in the mirror to ensure the silver chains aren't on my human skin before I get dressed. My hair is still black, and my scars and bruises didn't heal; I'm not surprised, though, the Mark is still firmly sitting on my neck.

Without saying a word, I push past everyone and make my way to the kitchen, needing food. I feel them all watching me as I open the freezer, take out the chips and put them on a tray; I place them in the oven.

When I have set the timer, I turn to face everyone.

"We need to make a plan to get Alec back." I say as everyone sets themselves into the kitchen chairs. Dayton walks over to me and pulls me into a hug. Sparks erupt on my skin, and I gasp; we pull away and look at each other. No pain appears, and I smile. This is what it's meant to be like with your Mate, the sparks and the intense feelings and the lack of pain. He pulls me in for a proper hug, and I settle in. This is what I needed. I just needed a second to process, and this hug is what calms me.

Then the burning starts.

I pull away, but the burning doesn't stop.

"Little Rogue?"

I find it difficult to breathe and claw at my throat like someone is strangling me.

I scream as my whole body felt the non-existent fire lick my flesh.

Lilla

As suddenly as it started, it stopped. I breathe heavily, trying to catch my breath. No, no, no! I start shaking my head as the tears fall. My chest feels heavy and my body weak, I'm struggling to keep my eyes open, but I fight the inevitable.

"How has this happened?" I scream out as I start to sob uncontrollably. I know this feeling all too well, a feeling I'll never forget. Dayton comes forward to comfort me, but I step away, already feeling the pain, dull as it was before I shifted.

"It seems Drake didn't underestimate you; we underestimated him," Emily says, watching me with sorrow in her eyes.

"He knew how powerful you are. He knew you would shift one day, it seems he planned for it." Cain adds.

"What is going on?" Dayton says through gritted teeth, he feels my pain and sadness, and he knows he can't do anything to take it away.

"Imagine the Venom Mark as a binding contract with clauses to cover all situations. That's what he's done. The Venom Mark is a powerful tool we only use on the most dangerous creatures; however, when we Mark someone with it, we can create clauses that can be and do whatever we want. It's like we are writing a contract between us. Drake knew she would break free; he knows how powerful Lilla is, he knew it wouldn't work to its full effect, and she'd meet her Mate, so he created a clause, she meets her Mate, and he dies three weeks later. Or, to make her suffer, she goes through the pain of shifting without shifting. If she does manage to shift one day, then the Mark renews." Blake explains to us all as I struggle to keep standing.

"What do you mean renews?" Russell asks; my heart goes out to him; his Mate has been taken, and instead of us getting him, we are once again dealing with me. He has the patience of a Saint.

"Like a refresh. She hasn't broken it, she bent it slightly, and the Mark snapped back into place. It'll be like she just received the Mark."

I hear the oven timer go off; my chips are ready. I move towards the oven but instead, I fall to the floor, my legs unable to support me. I smack my head on the kitchen floor, and everything goes black.

*

"Please don't do this, Little Rogue!" Dayton begs, but I shake my head, and with a cold voice, I say the words I had always feared I'd hear.

"I, Lilla, Rogue, reject you, Dayton, Alpha of the Freedom Howlers Pack as my Mate." The pain is excruciating, but I keep up my emotionless mask as I watch his face crumble and my big, bad Alpha starts to cry.

Lilla

The dream I had had last night was unsettling. I wouldn't have thought I'd ever reject Dayton, but that dream had felt so real.

I need to clear my head. I need to figure out what to do about Alec. We needed a plan.

I walk down the stairs to find the Ancestors talking with Rowan and Jace. They stop when they see me.

"I'm going for a walk," I say, and they nod and continue their talk. I try to listen, but honestly, my head is pounding after smacking it on the floor, so I can't concentrate.

"We need a plan," I point out, and they all turn to look at me.

"We are trying to decide on the best course of action; it's just hard when you don't want us killing them," Rowan explains; they still don't understand.

"The other day, I was in the Crescent Pack, and I ran into Luke. I grew up with him, he was my best friend, and I didn't recognise who he was without humanity. I watched as he struggled and fought it when I told him what Drake was doing to me. He has no humanity because an Ancestor has commanded him not to, but he fought the command, which could kill him because his emotions for me and what happened flooded through. We are not killing them; he is still my best friend; he is in there fighting, struggling every day. He doesn't deserve to die for what Drake is making him do."

They fall silent, so I leave them to think while I do the same.

*

I wander around the forest for about an hour when I find Russell sitting at the cliff's edge.

"Hey, you aren't going to jump, are you?" I asked, sitting next to him.

"I think I should be asking you that, considering you've done it once already." Russell chuckles, but then his face falls back to sadness.

"This is the only place I feel at peace," I tell him, and he nods in understanding. "Can I ask you something, kind of private?"

"Of course," he looks at me with expectant eyes.

"Why haven't you two Mated? I would have thought it would be the first thing you'd do." I turn away, shy, and Russell sighs.

"When you Mate, you get to see all of their memories so you can understand and know everything about each other." Russell admits like it's obvious.

"I don't get it?" I ask it as a question, hoping he will explain.

"He didn't want to say anything to you, so I don't think I should."

"Say what? Why can't you tell me? Why does it have anything to do with me?"

He sighs. "Alec doesn't know much of what happened to you, only what your mother told him, and it wasn't a lot. Your secrets are not his to tell, but he didn't want to say anything and make you feel pressured into telling us. I don't want that either, so we agreed to wait." Russell looks at me with such love, and I smile before wrapping my arms around him.

I know what I have to do. I don't want to do it. I'm not ready, but everyone has to make sacrifices.

Pack meeting, everyone comes! I say forcefully through the Pack mind-link.

"Do you think they'll come?" I ask Russell, as he stands up, pulling me with him.

"You know, Wolves; we are nosy and curious creatures."

*

I stand on the make-shift stage that I had stood on a week ago when Alec and I joined the Pack, only this time I am alone. Dayton is here, I can feel his presence, but I can't see him, which makes me feel lonely. I breathe in and out a few times before addressing the three hundred Pack members.

"Of all the ways I pictured telling my story, this wasn't one of them. I always dreamed I'd tell my Mate, just him and me when I was ready. I imagined that he would be angry at what was done to me, but he would love me anyway, comfort me, and I'd be happy. That was never going to happen, though; I was never going to tell my Mate my story, I was never going to meet my Mate, so it seemed pointless to even dream about any of it.

"Then I met Dayton, and I let myself dream a little, but I knew that one day when I did tell him the truth, he would reject me. So, I pushed him away; well, I tried, but he promised never to reject me, so I hope that he will want to keep that promise by the end of this.

"I've decided to tell you all my story at once; it's easier to tell everyone the same thing instead of telling one person and having the story change as it passes around the Pack. I only ask that while I tell you this, that you don't make a sound, you save your questions and remarks for the end because if I get interrupted, I don't think I could find it in me to continue. This is one of the hardest things I'll ever do and the one person to who I'm dying to tell the truth, isn't here, but I figure telling all of you my story will save his life."

3 Years Earlier

I am woken in the night by screams followed by howls, howls of sorrow and howls for backup. My Dad bursts into my room, looking around frantically.

"Big, you've got to get up. Rogues are here, and I need to put you with your mother." *His voice is urgent, and immediately I am by his side, his massive hand around my delicate small one. I'm scared, and he knows it because he squeezes my hand reassuringly every few seconds.*

"You need to stay here with your mother. I have to go fight with my Pack," *he says as he pulls back a bookshelf in the front room to reveal a spot big enough for three. My mum is already in there, and she holds out her arms for me.*

"Why don't you stay with us, Alfa?" *I beg, but I know he has to fight with his Pack. He pulls me into a hug and kisses my forehead.*

"I am the Alpha, and I have to fight to protect my Pack, but I also have to fight to protect my two favourite girls. I can't lose either of you. Okay, Big?" *I smile at the affectionate name for me and nodding, I go to my mother.*

"I love you, Alfa." *I say using my nickname for him, which is simply Alpha, but it was an inside joke in Swedish. Like his for me, Lilla is 'Little' in Swedish, and when I told him I hated being called Little, he started to call me Big and ever since then, he hasn't used my name.*

"I love you too, Big." *He closes us in, and we are left in darkness. Time seems to slow while we are stuck inside this space. Neither of us speaks, we don't know what to say, and we are too scared for my dad to break the silence.*

Suddenly, we hear a noise on the other side of the bookshelf, and we stand up as it opens, ready to fight if need be. Relief washes over us both as we see my dad standing there. We run into his arms, but I can't help but notice he looks sad.
Of course, he looks sad; he lost his Pack members today! *My Wolf points out.*
The next couple of days pass in a blur of funerals and showing condolences for those who lost someone.
My Dad is acting different, he looks heartbroken, and nothing can cheer him up. When all the funerals are over, we are called to a Pack meeting to discuss what to do about the increase in Rogues, when my dad, my kind, loving Father, simply shrugs his shoulders and says the words that would change our Pack forever.
"We kill anyone that steps foot in our Territory, Human or Wolf, I don't care. If they are uninvited, they are an enemy, and they will be put down."

*

Later that night, my mother sat me down and explained that my Dad's Mate had died; the Rogues killed her while he was busy fighting the ones trying to get into our home. He protected us, and his Mate, my biological Mother, died.
I know I should be angry that they kept such a huge secret from me, but instead, I'm sad for my father; the idea of losing my Mate even though I had never met him caused my Wolf and me pain.
So, as the days went on and my dad became more distant and colder towards the Pack, I made allowances for him, both my mother and I did. It was a mistake because once we started making allowances for his behaviour, we couldn't stop. He became violent towards the Pack. Anyone who questioned him or simply got in his way when he walked down the street got a severe beating that left them in the hospital for months but no matter what, he never touched my mother and me.
He comes home, and even though he isn't the Father I knew, he still tries; he

would smile and laugh and kiss my mother and read me stories.

"Alfa?" I ask, and he looks away from the TV to pay attention to me.

"Why do you treat the Pack the way you do?" I ask, and he sighs.

"They are meant to be protecting the Pack when they fight, but they didn't protect my Mate, and she died because of it. They failed me." He says simply, and I frown.

"So why don't you treat us the same way?"

"If I were to treat you how I treat the Pack, then what was the point in me saving you. I choose to protect you and your mother over my Mate, and if I start mistreating you, it makes it all pointless. Besides, my Mate is your real Mother, and I can never hurt a piece of my Mate."

I simply nod and wrap my arms around his neck, unsure I agree with his reasoning. "I love you, Alfa," I say, squeezing tightly. He hugs me back.

"I love you too, Lilla."

6 months later

(2 and a half years earlier)

I let out a sigh as I walk down the street; everything is different. The town is meant to be filled with people laughing and joking, but instead, the people in town are scared, sad or emotionless.

No one looks me in the eyes; I am the Alpha's daughter. People who used to be my friends look down when I walk past, a sign of submission.

These people fear me or what will happen to them if they accidentally do something wrong towards me. The wrong words or actions could result in punishment, so it is safer for them to just bow their heads as I walk past. They also hate me. They hate what my father has done to them and not done to me. I don't blame them; I hate me too.

I'm not an idiot; I'm fully aware of the pain and suffering everyone is going through. What my dad is making them do. We have gone from one of the most caring Packs to one of the most vicious and feared Packs in six months. It isn't their fault; my dad makes them do the things they do.

He is making them kill innocent people who come into our Territory, the youngest was a new-born, and the oldest was a simple human woman of 98; everyone in this Pack has killed someone innocent; my dad made sure of it. Except for my mother and me, we were excused from any such activity, another reason they hate me.

If they didn't kill them, they would be punished, not simply put in jail, but the men who said no were beaten until they were so near death it's a miracle if *they survive, and if the men have Mates, they are commanded to sit and watch while my father rapes them, makes them listen to the screams and cries and commands them to ignore it. The men are helpless against him, the women too, that's the main reason everyone hates me. I'm the only one strong enough to stop him, yet I haven't.*

He has raped every woman in the Pack, except my mother and me, of course. He has beaten every Pack member and kills anyone who tries to leave. Yet I can't bring myself to stop him.

That makes me as awful as him, but he is my dad, and I keep thinking he will snap out of it, he will realise what he is doing and stop. Every day I hope that this will happen and every night, I go to bed disappointed in him, my mother and myself.

6 months later

(2 years earlier)

I couldn't do it. Kill a baby, for what? For my dad, is he even my dad anymore? My dad wouldn't have done this to the Pack; my dad wouldn't be commanding me to do this. My dad was sweet and kind and loving.

What could I do, though? Breaking an Ancestor command kills you; I'd seen it happen.

I'd rather be dead than live like this anymore. *My Wolf pipes up. She's right; I can't kill him, so I might as well kill myself.*

My Wolf and I use all our strength pushing against the chains of the command; they pull tighter, restricting my breathing. I push harder, feeling weaker the more I do.

Then, all of a sudden, I feel them snap. The chains you feel with a command are gone. Broken. Relief washes over me.

"Kill him!" *My dad roars in command, but the chains don't appear.*

Have I broken the Ancestor Command for good?

The baby starts crying, and I smile at him as I hand him back to his parents; everyone is staring, unsure what to do. I didn't even know what to do; it should have killed me.

"You won't hurt anyone else, dad," *I say softly but with renewed strength, knowing he can't make me.*

He lunges for me and grabs me by the throat; no one moves as he tightens his grip. Finally, he lets go, and I drop to the floor, gasping for air.

He grabs me by my hair and drags me all the way home while I hold his clenched fist to my head, trying to limit the pain.

He throws me through our front door, and I hold back a scream at the agony radiating through my body.

He walks towards me, and I close my eyes, readying myself for the pain; he grabs me by the hair again, pulling me up before punching me in the stomach. I don't fight back; there is no point; he's stronger than me.

His Wolf is taking over more and more.

"You little bitch! Going against me in front of my Pack! I will make you pay for showing me up like that!" He shouts, hatred lacing his words, and my eyes widen as he pulls down his trousers.

He's no longer your dad. *My Wolf screams at me urgently, trying to take over.*

"Daddy, please! Alfa!" I beg as he straddles me. He ignores me.

So, I let my Wolf take over; we can't let him do this anymore. To anyone. I have no choice; he isn't my dad anymore. I have to try to kill him, to stop him while I have the chance.

I use the only weapon I have available, my claws, I feel them grow, and I plunge them into his heart with tears in my eyes.

His face shows shock, anger, sadness, and emptiness as I pull my bloody claws out, and he collapses on top of me, dead.

I push his body off me and see I'm covered in blood. I stare at his corpse, waiting for some sort of sadness or remorse to fill me but instead, I feel relief and happiness that it's all over.

It is over, right?

*

It's been a week since I killed my dad. My mum hasn't left her room, grieving for the man he was. I was trying to sort out the mess he had made. Everyone was relieved when I had told them what had happened, he had caused so much misery and pain, and I had killed him. Everyone was healing from all they had been made to do. It would take a long time for anyone to get over it.

Luke and I were trying to come up with some excuse for what happened. An Alpha is dead; if the Ancestors find out, we need a reason that wouldn't get me killed.

So far, we were drawing a blank.

Lilla? An Ancestor is here; he claims he is your Uncle; he looks like our old Alpha. *Kieran, a young Pack member who just turned 16 and wants to prove his worth, nudges into my mind, and I sigh, looking at Luke.*

Send him to my house. *I inform him and block the Pack out as I face Luke.*

"Why would you do that?" Luke asks.

"He is my Uncle; he knows his brother dead. They've always had a special connection," I tell him, and he frowns.

"Special Connection?"

"The Ancestors weren't meant to be blood-related, so when they were born, as twins nonetheless, they messed up the Prophecy; my dad used to think that's why he had a Mate and could reproduce. He was the youngest, born a few minutes later, and so he became the exception to the Prophecy, at least that's what he believed; he couldn't explain any of it otherwise." I tell him, and he simply nods. At the knock on the door, I stand and try to relax, but I can feel the nerves rolling off me. I open the door, and I look at my Uncle.

"Uncle Drake!" I exclaim and rush into his arms. He wraps them around me and pulls me close.

"How's my favourite niece?" He asks, and I pull away, feeling my smile turning in to a frown as a slight nudge is breaking through the barrier I had put up in my mind.

I watch my Uncle's face, but it stays in a smile, and I relax slightly, "Could we have some privacy? I'd love to talk to my niece alone." He asks sweetly, and nodding my head, Luke leaves us.

"So, Uncle, how have-" my words are cut off as his hand wraps around my *throat.*

"You killed him!" He growls out, crushing my windpipe, and I claw at his hands to no avail. He slams me against the wall, "you killed my brother, you little bitch, he was nothing but loving towards you, and you killed him. Don't think I didn't notice how you twisted your memories!" He says with disgust in his voice.

I struggle to breathe, and my eyes widen. Realising he thinks I made the whole thing up; I begin to panic. He lets go suddenly, and I fall to the floor, trying desperately to breathe in the air around me, wincing slightly as it burns my lungs.

"Uncle-" I try to explain, but he kicks me, causing me to scream. Luke bursts in and looks at me on the ground, but before he can react, my Uncle speaks.

"She tried to kill me; she has a taste for it; she can't be trusted. Take her to the cells; I will be taking over as Alpha of this Pack." My Uncle commands, Luke simply nods and takes me away, ignoring my pleas.

6 months later

(1 and a half years earlier)

I have managed to perfect the emotionless mask. Every time Drake would beat me in the first two months, I had been scared, and my face had given me away, which made him feel more powerful; he relished in my fear and pain. I didn't want to give him anything, so I started to work on making my face emotionless. My voice was cold and distant, and more importantly, I worked on my actual emotions; if my face didn't give me away, then the fear and pain rolling off me would, so I developed a feeling of emptiness. It isn't the nicest feeling, but he gets nothing from me this way.

He still tortures me, and he has managed to break through my emotionless state each time, but I keep practising; there isn't much else to do here.

I hear him walking towards my cell, so I ready myself, my face turning blank and letting the feeling of emptiness take over, which involves pushing down my Wolf. She isn't thrilled about it, but she knows why I'm doing it, so she doesn't fight.

"How is Little this morning?" *Drake's voice sings as he opens my cell. I immediately lower my head submissively without saying a word. He grabs my arm and begins to walk, pulling me alongside him.* "It had come to my attention that this Pack is slightly... weak, and when I asked your dear mother, she informed me that it is you're doing." *Drake says; I continue to stay silent as he brings me upstairs and into the daylight.*

"It seems that no matter how much I command this Pack, they have a sense of loyalty to you that I can't command away. It is the one thing that is helping *them keep their humanity, and I don't want a Pack of humans; I want a Pack of Wolves." He continues to enlighten me as if I asked him to tell me.*

I look up from the ground to see where we are, and a feeling of dread washes over me before I can stop the emotion, and Drake picks up on it.

He chuckles as he makes his way through the crowd and pushes me into the middle of the ring, closing the gate behind him.

"So here are the rules: you will fight a Pack member of my choosing. To the death. If he wins, then all my troubles are over, and if you win- which I highly doubt because you are weak and fragile- but for arguments sake, if you win, then I will leave you alone tomorrow, no torture, no beatings." Drake says, and I drop the emotionless mask and shake my head.

"I won't do it," I say forcefully, as he glares at me. "You can't command me, and I won't kill a Pack member."

"They aren't your Pack anymore; they are mine! I am their Alpha!" He growls, "I don't have to command you because your Wolf will take over out of instinct." He tells me, clearly having thought this through. "Bring him in." Drake commands, and a man jumps over the fence surrounding us instead of walking through the gate. I roll my eyes at his ridiculous attempt at intimidation.

I don't recognise him. *I say to my Wolf, looking at the bodybuilder as he growls and begins to circle me.*

Me neither; he was probably brought in by Drake. *She surmises.*

I don't think I'm strong enough to fight him; Drake has been keeping me weak. *I say, and she growls at me.*

You have Ancestor blood in you. Even on your worst day, you can beat him! *We both know my Wolf is lying, but I can see her statement for what it is, a vote of confidence, so I just accept it and watch the man continue to circle me, growling every so often.*

I watch him watch me, and then suddenly, he growls and shifts. I jump at its suddenness, and as he stalks me like I'm his prey, my Wolf becomes agitated and angry, clearly hating being thought of as prey. I don't fight her as she takes over, and I shift just as he lunges for me.

As he was going for my throat in human form, he went over me, as in Wolf form, I'm just as little as my name says I am.

I turn and growl, making my fur stand on end to appear bigger and more threatening to the Black Wolf in front of me. He growls back, copying me, and I curl my lips back to expose my fangs and gums as a warning, hoping he will see my attempt at avoiding violence.

He doesn't, or he does and chooses to ignore it as he lunges for me again, but I manage to dodge him. He turns to face me, snarling, and I immediately crouch and prepare for another attack.

I snap at him, still trying to avoid a fight, but he isn't interested as he pulls back slightly before jumping and landing on top of me. I snarl and snap as he pins me down and his teeth sink into my skin, causing me to yelp out in pain. He ignores my whimpering and shakes his head, ripping my flesh.

We have to fight, or we die! *My Wolf cries, and I know she is right. I sigh slightly and go limp, which surprises the Wolf in front of me. He opens his mouth and pulls away slightly as I close my eyes and make myself breathe slower, letting him think I'm dying. I feel the satisfaction roll off him as he believes he has won, and I hear him walk away from me.*

Kill him. *I say, and despite the pain of my wound, which is already starting to heal, I jump up and pounce onto his back, startling him. I sink my teeth into his neck, feeling the venom leak into his bloodstream and without thinking twice, I pull away, bringing his flesh with me. I spit it out as he turns to me, anger in his eyes, but the venom now running through his blood is weakening him.*

He moves forward and collapses; I tilt my head and watch him die, and once his heartbeat stops, I shift back and turn to Drake. Someone throws clothes in my direction, and I dress quickly.

"I have the power of an Ancestor; you knew if I had wanted to kill him, then all I would have to do his bite him," I say accusingly, and he stares at me in shock.

"I had no idea you could do that. Ladies and Gentlemen, I give you the winner," he points at me, and silence fills the crowd. Hatred is in their eyes. This is what he wanted. There will be no loyalty for me now that I've killed one of our own; we all know the right thing to do would have been to knock him out.

"How did one bite kill him, Alpha?" Luke asks, and Drake turns to him.

"Ancestors, as you know, have certain abilities that make them stronger and more powerful than other Werewolves. One of them is venom; we can use it for many things, sedating a Wolf, changing a Human into a Wolf or killing a Wolf, it depends on what you want to achieve." Drake informs the Pack, acting as a teacher. He turns to me, curiosity etched on his face. "You could have sedated him, but you choose to kill him; why?" Drake asks, and everyone turns to me.

I look him in the eyes as I answer. "You would have made me kill him anyway." I shrug, and he raises an eyebrow.

"How could you possibly know that I would do that? I might not have." Drake says, innocently and I let out a humourless laugh.

"My Father -the one who lost his Mate, not the one before that- would have made me do it, and you are one in the same. He changed into a cold-hearted son of a bitch when his Mate died, and it seems you did too, and she wasn't even yours." I say, daring him to challenge me; when he doesn't say a word, I decide to speak. "Can I go back to my cell now?" He nods simply, and I make my way to the gate. "Remember, I get a day off from you tomorrow." I say as a Wolf grabs my arm to lead me back to my cell.

Drake speaks up to the Pack members just before we leave the training grounds. "Someone get me information on my brother's Mate!"

6 months later

(1 year earlier)

I wake in my cell, my whole body shooting with pain when I move. I groan and sit up slowly, the pain slowly fading, but I feel weak.

Memories flood back of Drake telling me about a Venom Mark and then his canines sinking into my collarbone. I reach up and softly search for it, wondering if it was a dream, but as my fingers graze the Mark and I wince as it stings, not a dream. My Uncle gave me a Venom Mark.

What do we do now? *I ask my Wolf, but no one answers, and it's then that I notice the empty feeling that I'm used to putting on when I'm with Drake is there without me needing to do anything. As I remember everything he said about the Venom Mark, I burst into tears and bury my head in my hands; my Wolf is gone.*

"Why so sad, beautiful?" A man steps into view in his cell opposite mine, the only thing separating our cells in the corridor. He is leaning forward, his arms resting through the bars, looking relaxed like he isn't in a prison cell.

I relax at the sight of him and walk over to the bars, sink to the floor, and he copies as he waits for me to speak. "He Marked me, Aiden." I say, my voice cracking and tears rolling down my cheeks.

Growls erupt around me from the prisoners. The man in the cell next to mine appears. "He did what?" He asks, a rumble sounding from his chest as I see his struggle with his Wolf.

I have been here for a year, and there are five other people in here, four men and one woman and as crazy as it sounds, we have all become friends. I suppose it's easy to become friends with the only people in your life not torturing you. I had told them my story, and they didn't believe me at first, but then when Drake came down for me and spoke about me killing his brother, they realised I was telling the truth. Why would I lie about it anyway?

"He called it a Venom Mark," I say into the silent prison. I look at the faces of five people squashed up against the bars of their cell, looking at me with confusion. "I told you how the Ancestors have this ability with venom; there are loads of things they can do with it. When my father was a good man, he taught me a few for my protection, sedating and killing with venom. It turns out that you can also create a Mark with it, which locks your Wolf away. I can't shift or talk to her, and God knows what else I've lost." I break down as the growls erupt around me again. I can feel the anger rolling from everyone, and I find myself smiling, despite my sobs.

These Rogues care about me. Rogues are known for not creating emotional attachments, for being ruthless and more Wolf than Human. They care about me more than my Pack.

At that realisation, I feel sick, and I run over to the bowl that is meant to be my toilet and throw up. I feel someone rubbing my back, and I see Christian, the man whose cell is next to mine, leaning against the bar as much as he can while comforting me.

I give him a small smile which he returns, "We are getting out of here." I decide suddenly, and immediately they all chuckle, pity in their eyes. "I'm being serious, I know this place like the back of my hand, and we are getting out." I say more forcefully.

"How do you propose we do that?" Aiden asks, and I shrug.

"I haven't figured out everything just yet but Marking me is the last straw. He said I'm Human, and if that's true, I won't survive much more, and I refuse to die here." I sound confident, and they all exchange a look before turning to me, nodding.

"Then let's get out of here, beautiful."

Over the next week, we make a plan and perfect it. I'm tortured daily by Drake; he hits me, cuts me, burns me, delighting in the fact I now don't heal.

The others are desperate to leave quickly when they see how much pain I'm in and how it's getting harder for me to move, but we hold out for the right day.

For it all to fall into place.

The day comes, so that morning when the guards turn up to take me to Drake, I am lying on my bed, and no matter how many times they call, I stay as still as I can, until eventually, one of them comes in to get me. As soon as his hand touches my arm, I spin around and hit him. He doubles back, surprised by the attack, and I hurry to grab the gun and knives he has attached to his belt.

I hold the gun up, and he holds his hands up in surrender; his eyes flicker to something behind me, and without looking, I fling the knife backwards. The cry of pain I hear tells me I hit my Mark. He must be closer than I think; he must be in the cell. I make a run for the cell door and close it, locking it before their hands reach the bars.

"You really shouldn't leave your keys in the lock; anyone can steal them." I say sweetly before unlocking the cell doors for the others. I give out the weapons I have, holding the gun back for myself, and we make our way out of the prison.

"That was awesome, by the way." Aiden says proudly, and I turn, offering him my first genuine smile in a long time.

"Thank you for teaching me," I reply, and he wraps an arm around my neck, pulling me towards him as he affectionately kisses my forehead.

"Let's get out of here." With his words, we burst out into the sunlight and ran, hoping we get far enough ahead before anyone noticed.

*

"Aiden, please... hold on, okay? Just hold on, for me." I beg, and I look around

for help. We are alone; the others are dead. We didn't get very far before Wolves started appearing and killing the escaped prisoners, we fought as hard as we could, but we were outnumbered. When Aiden went down, I ran over to him, forgetting everyone fighting around me, and when I looked back up, we were alone. This was all my fault.

"Beautiful, listen to me; I need you to run, okay? Before they come back because they are coming back, and they will kill you. So, run, for me." He says, bringing his hand up to wipe away my tears.

"I'm not leaving you, Aiden. This is my fault; I'm not leaving you!" I tell him forcefully, and he smiles sadly.

"This isn't your fault, we all wanted out, and you gave us the hope we needed; none of us wanted to die in a cage. If you stay here, they will catch you, and I'll die knowing I left you in their hands. I'm dying; I won't survive. You need to go." He tells me, and I frown. "Go Beautiful, run and stay alive; it shouldn't be hard for you, you will make an amazing Rogue, and except for this Pack, I can't see anyone wanting to hurt you." Aiden says, and I notice him become weaker.

"If I had my Wolf, I could save you." I tell him, he laughs before wincing, and we both tense when we hear footsteps in the distance.

"Go!" Aiden says forcefully, and I give in. I can't let him die worrying about me. I lean down and kiss his lips, and when I pull away, he is smiling.

"A kiss by an Angel, that was always on my Bucket List." He jokes, and kissing his lips once more, I run.

Alec

I wake up in unfamiliar surroundings, and immediately, I'm on high alert. I sit up on the bed and look around. I'm in a cell. I groan as I try to recall the last thing I remember. The Wolves, four – no five of them coming towards Russell and me. My wolf whimpers at the thought of my Mate, and I panic. Is he okay? Is he alive? I stand up and make my way to the cell door. I open my mouth to shout, but I hear someone speak before I can.

"I wouldn't do that if I were you," I peer into the cell opposite mine to see a man lying on his bed, watching me.

"Why not?" I ask.

"They get pissed when you make a lot of noise; they tend to punish you for it." He tells me, and I sink to the floor.

"Where am I?"

"In a prison cell," he states, and I give him a sour look. "Midnight Moon Territory," he tells me, and I groan again.

"Shit, that's bad." I tell him, but he doesn't say anything. "Why are you in here?" I ask, curiosity getting the best of me.

"They found me dying in their Territory; the Alpha healed me and then threw me in here for being a Rogue who trespassed. You?"

"I'm not sure, either punishment for leaving the Pack or he is using me to get to someone else. Why didn't he just kill you?" I ask, and he sits up, slightly amused.

"He wants to use me for something," He shrugs as if it's no big deal.

"What does he want to use you for?"

"To get someone back," at those words, his face becomes dark and his voice cold, so I do what I do best. Distract.

"My name is Alec," I offer a small wave. "What's your name?" He looks at me carefully before answering.

"Aiden."

*

"She was breathtakingly beautiful- scratch that- there are no words to describe her beauty." His voice sounds dreamy, and I smile.

"I know what you mean. I'm like that with my Mate." After introducing ourselves, I went back to lie on the bed.

He has been telling me about his life in this prison; he has just told me about the time he and a group of friends escaped, he and a girl being the only survivors.

"She isn't my Mate." Aiden says, and I raise my head to look at him.

"What?"

"She isn't my Mate." He repeats, still staring at the ceiling.

"The way you are talking about her..." I trail off, confused.

"I know, but I wasn't the only one who spoke about her like that. All the others did; even the She-Wolf was protective and loved her. We weren't in love with her; we just loved her like she was our family. Before she came along, none of us had ever said a word to each other, too broken to even try. She had made a Pack out of us, Rogues. She is remarkable."

"I want to meet her." I admit, and he chuckles.

"You will one day. That's why I'm here; Alpha Drake knows he can use me to get her back. She was very protective of us, and she loved us as much as we loved her- or in my case, loves her." Aiden tells me, and then he smiles sadly.

"Why was she down here in the first place? Did she trespass?" I take a guess, and he shakes his head.

"No, Alpha Drake just threw her down here, and he would torture her every day. It was like he was obsessed with her tears, her screams, her pain." Aiden says, sounding bitter, but I can't help but notice he avoided my question, still protective of the girl after a year without her.

"Do you want to know the sickest thing?" He asks, sitting up slightly and leaning back on his elbows. I nod as I copy him. "She is his niece." He says, and I sit up quickly.

"What?" I growl out, and he looks at me, confused at my sudden reaction.

"She is Alpha Drake's niece." Aiden says slowly, watching me carefully as a growl erupts within me.

I'm not stupid. I know she had a hard time here. I mean, he Marked her, for God's sake. From what my mother told me, I know she was poorly treated, but I didn't know how badly. Lilla never let me in on how bad it was.

"Are you talking about Lilla?" I ask, stupidly hopeful that it's someone else, despite her being my only sister.

"Yeah, Lilla, did you know her?" Aiden asks, and I stand up, growling even louder, wanting someone to come down here now, wanting Drake to come down here, so I can rip him apart.

"She is my sister!" I say before I let my Wolf take over.

*

"Can I ask you something?" I ask, and Aiden nods. It had taken me some time to calm down, and no matter how loud I was, no one came in. They were probably used to this sort of thing. Now I was lying on the bed using the thin sheet to cover my naked body because my clothes had ripped to shreds when I shifted.

"Do you know how Lilla got those bruises and scars on her?" It had been in my mind since Dayton had told me about it, but he had made me promise not to ask Lilla.

Aiden watches me carefully as he sits up. "I don't want to tell anyone her story, especially strangers, but I guess…" he trails off and rubs his hand over his face; he begins to talk again. "One of Alpha Drake's torturing sessions, when he took her Wolf, he loved that she couldn't heal." He shakes his head, repulsed by the whole thing. "We were surprised it didn't kill her." He says, anger lacing all his words.

"Why was he so mean to her? Why did he punish her so much?" I ask, feeling myself get angry again.

"I agree; from what she told us, killing her dad was the best thing for everyone." Aiden says, lying back down. It's my turn to sit up, unsure if I heard him right.

"What did you say?"

"What?" Aiden says, looking at me, his eyebrows knitting together.

"Damn, he ruined the surprise! I was looking forward to telling you!" Drake appears, acting like a five-year-old who didn't get their way, but he smiles at me with malice. "Your dear, sweet, innocent sister…" he pauses for dramatic effect, as I notice the spite laced words as he describes my sister. "She killed your father."

Dayton

"After a year on the run, I ended up here. I never planned on telling my past to anyone, certainly not like this. I could have gone to Dayton and told him, and he would have commanded you to fight, but I don't want you to fight because you have to. I want you to fight because he took a member of your Pack. I want you to fight because he is an Ancestor who uses his power for bad instead of good. I want you to fight because he took good, kind people and made them puppets for his own sick amusement. Drake needs to be put down." Lilla finishes, and the room is eerily silent. It's a fantastic thing to see, over three hundred Werewolves, speechless.

I am speechless too. My Wolf is angry with what she's been through and with myself for how I treated her without knowing her reasoning behind it. I struggle for control, but I want to see what everyone says. The one thing I've noticed that worries me and my Wolf is that as she talks, it stings. I tried to ignore it, but the longer she spoke, the more the sting bothered me.

Finally, one of them speaks.

"Are you crazy? He is an Ancestor, stronger and more powerful than us, and it is illegal to kill him!"

Lilla opens her mouth to speak when Ancestor Blake takes over.

"He has a point. It is illegal to kill an Ancestor," He walks over as Lilla glares at him, but he ignores her as he steps onto the makeshift stage next to her. Everyone is staring at him. They all knew the Ancestors were here, but to have them standing in front of them, addressing them is a different experience.

"But doesn't the fact that what he is doing is wrong and illegal affect your decision?" He asks, and the same guy as before speaks on behalf of everyone. "He isn't a threat to us, and fighting him would get us in his eyesight, and I would rather stay out of it. If what she is saying is true, then he is dangerous. Why would we start a war we can't win?"

Ancestor Blake opens his mouth, but Lilla lets out a snarl, which comes without a wince, and I feel immensely proud of my Mate.

"If?" At that moment, I can see the Rogue in her as her eyes narrow at the Pack member. "If what I said is true? Are you kidding me? You think I'm making it up?" I watch Blake step away from her slightly; I hold in a chuckle; even the Ancestor is scared of her.

"I-It j-just seems e-elaborate. Y-You being an A-Ancestor's child, they can't have children." He stutters, all life seems to drain from Lilla and I can see the vulnerable, fragile girl she tries to hide so well.

She opens her mouth but then closes it, unsure how to answer. Then with a sigh, she lifts her shirt displaying the bruises and scars that cover her from the abdomen to the ribs. She slowly turns so they can see that they cover her back and sides too.

"This is the torture he imposed on me daily, delighted when I couldn't heal." She puts her shirt back down and moves her hair off her shoulder. "This is the Mark I told you about, the one that locks away my Wolf. I didn't have to do the Wolf part of the tests to get in the Pack because I can't shift. Still think I'm making it up?"

"Okay, you were punished by your old Pack but the Ancestor thing... I just don't believe." He speaks, while others around him have their hands over their mouths in horror over what they have just seen.

The other two Ancestors go and stand next to Ancestor Blake, and there is an audible gasp as everyone feels a strong power emanating from the stage and sees their eyes. Purple, just like Lilla's.

"You all know who we are; we are the Ancestors. We need to sort out a lot, but you must know that everything Lilla has told you is true. She is indeed an Ancestor's daughter, as Alec is an Ancestor's son, and you have our full support when it comes to killing Drake." Ancestor Cain speaks, but no one moves.

Lilla sighs, "Alec is your Pack Member! Are you going to fight to get him back? They came into your Territory and took your Pack member, and you are going to be cowards and not do anything? I thought you were better than that." She sounds annoyed and disappointed as she shakes her head. "I thought this was meant to be one of the fiercest Packs in the country? I guess you guys are just cowards, and the stories are just that, stories." That seems to get through to them as I watch someone stand up.

"I'm in," he shouts, and one by one they stand until everyone in the room is standing and shouting the same thing; I have never been prouder to be the Alpha of The Freedom Howlers Pack than I am at that moment.

*

I sigh and drop the papers I hold when I hear someone knock on my door. After everyone had decided to fight, the Ancestors took over; they sent everyone home, saying they'd come up with a plan, and I had left them to it, asking Austin to catch me up later.

Now I was going through the papers on my desk, finances of my Pack and requests from Pack members. I had been neglecting my Alpha duties these past two and a half weeks since Lilla came into my life, and now is a better time than any to start bringing my attention back to it.

"Come in." I say, and Lilla opens the door. I open my mouth to speak, but she holds up her hand as she closes the door and stands in front of the desk.

"Don't speak. It will hurt me, which will only hurt you, so let me say what I came in here to say, and then I'll leave." I simply nod, trying to concentrate on her words and not the fact that her scent is starting to suffocate me and the stinging that runs through my body when she speaks.

"I know I'm starting to hurt you. As I told everyone my past, I saw that you would wince slightly when I spoke or look sick when you took a breath, and my scent overwhelms me. We only have one and a half weeks left until you die, and it's already starting to affect you." Lilla's face shows a pained expression at the thought of hurting me, and she looks at her feet.

"I'm sorry about how you found out about my past, I wish I could have told you by yourself, but I just saw it as the easiest way. So please don't hate me." She looks back up at me and smiles.

"You know, when I was little, I also imagined that when I met my Mate, he would say he loved me first, and then I would say it, and we would live happily ever after." She laughs a grave laugh, "That's what all women want. Even the most feministic women want the man to say he loves her first, and if I could, I would wait for you to say it, but we are running out of time. So, I came in here, knowing full well you can't say anything to me, that you can't reply to me, but I have to say it now, while I can. Dayton, I have known you for nearly three weeks, and I just want you to know that I am so madly in love with you it hurts." She says with a slight chuckle, and I smile as she wipes away the falling tears.

Say it back! My Wolf urges, and I open my mouth, not caring if she winces at my voice, I need her to know I feel the same, but before the words can come out, the Ancestors walk in.

"Oh, sorry, we just came here to speak with Dayton, fill him in and get his opinion." Ancestor Cain says, and Lilla smiles at them.

"It's fine; I just came in to tell Dayton something. I'm nearly done."

"Okay, we can wait outside?" Ancestor Emily offers, but Lilla shakes her head.

"No, it's fine; I'll be quick." She turns back to face me, nothing but sadness in her eyes as she takes a deep breath. I wait, slightly confused, I thought she had said everything she wanted to say, but I wait expectantly.

"I, Lilla, Daughter of an Ancestor, reject you, Dayton, Alpha of The Freedom Howlers Pack, as my Mate."

Lilla

My heart hurt, and I had this overwhelming feeling of sadness that just wouldn't go away. God, if this is only half done, how bad will it be when it's completed? At the moment, Dayton was refusing to accept it, which is what was needed for the Mate bond to be fully broken. After all, that's how the Mating bond works, two souls agreeing to love, so they'd have to agree to heartbreak too.

I can feel it weakening; it was already weak because my Wolf is locked away; it was currently hanging on by a thread.

I glance at the clock, six o'clock in the morning. I hadn't slept all night. How could I after what I'd done?

I had tried to block it all out, but it kept playing on repeat in my mind. I tried thinking about telling everyone about my past, but all I could think about was Dayton. His face when I said I loved him and his face when I rejected him. A tear falls down my face. I had hurt the one person I never wanted to. There is a knock on my door, and it opens; Russell comes in holding a box.

"I thought we could be heartbroken together?" he throws the box onto my bed before closing the door. I grab it and empty the contents on my bed. DVD's, chocolate and tissues.

"It's 6 am..." I tell him, and he shrugs his shoulders

"It's not like either of us will sleep anytime soon."

I look through the DVD's, The Notebook, My Girl and a Walk to Remember.

"I don't have a TV in here; who watches DVD's anymore?"

"We can steal a TV from somewhere?"

"I'm not leaving this room." I say, grabbing a chocolate bar and snuggling back in my bed.

Russell grabs a chocolate bar and joins me under the duvet.

"Why did you do it?" Russell asks after a while.

"He was in pain. I'm used to feeling in pain around him, that's part of this Mark, but I saw him wincing at my voice and struggling to breathe when we were in the same room because my scent was suffocating him. I could feel the dull pain getting stronger and stronger in myself. The Clause Drake set-up was starting to affect us. I knew I couldn't hear him talk because hearing me talk hurt him, and I was weaker. We were killing each other." I say as I let the tears slide down my cheeks.

"But you love him?" It's a question, not a statement, making all the difference. If Russell wasn't sure, would Dayton be?

"Yes, I love him. More than anything. But that doesn't change anything, it had to happen."

Abruptly Russell sits up and stares at me.

"How could you do that to him?"

I sit up, confused. "So he wouldn't die," I explain slowly

"No, how could you decide what was best for him? How could you decide what he wanted? You say you love him, but you didn't give him any choice. How is that better than what Drake is doing? You've taken away his choice."

"He still has a choice! He gets to choose if he should accept it or not! He gets to choose if he lives or dies!" I feel myself get angry. Low blow comparing me to Drake.

"You've put him in an impossible situation. Look, I get it, okay? I get that you thought you were saving him. Saving both of your lives, but you didn't ask him or talk to him about it. You just did it. Drake put you both in an impossible situation with this whole 4-week thing, but you put my Alpha in an impossible situation by rejecting him. You had time to figure it out."

*

"If he accepts my rejection, can we be happy again?" I ask the Ancestors, who have come to see if I'm still alive after not leaving my room for the rest of the day.

"Neither of you will end up like your dad if that's what you are asking." Blake says.

"How do you know that?" I ask, not entirely convinced. Russell's words were still ringing in my ears.

He was right. I made a decision that affected both of us by myself. I didn't know the consequences it could have. I didn't talk to Dayton or anyone. I just did it.

"Your dad and his Mate were Mated and Marked. If one dies after Marking, the one still alive change, they feel like nothing matters, and their love for anyone slowly dies. Rejecting a Mate and the other doesn't accept? The one who rejected is usually fine, they feel like something is missing, but they can move on. The one who didn't accept can't move on. They can still feel their Mate's emotions, which drives them insane because they can't be with them. It usually ends with a murder-suicide. Rejecting a Mate and the other accepting, they both feel like something is missing, but they can both move on. They don't go crazy or anything; they are stuck with that feeling forever." Emily explains to me; I wipe away tears. Great, if he doesn't accept, he goes crazy and kills himself and me. What have I done?

"Do you think I did the right thing?" I ask in a small voice.

"I think you acted a bit irrationally; we had time to figure it all out, but I get why you did it. You were watching your Mate in pain, you were causing it, and you could fix it. You probably should have spoken to him and decided together, though."

"I need one of you to do me a favour." I say, trying to sound confident as my heart breaks even more.

"Anything," Blake says sadly, already knowing what I'm going to say.

"I need you to save him from what I've caused. I need one of you to command Dayton to accept my rejection."

*

"I've been thinking about what you said," I mutter, taking a bite of my toast. I am in the kitchen with Russell having breakfast while the Ancestors are with Dayton. He looks at me with a quizzical expression, and I sigh. "About my irresponsible decision'" I remind him, and he makes an "o" shape with his mouth.

"You were right; I should have spoken to him and decided with him, but I've been a Rogue for a long time; it isn't natural for me to discuss things with someone. He was in pain because of me, and I could fix it. I did what I thought was right."

Russell sighs, "I know, I'm sorry for going off at you about it, especially when I know it's hurting you too; I just got mad because you have your Mate, and you threw him away, and I don't have mine, he was taken from me." I wrap my arms around him, trying to comfort him. We stay like this for a while until Dayton walks in.

"I, Dayton, Alpha of the Freedom Howlers Pack, accept Lilla's, Daughter of an Ancestor, rejection." I let out a gasp as I feel the thread of the Mating bond break, and before I can see his pain, he storms out of the room. He's gone as quickly as he came.

"You okay?" Blake asks, and I shake my head. Tears poured out of my eyes at the pain of losing him.

"I made a mistake," I admit as I double over, the pain getting worse and worse.

"It'll pass." Emily says, rubbing my back, but I simply grip my head.

This wasn't because of the mate bond; this was like before.

"Someone is in my head," I manage to get out and her hand freezes.

Sorry to burst in here, Little; I hope I'm not causing too much pain! Drake chuckles.

What do you want? I say, trying to focus, my head feeling like it's splitting in two.

Your brother is okay. He is running around free, happy to be here, with no desire to leave. I think he may know who killed your Dad! Oops! In my defence, I didn't get to tell him; Aiden did.

The pressure and pain in my head evaporate, but his words are still in my head.

I can't be in here. I burst out of the kitchen, running, trying to escape. My legs buckle, and I fall just outside the house.

"He has Aiden," I mutter as the tears fall.

"Who is Aiden?" Voices appear behind me, but I can't focus.

"Oh, God, Aiden." A broken cry falls from my lips, guilt and grief taking over. "He has my Aiden." I feel like I've been punched repeatedly in the stomach, so I curl into a ball, trying to protect myself. I let myself succumb to my feelings over everything that has happened, surprising myself when the one thing that hurts most isn't losing Dayton but the fear of losing Aiden again.

Alec

I hate her. She killed my Dad, and then she kept it from me. How could she? It's been a day since I found out. Drake had let me out, and I had showered and eaten, but sleep was impossible. I just couldn't stop thinking about it. I couldn't wrap my mind around this huge bombshell thrown at me.

"Alec?" I turn at my name and see my mum; I hug her tightly.

"I've missed you!" She chuckles, and I squeeze her.

"How are you? What have you been doing? How's your sister?" She throws loads of questions at me in excitement as we pull away

"I don't want to talk about her." I say, my face darkening.

My mother touches my face. 'Don't be angry with her; you don't know the full story.'

"Drake said–"

"Drake is lying. Don't trust what he says," she interrupts, whispering. She looked around, making sure she hadn't been heard. She's frightened.

"So, she didn't kill Dad?"

"She did, but she did it to save us. She had a good reason. He wasn't your dad anymore." Her eyes fill with tears, and I pull her into another hug.

We sit there for hours catching up; I tell her everything that's happened, about Russell, which causes my Wolf to whimper as we miss him, about the Pack I was part of, I even fill her in on Lilla drama. She tells me her side of what has happened here, about what happened with Dad and what Drake has been like.

I knew some of it from before when I looked for Lilla, although it feels like a lifetime ago. I had gone back to the Territory before Freedom Howlers when I was looking for Lilla after news had spread about our family and our Pack. I didn't make it far once I crossed over into the Territory before I ran into mum; she had briefly explained about Drake causing the Venom Mark and that Dad had died, but she had rushed me off the Territory so I wouldn't be caught, so the catch up wasn't detailed.

I was still angry with Lilla, but I started to understand why she had done it. I just couldn't understand how she could keep it from me.

What do I do now? Drake let me out, thinking my anger towards Lilla would be enough to keep me here; I'm sure he had plans to use me against her.

I needed to get back to Russell; I needed a plan.

*

"I didn't think I'd be seeing you again," Aiden says as I walk towards his cell.

"Yeah, well, I figured you'd miss me," I joke as I sit down outside his cell; he sits on his side of the bars, facing me.

"You and your sister are way too alike," Aiden groans and I chuckle.

"Right now, I don't know if that's a compliment or an insult." I say, and he sighs.

"From what Lilla told us, she didn't have a choice. Who are you more likely to believe, your sister whom you have known forever or Drake, who has turned your old Pack into what it is today?" He asks, and we fall into silence.

"I'm just so angry at her; she should have told me," I finally say.

"I know, but she would have been so scared to tell you. She would have wanted to, but how do you tell your brother that?"

"You say that like you know her."

"We were here together for a long time, no secrets between us."

We sit in silence for a while.

"Lilla will come for you, you know that, right?" Aiden finally says; I nod. Of course, she will. She'd never leave me here.

"In the meantime, build up that trust with Drake; she will need someone she can trust on the inside and get as much information as possible. Be her eyes and ears."

"That's not a bad idea," I say finally, and Aiden smiles.

"I'm a Rogue; dirty planning is my thing. There is just one thing I need you to promise me," Aiden asks, and I nod, waiting for him to talk. "Don't tell her I'm here; whatever plan she has for getting you out, she will change it if she finds out I'm alive. She will get herself killed trying to save me."

"You can't possibly know her well enough to know she'd do that!" I exclaim, thinking he is over exaggerating.

"I know it seems impossible to believe, I don't even believe it, but I'm in love with her and Mate or not, she is in love with me."

Dayton

I felt the sadness first, I didn't know where it was coming from, but before I could figure it out, I was called out of my office to help. Lilla was curled in a ball on the ground outside my house, sobbing. No one knew what to do.

I picked her up and brought her into the front room, I had tried to put her on the sofa, but she wouldn't let go of my shirt, so I sat and held her until her sobbing subsided.

We aren't Mates anymore. Why am I doing this?

The Ancestors are watching us with curiosity, but I just hold her.

Why do I still feel her sadness?

Why do I even care?

"Isn't Aiden that guy you met in prison?" Austin asks after a while. Lilla pulls away; she looks at me, shocked for a moment. I guess I'm not the only one wondering what we were doing.

"Didn't he die?" Aria chimes in.

Lilla stands up, wiping her tears away and taking a deep breath.

"I thought he did," Lilla says.

"So why take Alec? Wouldn't he just use Aiden to get to you? Why would he need Alec?" Rowan asks the room, confusion and pain in his eyes.

"To torture me some more." Lilla's eyes are closed tight, as if that will lessen the blow of that reality. We all watch her; I marvel at this creature. All she has been through, and still, she soldiers on. I shake my head. We aren't Mates anymore. I shouldn't be marvelling at her!

Why do I still feel for her?

"Drake knows me; he knows I'll do anything to get Alec back but add Aiden into the mix, and I have to choose. I can't save both; he will make sure of that." Lilla's legs buckle, and I move to catch her; she stares at me in shock again. I help her sit down and brush her hair out of her face.

"You still care for each other." Ancestor Blake says, it's a statement, not a question.

We turn to look at everyone, both of us feeling caught in the act, guilty.

"They can't; they rejected each other." Austin feels the need to remind everyone. I roll my eyes.

"Actually, we don't think you did," Ancestor Blake says

"You were there." Lilla stares at them

"I mean, we don't think it worked. When we learned about the Venom Mark, Lilla, we had suspicions, but they have been confirmed watching you both now," Ancestor Blake explains.

"Suspicions about what? Confirmed what?" Lilla says, running her hands through her hair. She is closed to losing it, too much is happening.

"Your Wolf is locked away. Think of it like she is in a box, and when you met your Mate, your Wolf being so powerful, managed to make a hole in the box, a tiny hole, where a small strand of the Mate bond got through. It wasn't enough to cause the sparks and the intensity the whole bond causes, but it was enough to connect you both.

"As Ancestors, we can see the connection between Mates, like string tethering you to each other, but yours was so thin and fragile we didn't understand it until we learnt you had the Venom Mark. A small strand was connecting you both but not the whole string. When you rejected each other, you broke the Mate bond that existed. That small strand. You didn't break the whole thing. The rest of the string is locked in the box. You still care about each other because your Mate bond isn't fully broken; you just can't reach each other."

"So he will still die; we can't break the bond." Lilla's voice is small, hopeless.

"We don't think so. At the moment, you aren't Mates. You broke the only part of the bond that connected you both. Until Lilla's Wolf is free, you aren't Mates at all."

"That doesn't explain why we still care about each other," I feel a headache coming on as I try and understand all this.

"It's like children that meet their Mates young. The mate bond doesn't connect until they are 18, matured, but they care about each other, love each other, and know they are made for each other. They can feel each other's emotions and know each other better than anyone else; there is no connection until they are old enough. It's a bit like that." Ancestor Cain explains. We all sit in silence, digesting all this information.

"So, what do we do about Alec and Aiden?" Lilla finally says

"Well, we make a plan to get Alec back, end of," Rowan says, next to me, Lilla tenses.

"What about Aiden?"

"What about him? I'm sorry, he isn't one of us, but our priority is to save Alec." Rowan shrugs.

Lilla stands up, clenching her fists.

"You better make it a priority to save Aiden."

"Look, I get that you guys made a special friendship locked away together, and you want to save your friend but grow up; we all lose people we don't want to lose."

Lilla has pounced at him and pushed Rowan to the ground before anyone can stop her. He doesn't move; I'm not sure if he is scared of what she will do or what I will do if he hurts her.

"Grow up? Coming from a member of a Pack who has never left. Aiden isn't just a friend. He is my first love. I love him, and we will save him."

There is a dull ache, but it isn't like before; it's more manageable, it bothers me, but it isn't the end of the world.

"What about Dayton?" Austin growls out. "In our world, you love one person, and it's your Mate. Your first and last love is your Mate!"

Lilla gets off Rowan, and he slowly stands up.

"I don't live in your world! I may have for the first 20 years of my life, but the last year I've spent living in the Human World as a highly trained Human with skills. Not a She-Wolf."

"You were a She-Wolf when you met him." Austin points out, not hiding his disgust with her from us.

"When I met him, I was a broken girl who had just killed the one person who was meant to protect her. She had everyone she loved, her whole family, turn against her. I was all alone when I met him, and he was there for me. Our Wolves built a connection because we were all we had in a desperate, lonely and scary situation. We didn't have secrets. I could tell him everything, and I knew he would still love me." Lilla wipes away the tears.

The silence in the room is thick.

"If you had to choose between Dayton and Aiden, who would it be?" Austin asks, and all eyes fall on her, waiting for her answer.

"Seriously? That's what is important right now?" She asks, looking around at us; her eyes land on me waiting for me to tell her she doesn't have to answer his question.

"Answer the question, Lilla." I say with a sigh, and everyone takes in a sharp breath.

Lilla looks like I've just pulled out her heart.

We may not be connected, but I could still break her heart.

"I'll answer the question when you call me Little Rogue again."

Lilla

"Making battle plans?" I ask, walking into Dayton's office and seeing them all surrounding the desk.

"We have blueprints, but we want the element of surprise which is impossible; they will know as soon as we step over the Territory." Dayton tells me. I step closer and look at the blueprints of my old Pack Territory.

"Where did you get these?" I ask, studying the surprisingly accurate sheet.

"We have blueprints for all Territories. Part of our job." Emily explains. I sometimes forget that the Ancestors are in charge of our whole world. It's weird to think that now that I've met them.

I pick up a pen and mark different spots on the blueprints with an "X".

"What are you doing?" Rowan asks, annoyed. It was clear that I wasn't exactly a favourite of the Pack now they knew about Aiden.

"When I was little, my dad taught me about all these hiding places he had created in the Territory should we be attacked. Each one with a tunnel that leads out of the Territory without being detected. He was getting death threats at the time and wanted us to know how to leave the Pack without being noticed if the Pack was taken over. The death threat was taken care of, but I used it to go out without my dad knowing."

"Your dad was smart," Cain says with a smile.

"How did he do that, though?"

"There is a loophole in the Territory lines we created that only we knew about to get in and out without anyone finding out, so we could check in on Packs that maybe weren't following rules but put on a show when we turned up. Don't go telling everyone, but you can't cross a Territory line without the Alpha knowing someone has left or entered obviously, but you can go under it."

Everyone stares at them, amazed by this information.

"These crosses here are the hiding spots, and these lines I've drawn here are the tunnels, the circles are the entrances outside the Pack. Anyway, you are welcome for that. Dayton, I'm going to visit Danny; please permit me to leave the Pack, save me from the pain."

"As Alpha of this Territory, I give Lilla freedom to leave."

*

I've been walking in Danny's Pack for a few minutes when I hear paws hitting the ground, and I'm surrounded in the blink of an eye. I search for Ollie or any Wolf I know, but I don't recognise them.

I take in their scents, they are part of his Pack, but I don't know them, which makes this more difficult. I didn't tell Danny I was coming.

"Is one of you going to shift, or are we going to stand here all day?" I ask, and the Wolf directly in front of me disappears behind a tree and reappears as a Human.

"State your name and Pack," he demands.

"You go first," I joke, and he frowns; the funny bone has been broken in this guy.

"You don't have permission to be here, so do as you're told." He growls out, and I roll my eyes. This is going to get boring and fast.

"I always have permission to be here, and don't tell me what to do." I say as kindly as possible, and he growls at me, clearly trying to show his dominance. Poor guy won't stand a chance.

"I want to see Danny now, please. Tell him his Little One is here." I ask, and he glances at the others who look as unsure as him. I sigh, and while they aren't paying me any attention, I move forward and wrap my hand around his throat.

"I don't take kindly to being disrespected by pups, and I just want to see my friend so you can either fight me or contact Ollie or Danny and let them know that Lilla is here," I say calmly, and everything falls silent.

"Let the pup go, Little One. It's their first patrol." Danny says, walking toward me with a smile and shake of his head while I release my grip.

"He was trying to tell me what to do... you know how I feel about that." I say with a shrug, and Danny pulls me into a hug, laughter rumbling through his chest.

"What are you doing here, Little One?" Danny says, pulling away. We begin to make our way to his house, and the Wolves get back to their training.

"I came to see you and get my stuff."

"Did Dayton let you go, or did you leave?"

"Do I smell like a Rogue?" I ask, and he sniffs.

"You asked permission?" He looks at me, shocked, and I roll my eyes.

"You make it sound like I always do what I want to do."

"Yeah, because that's exactly how you work." Danny says, and I push him gently, only making him laugh.

Once we get to his house, I say hello to his parents and Ollie before going to the room that was mine when I was here. They follow behind as I fill them in on everything that happened and answer their questions. They all stand around the bed, and at my nod, they lift it, and I begin to pull out my bags. Once I have them all, they put the bed down, and we stare at the bags.

"What is in all of them?" Ollie asks, and I smile.

"Weapons, lots and lots of weapons," I say proudly. I open one bag, go for the little pocket inside it, and pull out a key chain with six keys.

"What are they?"

"Keys," I answer, and Danny playfully hits me. "To the tunnels," I explain and place the keys in my pocket before looking through the weapons I had collected in my stay here. "My sweet babies, mummy's home." I say sweetly and excitedly. "So, you guys in?" I ask, looking back up at them.

"Would we ever say no to you?"

Lilla

"Remind me to tell Dayton to keep some of these for our Training Grounds!" Danny laughs at me. We sit on sun loungers, on decking built to watch over the Pups training.

"I will; it's a lot of fun watching them work."

We sit in silence, watching them fight one-on-one; I had decided to stay for a while rather than go straight back with my collection of weapons. As a Rogue, I didn't have any form of protection, but when I settled in with Danny, I made it a mission to collect as much weaponry as possible; you never know when you would need it. I couldn't carry any of it with me when I left, so Danny had kept hold of it. He always found it weird that I would feel the need to have protection when I am in a Pack but none when I'm running around as a Rogue.

I find the Pup from earlier, the one I tried to strangle. There is something about him I don't like; I just can't put my finger on it.

"Tell me about him," I say to Danny, pointing at the Pup.

Danny shrugs.

"There's nothing to tell. About a week after you left us, he ran onto my Territory, bloody and bruised. He ran from his Pack because of how they treated him, and I took him in; he is an amazing fighter, ruthless." Danny says, sounding impressed, and I frown.

Ruthless is never a good thing. I don't say anything, though, and I watch the Pup fight. Danny is right; he is a good fighter, his footwork, precision, and reflexes are near perfection. My eyes travel to his face, and I sit up quickly. I feel my heartbeat quicken as I begin to panic, and my mind blanks of what I should do; I try to reassure myself. Danny is here; my friends are here, but the longer I watch him fight, the more I panic.

I need – no – I want Dayton.

Dayton!

Are you okay? His voice has a calming effect on me, but the instant I see the Pup take down his opponent, his facial expression showing his anger and need to kill, the panic rises, making me feel like I can't breathe.

Come to Danny's, quick.

With a promise that he will be here as quickly as possible, I turn to find Danny looking at me, worried.

I need a plan.

"What's wrong, Little One?" He asks.

"What's the Pups name?" I ask out of curiosity; I know the answer. I can feel it, but I'm silently begging it's not true. It can't be.

He answers me, my eyes widening at the name, and I begin to breathe slowly as I try to control my breathing.

"What's wrong, Lilla?" his voice deeper, more severe as I continue to ignore his question.

"Can you let your Pack know that Dayton is coming, please?"

"Of course, but why do you need him?"

"My Dad's name was Derek; did you know that?" Danny nods, slowly not understanding my point.

"When Alec and I had to complete the tests, there was this one member named Derek, and I just saw red and nearly killed him. He hadn't done anything to me; his name just sent me crazy."

"I get that, after what your dad did." Danny smiles softly, still confused.

"Lilla? What's going on?" Dayton runs over and looks me over to make sure I'm okay.

"He's a Pup; there is something about him I don't like." My mind is racing; my words aren't making sense because this can't be true. Just because this Pup has my father's name, it doesn't mean anything.

"It was the worst day of my life. I thought I'd remember his face if I saw it. I didn't think I would have to; I didn't think he'd be here, training. I was up close, staring him in the face, and I didn't recognise him, but the way he fights. The emotionless expression, the way he's looking for blood, and nothing else matter. Ruthless, right?"

"Lilla, I don't understand!" Dayton is late to the conversation, and not sure why I called him.

"You have a mole, Danny," I inform him, and he looks at me, surprised.

"How do you know that?" He looks around like the mole will just wave at him.

"It was the worst day of my life," I repeat. "That Pup of yours, Derek, has the same name as my dad; my dad hated anyone in the Pack with his name. That Ruthless Pup of yours is the baby he wanted me to kill."

Lilla

"How is that possible?" Danny lowers his voice; Dayton glances at the Pup fighting, ensuring he isn't listening.

"You said it happened 2 years ago! How is he here fighting? You must be wrong." Dayton tells me. I feel myself getting annoyed. I don't mean to be; I get where he is coming from. I'm scared, and I don't like being afraid; I'm annoyed at myself.

"You forget, the Ancestors are very powerful. They have a lot of abilities, the ones we've told you about or seen, that's only scratching the surface of what they are capable of." I whisper angrily.

"What you are capable of," Dayton says; it's a statement, not a question.

"What I used to be capable of, but yes, I can do what they do." I answer him anyway. "Look, the Ancestors can manipulate ages. They can age Wolves up or down. They don't do it a lot because it has a huge impact on the mind and body of the Wolf."

We needed a plan.

I'm looking at my hands in my lap, trying to think. Dayton and Danny are talking, bouncing ideas around. I'm not listening.

I look up to watch the Pup train. He's pinned another Pup down; he's won the fight. He doesn't get off. Instead, he looks up, and his eyes find me. At first, I thought it was just a coincidence, that he just caught my eye, but he keeps staring at me, and a small smile appears on his face.

I stand up quickly, pushing past Dayton and Danny, knowing what the Pup is about to do.

I let out a gasp.

Everyone freezes.

He snaps the other Pup's neck.

The whole Pack felt it.

No one moves. This is Danny's job. He has to deal with it, but the Pup is still staring at me.

He stands straight and steps over the body. Danny moves forward, but I hold up a hand, stopping him. Dayton growls at me.

We can't kill him; I need you to trust me. I mind-link him, my eyes not leaving the Pup as he makes his way towards me.

It's me he wants now.

I crouch down slightly and ready myself to attack; he lunges at me, shifting mid-air; I move out of his way. He turns and watches me move; I notice he is watching my footwork, testing my reflexes, and I freeze.

It takes one moment of fear, that's all.

One moment in a battle that can cost you your life.

He lunges for me again; I don't move fast enough. He lands on top of me, bringing me down. I scream as his claws scratch at my skin and his teeth bite down on my shoulder. The pain makes me feel dizzy, and for a second, I lose focus. He bites down harder, and I scream again, struggling against him. Suddenly, the Wolf is gone, and I hear teeth snapping and growls as my eyes begin to droop and tiredness takes over.

Stay awake, Little Rogue. Dayton's voice in my head is the last thing I hear before I slip into unconsciousness.

Dayton

As I feel Lilla slip away from me, I expect to feel rage or panic over her state, but instead, I'm too focused on dealing with the Pup. I've knocked him out and called for Russell and Rowan.

"Get Pure Silver cuffs from Dan and take him back to our Territory. Put him in a cell. I'll deal with him when I get back." I say, and Russell and Rowan pick up the unconscious Wolf.

I turn my attention to Lilla; it's weird with her now. I love her, don't get me wrong, and I want to protect her, my Wolf and I do, but it's not the same feeling as before. I feel slightly empty, like a piece of me is missing, even though she is still here. She isn't my every thought or priority like before we broke the bond; it's weird to be in love with her but not have the same connection.

I see the blood pouring from her wounds, and the faintness of her heartbeat and panic rises within me. I may not have the same connection, but I know I will not survive if she dies. Life without Lilla seems impossible, Mates or not.

I pick her up carefully, and she immediately curls into me. I look at Dan, who gestures for me to follow, and we make our way silently to the Pack Doctor.

I look at her as we walk. Her face is scrunched up in pain, and blood ruins her top as it pours out of her wounds. I begin to worry more; she is losing blood too quickly and isn't healing.

The panic I feel rises as I realise that she can't heal; this isn't a Werewolf attacked in combat, this is a Human. I must remember to treat her as a Human. I mentally kick myself and pick up my pace.

Austin? Can you get the Ancestors, please? I ask, not entirely sure how to get through to them myself.

Dayton? Is there a problem? I almost drop Lilla when the weight of three new people enters my mind all at once.

Lilla is hurt! Badly! How quick can you get here?

We will be there in five minutes.

Five minutes? It takes at least ten to get to the border? I need to make a list of the Ancestors abilities.

The connection is lost, and the weight disappears, so I shake my head slightly to clear it. I glance at Lilla again, five minutes. Lilla can survive five minutes, I repeat, but I begin to doubt myself by looking at her pale complexion.

"Stay with me, Little Rogue. Please just stay with me." I beg as we walk into the Pack Doctor's office. From the look of concentration and determination on his face, he has been expecting us and filled in on the extent of her injuries.

I place her on the empty bed and turn to the Doctor. "Five minutes. Keep her alive for five minutes." I say, and he frowns at me along with Dan.

"What are you talking about, Dayton?" Dan asks.

"The Ancestors will be here in five minutes. They can heal her; they are the only ones who can heal her. She heals like a human." I try to catch them up, but I can see they are completely lost from the looks on their faces.

I growl lowly. "Just keep her alive." I command the Doctor, who quickly gets to work on Lilla.

"Dan, the Ancestors are coming to heal her, okay?" I say slowly, and he nods, realisation hitting him.

"How's it looking there? Can you keep her alive?" I ask, watching the Doctor, who, after studying her injuries, looks up at me with a grave face.

"She is missing whole chunks of flesh on her shoulder; she has claw marks across her skin. The Wolf that did this knew what he was doing. He knew the fastest way to kill someone; he knew where to aim his teeth and claws. He has punctured several arteries, so she will bleed out and die; I'm surprised she has lasted this long. There is nothing I can do. I'm sorry, Alpha Dayton, but you may want to say goodbye."

*

I hate funerals.

When my parent died, and they had a funeral, I felt numb. I didn't cry, I didn't feel sad, I just felt lost. Then as they were lowered into the ground, I began to panic. I hadn't said goodbye.

Everyone else had said things in the church about how great my parents were and what they will miss most. I didn't do it because I couldn't name one particular thing I would miss most, and I didn't have to tell everyone else how great my parents were because they all knew that anyway.

I hadn't said goodbye, and at that moment, I realised why funerals were needed no matter how much they were hated; it gave everyone the chance to say goodbye. I had missed my opportunity with my parents.

It was the first time my Pack saw me cry. I just broke down, fell to my knees and begged my parents to come back. Not forever, just long enough for me to say goodbye, tell them I love them and that I would miss them.

That's why I hate funerals. It's your last chance to say goodbye. After that, you can cry and grieve, but you can't say goodbye again; you won't have the opportunity to say goodbye before their bodies are turned to ash or buried.

"Are you ready?" Austin knocks on my door, all dressed in his suit. I turn to face him, my tie still not done. He walks over, and as my best friend, he silently ties my tie.

"How can anyone be ready for this?" I ask, my throat husky from the sobbing I had done.

"Good point." Austin clears his throat and steps away. I look in the mirror to see he has done it perfectly. I turn to thank Austin, and I take in his appearance. I haven't seen him much these past couple of days, but I can tell he has been crying as much as I have.

"Okay, we go out there together; we say our goodbyes, and we leave before we break down in front of everyone." I say, formulating a plan, Austin nods, but we both know it won't happen that way. Grief doesn't follow a plan.

I sigh, "Did I ever tell you how much I hate funerals?"

Austin smiles sadly. "This one you are going to hate the most."

Dayton

"Thank you all for coming. I know she would have appreciated it. Not many people here knew her, but please, if you want to say a few words about your Luna, do so. Lilla was difficult from the get-go. She had a thing for secrets and not trusting people. She was so scared of being rejected that she kept everything to herself. When I first met Lilla, she was lying on the floor with most of my Pack surrounding her, and she should have been scared or intimated, but Lilla... Lilla made jokes and sarcastic remarks. Then I introduced myself, and she passed out. I guess I'm just that good looking." I pause, and everyone laughs at my joke.

"From the second I met her; I knew she was for me. I would never want anything or anyone as much as I wanted her. My Wolf and I made a promise that day. A promise that we would always protect her, no matter the cost. I failed. We both failed. If we hadn't, we wouldn't be standing here today." I stop talking and turn to the closed casket behind me; I blanch at the sight. I never wanted to see my Mates coffin.

"I don't know what to say. This whole thing shouldn't be happening. She shouldn't be dead. I don't need to tell you all how much I will miss her because she was my Mate and she will be missed by everyone. I don't know what to say, but I don't want this to be over. If this ends, she is gone, and I can't... she can't..." I trail off as I break down. You are never meant to let your Pack see you cry; it's basically rule one in the unofficial Alpha handbook, but I don't care. Today I'm weak and alone, and I don't care about the rules. I feel a hand on my back and see Dan standing there, tears in his eyes. He pulls me out of the church into the fresh air and then pulls me into a hug.

"Go." He orders when we break apart, but I shake my head.

"I have to-."

"Just go. I'll tell everyone you couldn't handle it. I'll be their Alpha for today." Dan offers with a sad smile, and with another quick hug, I leave.

*

"You're early."

"I couldn't hold myself together. Dan sent me away." I offer my excuse.

"So why come here?"

"I didn't know where else to go." I shrug.

"Did it work?"

"Yeah, I think so."

"Good. You okay?"

"It was hard seeing the coffin. I knew it would be there, but that caused me to break down. The thought of..." I shake my head.

"I know. It's not nice, but it needed to be done."

"Yeah, I guess so." I agree. "I just don't think I can do this." I put my head in my hands.

"You have to; just remember, it's what Lilla would have wanted."

Alec

I said I hated her. I don't hate her. I love her. After everything, she has survived. She's taken out by a Pup.

They are all partying. Drake permitted them to party and drink; after all, we celebrated. He won. He killed her.

I've snuck away while they danced on her grave. I couldn't even pretend to be happy when Drake told me.

"Hey, so I was think– you okay?" Aiden interrupts himself when he sees my face. I sit on the floor, and he joins me.

"Alec, what happened?"

I open my mouth, but I can't say it. I feel a tear roll down my cheek.

"Did you know that Drake has members of his Pack infiltrated in Packs across the country? They tell him where Lilla is at all times." I say; Aiden frowns.

"I mean, it's smart," Aidan admits and shrugs his shoulders. He's right. It's brilliant.

"He didn't want them to do anything to her, just watch and tell him, and he could play his games with her. She thought she was free." I let out a sob.

"Alec, what's happened?" Aiden says more urgently.

"Alec?" I look up to see my mum, tear-stained face. She has an envelope in her hand. I ignore it and just look at her.

She bends down, so she is at eye level with me.

"You and Aiden are leaving tonight. Take the tunnels, he won't notice until tomorrow, and by then, it'll be too late. This is your window to escape, both of you. He doesn't need either of you now."

"You'll come too?" I ask, my voice small like I'm a little boy again and I don't want my mum to go away.

"Drake has taken everything from me. I won't have him kick me out of my home." She sounds defiant; she looks it. Lilla would be proud.

"I just need you to do me a favour, okay boys?" She glances at Aiden, who is watching us, with no idea what's happening.

"Of course," I sniffle, trying to act strong. Lilla was always the strong one.

"Take this letter to the address written. It says everything in there, but I think you should verbalise it. This isn't something that should be read. Once that's done, they will help you get home."

"Who is it?" I ask, not bothering to look at the letter.

"Just promise you will take it straight there. You will go through the tunnels now, while you can. You will get out of this Territory and hand-deliver this letter."

"I promise," I nod, and she smiles, takes the keys to the cells out of her pocket and hands them to me.

"I love you, my sweet boy," my mum kisses my forehead, grips Aiden's hand between the bars and leaves us.

"Alec, what the hell is going on?" Aiden asks. I sigh, stand up to unlock the cells. We have time for me to do this right.

With no bars separating us, I walk in, sit him on the bed and sit next to him. "Lilla is dead."

*

"This is the place." I say as we stand just outside another Pack's Territory.

"You ready?" I ask Aiden, who looks at me, unsure. He's finally free, but he has stayed with me. He didn't want me to do this alone.

I can see why you liked him, Lilla. You picked a good one. I had taken to speaking to Lilla in my mind. It's what has kept me going for the last week. We were cautious not to enter another Territory; we didn't trust that all of Drake's Pups had gone back. We didn't need one reporting about us.

"You sure we won't get killed?" Aiden says, narrowing his eyes at me.

"You're the Rogue, aren't Rogues used to going in other Territories?" I laugh at him. Aiden has kept my spirits up. He was hurting just as much as I was, but he looked out for me.

"Actually, Rogues like to keep to Neutral Territory, like we've been doing. When we screw up or feel brave, we end up in Pack Territory. That's how we die."

"Well, we promised my mum to hand-deliver this to the Alpha, so we can't die." I say, matter-of-factly.

"Not really how it works, but screw it. Let's go."

We both step into the Territory with a deep breath and begin our walk as prey, waiting for the predators to find us.

It's not long before they do.

We are walking, not a word shared between us when we hear the sounds of paws against the ground and soon the growls from the Wolves surrounding us. We stop walking and wait for them to come to us. We need them to know we aren't a threat.

"You are trespassing," a man states as he walks into view, followed by the Wolves.

"We are here to see your Alpha. We mean no harm; we just wish to speak with–"

"Why?" He interrupts.

"We have a message from an old friend. We were asked to bring this to–"

"Follow me," he interrupts again; he doesn't seem surprised.

Silently we follow them to a building filled with Werewolves crowded together. All of them are fighters, and they are defensive, ready to attack us if we step out of line. Aiden moves a bit closer to me. He is still way too weak to fight, and he knows I can command them, so, naturally he's using me like his personal sheild.

Wuss, I jab at Aiden in his mind-link, and he jabs me in the side with his finger.

"Alpha, these Rogues requested to see you." I roll my eyes.

"Do you honestly expect me to believe that he is your Alpha? He has the power of a Beta, nothing more." I say, and he growls at me. I raise an eyebrow at him.

"Look, I have a critical message from my mother, Lisa," I say loudly.

"There is more than one Lisa in the world," someone speaks, but I don't see them. That's the Alpha, not usually ones to hide, but I'm sure they have their reasons. I think I know those reasons. "There is only one Lisa that would send her son into another's Territory with a letter. I think. I don't know how many Lisa's you know," I start rambling; Aiden jabs me again.

"What's the message?" The voice says again.

I close my eyes to stop the tears.

"Not here," I whisper, eyes still closed.

I hear movement and a lot of shuffling. I jump when hands touch my face.

"You look so much like your mother," she whispers back at me. I open my eyes.

"Is she dead?" I flinch, so direct.

"Yes,"

"I'm so sorry for your loss," she says sadly, taking the letter from my hand.

"Your loss too," I remind her. Why doesn't she care?

"She was your mother, don't worry about my loss."

"No, sorry, my mum isn't dead!" I quickly correct, shaking my head as my mind briefly clears of my grief.

"Who died then?" She asks, confusion on her face as she pulls her hands away.

"Your daughter. Lilla, she's dead."

*

"Why did you leave?" I ask as we sit down for dinner. It had been a long day. She and my mother have been sending each other letters for years, how my dad or uncle didn't catch either of them, I'll never know.

"I wish I could have stayed and raised my daughter, but Drake... he hated that his brother was happy. He hated that his brother had a Mate - had everything he wanted. I knew if I stayed, Drake would find out Lilla was mine and kill her, so I gave her to your mother, and we managed to fool everyone into thinking she was hers. We told your father that I didn't want to raise a kid without him because we knew he wouldn't give you or your mother up. He was a good man. I planned the whole Rogue thing; it became too hard to watch Lilla grow up and not be her mother. Drake was beginning to suspect she was mine; he would have killed us, killed all of us out of jealousy. So, the members of my Pack - my real Pack, I never joined your fathers - played Rogues for the evening, and I went with them, leaving behind enough evidence to believe I had been killed by them."

"But how did Dad go crazy? If you didn't die, how did he become like that?"

"I rejected him, but he couldn't accept it; he thought I was dead. He could still feel me, and it drove him insane. He would have killed himself and me if I was found, so he just got worse and worse."

"You did all this because of Drake?" I ask, and she nods. "Then help us take care of him once and for all. Help us kill the man that killed your daughter, Layla."

*

"I don't think I can do this," I say, and Layla pats my back. We are standing outside Dayton's front door, I had expected someone to stop us when we went into his Territory, but no one did. Layla had left her Beta to look after the Pack and come with us to meet Dayton and talk battle plans; her Pack is fighting with us now.

I take a deep breath and knock on the door, which is opened immediately by Russell. It is like he was standing there waiting for us to knock.

"Alec," he breathes, and I run into his arms, relieved and happy to be with my Mate again. For a moment, I forget everything, the sadness I feel over losing my sister, the reality of the situation. Everything is forgotten, but all too soon, we pull apart, and reality crashes back down.

I turn to Dayton, expecting to see a broken man, but I'm shocked to see him looking... fine? Unaffected by her death.

"Alec, why are you here?" He asks suspiciously.

"I left Drake's Pack as soon as I could. I brought Aiden and Layla with me." I explain, pointing at the two Werewolves behind me.

Dayton opens his mouth, but the Ancestors burst into the room, eyes locked on Layla.

"You are meant to be dead." Emily growls, and Layla flinches.

"Ancestors, how nice it is to see you after all this time," Layla smiled sweetly.

"You are meant to be dead!" Emily shouts.

"Emily, I know you must be angry, but I did what I had to do. Drake–"

"Drake? Drake? Did you run because of Drake? Did you leave Lilla because of Drake? If he was an issue, you could have contacted us! You of all people have a direct line to us, but instead, you chose to run!" I have never seen Emily this angry before; she is seconds away from shifting.

"I don't have to explain myself to you!" Layla shouts back.

"No, but you have to explain yourself to me." We all turned our attention to the top of the stairs, where the small voice had come from.

I blink rapidly, wondering if I'm seeing things, but glancing at Layla and Aiden, I know I haven't gone crazy. I open my mouth to speak, but I haven't a clue what to say, so I just say the first thing that comes to mind.

"Lilla."

Lilla

"...just remember, it's what Lilla would have wanted." I say, and Dayton nods.

"I know; I don't want to go to war anymore because Lilla wouldn't want me to." Dayton rehearses the words he would be saying to Drake later. Dayton is far from happy about this; he wants to kill Drake now and get it over with. He wanted to kill the Pup that attacked me, but I wouldn't let him. I have a plan, but the result is still the same: Drake will be dead.

Dayton sighs and rubs a hand over his face.

"Are you sure I can't just kill him when I meet up with him?" He asks for the hundredth time. I walk over and stand in front of Dayton, placing my hands on either side of his face, forcing him to look me in the eye. "Dayton, you don't kill him. Okay? If you kill him, my life is over." I say seriously, and Dayton places his hands on either side of my face, copying me.

"Your life wouldn't be over; you would still have me." Dayton says softly. I drop my hands from his face to his chest and closing my eyes, I lean into him. Dayton wraps his arms around me, and we stay silent for a few minutes, just enjoying the comfort we give each other.

"You aren't enough," I mutter, and I feel his body tense at my words. He unwraps his arms and steps away from me, hurt by my words.

"I should be," he says.

"Dayton..." I say his name but find I have nothing to add, so I just leave the sentence unfinished.

"I love you, Lilla; you are enough for me. I should be enough for you."

"I'm enough for you because you have everything."

"I know I'm wealthy, Lilla, but things don't make people happy." Dayton says, and I roll my eyes.

"I'm not talking about things. Dayton, you have a Pack and friends you trust and call your family. You have a Mate who loves you so much it hurts despite having no connection to you anymore. You have a place you can call home, but most importantly, Dayton; you have someone who has been with you every step of the way. Who you love and hate at the same time because even though they are a part of you, they can be annoying when they want to be. You have the piece of your soul that I'm missing. You have your Wolf." I finish, tears in my eyes as the empty feeling fills me.

"You have all that too," Dayton says, and I shake my head. He doesn't get it.

"I don't have any of it. Despite being accepted into your Pack, I am the outsider, the Human Werewolf. I don't know them, I'm not their Luna because we haven't Mated, and I don't trust them because I don't know them. This isn't my home; this is just a house where I'm staying for now, and I don't have my Wolf. All I have is you, which isn't enough; it will never be enough." I say, and from the look on Dayton's face, I am hurting him with each word that comes out of my mouth.

"Dayton, I love you, I honestly do, but this isn't a fairy tale where love conquers all, where love is the most important thing in the world, where love fixes everything. In fairy tales, love wakes people from comas and makes a beast human again. We don't live in that world; we live in the real world, and in the real world, love — no matter how amazing the feeling — isn't enough to survive on."

"If you loved me, you would let me kill him." Dayton speaks softly after a while, and I sigh. He isn't listening to me.

"If you kill him, I will be left with nothing."

"You would still have me!" Dayton growls out, and I sigh again.

"No, I wouldn't; if you kill the one person who can take this Mark and give me back my Wolf, I will never forgive you." I say simply, hoping he would understand and listen to that.

"You would forgive me eventually." Dayton decides, and it's my turn to growl, which causes me to wince.

Blake, I need you to do me a favour.

Anything, he replies.

I need you to make Dayton understand where I'm coming from.

A few minutes later, Blake walks into the room and walks over to Dayton without saying a word.

"Forgive me for this, Dayton, but I need you to understand." I say, and he looks at me, his face an expression of confusion.

I simply nod at Blake, who, in one swift movement, grabs hold of Dayton and sinks his teeth into the collarbone, creating the Mark given to me.

*

"Lilla."

"I thought you were dead," Layla speaks up. Is this woman joking? I walk down the stairs and towards Alec; he pushes past Layla to hug me. He is happy I'm alive; I'm delighted he's back.

"What the hell happened?" He asks as we pull away. I open my mouth to answer, but a hand on my back makes me turn.

"My Angel," he says softly, with a small, awkward smile. I had wanted to fling my arms around him the second he walked in, but there was so much happening.

Besides, where do I even begin? My Aiden was here, in my Mates Territory. Alive. What do I say? What do I do?

I burst out crying, and he pulls me into a hug. My arms are pinned to my chest, and I grip his shirt as I sob. Holding on for dear life, in case he disappears before me.

"I'm here, I'm here, beautiful," he mutters repeatedly.

Eventually, we pull away and just stare at each other. What do we say? There is nothing and everything that needs to be said.

"Lilla-" Layla begins, ruining our moment. I raise a hand, stopping her. I can't just be happy for a second because I have more drama to sort through. "I don't want to do this right now. I'm having trouble wrapping my mind around this, so you will have to give me a little time." I say, desperate to get away from her, opening the front door.

"Of course," she smiles at me.

"If you will excuse me, I'm going to go do something – anything – else."

*

"Did you know that we have memories from newborns, but we just don't remember them?" I say, and the Pup looks at me as if I'm crazy.

"It's like they are stored away, they are there, but we can't access them. However, I know some people who can access them for me. The Ancestors have this neat trick where they can look at your memories for themselves, see what you have been up to, and share them with others. In this case, the Ancestors shared all your memories with me." I tell the Pup, who lets out a laugh.

"I'm sitting, tied up to a chair, and instead of torturing me or beating the crap out of me, you are talking about memories?"

I ignore him.

"Did you know that you are named after my father? That's why you nearly killed me. I froze. Don't worry, though. We told your Pack it was because you had the upper hand; it needed to be more believable for Drake. They think you are dead too because Dayton would have killed you for killing his Mate." He watches me carefully as my topic of conversation keeps changing.

"What has that got to do with memories?" He asks, not making the connection.

"The Ancestors have a lot of special abilities; one of them is they can make Werewolves age quicker. Normally it's done on Werewolves a few hundred years old and ready to move on, but they can do it on children. Like Drake did to you."

"What are you talking about?"

"You should be 2 years old by now; instead, you are the same age as me. I'm in one of your first memories; I'm standing above you with a knife in my hands, with my father telling me to kill you as a punishment. I didn't do it – I couldn't do it. You were a baby, a beautiful baby boy, and all I could think was that you could grow up to be this amazing person who would do good. I knew it could go the other way because, at the time, my father was running the Pack like Drake is, but I couldn't get rid of that nagging feeling that you would do good things.

"I always thought that no matter how my life turned out, at least I didn't kill that baby boy, but now I wish I had killed you because it would have saved me a lot of trouble, and you wouldn't have had to grow up as you did. I made a mistake saving your life, and I'm sorry that I did." I wipe the tears that are falling down my cheek. Tears for his sad existence, tears for my mistake, tears for what I'm about to do.

"So, you are going to kill me?" Derek asks.

Instead of answering, I picked up the knife from the table that I had told the others I would torture him with. "I'm sorry, but I tried playing nice, and it didn't work. To beat Drake, I have to think and act like him." I say as I walk closer, and just as the door opens and someone shouts at me to stop. I plunge the knife into his heart.

Lilla

"Lilla!" Layla shouts, but it's too late; the knife is in his heart. Layla runs forward, trying desperately to save the lifeless Pup's life.

"It's too late; he's dead." I say simply before making my way back to Dayton's house.

I get looks of alarm as I walk back, hands and shirt covered in blood, but I don't pay any attention. I let the empty feeling fill me, not wanting to feel a thing.

I open the door, and the talking stops; eyes widen at my appearance, and without a word, I walk to the sofa and sit down next to Aiden. He opens his mouth to speak, but Layla slams the door and starts shouting.

"What the hell, Lilla? You killed him!" she accuses, and I just stare at her. "He is dead," she says when I don't say anything, and I chuckle.

"Why are you telling me? I was there," I say, and the shock on her face tells me she wasn't expecting that response. She doesn't get it.

"You are more like your uncle than you think," she disgusts.

Anger shoots through me, and I struggle with the pain, but I refuse to show any weakness to the woman in front of me. I stand slowly, fists clenched at my sides.

"I am nothing like Drake," I say through gritted teeth.

"You stabbed a young pup through the heart, you are covered in his blood and you don't care, sounds like Drake to me."

"Don't you dare say that I don't care; I will not be judged by you! I will not be judged by the one person who caused all this shit in the first place."

"I didn't cause anything!" Layla argues.

"You are meant to be dead. I could forgive you because you were dead, but you aren't. Instead of fighting, you ran, even though you knew what would happen to my dad if you did."

"I did what I had to do."

"No, you did what you wanted to do. You left me to deal with all this shit because you were too much of a coward to face it! I did what I had to do in there. He couldn't be saved. He is meant to be two years old, and instead, he's 18. He was going to die a painful death. I don't kill for fun. I killed him because I didn't have a choice. I have to act like I don't care because I can't deal with it otherwise. I will act like Drake and think like Drake to get the job done, to get this war over with."

"Lilla-"

"If you knew me like a mother should know her daughter, you wouldn't think I was anything like Drake."

*

I head straight for the shower wanting to get the drying blood off my skin. I peel off my ruined clothes and put them in a pile to be thrown away. I step into the boiling water, not caring as it scolds me. Grabbing the sponge off the side, I scrub my skin raw, even after the blood has washed away. I clean my hair, tugging and pulling, desperate to wash away the evidence of my crimes.

I've killed before, but this was different. This was the Pup I had fought so hard to save. This was the Pup I killed my Dad to save. This was a Pup, a 2-year-old Pup. I'm on the verge of breaking down when I hear a knock at the bathroom door and someone calling my name.

"Lilla, please come out and talk to me," Aiden's voice makes me freeze.

The love I feel for him begins to suffocate me, and I hurriedly turn off the shower, conditioner still in my hair, and wrap a towel around myself. Opening the door, I jump into his arms, startling Aiden and nearly causing him to lose balance.

"It's okay, Beautiful, it's okay," Aiden whispers as he holds me closer.

"I've missed you," I say, tears springing to my eyes, and I bury my face into his chest.

"I've missed you too," he says, kissing my forehead. "Why don't you get dressed, and we can catch up." I reluctantly pull away and head to my wardrobe, nodding my head.

"So … how are you?" Aiden asks, shouting from outside the wardrobe.

"Good, thanks," I respond, pulling on a pair of shorts and a vest but not before catching a glimpse of my scarred and bruised body. I grimace; even though I was used to them being there, I wasn't used to seeing them. I always made sure to avoid mirrors, which wasn't too hard when you are a Rogue, but now, mirrors are everywhere, and every so often, I catch a glimpse of my naked body, and I hate it.

I feel myself getting angry, and I breathe in and out, calming myself down. A sharp pain hits me, and I double over, biting my lip so I don't cry out.

"Lilla, are you okay? You're taking a long time." Aiden says, his voice traced with worry.

"I'm fine; I'm coming now." I say, taking a deep breath and standing up straight. I walk back into the room and look at Aiden with a smile.

"Still as beautiful as ever," Aiden remarks.

"Still as cheesy as ever," I mutter, and he laughs. I sit on my bed and pat the space next to me, he climbs on and I snuggle into him, seeking his comfort.

"Do you want to talk about it?"

"She is alive," I state clenching my fists, feeling the anger rise again.

"How do you feel about it?"

I open my mouth to speak, but my stomach rumbles, causing us to chuckle.

"Hungry it would seem."

"Come on; let's go get you some food."

"Can we get lots of food and bring it back up? Make a little bedroom feast?" I ask, batting my eyelashes. and with a chuckle, Aiden agrees.

"Do you know how to get to the kitchen?" I ask as we leave my room, and Aiden looks at me suspiciously.

"Yes, I do; why?" He asks, and I smile.

"Race you," I shout before shooting off.

"No fair!" Aiden whines before I hear him beginning to run.

"I won!" Aiden shouts as he gets to the kitchen, and he turns to me with a triumphant look on his face. As I run in a few seconds behind, I smile at him before leaning against the closest counter to me, trying to regain my breath.

"You okay?" Aiden asks, concerned.

"A little tired," I admit and Aiden steps closer to me.

"Why are you tired? Have you been doing too much?"

"No, I haven't been doing much of anything; I'm meant to be dead. I shouldn't be this tired."

"When did it start?"

"My emotions haven't been right ever since you came back." I admit, refusing to look at him.

"Why?" Aiden asks, and I sigh, running a hand over my face. The pain gets more unbearable with each second.

"I don't know, but it doubles anytime I feel the slightest emotions."

I cry out in pain as I collapse onto the floor, unable to hold my weight. I hear my name being called, but the pain becomes too intense for me to focus on anyone or anything. I close my eyes, trying to calm down, but her voice sticks out. My birth mother's concerned voice calls for me with one last cry of pain. She breaks out.

Dayton

I open my eyes and groan; my head hurts, my muscles hurt, everything hurts.

"Dayton?" I hear Lilla's voice, and as I slowly sit up in bed, I see her standing at the end of it, arms crossed and a worried expression on her face. I open my mouth to ask her what happened and why I'm in so much pain when it all hits me. My hand flies to my collarbone, I wince.

"It hurts, to begin with... like a bruise. It'll be fine in a couple of days." Lilla tells me.

"Why did you do this to me?" I ask angrily, and Lilla flinches at my tone of voice.

"You want me to give up my Wolf forever; you want me to have you and know and believe that you are enough. You can't ask all of that of me until you have experienced what I have to live with." Lilla explains, and I sigh.

"When does this feeling of emptiness go away?" I ask, and Lilla looks at me with nothing but sadness.

She sighs, walks over to my side of the bed, and sits down next to my feet.

"It never goes away, Dayton; you just learn to live with it or control it."

"Control it?" I ask, not understanding how you can control emptiness.

"I can cover it with other emotions, and then at the end of the day, just before bed or whenever I don't want to feel something, I let the emptiness consume me." Lilla explains. I feel a pang in my chest. I never knew she had to go through that every day.

"No wonder you have days where you are too weak to move. How long am I like this for?" I ask, already feeling the part of me that is missing and wanting my

Wolf back.

"You're the Alpha of a Pack. I can't keep you like this longer than a day before people start to notice something. Just enough time for you to understand what I go through. Are you angry with me?" Lilla asks, looking at me with a worried expression.

"I wish I could say no, Lilla. I wish I could say I understand, but you didn't give me a choice; you didn't ask me. You just did it; how am I meant to forgive you for that?" I ask, and Lilla's expression changes to an empty one. The blank look I've seen many times before but only now understand how she can turn it on and off so quickly. Without a sound, she stands up and makes her way to the door.

"I wasn't given a choice either," she mutters and then walks out of my bedroom and away from me.

*

The silence is almost deafening. It all happened so quick, even I was shocked. No bones were snapping, no unbearably slow change. One moment she was screaming in pain and the next a beautiful four coloured Wolf was in her place.

"Lilla?" Alec asks, disbelief over what he just witnessed written on his face.

"She did it again!" Russell exclaims, his voice a mix of excitement and shock.

"Again? She's done this before?" Aiden asks, his eyes never leaving the Wolf in front of us.

"When Drake took Alec, Lilla got so angry she shifted," Russell explains.

"So, what made her mad enough to shift this time?" Layla asks, and Lilla growls in response.

"Lilla, come on, that's enough," I say, getting tired of the way she was treating her mother.

"She can be angry at Layla if she wants," Aiden sticks up for her.

"Look, Layla has her reasons, but-"

"Enough! While love triangles are very entertaining and watching you both argue about Lilla's problems is fun, we have bigger issues to deal with!" Ancestor Cain interrupts.

We all turn our attention back to Lilla.

"How is it possible? Is the Mark wearing off?" Alec asks, hopeful.

"No, I don't think so. Everyone knows that when Werewolves get angry, they lose control and shift; the more powerful they are, the easier it is to lose control. When a Werewolf has a Venom Mark and gets angry enough to shift, they will normally pass out from the pain. Lilla is the daughter of an Ancestor and an Original, she-"

"What's an Original?" Alec asks, apparently the only one bold enough to interrupt an Ancestor.

"The Originals are the first 5 Humans we changed to Werewolves. We each took a willing Human and turned them, but for them to continue on the species, we had to give them some of our... 'power,' I guess is the best word to use, not enough to be more powerful than us but enough to be more powerful than those they created. Layla was the first Human we turned; she's like the Ancestor's daughter. It means Lilla has power from her Mum and Dad. The Venom Mark isn't meant for someone so powerful." Ancestor Cain tells us. I sneak a few glances at Lilla, who is processing this information.

"Is this like last time? After a while, will she lose her Wolf again?" I ask.

"I believe so, she still has the silver chains around her, so the Mark is still in place. Once she shifts back, she will lose her again. Until the next time, she gets this angry." Ancestor Blake answers with a sadness in his voice for Lilla.

Alpha? There are Rogues on our Territory! Austin's voice fills my mind, and I groan.

"Shit, we have a Rogue on our Territory!" I repeat for everyone's benefit.

I'm coming! Lilla decides, and I nod, knowing there is no point arguing. I grabbed one of my jumpers hanging on a chair and passed it to Lilla.

"In case you shift back." I explain, she takes it in her teeth before I shift into my Wolf, and we both run together towards the Rogue.

*

As we get closer to where they are waiting with the Rogue, I shift back and put on my shorts.

I'm going to shift back too... I feel myself weakening. Lilla decides, and she disappears behind a tree.

"You know you don't have to hide from me, right? I'm your Mate," I say, and Lilla reappears in nothing but my jumper.

She shrugs shyly, an emotion rare for Lilla as she looks at the ground.

"You're self-conscious about your scars and bruises, aren't you?" I ask, and Lilla looks up at me with a sad smile.

"Yeah, but it's not just that," she says truthfully, and I frown, confused.

"What do you mean?"

Lilla looks around, "Now, really isn't the time, Dayton. We have a Rogue to deal with."

"Lilla, please, tell me." I'm practically begging, and Lilla sighs loudly, clearly not pleased.

"Look, I know I give off the impression that I'm confident, and nothing fazes me, but it's an act. An act every Rogue learns to perfect, but honestly, if I dropped the act, I'm a shy person who is ridiculously self-conscious about herself, no matter what other people tell me. I don't hide from you because of my scars and bruises, though they are a big part. I hide from you because... I don't believe other people when they call me beautiful or stunning, I never have, and I probably never will." Lilla shrugs, and before I can say anything else, she walks away.

I follow trying to process what she has said. How can she not think she is beautiful? I don't get it. We catch up to Austin and other men in my Pack, I look for the Rogue, but I can't see him amongst them.

"Where is he?"

"He got away, he is strong... Dayton, I didn't recognise him at first, but I know who it is."

"Who?" I ask, and Austin glances at Lilla before glancing at me.

"It's–" Austin is interrupted when we hear a twig snapping, and we all stand on guard immediately. We turn in the direction of the noise, and when the Rogue comes into view, with a smile on his face. My eyes widen in shock.

"Mason?"

"Hey there, baby brother."

Lilla

Had I heard that right?

"Brother?" I repeat, and the Rogue turns to me; his eyes narrow slightly, but then he smiles a dazzling smile. I could see every bit of Dayton in that smile; looking at them, you wouldn't guess they were brothers, but the smile gives it away.

"What do you want?" Dayton spits out; the anger is evident. I move closer and grab his hand, he relaxes, and some of the anger leaves his body. He holds my hand tightly, almost afraid to let go like I was grounding him. I was stopping him from shifting from ripping his brother to shreds.

"I heard about the war; it's spreading like wildfire. I figured you'd need help." He sounds sincere, an idea creeps into my head, but I stay silent. I'll mention it to Dayton later, now was not the time.

"We don't need your help. Get him off my Territory." Dayton growls; he drops my hand and walks away. I run after him.

"Dayton, wait, you have a brother?" I grab his arm, and he turns to look at me.

"No, I don't; I disowned him long ago." His voice is cold and distant, and I fight the urge to recoil.

"Why?" I ask, my voice small.

"It's not important."

"Dayton, why didn't you tell me?" I ask, trying a different approach.

Dayton chuckles, but it's just as cold as his voice.

"Pot. Kettle. Don't you think?" I flinch at his words, and this time as he walks away, I don't follow.

*

"Mason, right?" I say, catching up with Austin and the Pack members escorting him off the Territory.

He looks at me and nods.

"Why did Dayton disown you?" I ask, and Mason glances at me before looking back in the direction we are heading.

"Why are you so interested?"

"I love Dayton; I want to know why you make him angry." I admit, and Mason stops walking and faces me.

"You love him? Huh, isn't that interesting. I would never have guessed you two are Mates. You don't have that spark, that connection. You look more like two Humans in love."

"Is there a question behind that?" I ask, ignoring the Pack members trying to get us walking again.

"Why do you love him?" Mason asks.

"Why is that any of your business?"

"He is my little brother, I have to protect him," he says, shrugging, but the sincerity in his voice is evident.

"I could tell you how I love his laugh or the way he says things, and I do, but I can't explain why I love him. It's just something I feel, with every inch my body, the way my heart is full for him." I answer, and Mason stares at me for a minute before nodding and walking on. Clearly, my answer was acceptable.

"Did he ever tell you why he hates Rogues?"

"They killed his parents-your parents," I correct myself. Mason nods his head.

"It was just one Rogue, not loads like he tells everyone. That Rogue killed our parents and made Dayton disown me and hate me."

"Why?"

We all stop walking as we reach the edge of the Territory, and Mason turns and looks at me, "I was the Rogue."

He walks off the Territory, leaving me speechless, "It was nice to meet you... I never got your name, but it was nice to meet you. I did just want to help." Mason begins to walk away, my idea creeps back into my mind. I could say goodbye and then run my idea by Dayton, but he would never let me do this.

"Wait!" I shout, and he stops and turns back to me, curiosity written over his face. I turn to Austin, "Tell Dayton, I'll be back. I have an idea."

"What?" Austin looks at me, completely confused.

"Just tell him I'll be back. Promise him I'll be back." I say, and realisation washes over Austin as I step out of the Territory and towards Mason.

"Lilla, why are you doing this?"

"I have an idea. Just promise Dayton I'll be back." I walk towards Mason ignoring the calls of my name. I let the emptiness take over, so I don't turn around. Dayton will never forgive me for this.

*

Okay, so it wasn't the best idea I had, to go into the woods with a stranger in only a jumper! After what feels like hours later but probably only half an hour at the most, Mason stops walking and turns to me.

"Why did you come? Why would you leave your Pack, your Mate and come to the Rogues with me?"

I sigh and seeing a small bench, I sit down. Mason stays standing, watching me.

"Since I met Dayton, I have lied, kept things from him, called him a Pup in front of his Pack, rejected him, and forced him to accept it. I even took away his Wolf." Mason raises his eyebrows, surprised but stays silent. "He has been angry at me for all of it. He still is mad at me for some of it, but the worst thing I have done to him is bringing this war on his Pack, and he isn't angry at me for it. They won't win. I knew they wouldn't win when I asked them for help. We are fighting a losing battle, but I don't care. I will do anything to get what I need from Drake, and if that means the Pack has to die, then so be it.

"I used to care; when I was younger, I learnt all the names of my father's Pack so that when I left, I could still be part of their lives. I could ask about them, be updated on what's happening. It was so important to me. I want to care that much again. So, I'm trying. I want to give Dayton's Pack a fighting chance."

"That doesn't explain why you came with me," Mason says, sitting next to me; I sense others and see Rogues walking over and sitting down. Mason nods at them, and they all sit and listen.

"Drake's Pack is inhumane; they have lost the love and care for each other. They are machines. Dayton's Pack doesn't get that. They are a family. They fight like a family. We will lose. We need Rogues. Rogues will be just as ruthless as Drake's Pack. That's what we need to make this battle fair. You said you wanted to help, so help me persuade Rogues to fight with a Pack, to get involved in Pack business."

"We would never do that. Rogues don't get involved." One of the Rogues says.

"Well, I need to persuade them to." I shrug my shoulders. I couldn't go back empty-handed.

"Okay, I'll help. I said I would, so let us see what we can do!" Mason says, smiling at me. I start to smile back when it hits me. The pain intensifies. I double over, trying to breathe. The familiar burning sensation tells me everything I need to know.

I have just lost my Wolf again.

Lilla

1 month later

Mason lies down next to me without saying a word. We both stare at the star-filled sky.

"When I first became a Rogue, I was petrified." I tell him; still, he doesn't speak. "I was alone and scared that my uncle would come after me. I ran for the first day and night, refusing to stop, but by the second night, I needed to rest, so I found a small area and lay down on my back, and the first thing I saw were the stars. All my worries and fears just faded and instead of this empty feeling I'm used to, I felt at peace. Just staring at the stars made everything better.

"I decided that night I would kill myself because I didn't want to give up that peaceful feeling. The next day, I woke and went on my mission to die, so I found a cliff and decided to jump."

"What happened next?" Mason finally speaks when I don't continue.

"A friend saved me, he brought me back to his Pack, and I stayed with him for a while. He wanted me to stay but I told him I couldn't, that I needed to move on, but the truth is I missed the stars. When you are in a Pack, you live in a house with a ceiling to stare up at. There are no stars on the ceiling, Mason. It's empty and staring up at it just made me feel so empty and lost, so for a whole year, every night I would make sure I was sleeping somewhere, where I could see the stars."

"Then you met Dayton."

"When I first woke in his Territory, I told them I didn't know how I ended up there, but it was a lie. That night there were no stars, the clouds were covering them, and it was so dark that the things that go bump in the night, the things I was used to, scared me. I couldn't go to sleep without my stars, without feeling peace. So, I walked for the whole night; I kept walking, knowing that I would end up somewhere I would feel safe. I met Dayton, and I didn't feel scared or alone, and he made me feel peaceful."

"And now?"

"Now I don't miss the stars anymore; I miss Dayton. Mason, I think it's time we go back."

Dayton

Kill them. I tell one of my Pack members when he reports Rogues are just outside our Territory. **Once they trespass, kill them.** My tolerance for Rogues is non-existent.

It was low before I met Lilla, but I don't care anymore since she left me for my brother. She made her choice, so I made mine. Rogues can't be trusted. No matter who they are.

Alpha, they are just standing at the edge of our Territory.

What do you mean?

They are just standing there like they are waiting for something.

I let out a small growl, and everyone turns to look at me, curious at my sudden outburst. We are trying to organise everyone for the war against Midnight Moon, which Lilla left us with.

"Rogues are standing outside our Territory," I tell the room, and immediately everyone follows me towards the threat.

*

When we come into view of the Rogues, I silently thank the Ancestors for being here. At least 50 Rogues are standing in a crowd doing nothing.

"Alpha, what do you want us to do?" A young Pack member asks, and I stare at the Rogues for a moment.

"There is nothing you can do," I finally speak. "They aren't trespassing; they are in Neutral Territory." I shrug, and the Pup stares at me, unsure what to do with himself.

As I open my mouth to address the Rogues and ask them to state their business here, a Rogue comes forward, holding a tiny Rogue in his arms. She looks unconscious, her long black hair nearly reaching the floor even though the Rogue holding her is tall.

"Please help us. We don't know what to do. She just collapsed." The Rogue begs, walking as far forward he could go without stepping into my Territory.

"Why come here?" I ask, my Wolf perking up for the first time since Lilla left.

"He said to," the Rogue says just as the woman in his arms begins to stir.

"Ethan?" Her quiet and weak voice is heard by us all, and I immediately search for her scent, surprised I hadn't already caught it. I come up empty and frown; it is her; I would recognise her voice anywhere.

"Lilla?" Alec calls her name, and she turns her head slowly, smiling weakly when she sees us.

"Alec?" She turns her head back to the Rogue again. "Ethan, put me down, please."

He looks at her, unsure but puts her down anyway, and he supports her when she nearly collapses under her weight. She slowly walks forward, hesitating slightly when she steps into our Territory.

My Pack looks at me in confusion, unsure what to do, she is a trespassing Rogue, but she is also my Mate. Alec runs over and hugs her gently; she holds onto him for support when Ethan doesn't cross over with her.

"Lilla, are you okay?" Layla asks, and Lilla looks up at her mother.

"No, Layla, I am very weak. It would seem I'm having a bad day. Used too much energy."

"Where's Aiden?" Lilla asks, looking around, and Austin growls at her.

"You've been gone a month, and before you say a word to your Mate, you ask where Aiden is?" Austin says, with his teeth clenched and fists balled. Being my best friend, he is angrier with Lilla than I am.

Lilla turns to Austin, "Dayton doesn't want me anymore. What's the point?" Her voice is cold, making it seem like she doesn't care, but I know her too well.

"Why do you think I don't want you anymore?" I can't help but ask.

"I'm a Rogue in your Territory. If you still wanted me, I could have stepped into your Territory, and I would have been part of the Pack again, but I didn't feel any pain or shift, meaning you kicked me out of the Pack. I'm a Rogue... you don't want me anymore. Now, where is Aiden?" I can hear the hurt in her voice, but she looks at me even in her weak state, daring me to argue with her.

"He is back at my house," I tell her, and she frowns.

"Why? Why is he there and not here?"

"I think you should see for yourself." I tell her hesitantly, and immediately Lilla's face changes to one of concern.

"Lead the way." Lilla says, walking towards me with Alec's support.

"What about them?" I ask, and Lilla turns and looks at the Rogues.

"They won't do anything, they are here to help, but I get you won't want a bunch of Rogues on your Territory. They will just stay near the Territory with the rest of them, but they will be ready whenever you need them." Lilla explains, and I frown but decide not to question it when Lilla gets closer, and I see how exhausted she is.

"At least let me carry you?" I hate seeing her struggle and dying to touch her and be close to her.

She looks at me for a second before nodding, and I quickly pick her up, holding her as close to me as possible.

"Dayton?" Lilla says softly, and I look down at her.

"Yes, Lilla?" I say just as softly.

"I missed you, and I kept my promise. I came back to you."

"Yes, Lilla, you did."

"Then why do you hate me?"

"I don't hate you, Lilla; I can never hate you. I'm just angry that you left."

"I'm sorry, but I had to; I needed to get away from it all. I'm so sorry. I missed you every day, every second."

"I missed you too, Lilla."

"Hurry up with this being angry with me thing because I have waited a month to hear you call me Little Rogue." Lilla says, trying to sound demanding, but it comes across as pleading in her state. I go silent, unsure how to respond, and soon I hear her breathing even out, and when I look down, I see her fast asleep with a peaceful expression on her face.

Seeing Aiden can wait, Lilla needs her strength back before dealing with that, so instead of heading for Aiden's room, I head for Lilla's, where I gently place her on the bed and tuck her in.

I kiss her forehead, and she smiles softly in her sleep.

"You have no idea how much I've missed you, Little Rogue."

Lilla

I wake during the night and begin to panic. The silence is deafening. Sleeping outside isn't quiet; nature isn't quiet. Seeing my surroundings, I calm down and climb out of bed. I'm still weak, but the excitement of having a shower has won over.

As I take my time washing and getting dressed, I let my mind drift to the first morning I woke up here, and the first thing I did was take a shower. Not much has changed. I laugh when I remember Dayton's face when I was walking around in a towel.

Once I'm dressed, I glance at the clock by my bed, nearly six in the morning. No one would be up yet; I have the house to myself. What to do first... I think for a few minutes when my stomach growls, answering my question. Kitchen first.

I jump out of my skin when I turn the kitchen light on.

"Shit! You scared the life out of me!" I whisper shout, placing a hand over my racing heart.

"Sorry." Layla says, smiling at me softly.

"Why are you sitting in the dark?" I ask, moving around the kitchen, making food. "Tea? Food?" I ask her, trying to be friendly, maybe even establish a bond. The month away from her was what I needed to calm down and process.

"Just tea, please. I find it easier to think in the dark, fewer distractions." Layla shrugs.

"Think about what?" I ask, placing a tea in front of her and sitting down with my cereal and tea.

"You, mainly. Every morning, I sit in the kitchen and think about you, your father, and my mistake."

"Why at this time?" I ask curiously.

"It's the time you were born; it feels right."

I put down my spoon and face her, now is a better time than any to speak to her. "Why did you do it?"

"I don't know, I used to tell myself it was to protect you and your father, but that's not true. What you did, reject Dayton, that was to protect him. What I did was..."

"Selfish?" I finish for her, and she shrugs.

"I was going to say cowardly..."

"That too," I agree, and Layla watches me for a moment.

"You are so like your father. You have your morals, and if they are crossed... you don't forgive, do you?"

"No, I don't forgive. Sure, the petty things, like arguing with loved ones, I can forgive those because my love for them doesn't change; what I think of them doesn't change. It's the bigger things I don't forgive. When people aren't what I thought they were."

"Like me?"

"There was nothing to forgive when I thought you were dead. It was the Rogues fault for killing you."

"But I'm not dead." Layla states.

"But you aren't dead." I repeat.

We sit in silence while I finish my food, and when I get up to wash my plates, Layla speaks.

"Just so you know, Lilla... I am sorry."

"Why did you do it? Why fake your death and reject him? My mum said you loved him, so why would you give him up?"

"Drake isn't a very forgiving man. Runs in the family."

"What does that mean?" I ask, getting annoyed at the vagueness of her answers. Layla sighs.

"Twins have the same Mate. Did you know that? I don't know why; I don't know if that's something the Ancestors can fix or not. The Mate of twins has to choose between them. Seems cruel. The twin that isn't chosen will never have a Mate. Maybe you can have a word with the Ancestors about that because it's not fair. If they can fix that, they should. I chose Derek; it was always Derek; Drake never stood a chance. He never forgave us. He tried to be the bigger man at the beginning, but I think he got lonely. He tried to convince me that your father didn't love me; if he did, he wouldn't be with Lisa, he wouldn't have had a child with her. He didn't understand that that was why I loved your father.

"When I was making my choice between them, Derek told me about Lisa and that she was pregnant; he told me to choose Drake because he would never leave Lisa, he loved her too, and he had an obligation to her. That's why I chose him. Your father was so kind and loving, and he always tried to do the right thing, even if that meant he suffered.

"Anyway, Drake got bitter and cruel and angry; he just couldn't wrap his head around why I chose his brother instead of him. He got worse and worse, and when I found out I was pregnant with you, I knew Drake could never find out; I could only imagine what he would do to you. So, to keep you safe, I gave you to Lisa. It was the hardest thing I have ever done. Drake was getting worse with me; I was scared for my life and yours if he ever figured it out. I joined a Pack, and they helped me fake my death. I rejected your father and ran. I could never tell him what I had done and because he didn't know, he couldn't accept the rejection, and he went crazy. I thought I was protecting us all." Layla finishes off.

"He figured it out when he was torturing me; he had me kill a member of my Pack, so they wouldn't be so loyal to me; it was the one thing they were holding on to when he was trying to make them inhumane. It worked, I mentioned my dad's Mate, and he commanded the Pack to get him all the information on her. On you. I figured that meant he had no idea about you. But he did; I just misunderstood what he meant. He knew who you were; he just wanted all the information on you, and that's when he figured it out. Some Pack members knew I was yours; my father had trusted them enough. After that, he took my Wolf, put in clauses, tortured me every day, figuring out how strong I was to help with his clauses on my Mark.

"If you had stayed, you and my father had talked and figured it out, you could have beaten Drake." I tell her as tears are sliding down her face after hearing what Drake did to me.

"We don't know that," Layla tells me.

"Get out. Go back to your Pack. Be strong and selfless, something you never were for me. You will never be my mother. I have one who is fighting every day for her Pack, her home, and her children. You are what you have always been, 'the other woman'. I'm not even biologically hers, and still, she fights for me; I don't need two mothers, I don't have two mothers. I have one mother who loves me, fights for me, and she would never have done what you did." I say, standing up and throwing my plate into the sink. The noise makes Layla jump.

"Lilla-" Layla starts, but I interrupt her.

"I want you gone before anyone wakes up. This is my Pack, my family, and my life, and I don't want you in it."

With the words finally said, I leave the room and search for what I've wanted since I came back, for whom I have wanted to see.

Aiden.

*

As I walk past the front door, it opens softly.

"Doc?" I say, surprised, and his eyes widen.

"Lilla? I thought you would still be asleep."

"Had enough of that for now. What are you doing here?" I still wasn't his biggest fan after our last encounter.

"Erm... well..."

"Lilla?" I turn to see Dayton, and I can't help the smile on my face.

"Dayton... why is Doc here? I saw everyone less than 24hours ago. None of them can be injured, surely?" I ask, and Doc and Dayton exchange a look; suddenly, it dawns on me.

"Dayton, where is Aiden?" I ask, panicked and Dayton sighs.

"This way, I'll take you to him." I follow Dayton up the stairs and to a room the furthest away from everything. My heart is pounding so loudly, I'm sure they can both hear it.

He opens the door, and I walk in, gasping at the sight.

Aiden is lying down, hooked up to all sorts of machines; his skin is so pale that he looks almost see-through, his veins coloured silver instead of blue. The Ancestors are watching him, and when they see me, the sadness is evident on their faces. They know how much he means to me.

"What happened?" I ask, never taking my eyes off Aiden, lying unconscious in bed.

"Drake visited us to gloat, he ran into a few of my Pups with Aiden, and he injected him with Pure Silver. Punishment for escaping." Dayton explains.

"Why aren't you doing anything? Why haven't you saved him?" I shout at the Ancestors.

"He has too much Pure Silver in his system, we may be able to handle a larger dose than normal Wolves, but this would kill us." Blake tells me.

"How long does he have?" I ask Doc.

"A week at the most. He is in a lot of pain, and the Pure Silver is slowly killing him. The humane thing to do would be to end his suffering." Doc says, and a growl slips out of my mouth.

"No! We have a week to fix this!" I shout.

"Lilla, we have been discussing this; the best thing for him is to let him go."

"The best thing? None of you know him; how can you decide the best thing for him?" My voice continues to rise, my hands shaking with outrage.

"Either way, Lilla, he is dying. We will leave the choice up to you, but you may want to say your goodbyes."

They all leave me with him after that, and that's when I let myself cry. I walk over and sit on the edge of his bed, trying to be brave.

"I know you can hear me. When Drake injected me, and I was unconscious, I could hear you, and it gave me hope, so I'm here giving you hope. You can fight this, Aiden, because I can't lose you again! No one understands how I can love you and Dayton, but you get it. We never were a couple, but you are my first love, and I am in love with you. You are my best friend. I can't lose you!" I beg him, tears streaming down my face.

Someone knocks on the door and quickly wipe my face of the tears. "Come in."

Doc walks in and looks at me apologetically. "Sorry, I have to check his vitals; if you want me to keep him alive for the week..." Doc says, and I nod fighting a scowl at his passive aggressive comment.

"I know he is in pain; I've been through it, which is how I know he can survive." I tell Doc, and he sighs.

"How did you survive so much Pure Silver in your system?" He asks, and it clicks in my head. I stand up quickly and lean forward, right in Aiden's face.

"Listen to me, Aiden, I can fix you! I can make you better; just hang on one week, okay? I can make you better; all you have to do is fight!" I demand, I kiss Aiden's forehead and go looking for Dayton,

"Hey Lilla, where's Layla?" Blake asks as I walk into the front room.

"Gone." I say quickly and look to Dayton.

"You need to talk to Mason."

"What?"

"You need to talk to Mason! He has agreed to help us if you talk to him."

"I'm not talking to him, Lilla. He killed my parents!"

"I know, and I'm sorry, but I can save Aiden; all you have to do is talk to Mason, and all the Rogues will help us, which means I can get Drake, get my Wolf back and save Aiden!"

"How can you save him?" Dayton says, his tone of voice and facial expression telling me he thinks I'm in denial.

"I was tortured every day by Drake injecting me with Pure Silver; it was painful, but he gave me more than he gave Aiden and didn't kill me. When I have my Wolf, no amount of Pure Silver can kill me."

"I'm not talking to my brother!" Dayton tells me, despite what I've just said. I grab him by the throat, losing patience.

"All he is asking is that you talk to him, not forgive him or become best friends, just talk, and you will talk to him! Even if I have to command you to do it, Dayton. I am not losing Aiden because you are being too stubborn!" I growl out.

Dayton slowly nods, his widened eyes tracking my movements. I let go of his throat, calming down.

"Thank you." I whisper, relieved before making my way back to Aiden.

Lilla

There is blood everywhere. None of it is mine. Most is of those I've killed; the rest is those I've tried to save. Tried, but without my Wolf, I can't save anyone. We have lost many loyal Pack members and many loyal Rogues. We have lost friends, Mates, parents and children. Everyone has lost someone, me more than most. I've lost people I know from my new Pack, and I've lost people I've grown up with from my old Pack. I just keep losing people; wherever I look, someone else I recognise or know is dying. This is war, though, I have to keep reminding myself, but even so, it is unbearable.

"Mason?" *I call his name, surprised to see him standing outside my house, I have come to find my mother and deal with Drake, but I don't understand why Mason's here.*

"Hey, Lilla," *he says casually as if we have bumped into each other on an ordinary day out, not in the middle of a battle.*

"What are you doing here?" *I ask, and Mason smiles at me.*

"I'm here to kill Drake. He took everything from me, and I want to be the one to kill him."

"You can't kill him! I need him alive!" *I begin to panic. I've come so far; I've nearly won. I can't lose now.*

"I thought that was the whole point?"

"It is but not now; I need him for something. Once he gives it back to me, you can have him and kill him, but you just have to wait a little longer." *I beg, but Mason doesn't answer.*

"Well...isn't this a nice, little gathering," we both turn to see Drake watching us on the other side of the road. "I am so glad I decided to come now. Mason, it's been a while... tell me... how are your parents?"

Mason growls in response and lunges at him before I can even react. I watch them fight, shouting and begging for neither to kill each other.

"Lilla?" I turn to see Dayton walking over with the Ancestors, Austin, Aria, Alec, Russell, Jace and Rowan.

"Dayton," I breathe out his name in relief and run into his arms, happy he is alive. I take in his smell as he does the same. Just for a second, everything is fine, and then I realise I don't hear any more fighting. I turn around abruptly and see Mason holding Drake by the neck, part of me is shocked; Drake is an Ancestor... how did he beat him? The other part? Panicking.

"Mason, please don't kill him. Not yet." I beg, but as I step closer, I realise Mason isn't there anymore; it's his Wolf, his very angry and violent Rogue Wolf.

"He deserves to die. We can't keep him alive any longer; think of all the bad he will do." How did his Wolf just speak?

Before I can even argue, Mason slits his throat with his claws.

"No!" I scream and run forward, collapsing next to Drake's body. I pull him onto my lap and begin to cradle his body. "Please don't die! Please don't die!" I beg the already dead Drake.

"Lilla..."

"No! He can't die! He can't!" I cry as Dayton pulls me away from the body.

"He can't die, Dayton!" I continue to cry, and Dayton pulls me closer to him. "I need him!"

"Lilla?" Alec calls me, and I turn to him. "Lilla?"

"Lilla! Wake up, Lil!" I open my eyes to see Alec talking loudly. "You were shouting in your sleep. Are you okay?"

"Bad dream, I guess." I shrug, trying not to think about the dream — no, the nightmare. I get up slowly, my muscles aching after spending the night on the sofa. I slowly make my way to the kitchen and make coffee for Alec and me.

"What was it about?" Alec asks once I sit down, handing him his coffee across the table, which he takes gratefully.

"Drake... he was killed." I take a sip, loving the taste of hot coffee first thing in the morning.

"Why is that a bad thing?" Alec asks, and I look over my mug at him.

"He was killed before I got my Wolf back," I say, and realisation dawns on Alec's face.

"Ah," he says simply, and we fall into a comfortable silence. After a while, Alec speaks, looking nervous.

"So, you killed Dad..." he says before trailing off.

"Yes, I did."

"Sorry, it's just we have never spoken about it. I was with Drake, and then you died; we haven't had a chance."

"Are you angry with me?" I ask, and he shrugs.

"I don't know. I was, to begin with, but I've had time to adjust and calm down. I just don't understand why you did it."

"You don't understand why I did it?"

"All I know is what Drake told me, and he told me you killed Dad for no reason, but Aiden told me you would have a good reason to do it, so I'm asking you... why did you kill Dad?"

How do you tell your brother what kind of monster your father turned into?

"Didn't Russell tell you?"

"No, I wanted to hear it from you, and besides, he wouldn't."

I let out a deep breath and steady myself. "Okay... then let me begin with when you left."

*

"Hey," I say as I walk into the kitchen to see Dayton in his own little world.

"Hey," he says back, as I sit down opposite him.

"You know, when I first came here, Austin told me that you are one of the most vicious Alphas in the country. I panicked, thinking I was back in my old Pack." I chuckle slightly. "I didn't believe him; I thought he was just trying to scare a Rogue, especially when I see how you are with everyone, your friends and your Pack. You have a temper, but I couldn't see you as one of the most vicious Alpha's.

"Until I became a Rogue again, I was asked if I had found my Mate or what my story was and as soon as I mentioned your name and your Pack, the fear on the Rogues faces was shocking. Rogues are petrified of you; I couldn't understand it until they started telling me the stories. The things you did to Rogues, the rumours that spread because of it–"

"I know, it's disgusting." Dayton interrupts me, but I shake my head.

"Actually, I get it. I get why you would do that to Rogues, why you would hate them. Rogues killed your parents, after all. No, sorry, a Rogue killed your parents, just one, but it made you hate them, more so because he was your brother, right?" I finish, finally getting to the bottom of the story, to find out the truth that neither of them will tell me.

Dayton stares at me before his shoulders drop, and his head falls forward, almost as if he is giving up.

"I was 18, Lilla, 18 years old and made to become an Alpha because my older brother killed my parents for no reason. I will talk to him — for you — I would do anything for you because I am completely one hundred per cent in love with you, even though you rejected me, kept so many secrets, killed your Alpha father, have no Wolf and ran away with my brother. I told you once — a while ago now — I said to you that there is nothing you can do that will make me reject you except for killing an Alpha, but I was wrong.

"Little Rogue, there is nothing you can do to make me reject you, nothing at all. We don't know how this battle will end, but Little Rogue..." Dayton stands up and walks over to me; I turn in my seat as he bends down in front of me. I sit there in shock; this is not how I thought the conversation would go. I feel like I have whiplash from the change in subject.

"You may have rejected me, you have broken any connection our Wolves may have, but I don't care. I love you, and I want to marry you more than anything. So, Little Rogue, I planned to do this in a more romantic setting than in my kitchen, but I can't wait any longer.

Little Rogue, will you marry me?"

Lilla

"Marry you?" I try to sound calm, but my voice is high-pitched and panicky. I immediately scan the room for an exit, the Rogue in me ready to run. I clear my throat, "You want me to marry you?" I ask, my voice at a more appropriate level as I stand up and step around him.

I pace the kitchen floor, trying to wrap my head around the fact he has asked me to marry him.

"What's the big deal? I love you, you love me, right?" Dayton asks, standing up, looking at me with uncertainty written across his face.

"Are you kidding me? We have been arguing non-stop since I got here. You have been angry with me for most of my past, and have you even forgiven me for running off with your brother?" I ask, trying to make him see sense.

"We are Mates, all of that can be fixed, we will end up together anyway, why not get married now?"

I groan and run a hand through my hair. "We have only had one date, and even that turned into some dramatic event. Dayton, we have both lied to each other repeatedly, and I still don't know much about you. I don't have my Wolf back, and the way things are going right now, that is probably never going to happen. Dayton, can you honestly tell me you are asking because you love me?" Tears spring to my eyes.

He hesitates for a second, which is all the answers I need.

"Dayton, I love you, but we are a mess right now, I would love to say yes and marry you, but I can't do that knowing that the only reason you are asking me right now is that you don't want to die alone. Saying yes is permitting you to die. I want you to live; I want you to fight. I want you to ask me when this war is over, and I have my Wolf, and we have the rest of our lives to sort out our mess. Ask me again when you are asking out of love." I finish speaking and wait for him to argue, but he stands there unsure of what to say, and so with a sigh, I leave him alone in the kitchen.

*

Mason? Where are you?
Just outside the Territory, where we stayed the first time I met you. What's wrong?
I need you. I start running, feeling like I'm trapped. I need to get out of this Territory; I need to be free again.
The weight feels like it lifts as soon as I step out of the Territory. I see Mason running towards me and jump into his arms, holding onto him tight as he asks what's wrong again.
After a few minutes, I pull away and beckon for him to follow, which he does silently. After half an hour of walking, we reach a cliff, and I sit down at the edge, my legs dangling over it; Mason copies me.
"What's wrong?" He asks again.
"Your brother is scared." I say, lying down on my back, legs still dangling over the edge. Mason watches me.
"Aren't we all?" he frowns.
I shrug. "We are gonna lose." I tell him matter-of-factly.
"We have a shot. The Rogues are exactly what we need. We balance out the numbers, and they will be just as ruthless; we are permitting Rogues to kill a Pack without repercussions."
I smile sadly and sit back up.
"Your brother asked me to marry him."

"He what?"

"He's scared of dying alone; he's scared that there won't be anyone left to lead his Pack if he dies."

"There might not be anyone left to lead."

"You just said we could win!"

"Doesn't mean people aren't going to die, Lilla."

We fall into silence at the thought.

"Is that why you said no?" Mason finally speaks.

"Who says I said no?" I ask, raising an eyebrow.

"You wouldn't be sitting here telling me about it. If you had said yes, you would be celebrating right now."

"That's part of the reason," I admit. "I want him to ask me when this is over, out of love."

"What's the other part?"

"You." Mason whips his head around, surprised.

"Lilla, I didn't realise you felt–"

"Don't be disgusting!" I sit up and shove him in the shoulder. Mason chuckles before turning to look at the horizon again.

"Why me? You want us talking again, so you aren't in the middle for the rest of your life?"

I stare at my hands, worried about asking because I know the answer.

"I had a dream last night that we were fighting this war, and everyone around me was dying, and I couldn't stop it, but I wouldn't let it go to waste. So, I went looking for Drake to get my Wolf back. You killed him before I could." I stare at Mason as he closes his eyes, knowing what I'm about to ask.

"You are gonna kill him, aren't you?" I ask softly.

"Yes." Mason answers without missing a beat, his voice full of conviction.

"Before I get my Wolf back." It's not a question.

"He can do so much damage if we don't. He already has done a lot of damage. I can't think of you; I have to think of everyone else. Unlike all the other men in your life, I'm not under your spell or feel the need to make everything okay for you. My main concern is the many, not just you." Spoken like a true Alpha.

I stand up, hurt at his words and what they imply. "I don't expect people to do everything for me; no one is under my spell. The world doesn't revolve around me, and I know that, but Mason, this is my Wolf I'm talking about and–"

"And it is selfish for you to be thinking of yourself and your Wolf instead of everyone else." Mason stands up, following me.

"So what? Maybe I want to be selfish? Maybe I want to be the selfish one and get what I want for once in my life! Mason, listen closely when I tell you, you will not kill Drake until I have my Wolf back, and I promise if you do, I will have an Ancestor take away your Wolf from you and keep you locked away, forbidden to leave the Territory. I promise you I will make your life a living hell if you kill him before I get my Wolf back." I turn to walk away from him but stop when his next words hit me.

"Now you sound more and more like your uncle."

People have got to stop saying that to me.

Dayton

"I'm only doing this for Lilla," I inform my brother as he takes a seat in the chair opposite. We are in my office, and I feel confident sitting in the "Alphas" chair, while my older brother, The Rogue sits opposite –below me in rank.

"Of course, you are." Mason says, rolling his eyes.

"What do you mean by that?" I ask, already defensive.

"It's just something I've noticed, that's all." Mason shrugs as his eyes survey what was once our father's office, what should have been his.

"What have you noticed?" I can't help but be curious.

"Everyone drops everything for her; they would do anything, probably jump off a cliff or shoot themselves in the foot if it meant Lilla being happy."

It's my turn to roll my eyes. "That's a slight exaggeration!"

"Is it? You are all going to war against the most vicious and feared Pack run by an Ancestor for her. Have you seen how many Rogues she has fighting for her? She says they are doing it for me because they see me as a Rogue leader, but I'm not the one who asked them; she is. I asked, and I got a no, which makes sense. Rogues aren't ones to get in the way of Pack Business without getting something out of it, but Lilla asked, and immediately they fell into place... everyone seems to want her to be happy and have everything she wants, and I love Lilla. I do, she is a great girl, like a sister to me, but I don't feel the need to do everything for her like everyone else. I just don't get it." Mason shrugs, and I smile.

"I may hate you; I may not have seen you in 3 years, but you are my brother, and I know when you lie." I tell him, and my brother looks at me innocently. "You are right about Lilla," I continue. "Everyone does everything for her because our Wolves are wired to protect her, to please her — including the Ancestors because she is the most powerful Wolf — our leader who is vulnerable and being threatened. We all know what we are doing for her, even Lilla is aware to some extent, but unlike you, we don't fight it. Lilla is the leader not only of Packs but of Rogues, which is something we all need, so she is to be protected by all."

"Is she aware of it?" Mason asks, and I nod.

"Lilla is aware, but because of her past, she refuses to admit it because she doesn't understand why people would look out for her, she sees herself as the person who has to protect everyone, and no one is to protect her." I tell him, and he frowns.

"What about Drake? He doesn't feel the need to make her happy and protect her."

"That's what I thought, but the Ancestors told me he does, he may have done some awful things, but he won't kill her. If he wanted her dead, she would be dead by now." I explain with a frown. I hate the idea of Lilla being dead; my Wolf growls, not liking the idea either.

"That makes some sense, I guess." Mason says.

"We aren't here to talk about Lilla, though. We are here to talk about your traitorous act." I change the subject, wanting to get this over with as quickly as possible; we aren't playing catch up between brothers.

"Right... Would you believe me if I told you I killed our parents to protect you?" He asks, and I shake my head.

"No, I wouldn't, but I promised Lilla I would hear you out, so you might as well explain." I tell him, and he nods.

"You are probably right about me needing to make Lilla happy. My Wolf practically screams at me when I make her upset, but as much as I want to do as she asks and not kill Drake, I have to because it was our parent's last wish."

"What do you mean?" I ask, sitting forward, not a hundred per cent sure if I believe him or not, but curious nonetheless.

"I mean, there is a reason I hate Drake so much... Dayton, he commanded our parents to kill us, he wanted a Pack, and for some reason, he wanted us dead, you more specifically, so I killed our parents to protect you."

*

"I have to ask... Why did you tell everyone you killed the Rogues that killed your parents?" Lilla asks, folding her legs as she gets more comfortable on my bed; she sits opposite me while we talk.

I have just finished telling Lilla about the conversation between me and my brother and how I didn't know if he was telling the truth... or if I could trust him.

"I've known that he killed them, but as much as I hate him, I couldn't kill him, so I banished him. Only Austin knew the truth. I told everyone he ran away, couldn't handle what had happened, but there were certain expectations from me; I had to find the Rogues and kill them. I hate lying to my Pack, but I felt this need to protect Mason, no idea why. Anyway, one day I came across a few Rogues attacking a family, and I killed them; Austin then came up with the idea to say they were the ones that killed my Parents, make it seem like I had finally killed them, got my revenge. So, we could all move on." I explain, and Lilla nods slowly.

"So, do you believe him?" Lilla asks, bringing the topic back to today's conversation.

"I don't know. I honestly don't know what to think. Do you believe him?" I ask, hoping she can decide for me.

For a second, Lilla watches me before she stands up and begins to walk out.

"I want to show you something; come with me."

Without another word, I follow her, we walk out of my house, and when we reach our destination, I have to withhold a shudder. This place is not somewhere I would come back to in a hurry.

We were standing at the cliff where Lilla had jumped off when she first met the Ancestors; this is where, for a brief moment, I lost Lilla.

"Why are we here, Lilla?" I ask, and she turns and faces me.

"I've told you I dream a lot, right? I have dreams that seem so vivid and real that I act on them, follow them, or try and prevent them." I nod in response, knowing all this but not understanding what this has to do with Mason. "Ancestors have the gift to see the future. Not everything, but certain things, of their own life or the people they care about, but they don't get to choose what or when they see it. It normally comes when they sleep, so it's like a dream." Another Ancestor ability explained, but I'm still confused.

"So, what has this got to do with whether you believe Mason or not?"

"Drake is an Ancestor; he can dream of the future. Mason said Drake commanded your parents to kill you both — specifically you. It is possible; Drake had dreamt a piece of my future, of you. I have to say, I believe him because I know what Drake is capable of." Lilla says, and I watch her carefully.

"So why bring me here to tell me that?" I can't help but ask.

"I had a dream last night, someone attacked your house; while we were having our conversation about Mason, they drugged us and took you. So today I spoke with Austin, and we set a trap for them at the house, and Austin and I agreed we shouldn't be there, just in case."

I look at her in alarm.

"I have to go help my Pack! I'm the Alpha I can't hide." I start to turn, and she grabs my arm, stopping me.

"Don't think of it as hiding; think of it as protecting me."

I go to speak, but pain shoots through my leg, causing me to scream. I turn to see a Wolf snarling at me, his mouth covered with my blood. Another Wolf runs at me, teeth bared as the other Wolf lets go, and I fall to my knees. I try to shout out for Lilla to run, but I can't get the words out for some reason. My vision begins to blur, and I try opening and closing my eyes several times, but my vision remains blurry.

We've been drugged! My Wolf informs me sleepily. I fall to the ground, finding it challenging to keep myself on my knees, just wanting to lie down and sleep.

"Dayton!" I hear Lilla scream, and I try so hard to stay awake for her; I have to fight. I have to fight for Lilla! Despite what I'm thinking, despite wanting to fight for her, my eyes begin to close.

Before I finally give up and let sleep takeover, the last thing I see is a Four Coloured Wolf.

Lilla

I tear them apart, limb from limb, my mouth tasting the metallic substance. How did they find us? No one knew where I was taking him. Austin and I had a plan!

Hello? Anyone? Help! I shout, broadcasting it out to any mind link — even blocked ones — just needing someone in this Territory to help me.

Killing the last Wolf alive, I run over to Dayton, who is lying unconscious. I nudge him with my snout but get no response. I sniff him and growl when I smell the distinctive odour of a paralytic healing drug. It stops Wolves from healing, it's illegal and dangerous and complicated to get hold of, but they have managed to use it on my Dayton. This has Drake written all over it.

Instead of waiting around helplessly, I decide to make a new plan. I shift into human form and strip Dayton off his shirt to cover myself up.

Okay, to anyone listening. I need help, Dayton is injured, and I can't move him on his own. I need someone to help me. Please! We are where Alec saved me. I broadcast again, deciding not to name where I am but to give a clue. I don't know who is listening, and I don't want enemies coming for us now.

I check Dayton over but can only find the one injury to his leg, which isn't healing. I let out a cry of frustration. I can't do anything! I can't save him! I'm useless.

I begin to laugh hysterically. I'm the most powerful Werewolf in the world, and I'm useless.

When I hear a twig snap, the laughing stops abruptly. I tense and look around, waiting for someone else to attack. Nothing happens, but I know better than to relax.

A Wolf slowly emerges from the trees and, seeing me, begins to growl. His eyes land on the bodies of the Wolves I had shred to pieces, and he growls louder.

Not a friend then. I sigh and stand up, readying myself to fight him. His head turns to the side as he watches me move, and slowly he begins to match my movements to his.

"Midnight Moon, am I right?" I ask, and he watches me for a few moments longer before nodding his head at me.

Who do you think I am? I ask him through mind link, wanting to start a conversation with him.

Should I know? He replies, his voice deep and bored.

No, I was just curious why a Midnight Moon Pack Member would be trespassing.

Our Alpha wants your Alpha dead. The Wolf answers, and I frown.

Why?

That isn't any of your business. Nor mine.

So, in other words, you don't know.

All I know is that our Alpha wants the Alpha of the Freedom Howlers dead; as a Pack member, I am not here to question what he wants but just do it.

To kill him, you have to go through me. I threaten, and Wolf's laughter fills my head.

I don't see that being too difficult. He says before running at me, teeth on show and ready to attack.

Before he can reach me, another Wolf appears, barging into him.

"Alec," I breathe, relieved I'm not alone anymore.

The Ancestors appear, Cain and Emily begin to search for more Wolves trespassing, while Blake picks up Dayton and begins to carry him back to the house. I follow close behind, worried for Dayton and Alec, but more importantly, concerned because Drake isn't finished with us.

*

"How is he?" I ask Doc as Dayton lies unconscious in the hospital bed.

"He has lost a lot of blood, and at the moment, we are waiting for the paralytic healing drug to leave his system for him to heal." Doc informs me.

"How long is that going to take?"

"It could take up to a week."

"A week? Does he bleed out until then?" I ask, my voice slightly higher than usual.

"We won't allow him to bleed out, Lilla. Just trust that we will take care of him."

Without another word, I stand up and walk away. Trust. I need to trust him? Is he crazy? I don't trust people. I'm a Rogue with a messed-up life. With a father, birth mother, uncle and Pack who went against me. Does he think I'm going to trust him?

I don't have a choice; Dayton's life is in his hands, and there is nothing I can do.

I walk with nothing but a feeling of helplessness, and I keep walking until I reach my destination: Midnight Moon Territory.

Lilla

I walk into the room, memories flooding me; this is where I was meant to kill the baby, where I broke the Ancestor command. The Pack turns to see who has interrupted; mouths open in shock. Their Alpha stares at me, speechless.

"I have to admit; I thought I'd get caught the second I came onto your Territory." I say, walking further into the room.

"You are meant to be dead." Drake finally speaks, still in shock.

"If you thought I was dead, why are you still after Dayton?" It's funny; I thought I'd be scared of him or being here. They could quickly grab me and throw me in a cell, but for some reason, I feel confident, empowered.

"We are still going to war; killing the Alpha would stop that." Drake tells me so calmly like he is telling me the recipe for a meal.

"Well, I'm sorry to disappoint you, but he isn't dead, just wounded."

Drake shrugs. The Packs heads are turning between us like we are playing table tennis.

"Can you honestly tell me why you are doing this? Is this all seriously because you didn't get the girl?"

Drake chuckles. "You stupid little girl, you think you can play with the adults, but you don't even know the game."

I frown. "Then tell me."

Drake eyes me for a second, he knows I'm not scared, and he almost looks impressed.

"I'm doing this to protect you." Drake says softly. I stare at him in disbelief. Does he expect me to buy that?

"You have got to be kidding me?!" I burst out, and start laughing. I have no idea why but laughter just keeps spilling out.

"Lilla, you need protection, whether you believe me or not."

"Protection from what?" I ask, still laughing.

"Dayton." Drake says, and the laughter stops. For a second, I believe him because of the way he says it. He looks and sounds so sad and worried, like giving me this piece of information is the hardest thing he has ever had to do.

I snap out of it.

"Why do you need to protect me from Dayton?" I asked, humouring him.

"I'm not meant to tell you; I made a promise to your father." Drake says, and suddenly, this is no longer a joke.

"What do you mean?" I ask, my voice barely a whisper. Drake stays silent like he is weighing up the pros and cons on whether to tell me or not.

"The moment you were born, your father started having dreams about you, about your future. What he saw scared him, and he tried to fix the original problem, but it was too late. So, he planned out your life, everything I was to do to you, the torture and taking away your Wolf, even your escape from the prisons and the people you met. He even planned his death into it, although none of us was prepared for what he did, who he became. I adjusted, though, and everything was going to plan, except Dayton. He is still alive." Drake summarises, and I stare at him. I know better than to believe him, but he couldn't be making this up on the spot, surely?

"You're lying; I don't need protection from Dayton. Why would I? What 'original problem' could my father not fix?"

"Maybe we should talk in private?" Drake offers, and I immediately shake my head. I am not being left alone in a room with Drake.

"No, the last time I was left alone with you, you took everything from me.

Explain yourself in front of your Pack."

Drake sighs and then offers me a seat; I refuse, wanting to stay standing.

"Dayton's parents were traitors to the Ancestors; they disagreed with our rules and tried to go against us. They killed the first people each of us changed, which were considered our children in our eyes. The only one they didn't get to was Layla, we managed to save her, which is how your father and I met her, but that's a different story. Instead of killing them — something so quick and easy — we decided to punish them. They had killed our children, so we decided the best form of punishment was to command them to kill their own. To begin with, that was a good idea, but it didn't feel like justice, so we decided to command them to kill their youngest; that way, not only would they have killed a child, their other child would never forgive them. It was the perfect punishment.

"Your father started dreaming about your death that night. Certain choices lead to different futures, and because of our choice, your future meant you were dying young. We tried to change it, but it was too late; Mason had killed them to save Dayton by then. I have no idea how he found out; you'd have to ask him that. Anyway, it was too late, your father had seen Dayton kill you because Ancestors killed his parents, and they were the reason he isolated himself from his brother. He blames you because he is angry; his family always did have a temper. Your father started to make plans after that."

"What plans?" I ask, feeling sick. It's all so specific, every detail. I can't decide whether he is lying or not.

"He planned out everything. They were to kill Dayton before you met him, but your father knew that wouldn't work, so he wanted me to take away your Wolf. He wanted me to torture you, find out how strong you were and how strong the Mark would have to be. He wanted me to keep you locked up so that you would meet Aiden and fall for him so that when Dayton did die, at least you could find happiness with Aiden."

"So why take my Wolf?" I ask, struggling to let everything sink in.

"So that you couldn't get too attached. If your Wolf is locked away, you can't fully connect with your Mate; even if you met him, killing him wouldn't hurt as much as it would if you had your Wolf." He has an answer for everything.

"So, you are trying to kill Dayton so he won't kill me?" I ask in a small voice. I sink my head into my hands, feeling dizzy and sick and not knowing what to believe. "

Then why be so happy that I was dead?" I mumble through my hands; he can't be telling the truth; Dayton loves me. He wouldn't kill me; surely he would have by now?

"I have a reputation to maintain, but I wasn't happy; you are my niece; why would I be happy about your death? Lilla, I would never have done all of that stuff to you unless it was to protect you. My Wolf and I argue every day over it, and the only reason he doesn't hate me is that we are protecting you. Lilla, I know I have no right to ask this of you, but I need you to trust me." I lift my head and stare at him, look him in the eye, and think for just a second before I nod my head.

"So, what do I do?"

"You go back to Dayton. You act like nothing is wrong. You get ready for war, and Midnight Moon will win when it happens. We are stronger, smarter; I taught them how to fight myself."

"You taught them how to be inhumane!" I find myself spitting out, and he sighs.

"I command them to act like it but never let them become so. I needed you to believe you had no one to come back to. So, you wouldn't save them; that would have messed with the plan. After the battle when Dayton is dead, I will give you back your Pack and your Wolf." Drake says, and I study him for a moment.

"Promise?" I ask, wanting to hear him repeat it.

"I promise."

Lilla

When he comes for me, I'm standing at the edge of Midnight Moon Territory. I feel like a wild animal as he strolls towards me, worried he will scare me, while I stare at the Territory that used to be mine.

"What are you doing here, Lilla?" Mason asks, and I sigh as I turn and face him.

"I just started walking and ended up here. I didn't step over; I've just been standing, thinking." I lie, he nods in understanding, but his eyes tell a different story as he continues to watch me carefully like I'm going to step into the Territory any minute if he makes a sudden movement.

"Shall we go back? Dayton is healing, and they could do with a leader without him," Mason says, and I smile.

"Dayton is healing? I haven't even been gone a day." I begin to walk with Mason back to Freedom Howler Territory.

"The Ancestors are helping, trying to speed up the process. The drug will be out of his system in a couple of days now." Mason informs me, and I nod, smiling a small smile.

"About what I said..." Mason begins, and I stay silent, curious about what he says. "I didn't mean it, okay?"

"You did mean what you said; I'm okay with it. I need to be like Drake to beat him. Compare me to him all you want."

Mason studies me for a moment before nodding, and we begin to walk in silence until I build up the courage to ask him what I had been dying to ask when he first told me about his parents, what has been racing in my mind since speaking to Drake.

"How did you know that your parents were commanded to kill Dayton?" Mason's steps falter for a second before continuing his walk.

"My parents were traitors to the Ancestors. They didn't believe in many of the things they were taught, they didn't like the rules, so they decided to make their own, which got them in trouble again and again. Dayton and I, however, loved the Ancestors; we thought they were these amazing mysterious creatures. From all the kids' stories, we could never understand why our parents hated them. Then they pushed it too far; they decided to protest against the Ancestors' new rule, something about Rogues?" Mason looks at me, wondering if I know what he is talking about.

"Rogues are to be killed if they step foot in a Pack's Territory, no matter the reason." The rule meant that Alphas didn't need to be present when Rogues entered their Territory. The rule didn't last for long; too much blood was shed.

"That's the one. My parents disapproved, they protested, but the Ancestors ignored them like they always did, so my parents acted. They killed the first person each Ancestor changed, the Ancestors were angry, and we didn't hear from our parents for days. I was so sure they had been killed, so I stepped up as Alpha, then one day my parents came back, but something was off about them. I kept an eye on them and watched as they tried to kill Dayton; I killed them to protect him. I had to choose them or him, and it was the easiest decision I've ever made."

"How do you know all of this?" I ask.

"I've met the Ancestors before. After I killed my parents, they walked into my Pack completely undetected. I thought I would be killed for killing the Alpha, whether they were my parents or not, but instead, they sat me down and explained everything to me. They even tried to stop my parents, but they were too late. They asked me if there was anything they could do, so I had them make Dayton forget how traitorous our parents were, make him believe they had come back from vacation, and then I had killed them. I told them to make him believe I had gone Rogue so that he would become Alpha."

"If the Ancestors were taking his memory, why not take the memory of you killing them?" I can't help but ask, it seems like the obvious solution. It's what I would have done.

Mason shrugs, "I guess it was a way of punishing myself. I know I did it to save him, but that doesn't make me feel less guilty. You must get that? I wanted to punish myself, and the best way was to have Dayton punish me and hate me forever. So, I let him banish me from the Pack and move on without me. I checked up on him from time to time, and he grew into one of the most amazing Alpha's I've ever seen. I'm so proud of him." Mason finishes, his voice going soft, laced with the pride that he felt.

"Are you ever going to tell Dayton the truth?" I ask, and Mason sighs.

"I tried and failed. He doesn't believe that I was saving him from them; he won't ever believe our parents were traitors."

"Couldn't the Ancestors unlock the memory for you?"

"I guess... but it'll mean he will have more questions that I can't answer."

"Why can't you answer them?"

"Because he may never forgive you for being the reason his parents are dead."

*

When we arrive back, Mason begins to walk in the direction of Dayton's bedroom but stops when he realises I'm not following him. Instead, I head for my room, where I have a shower, and change into more comfortable clothing. Without even a glance at my bed, I leave my room and stop. I look to my right, where Dayton is lying unconscious in bed, and then I look to my left, where Aiden is lying unconscious in bed, and without another thought, I turn left.

When I enter his room, Doc is there checking his vitals; I ignore his raised eyebrow and climb into bed next to Aiden. As I curl into his side and close my eyes, I try to block out all the machines, my mind racing with questions and problems I don't have the answers or solutions to.

"I thought you would be at Dayton's bedside?" A voice questions from the door; I open my eyes to see Blake standing there.

"I'm tired; can you lecture me when I wake up?" I asked, closing my eyes and trying to fall asleep.

"Dayton is your Mate; he is in pain and needs you. Why are you here?"

I try to ignore him, but Blake continues to try and make me feel bad; after a few moments, I sit up and snap at him.

"I'm here because Dayton will be fine in a couple of days; he will wake up. Aiden is dying; he may never wake up. So please save you're disapproving looks and let me sleep!"

Blake's expression softens, and he goes to leave, but I call him back. I have to ask; I have to know the answer; maybe I'll finally be able to sleep.

"Did my dad love me? I know you didn't know we existed, I know you didn't know us then, but you knew him. In your opinion, from the man you knew and the memories you've seen, did he love me?" I ask, choking on the last words, tears rolling down my face.

Blake sighs and walks over to the seat by the bed. I turn over and wait for him to answer. When you learn things about your past, you know the right questions to ask to get people to tell you the truth.

"We knew you existed; we just didn't know you were biologically his. We can't have kids, so we didn't question it when he told us he had adopted you. We probably would have if we met you, but your dad never let us; most likely, he was scared of how we would react." Blake stopped talking, and I waited patiently while he mind-linked someone; he seemed torn.

"Your father started having dreams about your future, about your death, over something we did - something that doesn't need explaining now - he tried so hard to fix it, but he was too late. He loved you so much; he planned your life to keep you alive. There are many ins and outs, but they aren't important right now. You weren't even born yet, but he loved you so much. He used and abused ALL his power just to prevent your death.

"So, Lilla, in my opinion, you were your father's entire world; both you and Alec meant everything to him." I have tears running down my face, and Blake smiles at me.

"I'll leave you to sleep. We can talk more when you wake, answers any questions you may have." Blake says before leaving me alone.

I continue to let the tears fall as I grab a pillow, and with Blake's and Mason's words running through my mind, I scream into it because Drake was telling the truth. Every word that came out of his mouth was true. So, I screamed into the pillow, my heart breaking because Drake was telling the truth.

Lilla

Dayton is going to kill me. I am going to die at the hands of my Mate. The words keep running through my mind as I lie next to Aiden. I had tried to sleep, but my mind was working overtime, making it impossible. I was arguing with myself. Part of me believed that Dayton would never in a million years hurt me, especially because of something the Ancestors did, but another part of me, a much louder part of me, knew that he would. He couldn't even forgive his brother for murdering them; he would never forgive me for what my family did. He has a short temper, something I've loved pushing since I got here, but I know how far I can push, and this would be too far.

I get out of bed and glance at the clock with a sigh. It reads 3:00 AM. I head to the kitchen for a cup of coffee, knowing that caffeine was the only thing that would get me through the day.

I see the Ancestors sitting at the table, each with a cup of coffee and one space empty with a cup in front of it. I sit down and blow on the steaming cup, grateful that they had it ready for me because I am exhausted.

"Talk to us," Cain says, and I watch them all stare at me expectantly. The tears start trailing down my face before I even have a chance to breathe; I wipe them away violently and sigh.

"I can't do this anymore. I just need everything to calm down for five minutes. Everything has been so hectic for so long now; I just need everything to stop. I honestly thought it would when I met Dayton. I had a deluded little dream that I could stop and relax for a bit. It was a stupid thing to dream about, but it is all I want. It's just one thing after the other, and I just haven't got the energy."

"I know it's been hard, Lilla, all you have to do is get through this battle, and everything will be fine. You will feel better when Dayton wakes up; when your Mate recovers, everything will be better." Emily says, and I laugh because what else can I do? The Ancestors look at me as if I'm crazy, and I probably have gone crazy, but I don't care.

"What's so funny?" Emily asks, and once I stop laughing, I explain exactly why what she said is ridiculous.

"It's funny because when Dayton wakes up, Mason will tell him the truth about his parent's death, and one of you is going to unblock the memories of it, and then Dayton will kill me. So, Dayton waking up won't make things better, although at least I'll finally be able to rest." I say before I laugh until tears are streaming down my face.

*

"Why does Mason have to tell the truth?" Blake asks a little while later; when I've calmed down and we are on our second cup of coffee.

"You can't keep something like that from him. It's not something I'm willing to lie about or cover up."

"You lied about your father's death," Cain mutters, and I kick him under the table.

"Yeah and look how that turned out! Alec trusted Drake, and I wish I had told him sooner; I wish I had been the one to tell him. If I could do it over, I would tell everyone from the beginning. I've learned my lesson. Dayton needs to know, and he needs to find out the truth from his brother."

"Okay, I'll help Mason tell him the truth," Emily offers. "I mean, I was the one to block them in the first place; I should be the one to unblock them." She finishes with a shrug, and I can't help but raise an eyebrow at her casual response to blocking someone's memories.

"Thank you," I say, and she smiles at me.

"What are you going to do when he gets mad? You will defend yourself, right?" Cain asks, and I turn and look at him.

"I'm hoping it won't come to that. No, I'm choosing to believe that he loves me enough not to kill me."

"But if he does, you will defend yourself if he tries to kill you?" Cain asks again, more forcefully.

I let out a sigh and shrugged, "I'm not killing him, I can't kill him, but I honestly don't know what I will do."

*

I walk into Dayton's bedroom, and my heart tugs as I see him looking so ill and lifeless. Even though I know he will kill me when he wakes up and finds out the truth, I still want him to wake up; I hate seeing him like this.

I sit down in the chair beside his bed, feeling uncomfortable and out of place, not like how I am in Aiden's room. I watch his chest rise and fall as he breathes evenly and it brings me some peace. I don't know why I'm here, but I ended up in Dayton's instead of walking to my room.

"I've changed," I say as if he can hear me, desperate to talk to someone about what's been weighing on my mind for a while now, and who better to listen than my unconscious Mate?

"When I woke on your Territory, I was feisty and sarcastic, and now? Now I'm not that person, I don't feel like that person, and I don't know how to get her back."

I wait expectantly as if Dayton will open his eyes and reply with words of wisdom or something, but, of course, he just continues to breathe steadily.

I lean my forehead against the edge of the mattress.

"I need to get some of me back; I need to do something other than sitting here waiting for you or Aiden to wake up. I was like this once before, ready to die because all I wanted was peace in a chaotic world. Danny brought me back; he made me whole again. If I could, I would go to him, but I can't have you waking up and me not being here because, despite everything, I do love you." I whisper the last part in his ear as I stand over him and kiss his forehead before leaving him alone.

*

"You know, I'm surprised you don't want to kill me," I say, walking into the front room and sitting on the sofa next to Mason. He puts the TV on mute and turns to face me.

"I don't hate you for something that you didn't do. The Ancestors did it; I can't hate you for that."

"I'm hoping Dayton will see it the same way," I admit, and Mason looks at me with pity.

"I don't think he will. Dayton had a different relationship with our parents than I did."

"How so?" Mason shrugs.

"Dayton was the golden child; he was the one with the good grades and the whole 'good person' thing. He was the one my parents wanted as the next Alpha, he was the child my father took to Gothenburg, or my mother took to meet other Luna's and their little girls in case they would be Mates one day.

"I was the disappointment, the kid who slept with any girl because I could, and the one who ignored my Alpha duties and just did whatever the hell I wanted. I was the rebel, always pissing my parents off." He chuckles as if the whole thing is like a good memory as he talks.

"How? What did a young rebel Mason do?" I ask with a cocked brow and a smirk.

"Oh God, anything and everything, but I did do this one thing that got to them, and I don't think they ever forgave me for it."

"What did you do?"

"I rejected my Mate."

"Why did you do that?" Trying to keep my voice level and hide my shock.

"I told them it was because I didn't want a Mate, but I just didn't want to admit the truth. My Mate practically begged me to reject her; she was in love with someone else. Some guy who had lost his Mate loved each other, so for her sake, for her happiness, I did what she asked."

"I can't believe you did that for her." My heart hurts for him but I can't deny that I'm annoyed at this woman I had never met because she didn't love him.

Mason shrugs, "I got over it; now I don't think I believe in the whole Mate thing. Sometimes, like with my parents, it gets it right, but sometimes, like with your parents or even you, it gets it wrong. Your dad loved your mother before Layla came along and long after she left. You love Aiden, and don't deny it.

"Aiden should have been your Mate, and my Mate should have been Mates with that guy she loves. Your father's Mate should have been your mother, not Layla. Dayton's should have been Katie; you never met her, but it was his first girlfriend, and he loved her, and she loved him before she met her Mate and moved to his Pack. I just think that the Mate connection is broken; it doesn't always work."

"Who should be your Mate? You're picking everyone else's, but who should have been yours? You must have loved someone once?" I ask, but before he answers, Emily walks in.

"Mason, did you want to go over the plan for when your brother wakes up? You need to decide what to say and when you want me to unblock the memory." Mason nods and begins to follow Emily out. When he gets to the door, he turns and faces me.

"In answer to your question, the girl that I would pick, I couldn't have; she already has two guys completely in love with her. I couldn't do that to them, or more precisely, I couldn't do that to my brother."

Dayton

"Little Rogue?" I call as I search the house; I hear a muffled reply and follow it into the main bedroom, where Lilla is standing in her underwear, her hair up in a messy bun with clothes surrounding her.

"What are you doing?" I ask, and Lilla looks at me in desperation.

"I don't have any clothes to wear!" Lilla says, staring at me accusingly as if this was somehow my fault.

"What do you mean?" I ask as I gesture at all the clothes piled on the floor.

"I have clothes! I just don't have any suitable enough to meet your parents!"

"Right... you do know my parents are dead, though?" I am almost surprised at myself for not feeling as sad as I usually feel when I mention them. Lilla gives me an 'are-you-stupid?' look, something I was growing used to.

"That doesn't matter! I have to look presentable meeting them whether they are dead or alive!"

"Lilla–" I start, but she puts a hand up to stop me.

"I have to look like a Luna!" She explains, and I frown.

"Why?" I ask; she was never bothered about looking like a Luna before; what's changed?

"I have to look and act like a Luna because you aren't here! Someone has to run the Pack! They need an Alpha, Dayton!"

"What do you mean? I'm right here, Little Rogue?" I say, moving forward, but Lilla shakes her head.

"Look around you, Dayton. Does any of this seem real to you? Since when do I stand in front of you in my underwear? I'm too self-conscious about my scars and bruises. Speaking of which, where are they?" Lilla asks, looking down at her perfect body. No scars or bruises to be found. "My hair is up in a bun instead of hiding my Mark, which isn't there." Lilla continues to point out the imperfections in her perfect self.

"I don't understand..." I say, shaking my head slowly.

"Dayton, look at me, look at this, none of it is real. I need you to think hard about the last thing you remember. Can you tell me what that was?" Lilla asks, and so for her, I do as she asks.

"I was... no, we were talking? We were outside talking about... about... Mason! You were showing me something about telling the future?" I ask, and Lilla nods. "Then there were Wolves, and they attacked us? You shifted!" I say as I remember her multi-coloured Wolf, and Lilla nods again. "Am I dead?"

"No, you aren't dead, you were given a paralytic healing drug, and you are unconscious at the moment."

"So, you aren't Lilla, are you my subconscious or something?"

"No, we aren't in a movie Dayton! I'm..." Lilla stops talking and then shrugs, "Screw it, you won't remember any of this when you wake, I might as well be honest. I'm the Ancestors. As in, all three of them. We can take over your mind to talk with you, one of the many gifts that we possess. It takes all three of us to do it, and we don't do it very often because it's draining, but we needed to talk to you."

"About what?" I ask, and the Ancestors version of Lilla looks up at me.

"Okay, look, you need to wake up. We have many things to discuss, but more importantly, Lilla needs you. She is falling apart; she doesn't know what to do or believe or think, she's losing her mind. Wake up."

*

I'm tired. That's my first thought when I wake up. I'm so unbelievably tired;

I try to fall back to sleep, but someone speaking to me ruins that perfect plan.

"You're awake; that's good!" I let out a growl as I open my eyes, seeing my brother sitting at my bedside.

"What are you doing here?" I ask, my voice hoarse and dry. I reach for the water on my bedside cabinet.

"My little brother is injured; where else would I be?"

"Somewhere you are wanted?" I bite out. He can't honestly expect me to be grateful that he is here.

Mason lets out a dejected sigh. "Against my better judgment, I will have to hope love conquers all and that you mean it when you said you'd forgive Lilla for anything. Dayton, I wish this could wait, but we don't have time. Emily will give you back your memories after I've told you the truth about our parents."

*

"What are you doing here?"

"I wanted to make sure you were okay." Lilla says, standing at the end of my bed and looking at the floor rather than me.

"I'm fine." I snap, and Lilla flinches.

"Dayton, I'm–"

"Don't apologise. I don't want to hear it. I don't even want you here. I now have no choice but to fight Drake and his Pack because the war isn't just with you. It's with my Pack, but I want you gone after that. I can never forgive you for this. After this battle, if you ever set foot in my Territory again, I will kill you, Mate or not."

Lilla

"Get up!" Alec says as he pulls off my duvet. I groan and put a pillow over my head, trying to keep the light out. He pulls that off too.

"Lilla, get your arse out of bed now!" Alec says, hitting me with the pillow in his hands.

"I don't want to." I whine like a 5-year-old child.

"Lilla–"

"Alec, just leave me alone!" I snap, sitting up, so I can look him in the eyes, annoyance rolling off me.

"Lilla, you have to get up," Alec says, his voice softer than before, once he takes in my swollen red eyes from the exhausting cry I had last night. I'm not ashamed of it; I spent most of yesterday and last night crying because I'm heartbroken and wanted to wallow.

"Why? Why do I have to get up? Why can't I stay in bed all day? Is there an actual reason, or did you just not want me to spend all day in bed? If it's the latter, then you can get the fu–"

"Aiden's awake," Alec whispers, watching me as I stare at him, trying to decide whether he is joking or not. When I realise that he is serious, I push him out of my way and run towards Aiden's room, excitement building at seeing Aiden speaking to Aiden and hearing his voice.

I burst into his room and froze. I frown. Aiden isn't awake. Why would Alec lie to me? I turn around to see Drake with a smile on his face.

"Sorry, did I say Aiden? I meant Dayton, my bad." His laughter fills the corridor, and I put my hands up to my ears to block it out, but it only gets louder and louder until I find myself screaming for it to stop.

*

I bolt out of my bed and run to Aiden's room; the need to check he isn't dead is suffocating. Seeing he is breathing, I take a deep breath, relieved. I lie down in bed with him, my head on his chest, listening to his slowing heartbeat.

"I need you not to die, okay? My heart hurts enough from losing Dayton; I can't lose you too. So, please, don't die." I whisper into the darkness, letting the tears run free.

"I thought I would find you in here." A voice says from behind me by the window.

"It's not exactly a surprise; I've been spending most of my time here recently anyway." I reply, wiping the tears away and sitting up.

"I'm surprised you are still here; Dayton made it clear he didn't want you around." Mason sits down in the chair by the bed.

"Technically, he said I could stay until the war is over." I tell him matter-of-factly.

"Are you okay?"

"Of course, my Mate doesn't want me; who wouldn't be okay with that?" I reply sarcastically. Mason just watches me, waiting.

I let out a sigh and tighten my arms around Aiden's stomach.

"I don't blame him; I knew he would; it just hurts." I shrug like it's no big deal.

"I'm sorry he's treating you this way," Mason puts a hand on my leg, trying to comfort me. I pull my leg away.

"You don't love me." I tell him matter-of-factly, and he raises an eyebrow.

"How do you know what I feel?"

"You know, despite everything I have done to Dayton, all the secrets and drama I have brought to his Pack. I started this war, I'm the reason your parents are dead. Yet he didn't kick me out straight away because he knows I have to get my Wolf back. He is still putting me first; despite everything, he is still putting me first. That's the sacrifice of love. Your needs and your happiness aren't as important. If you loved me, you wouldn't be hell-bent on killing Drake before I can get my Wolf. You refuse to sacrifice anything for me; you make a point of not sacrificing for me."

"I don't have the luxury of doing that," Mason states, standing up and walking around the bedroom.

I frown, "Yes, you do; you just don't want to. It is more important for you to get your revenge on Drake for what he did to your parents than me to get my Wolf back. You won't sacrifice it. It has nothing to do with luxury. You don't love me. So that comment you made earlier was laughable."

I stand up, and Mason is standing in front of me before I can blink. So close to me, I can hear his heart beating. I go to speak, but before anything comes out of my mouth, he leans down and kisses me.

For a few seconds, I get swept up in the moment. For a few seconds, I don't care. Then the few seconds are over; I snap out of it and push Mason away. He doesn't stop me.

"I'm sorry, I had to test it. I had to see if there was something there."

*

I walk into the front room with a cup of tea to see Austin had the same idea. He is sitting on the sofa with a mug in his hand, not noticing that I've just walked in as he is so lost in thought. What is it about the early hours of the morning in this place that makes everyone so contemplative?

"Hi," I say softly, and his head snaps in my direction.

"Hi, you're up early," he comments, and we both glance at the clock that shows 5:00 AM.

"I could say the same for you." I sit at the other end of the sofa; he watches me carefully.

"Couldn't sleep; I have a lot to think about. What about you?"

"I had a nightmare about Aiden and Drake," I shake my head as if that will get rid of the horrible dream.

He nods slowly, "Then your Mates brother kisses you; people just fall in love with you, don't they?" He is asking in a light-hearted way, but there is something in his voice that I can't place. I feel the need to tread very carefully.

"You heard that?"

"I may have been in my own little world, but a good Beta still pays attention to his surroundings. It makes your choice more difficult now, doesn't it? You now have three people to choose between, and it used to be two." Austin says, watching me place my cup on the coffee table and run my hands through my hair.

"It's still between two; Mason doesn't even come into it," I say and then frown and turn to face Austin. "You know when you asked me to choose between Dayton and Aiden?"

He nods slowly.

"I would have picked Aiden." I tell him truthfully.

"I know. I didn't know then, but you have shown it every day the last couple of days. You spend most of your time with Aiden; even when Dayton was unconscious, you went in once. You made your choice." Austin shrugs like it's no big deal. Odd.

"I spent every day with Aiden in the cells, watching as he was tortured, in pain, or knocked unconscious. When I see him like that, do you know what I feel now? Numb. I can visit him every day because I'm used to it. Dayton, I've never seen broken or bruised. Seeing him like that pains me, scares me, and frustrates me because there is nothing I can do to help him. I didn't visit Dayton because it was too hard to see him like that."

Austin nods, finishes his tea, and gets up.

"I better get back to bed before Aria wonders where I've gone."

As he gets to the door, he stops and faces me.

"So that you know, I've spent most of tonight trying to think of a way to convince Dayton that he has made a mistake letting you go. You are the best thing to ever happen to him, and to lose you would be the stupidest thing he has ever done."

Lilla

I wake abruptly to an ear-piercing scream and immediately look around for the threat. I was still on the sofa; I must have fallen asleep soon after Austin left. I hear the scream again. I didn't imagine it. I listen to footsteps running upstairs. They stop, and I hear a door open.

"Lilla?" Dayton shouts urgently.

"I'm downstairs," I shout, and the footsteps all race down the stairs. Dayton, Austin, and Aria appear.

"Are you okay? We heard you scream, and you weren't in your room?" Dayton asks, looking me over, making sure I wasn't injured. He still cared, despite everything.

"I didn't scream," I tell them, and they frown; they don't believe me.

"Lilla?" Alec bursts in the front door with Russell. He sees me on the sofa, with everyone around me, and runs over to me. "What's wrong? What happened?"

"I didn't scream." I say again with a firmness to my voice.

"Are you sure?" He asks.

Why doesn't anyone believe me?

The Ancestors come running in before they can open their mouths; the piercing scream is heard again.

Mason comes in behind the Ancestors, looking a little pale.

"See, it wasn't me!" I say, pointing at my mouth as proof.

Jace comes running in.

"Oh, for God's sake, it wasn't me!" I cry out.

Seriously am I the only one that screams around here?

Jace looks at me, confused. "I know, it's one of the Rogues outside the property. She is in pain, but she won't let Doc look at her; I figured you two should speak to her." He points at Mason and me.

My eyes shoot to Mason and the unspoken words of urgency are evident on our faces. We immediately follow Jace as the rest turn behind us and follow us out to the clearing.

"She kept asking for fruit," Jace tells us as we walk. "She kept saying... pears? No, that's not right. Strawberries?" He continues to ask himself, clearly not remembering what fruit this Rogue wanted.

"If she's in pain, why is she asking for fruit?" Alec asks, confused.

"I have no idea; she keeps saying I need... what was it?" Jace begins mumbling to himself, trying to figure it out.

We all walk in silence while he tries to figure it out.

"Peaches! I think it was peaches!" Jace says triumphantly.

I stop abruptly, grabbing Jace by the arm, making him stop too.

"What did she say exactly?"

"I told you, she asked for peaches." Jace tells me, frowning at me.

"What actual words did she use?" I say through gritted teeth.

Jace thinks, "I'm looking for peaches; please get me peaches."

I feel physically sick.

"What's wrong?" Alec asks.

"She's not asking for fruit."

*

"What about you? Do you have any family?" I ask as we get to know each other. We might as well; we were stuck together for a while.

"A sister, she is younger than me. Her name is Sierra. She is probably looking for me." He frowns. "She probably won't stop until she finds me."

"It must be nice to know that your sister is looking for you?" I ask, wishing I could say that my brother knew I was missing.

"Yeah, it is. My sister is smart; she won't ever walk into a Territory and ask for me by name; it's too dangerous that way." He tells me; I nod; before I met him, he was a well-known Rogue, always causing trouble in Packs; he was hunted, so never stayed in one place too long.

"How will she ever find you?" I ask, and he smiles.

"She asked me the same thing the first time I ran, so I came up with a code word and promised to tell at least one person I trust whenever I settle down. So even if I move on before she finds me, she can say the code word, and they can point her in the right direction."

"How did you come up with the code word?"

"It was the first thing that popped into my head, to be honest."

"What was it?"

"Peaches."

*

"Sierra?" I ask, moving cautiously to the woman curled up in a ball in pain.

"You know me?" She asks.

Her face is pale, ashen; her thick brown hair flows around her in ringlets. In any other situation I would tell her that she has hair I would die for.

"Yeah, I know you; he told me all about you." I say softly, kneeling in front of her. She smiles, relieved before letting out another scream.

"Where does it hurt?" I ask, and slowly she unfolds herself, letting her legs straighten. I see the dark and wet patch on her clothes as she does.

"Shit," I murmur. I make her jump at my sudden movements as I close the gap between us and lift her shirt. There I see the bite mark. A Wolf has bitten her.

"It hurts." She mutters.

"Okay, I need you to trust me, okay? That man over there, he's the Pack doctor, he can help you, you have to let him," I tell her; she watches me for a second and then nods.

"If my brother trusts you, then I trust you," Sierra says, and I smile at her.

I looked at Doc and gestured for him to come over. She grabs my hand while Doc assesses it. He glances at me and shakes his head slightly. It's serious.

She's lost too much blood; she isn't healing. She's dying.

Doc mind-links me; I'm slightly shocked because he hadn't done it before.

I'm not letting her die.

"Okay, I need you to trust me a bit more, the cut you have is serious, and you aren't healing, and the Doc can't do a lot to help. Do you see that woman? She can heal you, but she has to bite you first, okay?" She nods but begins to shake with fear.

I call Emily over, and without question, she bites down on Sierra's neck.

As she does, Sierra begins to fall asleep, and with one last squeeze on my hand, she is out.

"Can you bring her back to Dayton's, please? Put her in my bed." I ask Blake, who nods and picks her up.

"Who is her brother?" Dayton asks, and I turn to face him; I forgot he was there and am surprised he spoke to me.

"Aiden."

Dayton

Let me know when you are ready, and we will cross over. I mind-link to my people in charge of a section of Werewolves, all at different parts, surrounding the Pack. Most were at the tunnels, where they could get in undetected. I had many Werewolves with me, mainly my Pack; Lilla and Mason had mostly Rogues; I doubt they would listen to anyone else.

The Ancestors had set up an open mind-link, so we could all communicate without any issues. We had my whole Pack, all the Rogues that Lilla and Mason recruited, and Dan's Pack.

A lot of people are going to die today.

We had more men than Drake, at least 500 more, but there was a reason people didn't fight Drake's Pack. It took less than a week for Pack's across the country to learn not to mess with his Pack. That's how ruthless they are.

Lilla?

Yes, Dayton?

I don't know if we are going to survive this. So I need you to know something.

What?

I love you

*

As I throw off the Wolf, I decide to shift. Being a Wolf will be easier. I hear a growl and turn to see a Wolf with his teeth bared, his legs bent in a crouch position as if hunting his prey. I am not prey, and I show him by making myself seem larger, the hair on my back bristles, and my lips curl back, exposing my fangs.

It's what all Alpha's do to warn the lower rank from fighting them. The pup ignores my warning and lunges for me.

I dodge him and snap at him; he only lunges for me again. He manages to smack into me; nothing happens except my paws moving a little. Getting irritated with the pup, my teeth clamp down on his neck hard until he stops moving.

I throw him to the side, out of my way, and look around for my next target. I find myself lost in all the red. As if someone had painted a pretty picture but then decided to throw red paint on it. The grass, the bark of the trees, even a bird sitting on a branch is smothered in blood. Nothing is it's colour of origin.

Dayton! I turn to see Blake's Wolf throwing a Pup to the side. **Mason!** That is all he manages out before another Wolf attacks him.

I immediately search for the black Wolf. I see him running after another Wolf— a black, grey, and white one.

Go! Before he kills Drake and Lilla doesn't get her Wolf back. Go before all of this is for nothing.

I immediately push off my hind legs, jumping over the pup I've just killed. I kill anything that gets in my way, my sights set on Mason and Drake's direction. Just as I catch up, my Wolf decides to speak.

This seems too easy; maybe we should go back?

Why would I do that?

What if this is part of Drake's plan? What if this is a trap?

Lilla

When we get the signal, we all open the doors and begin our way into the outside. We surprise them at first. They weren't expecting anyone to use the tunnels; they weren't expecting anyone else full stop.

Most of the Werewolves had shifted already; I, for obvious reasons, had not. They all start to run past me into the fight. I freeze; so much blood makes me want to throw up. I had fought before, against many people, and obviously, I had killed before, but this looked like a massacre.

All of this just for my Wolf? All of these people will die because I refused to give up my Wolf?

What have I done?

Before getting caught up in my thoughts, I'm brought to the floor by a Wolf, who growls and snaps at me. I don't react, stunned by the abruptness of it. All of a sudden, the Wolf is gone. I sit up to see another Wolf ripping into his neck. The Wolf turns and growls at me.

"Luke?" I gasp, and he snaps at me.

Thank you, I say opening up a mind-link between us. There is hope for this Pack, I found Luke's humanity, and he held on to it long enough for me to get there. There is hope.

Out of the corner of my eye, I see a Wolf running at Luke. I return the favour by pushing Luke out of the way. I'm slightly surprised that the Wolf is from Midnight Moon Pack and not one of those fighting with us, but if they saw Luke save me, they are out to kill him.

The Wolf snaps at me, his teeth getting closer and closer to me. I swing my leg around and kick him in the side. He growls at me, and I arch an eyebrow, taunting him. He runs at me, but I push off the ground and land on his back just before he reaches me. For a moment, I can imagine it looks like I'm riding a Wolf, and I almost laugh at the idea.

The Wolf almost manages to throw me off, so I sink my teeth into his neck without hesitation. Using the one part of my wolf I have left. The one part of my wolf that I don't use unless absolutely necessary.

Even though he locked away my Wolf, the one thing I managed to keep is my Venom, and I am thankful for that, I can't help but think, as the Wolf below me becomes sluggish and a few seconds later drops dead.

As I retract my teeth from his neck, I feel a hot breath on my neck and freeze. A growl erupts from the Wolf standing over me, and I try to think fast. I turn my head and come face to face with the Wolf's razor-sharp teeth. I breathe slowly and try to think of a way out of this, but I draw a blank.

The Wolf lets out one last growl before going for me. I let out a scream as his teeth sink into my skin. I feel myself being lifted off the dead Wolf, and I scream again as the pain radiates through me. I'm dropped to the ground with a wince.

I need a plan, but the pain stops my brain from working. Come on, Lilla! Think! I shout at myself, but still, my mind won't cooperate. My vision blurs, and the Wolf is gone when it becomes clear again. I lie on the floor, just breathing through the pain. I don't heal. That's my problem. I won't heal without my Wolf.

Then I remember why we are all doing this. We are fighting this battle for my Wolf, so I can be healed when I get injured so that I can shift. So, I can be strong. So, I can be me.

"Lilla! Shit! Hold on one second. I'll heal you." I hear Blake's voice, but my eyes are too heavy to keep open.

"Lilla? Shit! Lilla, stay with me!" I fight the urge to sleep and feel his teeth sink into my neck, just above my Mark.

*

As I run onto the street where I grew up, I freeze.

This is the setting from my nightmare.

This is when Mason appears holding Drake by the neck.

This is when Mason kills my only chance at getting my Wolf back.

I slowly walk towards my house, cautiously as if they will jump out at me. No one appears. I decide to go in, completely thrown that no one was here and that nothing I saw has come to fruition. I began to walk back down the street and found an empty house to search.

I let out a yelp when I turn the corner and nearly smack into a pup from Drake's Pack. He growls at me and gets ready to attack, but I have him against the wall by his neck before he can.

"Where is Drake?" I ask, but the pup only growls. I squeeze a little harder.

"Listen to me, pup; if you don't tell where he is, he will die. I'm trying to save his life." The pup only growls again.

"Tell me where Drake is now!" I command. I drop him as burning pain runs through my muscles, feeling weaker from it.

"Alpha Drake is in the Torture Cells." I ignore his obvious hint at calling Drake 'Alpha' and make my way to the cells, panicking.

Why would he be in the torture cells? The only person I can think that he would hold there is my mother.

I rush into the prison cells, calling for her, knowing that she will hear me from the Torture cells if she is there.

As I open the cell door, I begin to shout her name, but the sound gets stuck in my throat as I see the sight in front of me.

*

"Lilla, I'm so glad you could join us!" Drake welcomes me cheerfully as I stare at the sight in front of me in shock.

"What's going on?" I finally manage to find my words, and Drake smiles at me — the same smile I got just before he took my Wolf.

"You and I are going to play a game. Like the one we used to play when you were a child. Do you remember?" He asks, and I nod slowly.

Whenever Drake visited, which wasn't much when I was younger, he would always bring three gifts. He would line them up for us all to see and make us choose. It wasn't a game, but it was half the fun of getting the gifts.

"Instead of playing with gifts, we will play with people. Let me introduce them!" Drake says, his excitement evident by his tone of voice, and he is practically jumping around.

"First, we have Aiden, your first love; he would do anything for you. He even gave up his freedom for you. Unfortunately, he is dying, but if you pick him — maybe you can save him!" Drake says, talking like a game show host.

"How did you get him here? He was at Dayton's house in bed; how did you get him?"

"Your Pack is very Ancestor friendly since the Ancestors showed up — they brought me to him with only a little bit of persuasion." Drake informs me before moving on to the next person. Meaning he commanded them.

"Next, we have Dayton, your soul mate. Again, he would do anything for you, he has forgiven you for almost everything you have done — except being the reason his parents are dead, but they do say love conquers all.

"Lastly, we have Mason, he was a bit late to the game, but he loves you, nonetheless. He has looked out for you from the moment he met you; he wants you to be happy."

Dayton and Mason are watching me, but neither says a word.

"Okay, so I will let you pick one guy, the one you want to spend forever with. I will give you back your Wolf and let you and your chosen love live happily ever after, so make your choice wisely."

"What's the catch?" I ask, my throat dry. How was I supposed to pick?

"The catch is that I will kill the two you don't pick. Right here, in front of you." Drake finishes explaining with a smile spreading across his face.

"You sadistic son of a bitch!" I spit out.

He laughs at me.

"Why do they look weak?" I ask, and Drake walks over and stands next to me.

"I had to give them a little bit of that pure silver — not Aiden — he has had enough, but the other two wouldn't come willingly. So, come on, Lilla, choose. You said you would do anything to get your Wolf back. Well, this is the anything."

Drake

There are many reasons Packs go to war. Some Alphas are just bloodthirsty and are always looking for the next fight—some Alphas like the thrill of cheating death repeatedly.

They tend to be the minority.

Then some fight for something or someone. They believe in their cause. They tend to be the majority.

There is always the bad guy, the guy who hurt that someone in some way or took that special something of their Alpha's, but the bad guy... maybe he has a point of view... perhaps he thinks he should be the good guy.

The bad guy believes what the good guy believes; that what they are doing is right for them and the people they love, for their cause.

I read once, somewhere, that everyone is the good guy. It just depends on the point of view.

It's true if you think about it.

Lilla, my beautiful niece, is fighting for her old Pack, her old home, her Wolf. She is fighting for all the unjust that has happened to her, that I have done to her. I get how she can be perceived as the good guy in this; if this were a book, I would say she was the good guy, but what about me?

I'm fighting for what Lilla has done, for killing my brother, an Alpha, and Ancestor. Killing him is illegal, and no one would have thought twice if someone else had done it and I had taken their Wolf and Pack, but because it was Lilla...

From my point of view, I'm the good guy, and Lilla is the bad guy, but what does it matter?

No one cares about what I think or my point of view because I'm the bad guy... so why not?

Why not torture Lilla again and again? Why not take her Wolf? Why not make her life a misery every chance I have? Why not turn her Pack against her?

Why not live up to everyone's expectations?

Blake

"Has anyone seen Lilla?" I shout, and the people around me turn and look at each other. The war was over; we had won, but now I couldn't find Lilla; I was worried. The Midnight Moon Pack had surrendered not long ago when it became apparent they were losing, more than half of their Pack was dead, and the rest were injured. They couldn't continue to fight us.

I began to search for Lilla, in the injured and the dead, Austin, Alec, Russell, and a few other Wolves I didn't know were looking too.

"Has anyone seen Dayton either? Or Mason?" Austin asks, and I freeze.

"Shit! Drake!" I shout, and immediately we begin to run, all of us making our way to where we know Drake will be dying and Lilla will be losing her Wolf.

Out of the corner of my eye, I see movement and turn my head to see Lilla emerging from a metal door covered in blood.

I stop running and face her, "Lilla? Are you okay?" I ask, running over to her, but she puts up her hands, stopping us from getting close.

"It's not my blood. None of it is my blood." She manages to say before she breaks down in tears. Heart-wrenching sobs escape her, and none of us knows what to do or say.

"Lilla, what happened?" Alec asks as I pick her up and sit her on the wall just by the door.

"He wanted me to choose. He told me to choose. Told me I didn't have a choice." Lilla says between sobs.

"What do you mean?" I ask; I try to step away, but Lilla grabs my shirt, not letting go, so I sit down and place an arm around her. She leans on my chest, and we all watch as Lilla cries.

"We had a plan, Blake. A good plan, and Drake wasn't meant to know the plan, but he must have. How else did he know to change it?" Lilla asks frantically, and I shake my head. She is right; we had a plan.

"What happened, Lilla?" I ask more forcefully, pulling her away from me and holding her by the shoulders.

"Drake had Dayton, Mason, and Aiden, and he wanted me to choose between them to get my Wolf back. I refused to choose at first, but he told me if I didn't, then he would kill all of them. I had to choose who I wanted to spend my life with, and he would kill the other two. It wasn't part of the plan, Blake!" Lilla says before breaking down again.

"Who did you pick?" Austin asks, and Lilla turns to him shaking her head.

"Lilla! Who did you pick?!" Austin shouts, and Lilla's eyes turn vacant, cold, and emotionless.

"I didn't pick anyone."

Lilla

"I won't do it. I won't choose. You can't make me!" I say, shaking my head; Drake just laughs.

"I can't make you? If you don't choose, I will just kill them all. It's a simple solution." He shrugs while I stand there.

How do I choose? How am I meant to choose between them? I begin to panic, and Drake sighs dramtically.

"How about we ask their opinion? I mean, I can pretty much guess they all beg for you to pick themselves but might as well ask. See, look at me being all helpful!" Drake says, proud of himself for his seemingly helpful advice.

"Aiden, we can't ask, so what do you think he would say? I think he would beg you to choose him–"

"Then you don't know Aiden because he would never do that. He would tell me it was my choice not to feel bad and that he would love me anyway." I say, tears running down my cheek, which I quickly wipe.

"Okay, we can disagree on that one. Next Mason, what do you say?" Drake asks, and Mason looks at me, almost pleading.

"Pick Dayton, please. Pick my brother, he is your Mate, and you love him. Please pick my brother." Mason says, his voice breaking slightly.

"What does Dayton say?" Drake asks, obviously loving this whole spectacle.

"Pick me." He says simply, and I frown. I would never have expected Dayton to say that. "I'm telling – no – I'm ordering you to pick me." He says, lacing his words with an Alpha command, something we both know doesn't affect me.

Why is the ordering me to pick him? He knows I hate being told what to do. He is doing it on purpose.

Something switches in me.

"There you go. Two for Dayton, I guess that's your answer. So, pick and get your Wolf back." Drake says, almost giddy with anticipation.

"You know what, Drake. Keep my Wolf. I don't want her anymore." I say, exhausted.

Drake's smile falls.

"What?"

"No matter how this ends, whether you kill all three or two of them, giving me my Wolf back will only cause more misery and pain that I don't want. So, I don't want my Wolf."

"Then all of this is pointless, all this fighting, this war, us sitting here is pointless." Mason growls, annoyed.

I shrug, "I don't care. If you give me my Wolf back, I'm just going to be living in hell; she will never forgive me. I don't want her back, so keep her; I'd prefer to live as a human than suffer the pain and misery having her back will cause."

Drake watches me carefully. "So, giving you your Wolf will be more painful and cause more misery than you feel now..." he repeats, and I nod.

"You shouldn't have told me that." Before I can blink, Drake is in front of me, and I scream as his teeth sink into the Mark he created.

*

Wakey, wakey. A voice sings, and I let out a groan.

Really? I thought you would be more excited to get me back! The voice says, and I smile.

Well, hello stranger! What have you been up to?

Nothing much, been doing a bit of this, a bit of that. I'm sorry I haven't spoken to you in a while; I've been SUPER busy!

I chuckle in response.

Okay, so what's the game plan here? You didn't mean what you said, right? That you didn't want me?

I hear the hurt in her voice, and I'm quick to reassure her.

No! I didn't, I promise. You know I love you. How did you know what I said, though?

Once Drake gave me back to you, I got your memories; it's why you blacked out. It was so cool! It was like a TV show! Seriously you have been very busy! Let's focus on the situation at hand. What's the plan, Batman?

Oh, how I've missed you! I slowly stand up and begin to chuckle.

"What's so funny?" Drake asks, watching me.

"I played you. I managed to play you." I say, and I smile at him.

"What do you mean?"

"I don't want my Wolf; it will cause me too much misery." I say again, with a melodramatic cry and Drake's eyes narrow. "I played you. Of course, I want my Wolf back. Why wouldn't I want my Wolf back? She wouldn't hate me; she's my Wolf, for God's sake!"

"You're lying!" Drake shouts, and I laugh again.

"I've been playing everyone from the beginning. I got to Aiden in the cells and look how that worked out. He gave up his freedom for me. Mason, I had wrapped around my finger from the second I met him, and I got a bunch of Rogues to fight with me. As for Dayton, he was the easiest to manipulate. I'm his Mate, all I had to do was bat my eyelids, and he would do anything I pleased. Thanks to you taking my Wolf, I had to learn to play people to get what I want." I say as cold as possible, and Drake looks at me, shocked.

"That's... I'm..." He trails off, lost for words, and I smile at him.

"You've lost Drake. I got my Wolf back. I won, and you've lost. The games over." I explain, and Drake shakes his head.

"I can still kill them! All three of them! I can kill them now!" Drake says, moving closer to the three men.

"I have my Wolf back, Drake. I'm the most powerful Wolf in the world so go on. Kill them... I dare you."

Lilla

"Really? You want to put the lives of the people you love on the line to prove what?" Drake asks.

"For goodness' sake, Drake, why aren't you getting this? I. DON'T. CARE. I have my Wolf back; I have been playing everyone from the beginning to get her back, and now I have her. I. DON'T CARE." I tell him, getting slightly annoyed, and I can't help but relish in the fact that I don't feel any pain anymore.

Oh my God. I forgot how dramatic you could be. My Wolf says, and I can imagine her rolling her eyes.

I always like playing the over-dramatic girl. Don't tell me you haven't missed me?

"You don't care? You, Lilla, the girl who would move heaven and earth to make people happy even if it meant you were unhappy, doesn't care whether I kill these three Wolves?" Drake says, not believing me.

"Drake, I'm not a girl anymore; I don't expect rainbows and unicorns. I've grown up a lot over the years, thanks to you and your brother. I know how shit the world is. I know that I can't make everyone happy. I know that there is no point wasting my energy on it, but I might as well make myself happy. Which is what I've done, I have my Wolf, so I'm good."

I cross my arms over my chest and cock my hip.

You know I didn't think I meant that much to you. It brings a tear to my eye. It also makes it awkward because you have been doing everything

possible to find a way to get me back, and I've been chilling out...really awkward.

"You aren't the girl I remember; you aren't the girl my brother raised." Drake says, sounding shocked, and I let out a laugh.

"Whose fault is that?" I ask, and I watch as Drake shrugs, a frown marring his face.

"I did what I had to do." He says casually, and I stare at him with an open mouth.

"You had to torture me every day, did you? You had to block my Wolf? You had to bring so much misery to me?"

"You killed my brother! Stop making out like you didn't deserve it! He was an Ancestor and an Alpha. You are lucky to be alive!"

I feel the anger rise in me, and I struggle to keep myself from shifting. "He tried to rape me. He raped and murdered people in his Pack for no reason! He was a monster, a rabid animal that had to be put down." I say, and Drake lets out a thunderous growl.

"Enough! Enough of your lies!"

"I'm not lying! You've seen the memories; you've seen what he did!"

"You twisted your memories! You tampered with them! Your father would never do the things you said he did."

I let out a sigh, the anger slowly ebbing away, being replaced with exhaustion at having to have this argument. "You know what, Drake, believe what you want. I don't care anymore. You'll never believe me, so do whatever." I say with a shrug.

"Okay." Before I have time to register anything, Drake is in their cell and slits Mason's, Aiden's, and Dayton's throats. When he is finished, Drake drops the knife and smiles at me.

"Do you still not care?"

Letting out a laugh, Drake disappears. I'm frozen on the spot; I don't know what to do. He killed them all, and I can do nothing but stand and watch the blood run down their necks and life drain from their eyes.

*

"No, they can't be dead. Dayton can't be dead." Austin shouts at me, tears running down his face. "Why don't you care?" He shrieks when I don't say a thing.
"I do care," I say softly, and Austin scoffs.
"Why tell Drake that you don't if you do?" Someone asks; I'm not sure who, I don't recognise them. I had stopped crying now, my cheeks stained with tears, my throat was burning from the sobbing and the talking. It was nothing compared to the pain in my heart.
"Drake kills the things you care about. I had to convince him I didn't care. Dayton and I had a plan. He had to pretend to hate me so that it would be easier when I told Drake to kill them all. We had a plan." I say again, trying to convince myself.
"Drake killed them anyway, so what was the point?"
"The point was Drake still wanted her to choose." Everyone turns to the voice in the metal door that I had walked out of. "Lilla has the power to heal people, to bring them back from the brink of death. Drake knew she would only have time to save one; he made her choose."
"And she chose you?" a voice calls from the crowd surrounding us.
"I was always going to choose him."

*

Oi, snap out of it and save them! My Wolf shouts, and it's what I need to snap into action.
I don't have time to save all three, do I?
No, two if you're lucky, but the question is, who do we save first? My Wolf asks, and without even thinking, I run over to the guy I would choose. The

guy I've known deep down that I would always choose—the guy I couldn't bear to live without.

"Dayton?" I call his name, willing him to respond. With a flicker of his eyelids as he attempts to open them, I sink my teeth into his neck. My Wolf and I begin to heal him; I feel the spilled blood dry and the cut heal. When the cut is completely healed, I pull away, his heartbeat is strong. I stare at him, willing him to wake up, but he doesn't. It may take a while, but I've never been the patient type.

Try and heal one of the others. My Wolf pushes me forward.

Who?

I don't know. It's up to you.

Really? You haven't got an opinion?

I didn't say that, but we both know who I would choose, but you need to want to pick him too.

Dayton will kill me. He won't forgive me.

Do what you have to do, Lilla. My Wolf says, so before I change my mind and before it's too late, I sink my neck into the guy I choose to save.

I think that part of you is still the girl Drake expects you to be. You still want to make sure people are happy, even if it means sacrificing your happiness.

I walk over to Aiden and stare at his lifeless body as she says it.

He would have survived if I had picked him first; I could have saved the other two if I had chosen him first because the others were stronger. I say as the tears begin to fall.

"My poor, poor Aiden," I mutter. "I'm sorry, I'm so sorry." I say before I begin to cry, my heart aching at losing him.

Lilla, I know this hurts, but you have to go after Drake and kill him. My Wolf says, but I shake my head.

I can't leave him. He should be alive. There has to be a way to save him. He did everything he could to make sure I stayed alive, and when the roles were reversed, I let him die. I lean my forehead against his.

"Aiden, I'm so sorry. Please forgive me. You know I love you. I'm so sorry." I kiss his lips, saying my final goodbyes.

Dayton

I wake up and groan—everything aches. My throat is the worst, though; it feels as if someone ripped it open — oh wait, they did.

I see Mason sitting next to me, his heart beating strong. Aiden is next to him, but I can't hear his heart beating.

Hey, get it together. Our Mate is outside, her Wolf is there too, and she is in so much pain. Go to her!

I get up and head out of this horrible place with another groan. I can't believe it exists; I can't even begin to imagine the memories it brings back for Lilla. As I move through the door, heading outside, I hear people talking.

"Drake killed them anyway, so what was the point?"

"The point was Drake still wanted her to choose." Everyone turns to face me; I notice that Lilla doesn't. "Lilla has the power to heal people, to bring them back from the brink of death. Drake knew she would only have time to save one; he made her choose." I say, and I feel an overwhelming sense of sadness that I don't recognise as my own.

It's Lilla and her Wolf. My Wolf informs me.

"And she chose you?" I hear someone say. I go to answer even though I don't have a response, but Lilla answers first.

"I was always going to choose him." She says, and my Wolf and I work to hide our excitement and happiness at the statement.

"You could have fooled us." Rowan says sarcastically under his breath, and within seconds he is on the ground with Lilla on top of him.

"Don't. Don't make petty remarks about whom I chose or how surprised you are because I'm not in the mood. I love Dayton; my Wolf loves Dayton. We were always going to choose Dayton; there isn't a doubt in my mind, but I couldn't let Drake know that, otherwise, Dayton would have been dead a long time ago, and I wouldn't have been able to save him. Dayton and I had a plan, and it worked. He doesn't hate me, never hated me, and never will hate me." Lilla growls out. Rowan struggles beneath her; he is one of the best fighters in the Pack, which is why he is our trainer, and to see him struggling beneath Lilla is shocking.

"What about Aiden?" He asks, and we all watch as all the anger and energy seep out of Lilla. She lets go of him, and Rowan stills, watching her too. He sits up so he is at eye level with Lilla, and without a word, he wraps an arm around Lilla, and we watch silently as my Little Rogue breaks down.

*

"Against my better judgment, I will have to hope love conquers all and that you mean it when you said you'd forgive Lilla for anything. Dayton, I wish this could wait, but we don't have time. Emily will give you back your memories after I've told you the truth about our parents."

"What truth?" I ask.

"I know I told you some of it. I told you that Drake commanded our parents to kill us, but it was all of the Ancestors. Our parents were traitors; they fought against the Ancestors and killed the first Werewolves that the Ancestors changed — except Layla. They went with the whole 'an eye for an eye' thing as punishment. Our parents killed their 'children,' so they wanted us to be killed but decided to command our parents to do it. Then Lilla's dad started dreaming about her death and saw how it would play out because they killed you, so they tried to stop it. I was suspicious when they came home because, well...it all seemed too easy, so I kept an eye on them, and I watched as they tried to kill you.

I couldn't lose you, Dayton. I would rather have my brother than my parents, so I killed them.

"I hated myself afterwards, even when the Ancestors turned up to explain why it was their fault, the blood was still on my hands, and as punishment to myself, I asked them to rewrite your memories. I'm sorry, Dayton." Mason finishes.

I didn't believe him; my parents weren't what he was describing.

"Emily is going to give you your memories now." Mason says, and suddenly, a sharp pain hits me.

"Mason! Mummy and Daddy are back!"

My child's voice sounds through my head, and I watched scene after scene play out, exactly how Mason described it.

Expect one. A memory of Lilla talking to a younger me.

"Dayton, listen to me. I know you won't hate me for this. I know you will love me because we both know it wasn't my fault. I have a plan. It's a good one, but it means you have to pretend to hate me. It means you have to break my heart. You and your Wolf can't even show a glimpse of love for me and if you do, pretend you are finding the whole thing difficult; I don't know, figure it out. I love you, Dayton, but for Drake to believe I don't care anymore, for him to think that I don't want my Wolf back, I need him to think you hate me."

As I focus on my surroundings, I look at Mason and Emily — we had all stopped saying "Ancestor" before their name per their request — I gave a small nod and asked to be left alone to process all the information.

Lilla was right; I don't hate her; none of it is her fault.

I get why Mason did it; although it would take me a while I could see myself forgiving him. After a couple of hours of rest, I decided I better do what was asked. I had to break My Little Rogues heart.

*

Lilla stopped crying and pulled away from Rowan as if a scent had caught her attention. She wiped her tears and began to growl, and I couldn't help but notice that a wince didn't follow the growl. I watched as the Wolves began to step away, almost unsure of whether they should be scared of her or not. Even I wasn't sure.

"Lilla?" I asked with trepidation, and she turned to me, but she looked like she didn't recognise me, like I was a stranger. Gone were her beautiful purple eyes; instead, they were blood-red.

"I want him dead. I want to kill him myself. I want to feel his bones crush beneath my fingers; my teeth sink into his flesh and blood pouring into my mouth. I want to feel the life slip away from him knowing that I killed him."

"Okay, then we will find him, and he can do that." I reassured her, almost frightened of her myself.

"No, I want to kill him, but I won't. Instead, I'm going to lock him in your cells and torture him every day; I'm going to inject him with Pure Silver and cut him and beat him so that his Wolf is too weak to heal him, and then when he is losing his hope, when he wants me to kill him, I'm going to take his Wolf from him."

"Lilla–"

"No matter how much he begs, I will make sure he lives forever without his Wolf, without company, and his Ancestor powers. I'm going to rip away everything that makes him scary, everything that made me fear him, and even then, it will never be enough punishment for taking Aiden away from me."

"Then you are no better than him," I tell her, but Lilla grins with a maniacal gleam in her eye.

"So people keep telling me."

Lilla

"Are you hungry?" Dayton asks as we step into his house. I shook my head; food was the last thing on my mind. I wanted to sleep. I wanted to curl up in a ball in bed and sleep until the pain in my heart went away.

"Lilla?" I turn to see Sierra sitting on the sofa, watching me expectantly. I push the feeling of wanting to run in the other direction and face her.

"Sierra," I breathe out her name, and she stands up.

"I am so sorry, Aiden was taken. An Ancestor came in and took him. I couldn't stop him. I was hoping you would find him and bring him back. Did you?" The hope written across her face feels like a blow to the stomach. All she wanted was to be reunited with him, and now I've taken that away from her.

"Sierra... why don't you sit down with me?" I gesture to the sofa she has just stood up from.

"Oh God, you were too late, weren't you?" Sierra says, sinking into the seat. I sit down next to her, and we face each other.

"Sierra, I'm so sorry, but I'm afraid... I'm afraid Aiden is... Aiden..." I trail off, unable to say the words, my voice catching.

"He's dead, isn't he?" Sierra whispers, and I nod as the tears fall down my cheek. "How?" She asks, her voice hoarse as she tries to stop herself from falling apart.

"Drake wanted me to choose," I say simply, and she frowns. "He wanted me to choose between Aiden, Dayton, and Mason," I explain, and she nods, glancing at Dayton.

"Obviously, you choose your Mate, but you would have chosen Aiden because you told me you loved Aiden; he was your first love." She says, and the pain in my heart deepens.

"He is – was – my first love." I tell her, but Sierra shakes her head and stands up.

"Then how did you manage to pick Mason over him? How do you manage to live with yourself knowing that you killed him?" Sierra is shouting now, and I stare at her. She's right; how can I live with myself?

You know why you chose Mason, Lilla. She can't see it now, but she will one day. My Wolf says in an unusual act of reassurance. **If not, we can always kill her, and we won't have a problem.** She finishes, the act of reassurance over and my Wolf back to normal.

Really, Kill her?

Okay, maybe that's a bit harsh! We could lock her away, out of sight, out of mind...?

You are lucky I know you are joking; if anyone else heard you right now...! I tell her, and my Wolf goes silent.

"I'm sorry, Sierra, I know he is your brother, and you have been looking for him for years, and I know you love him, I loved him too."

"If you did, he would be standing here with me now, instead of two brothers who HATE each other." Sierra says, pointing at the brothers as they stand there in silence. With another shake of her head, Sierra storms out. Dayton holds his arms open, and without hesitation, I walk over and into them.

"I'm going to make sure she is okay," Mason says, walking past us. I pull myself out of Dayton's grasp and grab Mason's arm.

"Leave her; she needs time to process it all." I say, and Mason looks at the door Sierra went through.

"But she's upset, and she's..." He trails off, watching the door she just exited before he turns and stares at me.

"I know, but Sierra has just lost her brother; the last thing she needs is to find out that he died so that her Mate could live."

*

"Are you hungry?" Dayton asks, walking over to the bed and lying in the space next to me. I was lying on my front, my arms tucked under the pillow. I mutter a no, and Dayton sighs. "You have to eat."

"No, I don't," I say automatically, and a small smile plays on his lips.

"Lilla, please eat for me?" He asks, turning onto his side and stroking the side of my face that isn't against the pillow.

"I'm not hungry," I say before turning my face over, so he can't see me. I hear another sigh before the weight on the bed disappears, and a few seconds later, the door shuts softly telling me Dayton is gone.

A tear escapes, I had been holding them in since I heard him coming up the stairs, but now I let them out. I'm exhausted. I haven't slept properly in days. Every time I close my eyes, I see Aiden dying, and I wake in a panic, my heart hurting as I remember it's not a nightmare. It's my reality.

I didn't know what was going on in the outside world, and I didn't care. After talking with Sierra, I hadn't left my room since. I hadn't showered; I hadn't even looked in the mirror, although I knew my hair was still black, and the bruises and scars were still there. My Wolf says I need to shift first before anything goes back to normal but as agitated as she is to run free, neither of us wants to leave the confines of my bedroom.

I close my eyes and try to sleep as my throat aches and my head pounds from all the crying.

"Why so sad, Beautiful?" I hear his voice and look around.

I'm back in Drake's cells.

"You're dead," I say, changing the words; Aiden frowns.

"They weren't the words; you are meant to say, ;'He Marked me' or something like that."

"But I'm sad because you are dead." I state, and Aiden sighs. The cells disappear, and he sits next to me on the floor.

"I know, but it's okay," Aiden says as I lean my head on his shoulder.

"It's not okay; I've lost you." My voice breaking. His arm wraps around me.

"I'll always be in your dreams; all you have to do is think of me," I wrinkle my nose and Aiden chuckles. "Wait, that sounded so cheesy."

"I think you are allowed to be cheesy when you're dead." I tell him, and he lets out another chuckle.

"My Little Angel." Aiden says on an exhale, and we fall into silence.

"I'm going to miss you," I say as the tears fall.

"I know, and that is okay, but you have to be strong. Hell, you are stronger than this. You aren't the type of girl to stay in bed and cry."

"No, I'm the type of girl who tries to jump off cliffs, so I don't have to feel anymore."

"Don't do that, okay? I couldn't have you dying too!" He pulls away and turns me to face him. "Lilla, you saved Mason instead of me because you knew I would never be able to live with myself if Sierra's Mate was killed to save my life. You did the right thing!"

"Sierra doesn't think so," I can't help but remark and Aiden rubs his hands up and down my arms.

"Sierra doesn't know you saved her Mate. When she does, she will understand."

"Great, so i just have to wait until she's 18. Do you think she'll find it weird that I start counting down the day's until next month?"

With a small smile from Aiden, we fall into silence and lie on the floor, heads touching as we lie diagonally.

"I'm going to miss you," I say into the silence.

"I know."

"I fought so hard to keep you alive, and then I killed you." A tear escapes, and I *wipe it away.*

"You didn't kill me; Drake did."

"I let you die. It's the same thing."

"Right, enough!" Aiden says forcefully. "What are you going to do when you wake up?"

"What?" I ask, turning my head to look at him.

"When you wake up, you won't want to get out of bed. So, we are making you a To-Do list. We will call it "Things you have to do when you wake." So first..." he trails off and looks me over. "You could probably do with a shower and a change of clothes."

"Hey!" I shout, hitting his arm.

"Oh, come on. It's true. Next...?"

"Okay, okay. Shower, change clothes, I should probably eat?" I ask, and Aiden nods.

"Good idea, next?"

"I need to shift."

"Okay, then?"

"I need to find my mum," I say, realising I have no idea where anyone is.

"Layla?"

"No, I don't care about her—my real mum. I haven't seen her since I ran. I don't even know if she made it out of the fight." I say, frowning.

"Okay, so find mum. Go on."

"Alec and the Ancestors, I don't know who is alive or dead. Once you died, I just didn't care anymore."

"Okay, check on loved ones in general, although I'm sure the Ancestors can take care of themselves. Next?"

"I should probably do something about the Midnight Moon Pack," sudden dread seeping through my pores. How am I meant to sort that issue out?

"Okay, good idea, keep going." Aiden continues, and I turn my head to face him.

"I have to plan your funeral and bury you."

"Oh, shall we leave that until last?" He asks, and I nod. "Next?"

"I have to find Drake."

"Definitely. Anything else? Although, I'm pretty sure we have everything covered."

"Dayton." I say his name with a smile which quickly turns into a frown. I sit up. "I don't feel any different towards him." I begin to panic, and Aiden sits up too.

"You probably need to shift first. You will get your hair colour and feelings towards your Mate back, and the scars and bruises will be gone."

"Promise?"

"Of course! My name is Aiden; I know everything!"

"You may be dead, but you still don't know how to be modest?" I say, and we laugh; it doesn't last long, but it feels good.

"You have a lot to do. You should probably wake up soon." Aiden says once our laughing subsides.

"That means I have to say goodbye, doesn't it?"

Aiden nods.

"I'll never see you again." I say, the pain in my heart growing.

"I'll be here. I've not got a lot on my plate, so I'll always be here."

I smile sadly. "Do you have to die?" I ask, the tears starting to fall.

"Yes, I do." He replies matter-of-factly.

"Why?"

"It's the way the world works," Aiden shrugs with a sad smile.

"It's not fair," I sound like a child throwing a tantrum.

"Life isn't, Lilla. You know that better than anyone." My mind flashes to another conversation I had about life not being fair, but it's gone before I can grab it.

"I don't want you to be dead."

"I know."

"Can we just lie down together for a while? Like we always said we would do back in the cells?"

"I'll tell you what. I'll stay with you, hold on to you tight, and keep you safe until you wake up, and then Dayton can take over, okay?"

I nod, the tears still flowing. I lie down, my head resting on his chest. I can hear his heartbeat thumping, and I treasure the sound. I turn in his arms and rest my chin on his chest, looking at him. Aiden waits patiently for me to say my final words.

"Loving you has made my life easier. It made my time in the cells bearable. Thank you. I love you with all my heart forever and always."

"Loving you made my life worth living. Having you get your Wolf back made dying worth it. You're going to do incredible things. I love you, Lilla; you were the love of my life. Mate or not."

I kiss him softly, tears running down my face.

"A kiss from an Angel, that was always on my bucket list."

Lilla

Morning! I let out a groan.

You are way too chipper for the morning. I grumble back to my Wolf.

I look up at the ceiling. I have no motivation to get up. I just can't be bothered. I feel better after I dreamt about Aiden; I got to say goodbye. It still hurts to think of him, but it's good to get a little closure.

We have a To-Do List, so get up, lazy butt! Hey, that rhymes! I am just so smart!

Oh my god, I haven't missed you in the mornings. And it doesn't rhyme!

We need to go for a run. I've been caged for too long! My Wolf shouts, and I groan again before getting out of bed. Food and shower can wait until I've been for a run. My Wolf needs it, and honestly, so could I. It'll do me a world of good.

I glance at the clock on the TV before I leave to see it says 7:00 am. Out in on the stairwell, I'm surprised I haven't seen anyone yet. Usually, I would have bumped into an Ancestor or something. Instead of overthinking it, I decided to enjoy the peace and quiet and make my way out the front door.

I head towards the forest and the safe enclosure of the trees and let out a deep breath; I try to shift.

There is no special way to shift. You don't imagine yourself as a Wolf and then bam! You're a Wolf. It's simple. When you get outraged and begin to shift, your Wolf pulls your human side back and out of the way. When you both want to shift, your human side is stepping out of the way while your Wolf steps forward. All I have to do is let go.

Your first shift is painful; everyone knows that. It's the first time all your bones are snapping and reforming; it will be painful. You don't expect that it still hurts no matter how many times you shift, no matter how often. It doesn't hurt as much, but the pain is still there. How can it not? Your bones are still snapping and reforming. You don't scream and cry every time you shift; you just get on with it.

This was like my first shift. Actually, this was worse than my first shift because I wasn't expecting it to be that bad. You know it will hurt on your first shift, everyone tells you. I thought it would be like that, maybe a little easier because I've been shifting recently, and my Wolf had tried to break out so many times. No. It was the most painful thing I have ever experienced. It was worse than my first time shifting and worse than being tortured by Drake.

As soon as my Wolf stepped forward, the pain radiated through me, making my skin burn. My tibia was the first bone to break. It ripped through my skin, causing blood to pour down the rest of my legs and my feet. Slowly, the rest of my bones followed, my skin ripped to shreds and replaced by fur. My teeth pulled and stretched; I always hated toothache. My nails grew to claws; I always liked that bit; I love having claws.

What feels like an eternity later, I am my Wolf, she is me. My senses are heightened. The smell if the grass under my feet is heavenly. The feel of the breeze in my fur as I stretch my achy limbs pulls a toothy grin to my face. To begin with, I walk slowly. For some reason, I feel like I might have forgotten how to walk. Once I am sure of myself, though, I run. I let out a howl and let loose. I have my Wolf back.

I have a lot of energy; more than I know what to do with. I'm used to having destinations and things to do, people to kill. Now I have nothing to do but run around like a pup.

So, that's what I do. I run around like a pup because I have my Wolf back and energy to burn. When I reach the cliff, I stop for a rest and lie down.

I have missed this. You and me being together. It was so lonely where I was. My Wolf tells me.

Where were you? What did it look like for you?

It was like I was trapped in a cell in the middle of nowhere. Pure silver bars kept me closed in, although I attempted to break them to get out and managed to bend them to make a hole. Darkness surrounded me, and no matter how many times I called out to you, I couldn't quite reach you. It was awful.

I'm sorry. I was trying everything possible to get you back. I've missed you so much.

I know. I have your memories; I saw everything you did for me, making me love you even more.

So, what do you think about Dayton?

He loves us. So does his Wolf. He has been incredibly patient throughout this whole ordeal, and I love him for it. We are unbelievably lucky that he is our Mate.

I have to agree with you.

I miss Aiden, though. I loved Aiden just as much as you did, and I miss him, but I understand why you did what you did.

If it was up to you...what would you have done?

I wouldn't have done anything differently because the idea of Aiden never forgiving himself for letting Mason die would be a worse pain than having him die.

We fall into silence, and for once, without having to jump off a cliff, I feel at peace. I hear someone move behind me, and I am immediately on high alert, although I don't react. I catch the scent and growl. I stand up and turn around to face the intruder.

"I give you your Wolf back, and this is the thanks I get?" He asks, and I just growl in response, watching his every move.

"Honestly, the youth today are so ungrateful!" He shakes his head in disappointment.

I'm going to kill you.

"Is that the way to treat your uncle? I told you; I've been trying to protect you!" Drake says and then bursts out laughing.

What was the point in telling me that? I don't understand why you bothered with that story when I came to see you. Why not just kill me?

"I mean, it wasn't just a story; it was mostly true. Remember, I told you, always tell as much truth when you lie. I wanted you to second guess everything; up until that point, no one had told you anything about your connection with Dayton's family. I told you so you would start asking questions that would ultimately lead to Dayton hating you. I knew you would pick him out of the three, but if he hated you, then you wouldn't ever be happy. Better than killing you."

Then why are you back?

"He doesn't hate you, and you could end up happy. When you agreed to be on my side during our little conversation, I wasn't the only one playing mind games. You don't deserve happiness after everything you did! So, after all our games, this can only end one way. With your death."

Dayton

"Okay, is everyone in agreement?" Blake asks everyone around the table.

We were in my office while Lilla slept upstairs. I was sitting at the head of the table with Mason, Alec, Russell, Rowan, Jace, and the Ancestors seated around me; Dan was sitting at my desk; he was yet to say a word. He watched all of us as we tried to decide what to do about The Midnight Moon Pack.

Austin and the others were out, keeping an eye on everyone. It was chaos at the moment, and they were answering questions, helping the injured, and trying to calm everyone down.

"Agreed." Almost everyone says in unison, although none of us were pleased with the decision.

"You should at least wait for Lilla; let her have a say." Dan finally speaks up.

"Lilla is in a state of depression; we cannot rely on her to make smart decisions." Cain respond, and Dan snorts.

"It seems no one in this room can be relied on to make a smart decision!"

"Watch yourself! I know we haven't acted like it recently, but we are still The Ancestors, and you should show us some respect!" Cain says, his eyes going slightly red like Lilla's had when she got angry; it must be an Ancestor thing.

"Then make decisions that deserve respect!" Dan shouts back.

"We are doing what is necessary!"

"Lilla will never forgive you." Dan says, his voice soft. No one replies; not even The Ancestors respond because they know he has a point.

"This is her Pack we are talking about!" Dan raises his voice, glaring at us, willing us to change our minds.

"No, we are her Pack!" I speak up, and Dan looks at me before shaking his head.

"If she were part of your Pack, I wouldn't catch the scent of a Rogue in your house!" That shuts me up; he has a point.

"All I'm saying is that Lilla lost Aiden, and she suffers because of it. I don't want to talk her down from the cliff edge because you all plan to 'get rid' of her Pack."

*

"Remember when we were younger? When we didn't have to make decisions and be responsible? Everything was so much easier!" I say, sitting next to Mason on the sofa.

We were doing better now that I knew the truth. We weren't the best of buddies, but I didn't want to kill him every time I saw him.

Progress.

"Maybe for you." Mason grunts, raising an eyebrow.

"What does that mean?"

"Mum and Dad's Golden Boy! Remember?"

"Well, I'm not the one who rejected my Mate..." I point out, and Mason sighs.

"I did it for her. I know I told Mum and Dad I didn't want a Mate, but the truth was she didn't want me. She was in love with someone else; I rejected her because she asked me to." We sit in silence, lost in our thoughts, when something crosses my mind.

"Wait, you had a Mate!" I say, and Mason nods slowly.

"How come you have Sierra too?" I ask, and Mason frowns.

"I don't know... I don't make the rules."

"No, you don't. We do." We turn our heads to see the Ancestors at the door staring at us.

"Did you give Mason another Mate?" I ask, and Cain sighs.

'Screw it; we might as well tell them the truth.' Blake mumbles, sitting opposite us on the coffee table.

"The truth?" I ask.

"The Mate bond is broken." Emily says, sitting in an armchair. Cain is the only one to remain standing.

"Broken how?"

"I knew it!" Mason says at the same time, sitting up.

"We created the Mate bond to stop blood being shed because of love triangles, greed, and lust. We created a connection between two Wolves that would be perfect for each other. Soul Mates. However, we also had to give people a choice, so we added the rejection. It had consequences, but ultimately it was up to each person." Emily explains.

"More and more people started rejecting their Mates for stupid reasons. They were throwing away their chance at happiness at having a Soul Mates, and as a result, the Mate bond has worn thin over decades." Cain takes over. "It's making Wolves confused. Making them mistake crushes for Mates as Mason did. She was never your Mate; the man she loves, the one she asked you to reject her for, is. We had to come up with a way to fix it. We had to find the Perfect Couple which could overcome every little thing and still comes out strong. We looked for years, we even considered using Lilla's Dad and Layla, but he refused because of Lisa."

"So, what did you do?" I ask.

Blake takes over. "Derek came to us. He had made up a story about a birth mother carrying Lilla, and he was excited. He told us that he had seen her future. He had seen her death and planned every detail to stop it. He then came up with the idea for us to use her for the Mate bond. He said he could plan out her life so that she has to overcome so much with her Mate. Then they would become stronger and make the Mate bond stronger."

"Wait, so the Mate bond is linked to mine and Lilla's relationship?" I ask, staring at all three of them in disbelief.

"As soon as you guys mate, the Mate bond will be strengthened. It's already getting stronger as the days go by."

"Oh, so no pressure then?"

*

"I'm just going to check on Lilla." I say to Mason.

After talking to the Ancestors, we had been left to think about what they had told us. Instead, we had gone to my office and were playing PlayStation.

"Okay. I'll set up another one, yeah?" Mason asks, and I nod in response. I know that we have a lot of work to do. The Packs are in shambles, and we have Rogues everywhere, but I'm reconnecting with my brother. A few more games won't hurt, especially this early in the morning.

"Lilla?" I call softly as I open the door. I wasn't expecting an answer, but I also wasn't expecting an empty bed.

"Lilla?" I walk towards the wardrobe, nothing. After coming up empty in the bathroom, I leave her room, calling for her as I make my way through the house.

My Wolf and I begin to panic. Where could she be? I search the whole house but come up empty. By this time, I've woken quite a few people up.

"What is going on?" I turn to Dan, who has just come out of the guest bedroom.

"I can't find Lilla!" Immediately the sleepy look is gone.

"Okay, we have to think about this. Where could she be?" He asks; by now, we are in the front room.

"I don't know." I growl out; my Wolf and I were very agitated.

"Have you tried mind-linking her?"

"No, I just thought it would be fun to wake the whole house searching for her and get my Wolf and me worked up. We want to look the old-fashioned way." I spit out sarcastically.

Dan goes silent as he thinks.

"What's going on?" Sierra walks in and looks around. Her eyes are puffy and red from all her crying.

"Lilla is missing." I explain.

"Oh, oh well. I'm sure I'll get over it." Sierra shrugs.

"Don't talk like that! Lilla has done nothing wrong!" I growl.

"She killed my brother!" Sierra shouted.

"She did it so–" I bite my tongue. Ancestor Rule – never tell anyone before they are 18 who their Mate is.

"She did it for herself. Lilla is the most selfish woman I have ever met!" Sierra says before starting to walk away.

"You know what? Sorry Ancestors, you can punish me. I don't care. Lilla saved Mason because he is your Mate." I say, just as the Ancestors walk through the door.

"What?" Sierra asks, turning to face me, her eyes flickering to Mason, quickly filling with tears.

"Sierra, Lilla had to make the most difficult decision between three people she loves. Her Mate, her first love, and my brother, none of it was an easy decision. She wasn't being selfish! Instead, she was thinking of everyone but herself. She was thinking of what was best for you, losing your brother or your Mate, she was thinking of me because she would never forgive herself for letting my brother die to save someone she loves, and she was thinking of Aiden and the fact that he would never forgive himself if Lilla saved him over his sisters Mate.

"If Lilla were being selfish, then Aiden would be standing here instead of Mason, you would never have a Mate, and I wouldn't be in a complete panic because I can't find my depressed Mate!" I growl the last bit out, and Sierra stares at me, stunned.

"I know where she is!" Dan says suddenly, and I turn to him to see his panic-stricken face.

"Where?"

"Where does she go when she is depressed?"

*

As we walk to the cliff, we all try unsuccessfully to pick up her scent. The Ancestors who are walking in front freeze. They let out a growl and start running. We follow quickly behind to the edge of the cliff.

There are two scents at the top of the cliff. One is Lilla's; I would recognise it anywhere, the other is familiar, but I can't place where I know it.

"What's wrong?" I ask the Ancestors.

"Blood." Emily says, ignoring me. The Ancestors sniff and look at each other in alarm.

"Blood?" Dan asks, neither of us wanting to hear the answer.

"Lilla's blood."

"Where is she?" I ask, searching for her scent. I begin to follow it but soon lose it as the other scent overpowers hers. Not a good sign. I hear the snapping of teeth and growling, and as I continue to walk, I come into an opening to see two Wolves fighting. Both are entirely covered in blood.

One Wolf is under the other, and as I scream her name, the Wolf on top sinks their teeth into the others neck, killing them instantly. The Wolf stares at me, blood around its mouth, before growling and taking off in the direction of my house.

"What the hell just happened?" Dan breathes next to me.

"I believe that's two for Lilla and zero for the Ancestors."

Lilla

Fine, let's fight. I've already killed one of you; I can add another to my list!
"List? What list would that be?" Drake asks with a smile.
I call it the Arsehole list. It's got a nice ring to it, don't you think?
"What a charming little girl you turned out to be." Drake says sarcastically.
Make no mistake, Drake. I'm not a little girl anymore! With those words said, I growl and run at him. He shifts before I reach him. His teeth clench down on my shoulder, and I howl in pain. Immediately he drops me and starts to cough.
Your blood is still laced with Pure Silver! He mind-links, disgusted.
I've only had my Wolf back a couple of days; we are still healing from everything you've done to me. Did you want to wait until it was out of my system? I'm pretty busy over the next couple of days, but I'm sure I can pencil you in. I talk to keep him distracted as my wound heals.
You've always been a sarcastic little bitch, haven't you? Some things never change.
Then we are even because you've always been an arsehole.
You should show some respect to your elders! Drake says on a growl.
And you should respect the most powerful Werewolf to prowl this earth, but you don't see me complaining. I had started strolling away from the cliff. The cliff was my sanctuary; I wasn't having it ruined by fighting Drake there.

Do you really think you're the most powerful Werewolf?

I don't think. I know! I say before turning and using my sharp teeth; I bite down on his shoulder. He growls and shrugs me off. He lunges for me, but I dodge him. As he tries to regain his posture, I go for his hind leg. He howls and tries to shake me off. I bite down harder, he goes still, and I relax my grip. He kicks back as soon as I do; I stumble and shake my head, letting out a noise that sounds like a sneeze.

In the time it takes me to recover from the shock, Drake has me flat on my back. I start to snap and growl, but Drake has his total weight on me.

You may be more powerful, but I'm stronger! Drake snarls.

Then kill me. Get this over and done with and just kill me. I stop struggling and close my eyes, waiting for the pain before the end.

I open my eyes to see Drake looking at me sadly when nothing happens.

What? I bark out.

He was right about you.

Who was? I ask, getting whiplash at the change of conversation.

He said that you had given up. That after losing Aiden, you had lost everything and had given up.

Who told you that?

My inside guy.

Your inside guy?

How else do you think I've been getting into your Pack unnoticed or knowing all your plans? Except for the one he didn't know about, of course. Very sneaky, by the way, how you got your Wolf back. I was impressed.

Who is it?

I see a flash in my mind of the traitor, and I gasp. Anger fills me, and I push Drake off of me using all my strength. He struggles to his feet but I jump on top of him. My front paws on his back, my back legs on the floor holding me up. He turns slightly, driving his head into my ribs. I wince but stay on top of him. He does it again, only harder. I fall off of him.

We both jump onto our hind legs, and his teeth sink into me as we fall back on all four paws. I growl and bite back until he lets go, and we both stare at each other, blood pouring from our wounds and staining our mouths. He pulls back his lips, baring his teeth.

I snarl, and we both lunge for each other. Our teeth knock against each other. His paw comes round to my face, and he lifts himself slightly to seem bigger than me.

I twist my head to look up and bite at his neck. His claws dig into my shoulder; the more painful it gets, the more I bite down. I began to pull on his flesh as he tried to let go. He is in the most vulnerable position, after all. He uses his paws to try and pull me away, and eventually, I let him, bringing fur with me.

He is weaker now, especially after the number of times he has bitten me with the Pure Silver still in my system. I jump up again and wrestle him to the ground. I'm on top of him, and I see fear in his eyes for once.

We both know this is the end.

I bite down on his neck with one last growl, releasing the venom that would kill him. I wait for his body to go still. Lifeless.

I catch Dayton's scent as the wind changes and turn to him. He is watching me; with a look I don't quite understand. I want to go to him, but I resist the pull and head for Dayton's house. It was time to deal with Drake's inside guy.

*

I open the door and stare at the group of people waiting around in the front room. All but one looks relieved to see me.

I shifted on my way back and was only wearing a baggy t-shirt, so without a word to anyone, I headed upstairs to wash all the blood off me and change my clothes.

"Lilla?" Austin calls to me and I turn to face them. "Are you okay?"

"I'm fine. Drake is dead." I add and watch the traitor's face; he looks lost suddenly and sad. I turn away.

"I'll explain later. I just need to shower." I say and disappear upstairs.

I close the bedroom door behind me and let out a shaky breath.

I strip and head for the shower. I let the scalding hot water burn my skin as it washes away the blood. I rub my skin raw, trying desperately to rid myself of all the blood on my hands.

Without any warning, I begin to sob; tears mix in with the water as I cry until I'm clean. The scars and bruises are gone, and as I get out of the shower, I glance in the mirror to see I have my blonde hair back.

I stare at myself, trying to readjust to the hair colour, but I can't help but think of how much I already miss my black hair.

Funny that.

*

"So, what happened?" Austin asks as soon as I come downstairs. Dayton, Dan, and the Ancestors are with them all. They all look at me weirdly, which I have no doubt has to do with my hair.

"Right," I say and then clear my throat, ready for business. "Drake is dead. I killed him but not before he told me he had a guy on the inside. It's how he got in and took Aiden; it's how he got into the Pack to fight me today. It's how he knew almost all of our plans. It's why he tried to convince me that he was the good guy trying to protect me when I went to see him. He had been updated, and he knew to make me second guess everything, to maybe start to trust him. Luckily, I didn't fall for it; the inside guy didn't know that either because I didn't tell anyone I saw Drake. I didn't tell everyone what I was thinking, just as well.'

"Who is it?"

"Is it one of the Rogues that you brought in?"

"Drake showed me; he showed me his memories before I killed him."

Everyone looks around suspiciously at each other.

"Okay, so, which one of us is the traitor?"

Traitor

I didn't plan on being a traitor. I love my Pack; Dayton's parents took me in and made me what I am. I was alone, with no family. My parents dropped me off when I was a small child; they didn't want me to grow up a Rogue; it was too dangerous. All I had, was a picture of them and a letter. Dayton's parents raised me as if I was theirs; I've always been grateful for that.

Even when I wanted to look for my parents when I was older, Dayton did all he could to help me. They had settled into another Pack had another child; I met them only once, but it was a fantastic time, as short as it was. After that, I heard about their Pack, and I tried to go and visit and help them escape with their newborn, but they were caught.

All this time, I thought they were dead. I never heard from them again. Dayton helped me through that.

Then Lilla came along; I liked her a lot. She is precisely what Dayton needs. I have my issues with her, but that's me, trying to protect my best friend. My Alpha.

It's my job.

I'm his Beta.

Then she killed my brother.

Lilla

"What do we do?" Rowan asks the room. No one had spoken since Austin had been taken away to the cells, joining the Pack he betrayed us for. I was sitting on the sofa, not trusting my legs to support me. I see Aria, pale, seated on a chair; I look around the room. She had no idea what her Mate had done. She didn't know what to think or say or do. She was just staring off into space.

I feel for her. My Wolf pipes up.

It's my fault. I say back, sinking my face into my hands.

"We have to kill him; he's a traitor." Jace speaks up.

Aria lets out a small noise at the thought. He is still her Mate, after all.

"No more killing." I speak up, and everyone turns to me.

"He's a traitor; it's within your rights." Cain informs me.

"No more killing. I can't have more blood on my hands."

"So, what do we do with him?" Rowan asks. I sigh and stand up.

"Nothing needs to happen now. We all need rest. He is locked away; we will deal with him later." I make my way to my bedroom slowly. As soon as I close my bedroom door, I sink to the floor and cry. I cry for all the people who have died, for all the bloodshed. For the chaos I have caused. I even cry for my uncle.

*

A little while later, there is a knock on my door.

"Little Rogue?" Dayton's voice makes my heart sing. It's so different; now I have my Wolf. The sensations, my feelings, it's magnified.

Without getting up, I reach my hand up and open the door. Dayton comes in, sees me on the floor, and sits down next to me. I rest my head on his shoulder, and we sit in silence, digesting everything.

"Are you okay?" I ask in a whisper.

"How did I not know?" He asks, clearly beating himself up.

"It was my fault. I'm the reason he betrayed us." I want to take the blame, so Dayton doesn't have to.

"We need to decide what to do with him. Together."

"Moving forward, we should decide everything together, be in this together." I say, lifting my head to look at Dayton. He turns and looks at me before dipping his head down to kiss me softly.

"No more secrets, though. I've had enough of them to last a lifetime." Dayton says.

"If I had to do all this from the beginning, I would tell you; I wouldn't keep secrets. It's complicated everything."

"It wouldn't have changed the outcome," Dayton tells me, and I smile sadly.

"No, but I wouldn't have felt so alone."

*

We walk downstairs together with a plan.

"I'm going to talk to Austin." I turn my head to let Dayton know; he nods and squeezes my shoulder before I walk away.

"What's the plan?"

"I will talk to him and punish him; Dayton and I have agreed on it."

"What are you going to do?"

"Where is Aria?" Dayton asks.

"We managed to get her to take a nap; this has hit her hard."

"I'm going to take away Aria's memories of Austin, so she doesn't have to live with it, so she has a chance of being happy. If she wants, that is."

"And Austin?"

"Austin will spend the rest of his life in the cells. He doesn't deserve death; he deserves to be imprisoned alone."

*

"So, you decided to come to visit the betrayer? How nice of you." Austin says when we step into view of his cell.

"I'm here to tell you why I killed your brother." I tell him, and he raises an eyebrow.

I let out a sigh and looked around for a seat. There is none, of course, because cells aren't made for comfort. I sit on the floor and lean against the bars of the cell opposite his. Dayton stays standing, ready for anything that could happen, although I'm not sure what could, what with everyone being behind bars.

"Your brother, Derek, had the same name as my dad; he was named after the great Alpha Derek that everyone knew and loved, the ones that helped and took in your family. That is why your parents named him that."

"How do you know that?"

"After I refused to kill your baby brother and then killed my dad, they came to thank me, and they told me. They said if anything, it was a way to remember how great my father used to be, and if I'm honest, I was grateful; it meant a lot to me to know that someone would still remember that my dad wasn't always bad."

"That's nice for you, but now my brother is dead."

"He should have been two, Austin; your brother should have been learning to walk and talk, stumbling around on his little legs. He should have been playing with trains and cars, watching kids' TV. He shouldn't have been 20 years old, shifting and learning to fight. He shouldn't have been taught to find me and kill me."

"A gift from the Ancestors, right? They are the only ones who can age people."

"It is a gift. To be aged faster or slower is a special gift that the Ancestors try not to use because it is dangerous. If someone wants to age faster, then the Ancestors can do it but only a few months at a time. They can age up to a year in advance, but no more than that because your body needs to catch up. The organs need to catch up. Drake gave your brother a life sentence when he aged 20 years; his insides, his organs were still those of a baby. His body couldn't keep up; he would die a painful death. I saved him from that by killing him there and then. He wouldn't have survived much longer than he had, and it would have been a gruesome, horrible death. I did what I had to do to save your brother from a pain he didn't deserve. I'm truly very sorry."

Lilla

"I said NO more killing!" I growl out, and immediately everyone takes a step back. I don't blame them. I'm temperamental now that I have my Wolf back — it's like a newly shifted pup; their emotions are heightened and all over the place.

"Lilla, we don't have another choice," Emily explains calmly.

"There is always another choice!"

"There wasn't when you killed Austin's brother," Jace mutters. I let out a growl, and before he can blink, I have his neck in my hand, and he is gasping for breath.

"You seem to forget that I have my Wolf back, which makes me stronger, don't test me, Jace," I let go and turn back to the Ancestors.

"Find a way around it because you aren't killing anyone."

"There isn't a way around it," Blake tells me. "As the Ancestors–"

"No! I'm not letting the three of you hide behind that title. 'As Ancestors, we do this and that because we are the most powerful Wolves in the world, and no one can stop us!'" I mimic. "Find another way because we know I am more powerful than all three of you, and I can stop you. I will stop you from killing a bunch of innocent people."

Cain scoffs, his face reddening with rage. "Innocent? These people killed others for fun. That's not what I would call innocent."

"They were commanded to! They didn't have a choice! You can't break an Alpha command, let alone an Ancestor one."

"We can't just give Wolves with no humanity, humanity."

"Drake did; he took their humanity. Why can't you just give it back?"

"It doesn't work like that." Cain snaps.

"Have you tried?" I ask, and immediately they fall silent. They look at each other before shaking their heads. "Let me try, let me take one of them and see what I can do, let me try. They are all locked up in cells, what is the worse that could happen?"

"Lilla."

"Please? I can't deal with any more killing or dying," I say, my voice breaking and tears filling my eyes.

The Ancestors let out a sigh before they all nodded in unison.

You always were good at playing people.

*

"It's harder than you thought, isn't it?" Dayton whispers. He is standing next to me, Thomas sits in front of us, the young pup I brought from the cells.

"I don't even know where to start," I admit in a whisper. The pup was sitting on a bench in the training grounds, watching us and waiting for me to tell him to do something.

"Start with something little...?" Dayton asks, and when I look at him with a raised eyebrow, he shrugs his shoulders.

"Thomas, what did Drake command you to do?" I ask. I had already commanded him to answer anything I ask and do anything I tell him.

"He commanded us to do many things," Thomas answers vaguely.

"Like?"

"He would command us to kill little things, to begin with, and then move on to killing babies and toddlers to make sure our humanity wouldn't get in the way."

"In this situation, what would Drake have commanded you to do?"

"Kill you." He says bluntly.

"How about if you were to shake my hand instead, would that be okay?" I asked, lacing my words with my commanding tone behind them.

"I would do it because you command, but it would take me a lot of restraint to not kill you."

What a charmer!

I hold out my hand, and he takes it. He shakes it, squeezing it a little too hard before he lets go and sits on his hands. He is holding himself back. I tilt my head, and he copies me. Without saying a word, I sit down next to him. I sit close enough to feel him shaking next to me, trying to resist Drake's command in him.

"I want you to ignore Drake's command; I want you and your Wolf to forget about Drake's commands and only listen to mine. Can you do that?"

"I have to; you commanded me to."

He has a point.

Will you shut up? You aren't helping!

You know, you ignore me an awful lot for someone who missed me so much.

"I want you to see only the good in people. I want your first reaction when you see people that aren't a threat to be positive. Smile at them, wave, and say hello. I need you to restrain yourself from your instinct to kill people. I need you to start caring about people. Start with me. I need you to care about me." I finish, and he nods.

"I am tired; can I rest?" He asks, and I let out a defeated sigh.

"Come with us; you can stay in one of the guest bedrooms." Dayton offers, and we make our way back to Dayton's house.

"You will get there in the end, Little Rogue." Dayton says, wrapping an arm around my waist. It strikes me as something an average couple does and I can't help but grin to myself with the thought.

"How do you know that?" I ask, leaning my head on his shoulder.

"You don't give up on people. You, my Little Rogue, are too stubborn."

I smile softly as we walk to the house in silence.

Dayton

"How are you feeling?" I ask Lilla as I walk her to her bedroom.

Lilla stops at the door and looks at me with a frown on her face. "About what?"

"About having your Wolf back."

She makes an 'o' shape with her mouth and then, shrugging, she walks into her room. It's my turn to frown as I follow her in.

"Nothing to say? Just a shrug." I say sitting on the edge of the bed while she disappears into her wardrobe.

She reappears still dressed and comes and stands in front of me, I open my legs and pull her closer. Enjoying us having a moment alone.

"I have missed her and I'm so happy she is back but it's an adjustment, I won't lie. I'm not used to having someone constantly in my head." She points to her head as if I can see her how crowded her mind is.

Rude.

"Hmmm well…I can help distract you from your heavy mind." I offer, putting my arms on her waist and resting my chin on her toned stomach. She smiles and leans down for a kiss.

"And how you would you distract me?" She whispers, inches away from my lips.

"Well firstly, we need to get you out of these clothes, wouldn't you agree?"

"We? I'm perfectly capable of getting out of my own clothes." She teases, as

I slowly glide my hands under her top. I feel her shudder as my fingers trace along her narrow waist.

"With that heavy head of yours? I think I should do the gentlemanly thing and help you."

She starts to laugh. "Oh, being a gentlemen, is that what they call it?" Before I can respond, her lips capture mine with an unexpected urgency.

I stand up and slowly lift her top up, her arms stretch up, helping me to pull it off. With our lips parted and our breaths heavy, I look down, deep into her eyes as she grips the hem of my t-shirt and yanks until it's thrown somewhere over her head.

Her lips find mine, desperation pouring over us. Like we can't breathe unless our skin is touching. I undo her trousers and crouch in front of her as I slowly peel them down her legs, my eyes tracking her face for any hesitation. She lifts one foot before the other, shedding the last of her clothes until she stands completely bare with me at her feet.

I stretch to my full height and run my palms down the length of her arms. Lilla smiles a rare timid smile. My hands cup her jaw as I bring her mouth back to mine, reassuring her with my kiss. When she opens her eyes, there's an unmistakable sparkle before she hastily undoes my zipper and drops to her knees.

She stands and releases a heavy breath, meeting my eyes again. I lift her up, her legs automatically wrapping around my waist as her arms cradle the nape of my neck, and crawl across the mattress, placing her softly on the bed underneath me.

There's an electricity in the air, one I've never experienced before. Sparks and tingles erupt everywhere our skin touches. I feel like I know her body, like I've studied it for years. This is the cementing of the Mating Bond.

I start kissing down her body as her nails scrape across the top of my back. There's a deep satisfaction in knowing she is mine, a reassurance that after this, we will only grow stronger. A soft moan escapes her lips and I let out a lust-filled growl.

The world and it's worries slip away as we become entwined with each other, pleasing each other. Loving each other.

Knowing we are now Mates, we fall asleep with our arms wrapped around each other. Our hearts full.

Lilla

"Morning," I say, walking into the kitchen.

"Morning," voices sing back. I turn to see Alec and Russell sitting with huge grins.

"How are you guys?" I ask, making myself a cup of coffee. Alec is fine, he had a few cuts and bruises, but he didn't get injured much in the war, luckily. He told me our mum had made it out too, but he didn't know where she went when they all came to our Pack.

"Fine, how are you this morning?" Alec asks, raising an eyebrow.

"Fine, thanks." I sit down opposite them and sip my coffee.

"Not even a little bit tired? I mean, Alpha Dayton wasn't found in his room this morning..." Russell says, and I roll my eyes.

"Wipe those goofy grins off your faces. Surely, we can all behave like the adults we claim to be?"

Russell holds up his hands in surrender. "I was only asking if you were tired because it appeared you hadn't been to sleep; I was thinking innocently!" He looks at me with doe eyes, but the smile that spreads across his face catches him out.

"Besides," I add on a mutter, "It's not like you didn't all know that we Mated already. Luna, remember?" I point to my face.

"Okay, okay, enough. As lovely as it is talking about my sister's sex life, please can we change the subject?" Alec asks, the smile at least wiped from his face to be replaced with grimace.

"I have been looking for mum, but no one in this Pack has seen her." I tell Alec, and he looks up at me with a frown.

"Where is the majority of the Midnight Moon Pack?" He asks, just as Dayton walks in.

"Why?" Dayton asks; we had locked them all away because they have no humanity, and we couldn't agree on what to do with them. They are fed and looked after, but no one goes near them except the Ancestors and me because we can command them if they try anything.

"We can't find our mum," Alec explains, worry etched all over his face.

"I highly doubt she's in the cells; we would have noticed." Dayton says.

"Wait, who rounded them up and put them in the cells?" Alec asks.

"Austin did but–"

"Shit!"

Alec and I are up and out of the house before anyone can say another word.

*

"Mum?" Alec and I call as we run into the cells. Immediately there is a commotion as the Pack tries to attack us, arms outstretched through the cells. This is what they were commanded to do, after all. Kill me.

"We are never going to find her here. They are all too loud, causing too much trouble we won't be able to hear her." I just about hear Alec as he shouts at me.

I look around, trying to think of a way around it, a way to find her. The more I see them shouting and trying to grab and hurt us, the more I fear for my mum. The more noise they make, the more I think about my mum being in here; the angrier I become.

I can't think overall this noise! My Wolf growls, and I have to agree. How can I help my mum when I can't even think straight over the amount of noise they are all making?

"Enough! All of you shut up, stand still and quietly!" I use all my strength to command all of them in the room. I grab hold of Alec as I get weaker, and he holds me up. To my surprise, everything goes quiet, and everyone stands still.

"Shit! Just how powerful are you?" Alec asks as we slowly start to walk past the cells.

"I have no idea," I say in awe as I watch all of them.

"Mum?" Alec calls. I let go of him as he walks ahead. I stop in front of one of the cells and watch a member of the Midnight Moon Pack.

"Do you know where my mother is?" He shakes his head.

"Will you help us?" I ask, my voice barely a whisper.

The member looks me in the eyes. "Thomas said you were teaching him about humanity; is that true?"

"Yes, I am," I answer, frowning.

"Can you teach the rest of us?" He asks almost sadly.

"I hope so. I wanted to see how Thomas responded to it first, but I would love to teach all of you about humanity."

He nods, "I think I miss my humanity," he informs me, no emotion in his voice.

"The fact that you miss it means there is still humanity in you. That's a good start."

"Your mother is in the last cell, on the left-hand side."

"Thank you, what's your name?"

"My name is James," he answers. I open my mouth to say something else when Alec calls for me.

"Lilla! I found her! I need the key." I give James a small wave before running over to Alec, the weakness I felt slowly ebbing away.

*

"This Pack is a mess." I stare into the crowded meeting room. We have the whole of Dayton's Pack and the Rogues all squashed into the Pack Meeting room.

The room stays silent. "I'm glad you all agree. No one knows what is going on, and this Pack has almost tripled in size since the war. I am standing here to give you all answers. Firstly, all the Rogues will be leaving; they will gather their strength, make sure they are all healed, and then leave. They have no intention of joining your Pack, except Mason, of course."

"What about the other Pack? The one we fought?"

"They are all together and being kept separate from everyone while we try and find a way to give them back their humanity." I answer.

"How do you plan on doing that?"

"With a lot of patience and a commanding tone, I plan on re-training them." I tell them honestly. "You have all been amazing as a Pack. You have been hospitable and kind to all the Rogues, you have fought beside them and me, and I am eternally grateful for that. You are what makes an amazing and strong Pack, and I am proud to be a member and leader of this Pack."

"What about our Beta? Don't we need a new one?" Someone else yells, and this time Dayton speaks up.

"Yes, and I have chosen your new Beta, Big Brother; please take a step forward and introduce yourself."

Mason moves out of the crowd and gives a wave.

"If you have any issues, please do not worry or be hesitant; find one of us, and we will help you." I add before we finish the meeting. There are a few nods, and everyone slowly leaves.

"Lilla?" I look over to see Sierra standing there with a hesitant expression. "Can we talk?"

Lilla

I take us to Dayton's office, where I know we will be left alone. I start rummaging in his cupboards, looking for something strong enough to get us through this conversation.

"Ah," I say when I find what I'm looking for.

"Should you be supporting underage drinking?" Sierra asks with humour in her voice and a sly grin on her face; I shrug before filling our drinks.

"I won't tell if you don't?" I hand her a glass of whiskey. Sierra takes the glass, sniffs it, and then takes a sip; she grimaces at the taste. I take a gulp and relish it as it burns my throat; I haven't had whiskey in a long time.

"Dayton told me that Mason is my Mate," Sierra speaks first, and I nod with an understanding smile.

"He shouldn't have done that." The Ancestors had rules for a reason.

"I'm glad he did, he broke the rules for you, and if he hadn't, we wouldn't be sitting here talking now."

"That's true; you would probably still hate me." I say, and Sierra shakes her head.

"I never hated you. I was angry and sad, but I never hated you."

"Why not? I am the reason why your brother is dead; I would hate me if I were you."

Sierra sighs, "When you told me Aiden was dead, I was angry and upset, so I shouted and blamed you, but I couldn't get the look on your face out of my mind. The pain it caused you to say the words; I could never hate you for my brother's death; I think you hate yourself enough for the both of us."

*

"Really?" I manage to get out as we both laugh.

"I promise you, he was convinced he was pop-eye!" Sierra says, and we both laugh until our stomachs hurt. We had been swapping stories about Aiden, and Sierra's latest one was about when Aiden first got drunk.

As our laughter dies down, we stare at our glasses in silence. "You know Aiden used to tell me about you every night when we were locked in the cells. We would stay up when everyone else had gone to sleep, and he would tell me so much about you." I tell Sierra, her smile is heart breaking.

"He once told me that we were a lot alike, you and me." I tell her, and she looks at me with a quizzical look.

"I don't see it," she says, and I smile.

"I didn't see it either when I first met you; all I could think was, 'does Aiden not know me?' I see it now, though. He was talking more about how we deal with things. We lash out and hurt others because we are scared and don't want to hurt. You thought I would kick you out, didn't you?" I ask, and Sierra looks at me, sadness and guilt written across her face.

"I thought that maybe when the Rogues were leaving, you would ask me to leave too; I'm a Rogue with no tie to anyone here before I found out about Mason. Does that make me a bad person? My brother dies, and I think about myself?"

"No, it doesn't make you a bad person; it makes you normal and like me. I think Aiden knew us too well!"

"I have to plan his funeral, and I don't think I know him well enough," Sierra admits; I lean forward and grab her hand, forcing her to look at me.

"You are his sister; you know more about him than you think, and I will help you. Together we will give Aiden the best funeral he deserves."

*

"I don't know anyone in this room. Sierra is here, and a few others are here to support us, but the rest of you... I have no idea who you are. I have no idea how you knew Aiden or your relationship with him, and if I'm being sincere, I don't care. It just means a lot that you are all here; wherever you travelled from, you all took the time and effort to be here, and if Aiden was here, I think he would be in shock that you all did this for him. He didn't realise how amazing he was; how lovable he was.

"Sierra and I sat down together to organise this funeral, and we made it clear to each other from the beginning what we would and would not be doing. For example, I refused to do the invitations because, as I said, I don't know any of you or how you knew Aiden; the people I would have thought to invite are all dead, so that it would be a pretty empty church, right now. Sierra refused to do a reading or the eulogy because she wouldn't be able to get through it without crying, and I agreed with her based on the same reasoning. I wouldn't be able to get through it without crying, without breaking down in front of a roomful of strangers.

"This wasn't planned. I was sitting listening to an old friend – I think – of Aiden's give a reading, one of his favourite poems, and all I could think was that I had to tell everyone how amazing Aiden was. I convinced myself that you wouldn't even know how much Aiden meant to me and how great he was, and it scared me because Aiden deserves the best funeral ever. He deserves someone who loves him with all their heart to stand up here and tell you, and I think the best person for that is me.

"I met Aiden when I was going through one of the most challenging times of my life, we were in the prison cells of a Pack, both of us Rogues. We met other Rogues, the ones I mentioned, that are all dead now, he made living in a cell bearable. He made being tortured daily just that little bit easier to live with. That was just the sort of person he was; he made life worth living; even when you were done fighting, he would make you feel better and like you could fight that little bit more. Even if it was just by making up a silly nickname for the people who had us locked away to make me laugh.

"He loved nicknames; everyone always had a nickname because it was easier than remembering everyone's names. Sierra, his gorgeous sister, was nicknamed Peaches, and I'm sure he has nicknamed everyone here for some reason or other. He called me Beautiful, which sounds like a term of endearment, but it was my nickname. It was originally Beautiful Angel, but he shortened it because it was a mouthful to say all the time, but as long as we both knew it, he was happy.

"When he first nicknamed me, I remember being confused, I was filthy, and my clothes were ripped with blood all over them, and I had cuts and bruises everywhere, but still, he insisted on calling me, Beautiful Angel. After a couple of times, I asked him why and I remember his face more than anything because he looked at me like I was crazy, like I was completely nuts.

"You see, Aiden had this talent to make me feel amazing about myself even at my lowest point, and this was my first time 'witnessing' it. He didn't even answer me. He just gave me this look of his and then shook his head. I thought maybe he had misheard me or didn't hear me at all, I don't know, but I repeated my question, and this time with the look, the shake of the head, I got a sigh and an answer.

"He told me that being in the cells made him think about dying. What it would be like on the other side because he believed in God. After everything he had been through, he still kept his faith. So, he had these ideas about Heaven, maybe it was with family and people who had died, and you missed, or perhaps it was just like a town or city or something. He had loads of different theories, but with each theory, one thing stayed the same.

"He had this idea that Angels are in Heaven no matter what it is actually like. He told me that Angels were beautiful, they were only in paradise, though, and he honestly couldn't wait to die and meet them. He wanted to marry one; he knew that much about his afterlife. He was going to marry a Beautiful Angel, and that was one thing he couldn't wait for. Then he met me, and he realised he didn't have to die to meet one or marry one because he had found a Beautiful Angel while he was alive. He said he would be one of the lucky guys who was going to marry a Beautiful Angel on Earth and in Heaven.

"That is why he called me Beautiful Angel, that was how he saw me, and in those cells, it made me feel so much better because it was all I had to hold on to. Now I can imagine Aiden marrying his Beautiful Angel up in Heaven while his Beautiful Angel here is missing him with all her heart, and strangely it puts a smile on my face because he is getting what he dreamed of. He isn't trapped in a cell, he isn't lying in a coma, he is free, and he is happy, and that is what I wanted for him even if it meant leaving me behind."

I walk over to his coffin, put my hand to my lips, and then to his casket, where his head should be, and as the tears fall, I walk back to my seat and grab hold of my Mates' hands seeking his comfort.

Lilla

"I don't know how it's possible, but you get more and more beautiful every day," I hear my Mate say as I begin to stir.

"I don't know how it's possible, but you get cheesier and cheesier every day," I return, opening my eyes to find Dayton staring at me.

I feel the sparks as his eyes race over my face, and I find myself smiling, still not used to the intoxicating sensation.

"I try to be nice to you, and you are so mean to me!" Dayton feigns a hurt expression. I turn on my side, facing Dayton, and sit up on my elbow; he copies me, so our faces are inches apart.

"Are you trying to be nice or sweet talk me enough to get in my pants?" I ask, raising an eyebrow; Dayton frowns.

"It's the same thing, isn't it?" He asks, and I smack his chest; he falls on his back, laughing.

"So, when I'm nice to all the guys in the Pack, it's the same as me wanting to get in their pants?" I ask innocently, climbing on top of him.

His laughter stops, and he lets out a growl. "Maybe you need to stop being nice then," he says, and it's my turn to laugh as his hands wrap around my thighs.

"Does that include you?" I tease as I move my face closer to his, our noses barely touching. I watch his eyes turn a darker shade as they fill with lust.

"You, my Little Rogue, can be as nice to me as you want," a shiver runs down my spine as he calls me by my pet name.

Ever since we had Mated we have been closer than ever. Tingles and sparks and all the things little girls grow up hearing about when you find your Mate was finally happening, and we were loving every minute of it.

I'm inches away from kissing him when I stop and whisper, "Well, when you put it like that..." I pull away and jump off him.

He growls at my retreating back.

"Come back here, Little Rogue," the big, bad Alpha commands. I open our bedroom door, and just before I shift, I turn back to him.

"You're going to have to catch me first, Alpha."

*

"Not much has changed," I note, and Dayton sighs.

"Rome wasn't built in a day," he points out, ever the optimist.

"Rome didn't have Werewolves building it," I say, and Dayton chuckles.

"How do you know?"

"I'm pretty sure the Ancestors would have mentioned it." I say, arching an eyebrow in his direction. I look at my old Pack Territory. My brother was now Alpha of the Midnight Moon Pack, and he was stripping everything and starting over. The old grounds that hold nothing but bad memories were being taken apart and made new; the only thing that was staying were the houses, by popular demand. The Pack members who used to live here want to keep everything the same because, according to them, nothing bad happened in the houses. That was the only time life was good for them. As for any new Pack members - the Rogues who fought for us that don't want to be Rogues - new houses were being built to fit them all in. The old Pack members were slowly gaining back their humanity because I had them on a tight training schedule.

"Come on, let's see the Alpha!" Dayton says, dragging me along. I say dragging because I keep stopping to look at new things or talk to members of the Pack to find out how they are. Dayton wanted to get to my brother's house, get the business over with and go back to our Pack. Like most Alphas, he hated being away from his Pack for too long.

I, however, was dragging my feet on purpose, and Dayton knew this. That house was one of the last places I ever wanted to be.

*

"Would you like tea or anything?" Russell asks as he ushers us into my old home.

"Tea would be great, thank you." I reply with a plastic smile, and Russell turns to Dayton, who politely declines. "Okay, well, Lilla, you know where the front room is, make yourselves at home. I'll be joining you in a moment, and Alec will be down soon. Some Pack business ran over, so he is running a bit late." He disappears into the kitchen, missing my pained expression at his remark of making ourselves at home.

"Are you coming?" Dayton asks, and I shake my head.

"I need a moment; go ahead."

"Take your time, Little Rogue," Dayton says softly before making his way into the front room.

I stand still, unsure of what to think or feel. This house holds so many memories for me, and the sad thing is that they are mostly good but clouded by the bad.

I look in the direction of the front room and then at the stairs, curiosity getting the better of me as I climb them.

I take a shaky breath before opening the door; nothing has changed. As if reading my mind, I hear a voice behind me.

"I didn't know if I should get rid of it or not; I thought maybe you wanted to go through it and maybe keep some of it?" Alec explains as I walk around, my eyes tracing over all my old stuff, every so often my hand reaching out to touch something, not quite believing it is right in front of me after so long. My eyes and hands fall onto a picture of my dad and me, and I pick it up, my breath catching. My eyes water as I see our smiles, and the expression of such love on his face causes me to struggle to breathe. I sit on the edge of my bed as the tears fall, I feel an arm wrap around me, and I lean into my brother as he holds me.

"I am sorry, Alec, you know that, right? I don't think I've ever said that to you, and I wanted you to know that I am sorry that you don't have a dad anymore."

He holds me tighter, "I don't blame you, but I miss him. I feel guilty for missing him because of everything he did, but I miss him."

"I miss him too."

*

"What if I don't want to make a Treaty with your Pack?" Alec asks my Mate, and I roll my eyes.

"Alec," I say, and he shrugs.

"Your Pack is known for going to war with other Packs. Do I want to sign a Treaty with you?" Alec teases, and Dayton laughs and plays along.

"Isn't that the perfect reason to sign the Treaty?"

"How so?"

"Well, you're sitting here talking to me, not the Packs I went to war with." It's Alec's turn to laugh as he picks up the pen and signs the contract that ties both Territories. The agreement was a Peace Treaty but also a Link Treaty. A contract linked our Packs so that we could go in and out of each other's Territory without any trouble. Which meant I could pop by whenever I wanted. Other little bits are included, but it's all so boring I stopped listening and instead, silently admired my Mate and the way his muscles jumped with every subtle movement.

Once both Alphas signed both copies and had a copy, Dayton stood ready to leave, but Alec wasn't done.

"Before you guys go, there is one more thing…" He trails off, he isn't looking at Dayton but at me, so I raise an eyebrow in question.

"What, Alec?" I ask when he doesn't continue.

"There is someone who wants to see you, Lilla." He points at the door, and I turn round, a gasp leaving my mouth when I see who it is.

I'm in her arms before she can say a single word.

"I've missed you," I whisper as I breathe her scent in. She doesn't say a word, and she doesn't have to. Instead, she just holds me tighter, using the magic trick only mothers have of making all the pain go away.

Epilogue

Lilla

"Okay, Little Ancestor, please proceed with your report," Blake says, acting professionally. He would have succeeded if we weren't in my front room with cups of tea, the Ancestors in jeans and me in my lounging outfit – shorts and a vest top.

Their idea behind this meeting was to see how everything has gone over the last year. They left soon after Drake was killed, they had many 'Ancestor' things to do – whatever they were – but we spoke at least once a week, which helped me sort out all the mess because I could fall back on them.

They called me their Little Ancestor now because apparently, rebuilding two Pack's was something Ancestors do, hence the meeting now; they have this idea to train me to be an Ancestor. I still haven't agreed to it, but I haven't said no either.

"The buildings in the Midnight Moon Pack have been completely rebuilt, they have a new Meeting Hall, new shops, new houses for new members, and they have also revamped the school and are currently hiring teachers. I have finished my training with the Pack members; they have as much humanity as I could rebuild in their system. I have left a command in them that if they ever think or feel their humanity slip, they must come straight to me.

"Alec is rebuilding the reputation of his Pack, which, if I'm honest, hasn't been going great, but he now has Treaties with us, Danny and Alfie, which is helping their reputation immensely."

"That's great to hear; what is happening with our Rogue Situation?" Cain asks.

"It is all set up and ready for you three to agree to a Neutral Territory. I will, of course, show you around but it has food and clothes shops, bars and clubs, hotels, a church, and my favourite, a university. Once you agree and sign the contract, everything is ready to go. Most, if not all, the jobs are taken by Pack members across England, so we are building a housing estate so that the Members don't have to make such a commute."

The idea of the Neutral Territory, to begin with, was somewhere Rogues could go without immediately being bombarded and terrorised by Packs. It has become a neutral ground for Rogues and Packs; somewhere everyone can meet and not worry about breaking their Pack rules. The Neutral Territory only had a few rules:

No fighting.

Equality amongst everyone — Pack member or Rogue.

No Killing.

If any of the rules were broken, the rule breaker would have to answer to an Ancestor.

"That sounds great; we may pop over there to look tomorrow, but where can we find this favourite cook of yours for now?" Emily asks, eager to have some of Sierra's cooking.

Mason and Sierra had taken Aiden's old room when Dayton asked his brother to be Beta, something Mason was more than happy to accept. The brothers have been getting closer and closer ever since. Sierra turned 18 a month after the war, and thankfully there were no hard feelings between her and Mason, as far as I know and have seen, they are blissfully happy.

When they moved in, Sierra took over the cooking for us all. We are grateful that she did because she is a fantastic cook; I constantly told the Ancestors about her remarkable ability, and they were eager to try it.

I watch them all go to the kitchen, laughing when Dayton pops his head into the room.

"Shall we go for a run, Little Rogue?" Without a single second of hesitation, I nod. He grins mischievously.

"You better catch me then," with that, he was gone.

*

After about an hour of running around, Dayton slows to a walk, and we walk together, Alpha and Luna, side by side. When I realise where we are, I freeze; Dayton shifts and throws clothes in my direction before getting dressed.

As I shift, he talks, "Lilla, this place, as beautiful as it is, has so many bad memories for you and me. Every time I come here, all I see is you jumping, and it makes both my Wolf and I sick with the idea. I know you aren't as fond of this place as you first were; too much has happened here. Which is why I brought you here today."

Dayton had brought me to the cliffs; he was right; I used to love this place because it was peaceful, but too many people had disturbed it. Ever since I killed Drake, I had avoided this place.

"Little Rogue, I want to make this a place you can come to whenever you feel sad or angry or want to escape; I want to make it a happy place. I made a speech before and so you know how I feel about you. So, I'm going to keep this simple:

> Little Rogue, will you marry me?"

Printed in Great Britain
by Amazon